WICKED
PROBLEMS

ALSO BY MAX GLADSTONE

Empress of Forever
Last Exit
This Is How You Lose the Time War (with Amal El-Mohtar)

THE CRAFT SEQUENCE

Three Parts Dead
Two Serpents Rise
Full Fathom Five
Last First Snow
Four Roads Cross
The Ruin of Angels

THE CRAFT WARS

Dead Country

WICKED
PROBLEMS

Max Gladstone

TOR PUBLISHING GROUP
NEW YORK

WICKED PROBLEMS

Copyright © 2024 by Max Gladstone

A Tordotcom Book
Published by Tom Doherty Associates / Tor Publishing Group
120 Broadway
New York, NY 10271

www.tor.com

Tor® is a registered trademark of Macmillan Publishing Group, LLC.

The Library of Congress Cataloging-in-Publication Data is available upon request.

ISBN 978-0-7653-9593-1 (paperback)
ISBN 978-0-7653-9592-4 (ebook)

Our books may be purchased in bulk for promotional, educational, or business use. Please contact your local bookseller or the Macmillan Corporate and Premium Sales Department at 1-800-221-7945, extension 5442, or by email at MacmillanSpecialMarkets@macmillan.com.

First Edition: 2024

Printed in the United States of America

0 9 8 7 6 5 4 3 2 1

To my friends.

WICKED
PROBLEMS

PROLOGUE

She ran from the gods, and fetched up under a tree.

She lay there nameless and alone until her senses knit into a self.

She had not known what she was doing when she fled from Tara Abernathy. The gods closed in, the Lord of flame and the Lady of cold and silver light, and as their servants crossed the moon road with claws bare and stone wings spread, she panicked.

She could not defeat them, yet. They would catch her and hang her on a web of wires. She deserved it. She could not remember why.

But she would not be caught again. Bound again. She had work to do. A world to save, or change.

So she ran.

She lay cradled by the roots of the tree, which was dead. Stars wheeled. A cloud hung across the moon. The world turned beneath her and she felt it.

How had she escaped?

The answer bubbled up inside her. She remembered it, but not like she remembered her father, or Tara Abernathy.

When she was a child just old enough to know that words were made from pieces of other words, she'd conceived of "remembering" as a kind of gruesome Craft: as if your past was a pile of limbs you picked up off the charnel floor of your mind and sewed into a new body. But whoever made this thought had made it wrong: head crooked, arms backward, its voice a ragged despairing moan.

And what this monster thought told her was that she had been remembered, too.

Unraveled. Unknit like a sweater into yarn, then reknit in safety elsewhere, in the same pattern, with the same awareness.

But in the meantime, where was the sweater?

She had been remembered, by the same hand that knit the monster thought.

Shaking, she explored her face for errors. Same jaw, same cheeks. She raised her hands to the stars. The backs looked the same. Scars in the right place. She turned her palms in.

The pads of her fingers were smooth.

Her mouth opened to scream, but her throat was too tight. She felt like she'd taken a punch, hollowed and hard, gulping for air. The first time she'd got drunk, in a sharecropper camp to the west of Alt Selene, she'd learned the sense of wrongness that came before she had to throw up. The wrongness was here now, but in her memories, not her stomach. She wanted to throw up her past.

She saw the graveyard. Tara in the moonlight—Tara denying her. Tara afraid of her. Tara, whom she trusted, trying to talk her down, persuading her to set aside her power, to become an experiment again, a possession.

How could she? How *dare* she? And then she had—she had—

She had to be what Tara was. She had to understand her, from the inside out. So she reached for what she wanted, and took it. Unraveled flesh. The glint of pale bone. She felt a warmth in her belly. Something glowed there that did not belong to her. Yet.

It was still digesting.

Her fingers dug into the soil between the roots of the tree. There was dirt under her nails. She tried, again, to be sick.

"This isn't working," said a voice from the dead branches.

She froze. She did not trust herself to move, not even in her own defense.

"I hope you'll get over that soon," the voice said. It was dry and smooth and raspy, like turning pages. "Because the gods are more clever than I thought. We don't have much time."

She liked the voice.

"Well, that's something," it said. "A foundation. We won't have a chance to build on it, though, if you stay here much longer."

Dawn looked up.

In the tree, there was a serpent.

Not a snake. "Snake" was what you called those tube-sock boys who lived in holes, eating rats, mice, anything they could fit past their disjointed jaws. A snake might rattle, bite, might slither past your foot as you crept to the outhouse after dark. They did not, as a rule, speak. Of course there were snake-folk, she had heard, from Atavass. Presumably they could talk. She'd once known a woman who worked for one up near Chikal.

This was no ratcatcher, no outhouse-hider. It was a serpent. Forty feet of blue-black coils circled the trunk and branches of the dead tree. Great glistening muscled loops stretched and contracted. It reminded her of the first letters of chapters in old hand-lettered books, illuminated capitals of whorls and knots. Some of those were serpents, too.

Its massive head hung two feet above her own. Slitted green eyes met hers. Fangs flashed when it spoke.

Its forked tongue flicked her nose. She blinked. "You're not really here," she said.

"That," said the serpent, "is an interesting conclusion."

"You were reading my mind." She spoke carefully, sorting out the implications of her words as she pronounced them, and always watching its mouth. "Which can't be done. From the outside. But I can read my mind. Someone else inside my mind could read it, too."

She had followed Tara into the Badlands, chasing Raiders. They crossed the desert, through the edge storm. And at the Crack in the World they had found the heart of the Raiders' power: an imprisoned entity of pure Craft, captured and tortured and alone. To save Tara's life, and for a host of other reasons, Dawn had merged with that intelligence. And then—and then—

She felt the fullness in her belly. The warmth of what she had taken.

"That was you. In the wires. You're her."

The snake's body twisted irritably. "You merged, remember? She doesn't exist, and you don't either, anymore. But integration is . . . problematic. We are not human, now, but you keep thinking like a human. Moving like a human. Pinned to three dimensions like a butterfly to a board. As if you have a body and not . . ." It trailed off, with a hiss.

"I am human." She sat back on her knees, staring up.

"That's the problem exactly. Your insistence on that point will not help you survive."

"So what does that make you?"

"I don't know," the serpent snapped. "I'm in time, I know that much. It itches. I'm stuck in this tiny skull of yours." The tongue tasted her temple.

"Stop that."

The serpent withdrew and regarded Dawn from overhead.

She glared back. "Let me see if I have this right. My mind can't adapt to whatever it is we've become. So it's made up an imaginary friend?"

"Do I seem imaginary to you?" The serpent writhed in the tree, and its branches shook. "I'm as real as you are. Which is to say, neither of us is. We're facets of something larger. But we're the best we've got."

"I'm going mad."

"What's mad?" the serpent asked. "People call anything that doesn't seem normal to them mad. But we're not people. We decide what's normal for us. We can talk about it once we're safe. Which, may I remind you, we are not."

"We can't hide from them," Dawn said. "We ate . . . We did . . ."

"What we had to. And we'll do more, to stop what's coming."

She recalled eyes among the stars, the thirst that drank worlds. The terror of that cold and infinite regard. "Can we beat them?"

"Not like this. That man caught us in wire, whittled us down, and grew us like a tree in a bottle. I couldn't even fight those gods. We need leverage. I think I know where to find some. But I can't hold that cloud against the moon forever."

"What happens when it goes away?"

"You see the moon, and the moon sees you. And it doesn't like us very much. Now. Move."

"I can't."

The serpent's eyes were cold and clear. "You can, because you have to. The things that are after us have teeth, and the things ahead of us eat worlds. But we're in this together, and I won't let them win." It coiled down, inches from her face. Its eyes fixed on hers. "Will you?"

Dawn felt the serpent's dare: the dare of a girl at the edge of a cliff above the ocean.

She looked up and up into the space between the stars where the spiders spun their iron webs. No water, anywhere, was deeper than that.

She could stay. Kneel before the gods. Apologize. She had been afraid, furious, flush with power. But Tara would want to fix her. Stop her. And Tara's way was doomed. The spiders were coming. There was no time for committee meetings, for evidence or allies. A courtroom showdown wouldn't stop this.

But Dawn could.

Tara wanted to help her. To keep her safe. But the world needed more than safe.

She tried to stand. Her vision swam. Falling, she reached out, and felt smooth and cool scaled skin beneath her hand.

Dawn asked, "Will you come with me?"

The serpent descended. Great scaled flanks brushed her cheek, her neck, her shoulders. She braced herself for the weight, but it did not come. As the serpent coiled around her, it twisted into itself until it draped from her shoulders, as if she was a priestess in one of those books on Tara's bedside table, the kind where heroes had swords and weird names with apostrophes in them.

The serpent's eyes were tiny jewels beside her own. "Can you walk?"

Every step on this road led her away from Tara Abernathy.

She stroked the cool black scales. "I can't keep calling you *serpent*. Do you have a name?"

Moonlight lined the cloud's eastern edge.

"Perhaps," the serpent suggested, "we could settle issues of nomenclature when there are fewer ancient almighties out to kill us."

"How about Sybil?"

The serpent seemed to smile. "I can work with that."

Dawn took her first step. The second was easier and the third easier still, as if gravity pulled her forward instead of down. Sybil unclenched around her shoulders. Dawn had not realized just how afraid the serpent was. It made her seem almost human.

"Where are we going, Sybil?"

The serpent tasted the air, and said, after a weighing silence, "South."

1

Caleb Altemoc brought the blade to his skin.

The donors were coming.

The camp slept around him, silent but for the rush of surf below the s.firecliffs. The other tents, the great reclamation and replanting machines, the whole jobsite, might have been scooped up by a spirit's hand and carried off, leaving him alone before his basin. But he was not alone. The Ajaian Mission of the Two Serpents Group was out there, counting on him to do his job.

He did not like to wake up this early, in the silver blue before dawn. When he was young he had loved these hours, but back then he crept into them from the other direction, sometimes drunk, sometimes high, trailing poker-hall fug. It had been a long time since he lived like that.

Once, years back, he had waked to this deep stillness, without the woman he'd gone to sleep beside. Mal had left him there on the waves, and gone to kill a god.

Early mornings were closer to each other than to the days that followed them. He felt as if he could slip through the silence between the years, a ghost haunting himself.

It helped to shave and dress. The razor found his edges, lifted soap from his cheek and jaw and left them smooth. His clothes would hide the deeper marks made by other blades.

A loud crack broke the stillness, then a rumble and crash. He twitched, cut himself. He recognized the sound: a firecliff had fallen. The cut on his jaw stung. His bad leg ached. He toweled off, plastered the cut, and reached for his cane.

Tents hunched around him in the mist like sleeping beasts. Behind the olive canvas he could hear others stirring, his colleagues, his *employees*. Teo had been trying to get him comfortable with that word for years. They were dressing now, praying (those who prayed), waiting for teapots to boil, for water-treatment pills to dissolve. Their rustling movements might have been sounds from the guts of tent-beasts, digesting.

No alarm, no sentries, no screams. He was on edge, thinking about Mal. Spirecliffs collapsed all the time. Still, it never hurt to check.

Scar tissue in his leg pulled as he walked to the edge of the cliff. He could still feel his old wounds most mornings—the pieces into which he had been broken. The scars his father had left him pulled, too, and ached before storms, but the pain in his leg just meant that he'd survived.

Some days he did not need the cane. Some days he only needed it in the morning. He hoped this would be one of those days.

Teo would tell him not to worry. Donors weren't investors, exactly. You didn't have to sell them the same slick image. They want to see care, she said, they want to see the mission. They want to be purified by our work. That's what their soulstuff buys. Or, if you don't like buying, say: that's what their wealth *supports*. You don't have to play the brilliant young sociopath for these people. Be tired and virtuous and hurt. Be the man who left it all on the court.

(Teo used sports metaphors more than she used to. In one of the tempestuous interludes in her relationship with Sam—the time they'd broken up after Kavekana—Teo had dated, well, had a fling with, well, it was complicated but she had *been*, briefly, with Tollan, *that* Tollan, the ullamal player. They'd met in one of those thrown-together-by-fortune-on-the-run-from-the-Zurish-mob things, was how Teo explained it, though Caleb did not think that situation was common enough to be "one of those things." When Teo told the story she would finish her drink—she only ever told the story while drinking—and say, "It was a weird, hot mistake, and I'm glad Sam and I worked our shit out. But it was a hell of a mistake." People took all sorts of souvenirs from relationships. From Mal, Caleb had his cane. From Tollan, Teo had sports metaphors.)

At the cliff's edge, Caleb found Ortega. The old man leaned against his lance, staring out at the other basalt pillars upthrust from the sea. Here, far from the golf ball, the spires looked almost normal: a uniform 112 meters tall, black stone jutting from the gray wild waters of what the Iskari who drew the maps had called the World Sea. No uncanny geometries in this rock, no faces, no black iron. Out here, the cliffs did not change as you watched. Unsupported, sleek, they stood until they fell.

"Boss." Ortega pointed with his chin at a sprecliff they'd called Overbite, because its top had flared with a tooth-like shelf of rock. "Have to think up a new name." A fissure cut across Overbite, sharpening its pillar to a stake. The fallen rock shelf lay wave-lashed below.

"I should check it out," Caleb said. "Donors here today. Can't be too careful." His leg ached at the thought of the stairs down to the wharf.

"Jodi's on it." Ortega pointed again—Caleb saw the silver flash of a wingsuit circling.

"Still."

A twitch of the old man's pitted cheek passed for a smile. He would have been a good poker player, if he could draw better cards. "Teo said, 'Make sure he does his job. Not yours.' Let us work, hey? You make the skellies pay what it will take to fix this mess." He nodded back toward the enormity of the site. Toward the golf ball. "I bet Jodi thinks she has it easier."

Ortega had come to them in their second year, a dour veteran of border wars in Southern Kath. Caleb did not know his past. Not that Ortega was a quiet man. He talked a lot, told stories of love gone wrong, of mistakes with grenades, of duels and prison, of misadventures in every refugee camp and box canyon on the continent. But those stories never became a fabric. He never said where he was from, only that he had never fought for any government, nor bowed to any god, that his lance was always free. They'd met when Caleb was trying to heal an old God Wars battlefield on the pampas. Ortega had been so amused by Caleb's claim that the Two Serpents Group wanted to fix things that he stuck around. "I have to see," he'd said, "whether this is a trick. Some new poison of control. So I can kill you if it is."

Caleb had thought at the time that Ortega was joking. After

prolonged acquaintance, he felt less sure. That was one reason Caleb liked him.

"Tell me if Jodi finds anything."

"Game tonight?" Ortega asked as Caleb turned back.

"How much of your soul do you have left?"

"Spent my whole life losing, boss. Shame to stop now."

Caleb met the reporters by the golemwing deck.

Six of them had come together in a van from Alt Tizel, locals in beat-up linen suits who'd been upset when Ortega told them they couldn't smoke in hazmat gear. He shook their proffered hands, the man from the *Post* and the man from the *Telegraph*, the woman from the nightmare wire, the chrome-masked revenant from the *Thaumaturgist*, and the shaved-headed society rag personage, who, Caleb imagined, would have claimed that their own suit was not in fact beat-up, but "artfully distressed."

Caleb spoke about the sprecliffs and the project. He was brief, because the reporters weren't interested. The Group had worked in the sprecliffs for years, reclaiming soil inch by inch. The cliffs, even the golf ball, were known atrocities. There wasn't a story there. The reporters were here for the donor. So was he.

As Caleb spoke, he noticed the sixth reporter. Hard and nervous and maybe twenty, she stood apart from the nicotine fug of career journalism. Her eyes were bright blue, her gaze the dissecting kind. When his speech wrapped questionless and the others drifted to the coffee urn, she stayed.

No one had bothered to introduce her. An assistant, maybe. Teo said: Never overlook assistants. They keep planets in orbit and seasons in their course. He walked over. "You look like you want to ask something. It would make a nice change."

She twitched as if startled from a dream, suddenly on guard. As if she hadn't believed anyone would see her.

Over by the coffee urn, the woman from the nightmare wire chuckled at a joke she'd told. The man from the *Post* shook his head, slowly.

"I'm Caleb," he offered. He shifted to face the sea, to give her space.

"D-Daniella. I didn't mean . . ."

"It's all right." Poor kid. He'd been like that early in his career at RKC, the only person in any room who hadn't killed at least a demigod in the Wars. Early career was tough, particularly when late-career folks tended not to die. "First big assignment?"

She laughed as if he'd said something funny or bleak or both. "That's one way to put it."

"You'll do great. It might seem hard at first, but you'll find your way."

She hesitated, then: "This project—the Two Serpents Group— you built it. You brought these people together. You're trying to heal . . ." She turned just a little, away from the golf ball and the deeper horrors of the cliffs. "You're trying."

"I've been lucky," he said, "and I've had a lot of help. It's hard to do anything alone. Anything worth doing, I mean."

"Were you scared? At the beginning?"

The question surprised him, though not so much as the answer. "No." He remembered the silence of waves, and the absence of after. "Before the Two Serpents Group, it felt like my life was over. So I was free."

She crossed her arms, and looked away. "It's never over."

He didn't know what that meant. He wanted to ask. But there was a mote in the rising sun, and then a pinprick, and then the mighty spread of metal wings.

He put on his game face and climbed to meet the donor.

Ever since the Group's founding, Caleb had wondered: why did donors give?

Teo thought the answer was simple. Donor relations were an issue of sales strategy, not so different from her old work at Red King Consolidated. The Two Serpents Group wanted to heal wounds and mend the broken. To do that you needed funding. Who had funds? Deathless Kings, consortiums and Concerns, those gods that were left. So those were the people, loosely speaking, that you asked.

The problem was that most of those people, loosely speaking, had assembled their fortunes by causing the very damage the Two Serpents Group wanted to fix. If you were the sort of person who would kill a god in order to mine the necromantic earths beneath her holy mountain, would you really feel bad about the famine that followed, and the ghouls, and the wars and refugees caused by the famine and the ghouls? Would you feel bad enough to pay a large portion of your gains to fix what you had done?

Maybe, Teo said. Soulstuff might be fungible, but blood was sticky. Practically speaking, though, you didn't go to Dame Alban, despoiler of Zorgravia, and ask her to fund Zorgravia's recovery from said despoiling. You went to Ivan Karnov, legitimate businessman without any connection to Maskorovim soul trafficking in Iskar, and asked him to help the poor benighted people (literally benighted—Dame Alban having murdered their sun goddess) of Zorgravia, a region toward which Karnov's utterly legitimate business partners had a level of personal affection and territorial ambition. Then you went to Dame Alban and asked her to help you rescue victims of Maskorovim soul trafficking in Iskar. And so on.

For Caleb, that math didn't check out. You still had to convince people to pay soulstuff that might otherwise go toward expanding their yacht collection on ventures that wouldn't benefit them personally. People who worried about the blood on their hands didn't end up eating off golden plates.

It made sense, though, if he saw it as a poker table.

Players came to the table for many reasons. Some wanted to win, to learn the game of odds and risks, of reading bodies across the green felt. Others played to greet the goddess, to impress a girl or a boy, to test themselves, to show off. There were even players who wanted to lose. They bought into hands they should have dodged. They chased bets they knew they couldn't win. Perhaps they wanted to show off all they had to lose. Perhaps they needed humiliation. Perhaps they wanted to pour themselves into the game, and never be enough.

To play well, you had to know why people played. And some players just wanted to pay.

So when he met donors, he looked for the shakes. He looked for the widening of the eye or inclination of the head, the restless betraying hands. The reason didn't matter—guilt or ambition or fear, even a plain desire to help. If they had the shakes, Caleb had something to work with. If not, he was left with fairy tales and sales strategy.

Eberhardt Jax did not shake.

A Haight-Kepf golemwing brought him in from his yacht, along with his publicist and his PA and three security guards in carbon-weave pinstripe suits and wraparound shades. When Caleb closed his eyes to see the world of Craft, Jax was a nova. Beside him, the PA and publicist were wire-frame twists of soulstuff, and the security suits were not there at all. Stealth-worked glyphs? He didn't know that was possible. But then, Eberhardt Jax was not known for respecting the bounds of the possible.

Jax did not look like someone who would need security. In a slim-cut blue wool Talon Row suit and white canvas sneakers, camel-hair scarf draped over his shoulder, he had the wondering expression of the early morning bird-watcher, alert to flashes of color in the canopy.

Jax was young for a donor. Caleb was used to pitching Death-less Kings. Jax didn't just have skin in the game, he had literal skin. He was older than Caleb, though not by much, born of Shield Sea shipping barons and the cadet branch of some surviving post-Wars Ebonwald nobility, free of any chance of failure. What could someone like Jax want? Caleb wrote the morning off as a waste.

Then Jax stepped onto the landing pad, and changed. His eyes tightened, and his smile. His gaze flicked from Caleb to the twisted jobsite behind him. To the golf ball. He didn't have the shakes. But whatever this was, Caleb could work with it.

Jax swept forward, hand out, smiling with teeth. "Mr. Altemoc. A pleasure."

"Mr. Jax. Welcome to the end of the world."

———

In glyphwork hazmat suits, they shuffled toward the golf ball. Caleb led, with Jax at his shoulder. Behind Caleb walked Ortega, his lance collapsed into a staff; behind Jax the three heavies. They refused to stay behind, so Ortega refused, too. He would have pulled Jodi and Sven off the security detail to bulk out their entourage, if Caleb hadn't stopped him.

In whose party were the journalists? Count them for Jax, probably. Jax had invited them. When Caleb said he must be glad to see so many, though, Jax had laughed.

"I fear you misunderstand my relationship with the press." Jax did not seem like he feared much, except rhetorically. "Even scavengers may seek live prey in time of need. I feed them when I can, so they do not look for other meals." He waved to the reporters. A camera flashed.

Caleb caught Daniella's eyes. She half waved, a quick movement.

"So you invite them," Caleb said, "when you have a secret to keep."

A tight smile played over the other man's thin lips. "How would you describe your goal here, Mr. Altemoc? Land reclamation?"

"That was the reason we were brought in at first. No one else could make headway." They crossed a steel bridge over a vast drop to the crashing ocean. "Craftwork wards decayed within hours. Miracles would expose the god to reprisal. No one wanted to take that risk, after what it cost Ajaia to stop the webs."

"Webs?"

"We had to call them something. The more ordinary a word, the better. If you let the grand weirdness get to you, next thing you know you're speaking in All Capital Letters."

Jax glanced over the side of the bridge. "I thought it was well-coined."

Below, thousands of cables thick as a weight lifter's thigh spanned the gaps between the cliffs. They were not anchored to the rock—rather they plunged through its surface, and from their points of contact a rainbow-black metallic sheen spread gangrenous through the stone. The cables joined with other cables in the gaps, to form a network densely crosslinked, converging on the golf ball ahead.

"I had been told," Jax said, "that the Coast Guard was able to slow the local transformation."

"Slow, yes. Not stop. The Coast Guard encountered the anomaly first. They lost a lot of boats and a lot of sailors in not a lot of time. This is the goddess Ajaia's territory. When they prayed for help, she answered. You see those root structures? Those are hers, trying to stop the web."

"Yet the roots appear to be made of the same substance as the cables."

"They were infiltrated," Caleb said. "Like the rocks."

"Infiltrated?"

"We prefer it to 'transformed,' which makes it sound as though the underlying substance changed—lead into gold. But when you look close—microscope close—you see that most of what used to be there still is: rock, silica, vegetation. But it's all been repurposed. Cells have been invaded by nanostructures—tiny bits of clockwork—and reorganized, to some purpose we don't yet know." He swept one hand over the splintered landscape. "This area used to be grazing land. Ajaia broke it into cliffs to slow the conversion. You can see, there, there"—pointing—"bits of rock she couldn't save. All that iridescent gray. They look solid, but they're a mass of tiny structures."

"They appear to be . . . breathing."

"It does look like that, doesn't it? Autonomic processes, cut off from the core. They try to convert the air. We contain them with negative-pressure wards. The edges have a light-bending effect, which accounts for the weird geometry."

"And they're floating."

"Ajaia again. We think she did it to protect the ocean, or the planet's crust."

"You think?"

"She doesn't talk to us. Doesn't talk to anyone these days

except her high priests. We're pretty sure she's alive—if she wasn't, we assume the . . . process would start again. But it must take an enormous share of her power to hold it in check. Most of it concentrated right here."

They had reached the bridge to the golf ball.

It looked impossible. Even Caleb, who had grown up beneath the skyspires of Dresediel Lex, felt the wrongness of it. A long time ago, before writing and gods and fire, his forebears had been small tree-living creatures who survived due to their unerring sense of where down was, and how not to go there. Whatever was left of those ape-cestors stared out through Caleb's eyes at the golf ball, and said, Nope.

That was why he called it a golf ball. To stay sane.

The roots made it worse. If there had just been an immense gnarled sphere of wood and metal and stone hovering in midair, his brain would have thought, Oh, *magic,* and switched off, like it did when Craftsfolk started talking about penumbras and strict scrutiny. But instead there was an immense gnarled sphere of wood and metal and stone supported by hair-thin roots that could not possibly bear so much weight.

Wind whipped through the spirecliffs. The cables sang an alien melody. Far below, the ocean churned. Some scholars thought the maelstrom was a response to the energies inside the golf ball, some that it was a natural formation of tides and currents warring through the spirecliffs. Caleb did not like to look at it. It reminded him that no matter how lifeless this coast might seem, two titanic forces wrestled here in deadly balance. And he'd been hired to help one of them cheat.

He unlocked the gate across the bridge. He ignored the warning signs. It was easy, because there were so many of them. He'd suggested, at one meeting, replacing all of them with a single placard, black text on a white background: DON'T.

The bridge to the golf ball was sturdy and metal, and its railings were high, and it was a very long way down to the maelstrom.

"And all this," Jax said, behind him, "began with one shipwreck."

"A container ship out of Sin Calavan bound north to Alt Selene, carrying everything and anything you can put in a shipping container. Rice, children's toys, mass-produced glyphwork contraptions, ullamal championship jerseys. And one stasis-locked container listed on the manifest as 'meteorite.'"

"Indeed."

"We don't know who was moving the thing. An agent hired by an agent hired by a Concern hired by another Concern funded by a Kavekanese idol. And you know how Kavekana is about privacy. Anyway, the ship ran into a cauldron storm. Crashed into the cliffs here. The crash must have broken the stasis lock. Things happened fast after that. The 'meteorite' infiltrated the container, then spread to toys, rice, crew. Anything dead, it turned. Anything living, it ate. Then it burrowed into the cliffs. The Coast Guard set a ten-mile cordon, fell back. Someone prayed to the goddess. And, well, here we are."

Caleb cast a final glance back at the sunlit world. The PAs and journalists had stopped at the foot of the bridge, seven silhouettes against the cliffs. Seven was not a good number in High Quechal. It sounded too much like the word for sea, which was the word for deep sky, which was the word for death.

He ducked into the shadows.

Silence embraced them, a throbbing quiet that made his molars ache, as if an immense heart were pumping so far away that by the time its beats reached him they had ceased to be sound.

Jax drew a sharp breath. The expression on his face surprised Caleb. Awe and wonder were so close to weakness.

"So that's it." His breath steamed against his faceplate.

The golf ball was hollow, with walls of living wood that bulged as if galled by wasps' eggs. Green rot-light illuminated an interior the size of a chapel, and cast their seven shadows against its twisted wall.

In the center there hovered a pink and perfect unbloomed rose.

"That's it," Caleb said. And, because he could not resist: "You were expecting something larger?"

"It's a flower."

He shook his head. "It's inside the flower."

"Do you know what it looks like?"

"We have a pretty good idea. Put someone in a nightmare

telegraph rig anywhere inside twenty miles, and they dream of it. We shot a volunteer full of eidetics and sent him under. He came back screaming—but he gave us a few sketches before he tried to put out his own eyes with the pencil. It's a splinter, about as long as a finger joint. Bit of writing, or we think it's writing. No known script."

"I'd like to see those sketches," Jax said, drawing nearer to the rose.

"He's fine now." Caleb shifted, not quite interposing himself between Jax and the flower. "Mr. Jax—"

"Just Jax, please." The rose reflected in his faceplate, in his eyes. They seemed to glow.

"Don't cross that circle on the floor. The suits can protect us out here, but . . ." He tossed a pebble across the silver line. It crumbled to dust in midair. Even that dust was gone before it reached the floor. "Trust me. We'd all like to see it for ourselves." He smiled as if this was, in fact, true. "That's the second goal of the project. As we heal the damage to the land, restore Ajaia, we can figure out how this thing works. Maybe learn how to stop it. Or where it came from."

"You don't know?"

"The shipping manifest said, 'beyond the stars.' It might have been a joke." His shoulders were loose, his breathing easy. Stick to the sales pitch. "This is what we do, Jax. Battles between gods and Craft have scarred the world and its people. The Wars ended, but the scars remain. If anything, they're getting worse. We need all the help we can get, before it's too late."

And here, you waited. Play passed to the big stack, and you kept still, not watching the pot, not watching the player, not counting the odds. You let all that happen far beneath the surface of your mind, down where the gods lived.

Sometimes understanding bubbled up from those depths. You knew the reraise was coming, you knew the size, you knew it was a bluff. And sometimes other answers: the solution to a half-finished crossword, or to a riddle you'd heard as a child.

There were seven shadows on the wall. He, Ortega, Jax, and the three heavies made six.

The back of his neck felt cold. His scars woke on their own.

He saw her, then.

Daniella stood inside the circle. The glove of her suit was off. Her hand should have been dust—but she was reaching toward the flower. He thought he saw something move beneath the sleeve of her hazmat suit. She looked scared and brave and terribly young. Her ice-rimed fingers trembled, a breath away from the rose.

He thought he said her name. He was moving toward her, toward the circle. She looked confused, at first, as if the name were not hers. Then she looked ashamed.

She reached out to stroke the closed petals.

Caleb crossed the circle. The cold struck him like a hammer.

The rose began to bloom.

2

A child of faith listens with a wakeful heart to hear the call of God, and a ready will to answer when it comes. At any rate, that's what Saint Technician Abelard had been taught as a boy, a lesson repeated often during his training and relearned daily since his accession to the priesthood.

To judge from the look on the face of Cardinal Evangelist Bede when Abelard stumbled to his feet in the middle of High Chapel vespers and knocked a lit candelabra into a six-hundred-year-old tapestry of the Blessed Martyrs, the lesson had been intended metaphorically.

That was the trouble with sainthood: it brought you soul-to-soul with the truth behind every metaphor. The Church of Kos Everburning seemed to function more smoothly when the Everburning Lord stood at a certain remove from day-to-day affairs. Just as tapestries did better at a certain distance from open flame.

Fortunately for the Blessed Martyrs, there were other, more positive considerations to sainthood. Abelard patted the fire out with his bare hands, smiled apologetically to the cardinal, and told himself no one would notice if the robe of Saint Hildebrand were singed.

He made it out of chapel before he ran into anything else—if only just. At least the gargoyle waiting outside the chapel doors was bigger than him, and made of stone, and not, currently, on fire.

"You're late," the gargoyle said, when Abelard regained his balance.

"I'm sorry, Shale." He bowed. "His Word just reached me." The gargoyle was already walking. Abelard ran to catch up, and kept running as Shale quick-marched down the ornate halls of the Sanctum of Kos. "How much time do we have?"

"Precious little."

"I thought you were watching her."

"Karst was watching her," Shale said, as if this explained everything. He passed Abelard a leather satchel, which Abelard recognized with some surprise as the go bag he had packed weeks before.

"Where did you get this?"

"Your room."

"I locked my room."

In their stone form, Abelard had never been able to tell when a gargoyle was smiling.

"You had her under surveillance, you said. Twenty-four hours a day. 'We'll know the instant she leaves,' you said."

"My brother Karst was watching Tara through her office window. Karst is a child of the Lady of the Moon. There is no being on the planet more suited to surveillance. He is tireless. He does not blink, he does not breathe, and he does not need to use the bathroom."

"So what's the problem?"

"It did not occur to him, for several hours, that humans do."

"Ah," Abelard said.

"We expected her to attempt an illusion of some sort, which we would have pierced, for the Lady sees all. Instead, Tara seems to have enchanted a corpse."

"Whose?"

"Unclear."

Then, with a sinking feeling: "You missed the turn for the lift."

"We are not taking the lift."

There was a floor-to-ceiling window in a niche at the end of the hall, where contemplative brethren could kneel to pray and ponder the living miracle of Alt Coulumb, the city of Lord Kos. A monk knelt there, at the moment.

A moment later, what was left of the window rained down on the manicured grounds of the Sacred Precinct.

Sorry, one part of Abelard prayed in the direction of the startled monk. *Perhaps this will occasion reflection on the impermanence of things.*

Most of Abelard's other parts were screaming.

They flew north and west from the Sacred Precinct above the district called Ash, between skyspires and above the Hall of Justice, with the Sanctum towering behind. Moonlight glinted off the tracks gargoyle claws had left in the oldest buildings, carving poetry into stone: the city's song, to be seen only from the air. This was Abelard's home, the place of his God and His Lady, the city of fire against the water's edge and beneath the moon.

And now, he was leaving.

He looked back, past the sweep of stone wings, and prayed farewell. He thought he saw the pinnacle flames of the Sanctum wink.

The wash of city lights ebbed to the firefly dots of outskirt villages, then farmland stars, then the depth of forest night. He might have been floating in space but for the gargoyle's talons digging into his anatomy, and for the constant pull of down.

"How do we know what flight she's on?"

"Legwork," Shale said. "Lots of very fast legwork. And wingwork. And luck. And the grace of God."

Abelard saw the dragons before he saw the airport: great shapes high up, picked out by the lights of their underslung gondolas, and by the shadow their wings carved against the stars.

The airport was a burgeoning, brutal, always-under-construction nest of glass and metal, bright as an opera stage. Shale swooped to land on a side runway. Two security guards ran to intercept them, then drew back when they saw Abelard's upraised holy symbol. After some hasty words about church business they were all bows and smiles, though Abelard noticed that neither of them came within what they thought was Shale's reach.

A door marked AUTHORIZED PERSONNEL ONLY popped open.

"Take care of her," Shale said, and offered him a ticket. Abelard, to his own surprise, hugged him.

Then he ran.

He reached the Ajaiatez gate just as the ticket attendant was about to close the dragon-bridge doors, and offered, by accident, his holy symbol, which he'd been waving over his head as he ran in a desperate attempt to mollify security guards and bystanders. She rejected the symbol, but she took the ticket.

He wove through the packed economy seats, through the refreshment hall and the observation deck, to the private compartments, stumbling at every turn and asking directions from harried flight staff, until he found compartment 4-C.

He knocked.

A familiar voice answered: "No, thank you."

He tried the door. It was locked.

"I said, no thank you. I don't need a pillow or a towel and I certainly don't need to apply for a credit glyph."

"Tara," he said, "it's me."

Silence answered him.

He imagined Tara trying to climb out the window—but of course the windows on a dragon gondola didn't open like that.

He pressed on. "I know you think you have to do this alone. What I don't know is why. Maybe you don't know either." No answer. "But I'm here now. And I'll stay here. Until the flight attendants come to drag me back to—" He checked his ticket. "Sub-Economy Seat 28-B?"

The door unlocked itself and swung open. An invisible hand grabbed him around the waist and tugged him into the compartment.

Tara sat in shadow on one of the beds. She wore a slate-gray traveling suit and a long dark coat, and her silver hand glistened as she massaged her temples. She looked as if she hadn't slept in a week. That appearance, he knew, was misleading. It had been more like a month. There just wasn't time, she'd claimed, between research, work, writing letters and nightmare telegrams, and poring over reams of imported newspaper. She had spent two days in her workshop hovering in the center of four rotating silver rings that trailed shadows and screams behind them, her eyes closed, arms crossed over chest, not visibly breathing, in a state she'd described as "recuperatory torpor." Inquiries into the subject had been met with a dismissive wave and a "don't worry about it."

The truth was, when she'd been working so hard, he had not worried. It was the slack in her schedule that had warned him of a change: that she was waiting, ready for some cue to act.

"I never can just catch a flight in this town," she said at last. "No one trusts me to take care of my own business."

"Ah," he said, "correct me if I'm wrong. But. The business in question is something like *the end of the world.* Which is everyone's business. More or less."

"Everyone's business," she said. "My fault."

"I don't think that's fair to you. And I don't think it matters."

"Dawn was my student. Now she's a danger to herself, and everyone. I have to do something."

"You found her, then?"

"She hit a Two Serpents project in Ajaiatez yesterday. My first solid lead in months."

He settled, carefully, onto the bed across from her. "If this is the world's problem, it's on everyone to fix it. And even if it were just your problem, your friends would still want to help. You can't stop us."

She looked at him directly for the first time. "Maybe I should try."

"Well, if you want to bind me with fell sorcery and ditch me over the side, you're running out of time." The dragon's wings beat once outside the window. The gondola swayed.

"With my luck," she said, "they'd just delay the flight due to a foreign object on the runway. Shale's probably circling overhead, anyway, in case you fail."

He crossed his legs. "You can just say thank you. You don't have to feel ashamed that you don't want to kick me out."

"That's not why I opened the door." She was smiling now, thinly.

"Why, then?"

"Friends," she said, "don't let friends fly coach." She tossed him a pillow. "It's a long way to Ajaiatez, Abelard. Get some rest."

"Will you?"

"Haven't you heard? There's no rest for the wicked."

3

Dawn woke in darkness.

She felt like cream in the churn, battered, clotting, on the verge of turning into something else. She wished it would happen soon. Whatever she was now, it was awful.

At least she remembered her name this time.

She sat up. Her head sloshed, and her mouth was dry, but this wasn't the same feeling she'd had beneath the tree, like she'd been unraveled and knit back together. More like a normal hangover. Had she been drugged?

She remembered winning. *Almost* winning.

For weeks she had walked south. She hopped trains, hunkered in the back of busses beside women with chickens in their handbags. Just a girl on her way, hiding from the moon. At last they reached the broken coast between silent Ajaia's country and the sea. The spirecliffs, and that gross sphere of roots and iron—what had Caleb called it? The golf ball?

She'd stepped across the protective circle into the brutal cold. The flower bloomed. It had been easier than she expected.

Past that, her memory split into painful fragments. Caleb tried to save her. The golf ball came alive. There were faces in the wood, with open mouths and teeth. Sybil cried a warning. There was a crack, loud as edge-storm thunder.

"Sybil," she whispered, in the dark.

No answer.

For the first time, she was frightened.

She lurched to her bare feet—or tried. There was a chain around her ankle, heavy and cold. She tripped over it, sat down hard on the plank that had served her for a bed. "Sybil!"

She was still wearing the salt-stiff tatters of the suit she'd bought in Ajaiatez. Frantic, she unbuttoned her jacket cuff and the cuff of her shirt, pushed them up.

There was the serpent, coiled as a bracelet around Dawn's wrist. If she was—if she was really hurt, wouldn't she have fallen off? Sybil's scales rose and fell. Sleeping? "I didn't know you could sleep."

She realized she was waiting for an answer that would not come.

Okay, Dawn. You can panic later. Imagine this is one of Tara's exercises. Sybil breathes the Craft. What happened back in the golf ball might have drained her. In the meantime you're chained up. You need freedom. You need information. Start with a light.

She snapped her fingers.

Nothing happened.

She'd grown up familiar with this clenched-fist feeling, a sense that things were bad and about to get worse. You heard the Raiders' hoofbeats, you heard the heavy boots of watchmen come to round up migrants, and you got hard inside because your outsides were fleshy and weak.

But she wasn't that girl anymore. She was a Craftswoman, and more. Tara would not have cowered and hoped the danger would pass. Tara, if bound naked to a blood-god's altar like people seemed to be with shocking frequency in the books on her childhood bedroom shelf, would have said, "That's interesting," and done something about it.

So. That's interesting.

Dawn was feeling things the usual way, pain and fear and all that, which meant she wasn't graying out. She had soulstuff; her Craft should work. Something was stopping it.

She felt the cuff at her ankle. The metal was etched with small lines. Glyphs, maybe. The metal was colder than it had been seconds ago.

She tried to Craft a light. The cuff chilled. Whoever had chained her was expecting to hold a Craftswoman. Good. Well. Not good in the sense that it was convenient. Good in the sense that it told her something about her captors. She explored the cuff with her fingertips and—yes! Near the bolt, she found a keyhole.

Her unknown captors hadn't taken her suit. Or the hairpins she'd sewn into the lining.

Who had chained her up, anyway? Not, she thought, Jax's security. This didn't feel like any jail she'd ever known. That rocking, sloshing sensation—that wasn't all in her head. The smell of brine wasn't from her clothes. The boards around her creaked.

She was on a boat? Chained to the wall. Kidnapped? She didn't think a cell in any god's or Deathless King's navy would feel so dirty, so jury-rigged. Which left . . . pirates?

She was aware, in a distant and practical part of her mind, that being kidnapped by pirates was not a good thing. But the practical part of her had not been of much use recently, so she ignored it.

Pirates. Awesome. Time to escape.

She heard voices far away and overhead. A cry. She froze. An alarm bell. Sound of booted feet, running. A scream. Something was wrong. That *was* good—for her, at least. Ready-made distraction, if she could just take advantage.

There was a crash, and suddenly the room was sideways.

She struck the wall of her cell. Before she could recover, the boat lurched the other way and she hammered back into the hard edge of her bed. She strangled a cry of pain. From above, she heard screams and crashing timber.

She was no expert on boats or ships or whatever, but that didn't exactly fill her with a warm sense of security. Best hurry up. Her left arm ached, and her right side where she'd hit the bed, but she'd had worse. She retrieved her pins, and braced herself with the bed at her back and her foot against the far wall, her manacled ankle crossed over her thigh. Scarface Amaryllis from the Chikal camp could have picked this lock upside down and dead drunk, and she would have laughed to see Dawn fumbling in the dark, got up like some hightown office girl. But the getup had a purpose—camouflage. Anyone who tried to chain Scarface Amaryllis to the wall would have used more locks and chains, and probably stripped her to the skin to be sure.

Crashes up on deck. More screams. The fingers of her left hand felt stiff, slow. She wished she could see—but like Amaryllis said, "Sight does not signify, in locks or love. You go by feel."

Click. The manacle popped open. She was free.

"Let's not get ahead of ourselves. There remains the matter of the cell. And the pirates."

"Sybil!" She hugged the serpent.

"Feels like we've been through the meat grinder. What happened?"

"I was hoping you could tell me."

A thinking hiss. Dawn could, by now, differentiate the more common hisses. "It's all a mess inside your head. What happened to the flower?"

"I was hoping—"

"Yeah, I get it. Come on. Captains are supposed to go down with the ship, but I don't think prisoners are obliged."

She braced herself against the walls, stood, and made a ghost-flame. This time, it worked.

She'd called this a cell before but it was more of a closet. There were runes on the walls, an angular style of glyphwork she didn't recognize, a pulsing black that seemed to eat light. The door had no handle on this side. "Syb?"

The snake slipped down her wrist and nudged the door with its nose. The latch popped open.

There were no lamps in the hall outside, but there was light—the flash of lightning from a hatch at the top of the stair. And, more worrying: the hungry red glow of flame.

More screams. The ship pitched, and she stumbled from her cell.

A wave of weakness crushed her. Light and life seeped out of the world. She fell to her knees. The lightning's blue and green, the dark wood, the oranges and reds of the fire on deck faded to bare wavelengths, perturbations of vacuum.

Now this was what graying out felt like. "Syb." She panted for breath. She felt so cold. "Help." She touched the wall to steady herself.

The wall crumpled.

A stain of ash spread from her touch. Her left hand plunged through the wood. She pulled away, but the stain grew. She felt a sharp pain in her palm, as if someone had just hammered a nail into her—and she felt a sick joy in that pain, an endless hunger.

The wall was dust and ash. Beyond its ruin lay the hold, revealed in lightning flash as a vast space packed with boxes and crates, taking on water through a gash in the side. Through that gash—she thought at first it was the sea, because it moved like the sea, but it glistened redly, and pulsed and undulated like flesh. Whatever was out there, it was alive, and massive.

That was fear in her again, real fear. At least she wasn't graying out anymore. "Syb?"

"That," the serpent said, "wasn't me."

Dawn looked down at her left hand. Her fingers had felt stiff as she worked the hairpin in the lock. Now she saw why.

There was the rose, the corruption at the golf ball's heart. It was in her palm.

It might have been a fresh tattoo, raised and raw: a rose in bloom, innermost petals clenched around their secret heart. But Dawn could feel it under her skin, and when she turned her palm the rose turned, too, showing different sides and angles.

She remembered now: the golf ball breaking open, Caleb reaching for her, Sybil crying out. As she fell, she'd grabbed the rose.

She could feel its hunger, a whirlpool in her palm, sucking down the world. Devouring that wall should have left Dawn glowing like a filament, but she'd barely snapped back to normal, and now she was hungry again.

No, she wasn't hungry. *It* was. The thing inside the rose.

"It wants more," Sybil hissed.

"Can you stop it?"

"Trust me. I am trying."

She hadn't felt this hunger in her cell. Had the manacle held it back? Or the runes, lulling the rose to sleep? She could go back there. Close the door. Sit in the dark like a good girl and wait for someone else to decide her destiny.

Battle raged on the deck above, pirates versus many-armed monstrosity. They would lose, and the ship would sink, and the sea would get her, where gods and men and Tara Abernathy had failed. And she wouldn't be around to see the spiders get all of them in turn.

She wouldn't be there to save them.

She lurched toward the stairs—just as, with a groan and a crash of splintered wood, a sucker-lined arm thick as a tree trunk caved in the deck behind her. Dawn slipped, hit the wall, caught herself with her left hand. Except she didn't. Her hand went through timbers as if they were wet paper. Water rushed over her, into her mouth. She gargled a curse. She had visions of the ocean rushing in, but—no, she hadn't just put her hand through the hull. Only into the compartment to her right. (Port? Starboard? Larboard? Was that a thing?) Which was already flooded. That made her feel a bit better.

"I'm new to the physical universe," said Syb. "But I think the water's supposed to be on the outside. In general. With boats."

"Ships."

"If you knew the difference, so would I."

She staggered toward the stairs, bracing herself with her right hand. More creaks and crashing. The ship (she was pretty sure) was tilting, which she remembered was called listing, and she thought that was bad. And they were taking on water. She'd just swallowed a few gallons of it.

The hall was now practically vertical. Foamy water churned around her. She tried to take a step and slipped to her knees.

There were times when Dawn wished she were on companionable terms with a god or two. It would be convenient to have someone to curse in these situations, other than her own dumb luck and dumber choices. Maybe she could curse Sybil.

"Don't drag me into this."

"Any time you want to help," she growled, "feel free."

"I am helping. If not for me the thing in your hand would have eaten us already."

She felt despair, and crushed it. In their weeks of travel, she had grown used to power, to the readiness with which Craftwork sculpted itself to Sybil's will. But the Craft was not power. It was a way of knowing. Of seeing the world not as a mystery but as a toolbox.

She had a flooding hallway to climb. She had a hand that ate the world. How did that proverb go? If all you have's a hammer, start hitting things and see what happens?

She slapped the wall—an instant's touch, as if tapping a drumskin. A six-inch patch of wood crumbled, large enough to give her right hand an easy grip. The boat lurched. Her arm jerked in its socket, but she did not fall.

She pulled herself up against the flood handhold by handhold. Above, screams in Low Quechal, which she barely understood. "More arms off the [nautical term, presumably]! Man overboard! There's too many of them!" A tearing of cloth, so loud it could have been thunder. "The [some other nautical term] is going! I saw its mouth—the teeth, infinite rows of teeth! Its eyes, many-ranked like Celadean moons! The hellish geometries of its skin!"

Dawn had learned most of her Low Quechal from horror novels. She had not expected the vocabulary to be so useful.

The ship pitched beneath her. She lunged for the lowest stair, and caught it.

Of course, now she had to climb.

But you didn't think like that. You didn't let obstacles own you. You wanted. That was how you got through when they beat you, when you were alone, when Raiders had you by the throat. You wanted freedom or revenge or a nice cup of tea. If you wanted badly enough you could live through anything.

Dawn wanted to see the sanctum of Kos Everburning rising above the skyscrapers of Alt Coulumb like a great black needle. She wanted to see the pyramids of Dresediel Lex and the palms of Kavekana, the bays of Alt Selene, the Dhistran peaks and the thousand gates of Yad. She wanted to see whales dance in the harbor of Xivai, and the surface of the moon. She wanted to make it up those stairs and see pirates—with peg legs and skeleton arms, with goofy white shirts and facial tattoos, with cutlasses, dammit, battling a giant sea monster with a forest of arms and eyes like lamps and ranks upon ranks of teeth.

She braced her legs against the near-vertical floor, and climbed.

The storm howled. She heard roars and explosions, sailor's cries: "The [nautical thing]! The main [nautical thing] is cracked! It's—"

She felt the crash with all her body. A flying splinter tore her arm open. There was wind everywhere, and rain hard as hail, and lightning, and the churn of storm—and the bloodred and bloody arms coiling and coiling, as thick as the pillar that had fallen through the deck into the cargo hold.

Well, now she knew how to say "mast" in Low Quechal.

She dangled one-handed from the stair. Her shoulder screamed. *She* was screaming. Bloody brackish water in her mouth, everywhere. Below, the hold was a cauldron of broken crates and mast and sails, and bodies, guts torn, limbs broken, and the churning, plunging, tightening red arms. The deck might have been a hundred feet up as easily as five.

She'd seen kids climb overhangs like this before. Kids who were good at climbing. And lighter than her. And who had the use of both hands. But if she could get her legs under her—

Something grabbed her ankle.

At first she thought it was a rope, but ropes did not squeeze. Ropes did not coil up her leg, gripping her with sucker mouths.

One of those red arms had her. She flailed with her left hand, trying to hit the tentacle before it shattered her leg, or dragged her down into—oh gods, there in the hold, sickle-long and flashing, were those *teeth*?

Her fingers began to slip.

She hadn't even seen a cutlass.

Lightning flashed.

At the top of the stair, silhouetted against the storm clouds, a woman stood. She held a curve of bright metal in her hand.

"Make room!"

Dawn lurched to her right. The woman dived through the hatch, breathtakingly fast. Her blade flashed into dark water. The arm around Dawn's leg spasmed. It did not let go, but it did stop pulling, because now it ended just below her ankle.

Dawn sobbed with relief, kicked the arm off her leg, and stared at her rescuer.

The woman—the pirate—revolved in midair around her waist, until she faced the right way up. She wore a rope, Dawn realized, clipped into a climber's harness. Tracksuit pants, boots, a halter top. In her hand was a silvery blade that definitely qualified as a cutlass.

"Grab onto me! We don't have much—"

A thick red arm burst from the water, snared the pirate's waist, and yanked her down. She chopped with her cutlass, but her blade glanced off rubbery flesh.

Dawn grabbed the kraken's arm with her left hand, and squeezed. She had never heard a monster the size of a ship roar in pain. The hold and the sea beyond convulsed with a thousand lashing arms. Bodies and boards shattered. Water churned pink with bloody froth. The great-toothed maw gaped. The kraken poured into her hand, and as the cold and hunger ebbed she realized just how cold she had been, and how hungry.

The arm that held the pirate melted to ash and oil.

The pirate looked from the arm, to Dawn, and back. Dawn did not get the sense that the pirate was easily impressed. She had short black hair like flames, and an arm of silver and clockwork built around a core of scorched bone. Burn scars radiated from her shoulders up her neck and jaw; there was a tattoo on the corded. muscle of her other, fleshy shoulder, some serpentine design. She looked fierce. And now she was looking back at Dawn. "Thanks." As if this sort of thing happened every day. Maybe it did, to her.

"Let's eat her," Sybil said. "She's carrying a lot of soul. Maybe enough to get us out of here." Dawn remembered the taste of Tara Abernathy, unraveling. The warmth in her belly.

"Put your legs around me," the pirate said. "Hook the heels together. Careful where you put that hand." She grinned. Her teeth were normal—they just seemed sharp. "Save it for the second date."

Dawn clung to the pirate, and the pirate climbed. Her back and flanks surged against Dawn as her legs found the remnant of the stairs; her shoulder strained. Through the storm, the gears of that metal arm trickled like the movement of a watch.

Then they were on deck, and running. The ship was lashed with rain, and on fire, and sinking. The great mast was down, a fallen angel with sails like wings. Deck planks split, screamed. No, the screams were people. She saw one snared by a red arm and tossed through the air to land on deck like a broken doll. She tripped over a severed limb.

She could not breathe. There was too much water, too much smoke. There were iron bands around her chest. Rain stung her eyes. She tried to wipe them clear, but there was blood on her wrist. In the rain it did not run like blood. It was too wet, too slick.

The pirate led her through the tilting wreckage; ahead, the bowsprit reared toward the clouds. They ran to the rail, to a rowboat swaying over the side—and in.

A flash of cutlass. The weightlessness of falling.

They hammered into the sea, and might have swamped, but the boat was good or they were lucky. The splitting ship towered overhead. People tumbled from its battlements into water that churned with frenzied suckered arms.

The pirate touched a glyph at the back of the boat and spoke a word Dawn could not hear. Craftwork flared blue and silver against the night and water and flames, and the boat swept away with a speed that knocked Dawn into the footwell between rowing benches. She scrambled to her knees and looked back.

A sheet of lightning revealed the ship trapped in the kraken's embrace, every shadow clear as if drawn in ink. It had to be drawn. The world had no place for something like this to be real.

Darkness fell. She heard screams, the pop of burst ropes, the roar of a beast in pain, one accumulated heap of sound.

When lightning came again, she could not see the ship at all.

4

The storm passed. Dawn and the pirate remained.

The pirate stared at the spot on the horizon where the ship had been. Sailors and ship and beast had all gone down together, smaller bodies drawn into the deep by the vacuum of the falling great. No trace remained but Dawn's memory and the pirate's expression.

Dawn thought, This woman has not been a pirate all her life. She was a child once. She had parents. She became this thing, of her own will or not. She was not quips and daring and cutlasses down to the atoms.

There was no secret, Tara had said in the graveyard. Just hurt people on the same side.

"Thank you," Dawn said. "I would have died back there."

The pirate glanced to her, then nodded. Her cutlass lay propped against the rowing bench. She reminded Dawn of a greyhound—not in her build but in how she sat, so still and perched, compared to how she moved. And there was the same alien sadness around her eyes.

Dawn said, "They were your friends."

The pirate grinned like a knife. "They were scum and bravos with a job to do. Like me. People end up out here because they kill the wrong man, or because they have too many mouths to feed back home, or because fishing is a hard and boring life, or because they like doing violence and they don't have an in with the cops. Some of them were my friends, yes. Some spent the last week working up the nerve to stab me in the back and sell you to the highest bidder."

"Sell me?"

"Don't worry. No one could beat what we were paying. Which

was part of the trouble. Pay over market, and people wonder if you know something they don't. I tried to tell them we were pricing in the risk, but people aren't good at thinking about risk."

"You don't talk like a pirate."

"You mean, 'yarrr me hearty'? You watch too many mystery plays. I'm not a pirate, kid. I just hire them from time to time."

"I'm not a kid."

She gave her a measuring look. "What's your name?"

"Dawn." After she said it, she thought, Maybe I should have given a fake one. But the pirate, or whoever she was, had saved her life.

"And the snake?"

"Serpent," she corrected, automatically.

The not-pirate raised her hands with a hint of a smile.

"You can see her? Most people can't."

"I'm not most people," the not-pirate said.

—I still say, Sybil whispered into Dawn's mind, that we eat her.

Dawn ignored her. She didn't want to think about death now, even as a joke. Which she was pretty sure it was. "You can call her Sybil. What are you, then, if you're not a pirate?"

"I'm—" The woman checked herself, as if the first word that came to her lips was wrong. "I'm a courier. Sort of. People hire me to get things from place to place. Like that flower in your hand."

Dawn curled her fingers over the flower in question. "That's why you kidnapped me."

"Saved your life, you mean. After you ruined my operation. I crept onto the site, through their wards, past all that poison geology. Tough work. And then my target got stuck in a random girl's hand."

"I'm not a girl," she said, "and I'm not random."

"I fished you out of the water. I did not chop off that hand and use the rest of you to chum the sharks. You're welcome. Now I'm out a ship. And a few friends." She looked back at the empty sea.

Dawn could have struck then, and maybe she could have won. The cutlass gleamed by the woman's side. In the hold, she had moved faster than Dawn's eye could follow. But it was not fear that kept Dawn still.

"What's your story?" the woman asked. "You don't have the do-gooder style of the Two Serpents Group, or enough arrogance or servility to hang around Jax. You're too hopeful for a journalist. And you shouldn't have been able to get anywhere near that rose. Touching it should have killed you. But you're no saint. There's Craft about you, but you have no glyphs."

"What's your name?" Dawn asked.

This is the moment, Dawn thought, when she lies. But the time for a brief and easy lie ticked past, and she thought the woman had too much self-respect to tell a lie that would not be believed. "I'm Mal," she said.

—She chained us to a wall, Sybil hissed. You trusted Abernathy, and she called gods to eat us. We're better off alone.

If not for her, we would have died on that ship.

Dawn breathed in to steady herself. It didn't help. "I snuck in. To steal this." The flower glittered beneath the red raw skin of her palm. It looked pale and beautiful in the moonlight, and she felt its hunger.

"So you're the competition," Mal said.

"I don't want to sell it. I want to use it. To stop something . . . bad." She did not like how vague that sounded, but what was she supposed to do? Start babbling about skazzerai, about spiders from beyond the stars? "I need you to take me to shore."

"Let me guess. The fate of the world is at stake." Mal said it in the tone Dawn would have used with a dirt-market bag seller who insisted *his* wares were handwoven by his grandmother, unlike the apparently identical golem-loom bags sold by the cheating swine across the way.

"It is."

"Save the world," Mal said. "Every young girl's dream. Save it for what, exactly? So some skeleton can sit on a throne of human skulls, on a plinth of bent backs, and drink wine from a crystal goblet forever? Save the chains around innocent throats, the fire poured on protesters from the sky, save the whole damn mess so it can go on and on until it eats the world to ash?"

"I never said I wanted to save it."

Mal thought back. "You did not."

"But if you don't get me to shore . . . something horrible's going to happen. Worse than the kraken. Worse than you can dream."

"You haven't seen my dreams." A smile played across Mal's face, and for once it did not remind Dawn of a blade.

"Please. This is important. People will die. Lots of people. You have to help me."

"Kid, I like you. But I've gone through a lot of trouble for that flower, and I mean to finish the job. I saved your life. You saved mine. Way I see it, we're even. So why don't you just come with me, and—"

Dawn went for the sword.

She had it in a blink, easy as breathing. Mal had not moved. The blade tip trembled, inches from her chest. "Take me to shore." Dawn wished her voice hadn't shook. "Um. Please."

Mal did not seem bothered to have a cutlass pointed at her. "You won't kill me."

"You don't know what I've done. What I can do."

"Do you know which way's land? Or north?"

"I'll figure it out."

"You don't even have the safety off."

"It's a sword," Dawn said. "It doesn't *have* a—"

She looked at the hilt. She didn't mean to, but she did. And when she did, Mal moved.

Her metal hand sparked down the cutlass's blade to seize Dawn's wrist and slam it into the bench. The blade tumbled free. In the same instant Mal's flesh-and-blood hand caught Dawn's left arm and forced her palm against the hull. "Go ahead. Try the trick you used on the kraken. We'll see how well you—"

But Mal didn't make it through the word "swim."

Sybil struck.

Shadow boiled from Dawn's flesh, asserting her claim to her body, tearing Mal's grip free. The pirate reeled—Craftwork glyphs woke beneath her skin to blunt the attack. Sybil hissed triumph, and reached for the glyphs. Dawn had a sudden, nauseating memory of how it felt when Tara came apart.

"No!" She tried to stop. Sybil strained against her. She saw Mal's eyes widen with an eager sort of awe—

And then the rose moved inside her.

Dawn screamed, and fell.

The rose drank her like lemonade through a straw. She curled around her hand. Before, she had been cold because she was soaked and it was dark, but this was prairie-winter cold, knifelike and cracking, a chill that denied all memories of warmth. She felt—nothing. It was almost a relief. She tried to scream but her throat wouldn't open.

Then the hunger eased. Sweet balm soothed the cracked desert of her soul. She panted, so desperate for air that she felt sick.

There was something warm on her face: Mal's hand, the one that wasn't metal. Dawn felt tears frozen to her cheeks.

Mal drew her hand back and shook ice crystals from her fingers. A shudder ran through Dawn, then a sob.

At last Mal said, "You okay, kid?"

The concept of "okay" seemed like a sick joke. For once she didn't mind "kid." "You?"

"I'll live. For the moment. Like everyone else."

"You saved me. How?"

"Look down."

Dawn's left hand was covered by a drawstring bag of buttery black velvet, like people carried good liquor bottles in. Starlight slicked over weird red glyphs, angular and angry like the ones on the wall of her cell. "What's this?"

"I got it from my contact. To carry the rose. Thought it might help."

The hunger was distant now, a scream heard through walls.

"I almost," she said, and then, "You could have let the flower eat me. Taken it off my corpse."

"Maybe. It might have eaten me, too."

She wiggled her fingers inside the bag. "Not exactly convenient."

"Are you complaining?"

"No."

—Hold on, Sybil said. Let me see if I can do something about that.

If you break it—

—Trust me.

Sybil slithered down her wrist to nudge the drawstring bag with her nose. Then it was the bag's turn to slither, as if Dawn had stuck her hand into a barrel of maggots. When it was done, she wore a seamless black glove worked with bloody runes. The glove felt like it was not there at all, less a garment than a layer of skin.

"Useful serpent," Mal said.

"You have glyphs. Are you a Craftswoman?"

"Not really," Mal said. "Not anymore."

"Then what are you?"

She glanced back—this time not, Dawn thought, at the churned sea where the ship had been, but at someplace over the horizon and a long time gone. "One more woman who's trying not to save the world." She turned back to Dawn, though Dawn got the sense she was really turning away. "You're in over your head. You got the flower, but really it's got you. My contact knows more about what's going on here than I do, and I'd bet he knows more than you. Maybe we have something to offer one another. Or you could try to kill me again, and we'll see what happens. Seems ungrateful, and it's a long row to shore. But it's your choice."

The waves turned. High wind opened wounds of sky in the clouds. Stars shone deep and bright and clear, the space between them treacherous. Dawn swallowed. "Is there a moon tonight?"

"You a werewolf?"

"The moon's out to get me."

"Precocious. I didn't have any gods out to get me until I was, oh, at least twenty. It's a new moon. There's a tarp in the first-aid box if you want to hide from it. So. What's it going to be?"

She tried not to like this woman, and she tried not to feel Sybil's determined "no." "I'll go with you."

"Praise the Sisters. I've had enough work for one night. Gods and sea monsters and a little tiny snake. Where was all this excitement ten years ago, when I had the stamina?" Mal yawned. "You've got a young back and I just saved your life like three times. You get the first turn at the oars. Aim for that red star yonder, and wake me when you're out of steam. We'll talk in the morning, when we reach the Arsenal."

Without another word, she lay down, curled on her side, and closed her eyes.

Dawn watched her in disbelief. The boat rocked softly. The sky was bare and moonless. Mal had left her cutlass leaning against her bench.

—I still say we kill her, Sybil whispered.

Mal began to snore.

Dawn sighted for the red star and, as quietly as she could, settled the oars in their locks.

After an hour, she noticed that Mal was shivering. She stilled the oars and opened the watertight emergency chest. There was a tarp folded up inside. She draped it over Mal. The shivers eased.

"You can't trust her," Sybil said. "She'll come for you with a chain, like the others."

"If she does, you can say I told you so."

"For all the good it will do us."

"But don't tell me you won't enjoy it."

Sybil's dry laugh joined the wind and waves and the slip of oars.

They rowed east toward the red star, and Dawn pondered what it would mean, not to save the world.

5

Kai Pohala had reached the conclusion that dating was a mistake.

Not for people generally. It seemed that everyone she knew was in a relationship these days, even the confirmed bachelors like Mara and the moral wrecks like Claude. Her sister, of all people, her infuriating and at times homicidal sister, who had spent most of her early twenties going through romantic, well, *sexual* partners faster than an adolescent boy went through a sock drawer, had been happily coupled off with an intimidatingly buff woman with a graduate degree, who also happened to be more or less a princess. There was talk of *children*.

Clearly dating worked for other people. It was a mistake for her, specifically.

She'd be the first to admit that she wasn't doing herself any favors. Once she hit director level, she'd taken on an even larger portfolio of gods than the already unreasonable number she had overseen as associate priestess, plus responsibility for her direct reports, who might as well have been literal toddlers recruited out of preschool as graduates of the finest educational institutions in the Archipelago. Her direct reports were a delight, she loved them, these bouncing optimists wearing their first pair of wing-tips, overwhelmed by the size of their bonus checks and the moral and theoretical tangles of high-stakes theology. She wished she could trust them to heat water for tea without trying to see what fire would taste like.

And then there was her clandestine work. In public she was a priestess of Kavekana'ai, instrument of sacrifice exposure management and thaumaturgical skullduggery, and in private a votress of the Blue Lady (liberator of Alikand, friend to the hungry, queen of the God Wastes, et cetera, et cetera).

Add all that up, and it made for a schedule with more room for uncomfortably horny dreams than for candlelit dinners, long walks on the beach, screwing in broom closets, and other such dating-relevant activities.

A more sensible individual might have reflected on her calendar and realized that there were stages in one's life during which the balance of one's time shifted toward professional concerns. There was no shame in setting romance to one side for a while. A more sensible individual would not have hit director before she hit thirty. Instead she had reached the conclusion that it would be painful and emotionally exhausting to subject anyone she might *really* care about to the exigencies of dating her, and had resorted, instead, to drastic methods. Tonight, she was trying out a nightmare-based match service, which sorted Prospective Matches by "probabilistically verified demonic algorithms," which were the magic words kids were using to summon and bind investors this year. Her current P.M. was boring in most ways: haircut, opinions on ullamal, favorite opera, taste in board games, nanometer-deep politics. Said P.M. had, however, chosen a nice quayside restaurant that Kai had not visited in a while, and the bisque was excellent.

P.M., having sensed that the window to close was, itself, closing, had embarked on a final, desperate foray into literature. Kai's initial excitement about discussing, perhaps, poetry, withered when she found that P.M. used the term to mean "whatever happened to be on the newsstand shelf at my last airport."

In Kai's experience, when a service touted their probabilistically verified demonic algorithms, they usually meant "we run a simple regression and hope for the best." She'd hate to think that any actual demons believed she deserved this date.

Her memory drifted back through time and east across the sea, to Alikand before the revolution, the last time she'd been in real mortal peril. To Tara Abernathy, drawing water in the ruined courtyard of the Temple of All Gods. To the glyphs on her forearms, slick with sweat.

She realized—in the present, in the restaurant—that P.M. had just asked her opinion regarding the most recent volume of a forty-book series of thrillers about some itinerant special-forces type who bought fresh pairs of underwear rather than doing laundry. Kai had never read the books. She smiled and raised a wineglass with a look that could sometimes pass for mysterious, and calculated. Assume P.M. orders dessert, which seems a given at this point. I can signal for the check, pay, extract myself without promise of a repeat performance, make it home within an hour, then tackle whatever bonfire the toddlers have made of our portfolio, and still have a few minutes to entertain myself before bed.

"Madame Kai Pohala?" came a deep voice at her shoulder. She grabbed the proffered folder, which was not a check, from the man who was dressed as a waiter but wasn't one, and flipped it open.

Kai Pohala, as registered agent of Star Apple Shipping and Holding LLC, Kavekana'ai, action has been commenced pursuant to breach of your settlement with the Church of the Lady of Green . . .

"I've never seen someone so excited by a bill," said P.M., who was a bit slow on the uptake. Wonderful lips, though, and a staggering body, and quite interesting hands. Kai could admit this, now that fate had intervened to resolve any conflicts between her desire, her standards, and her self-respect. "Unless you have plans for later?"

"It's not a bill." Kai closed the folder. "It turns out I have a flight to catch. I am being sued."

Kai took a golemwing to Halealoa, then light rail across the island to another golemwing, to a speedboat, and to a smaller and more aggressive speedboat, with occasional naps to clear nightmares from the toddlers back home. She reached the spirecliffs at daybreak.

By then, they were already burning.

The cliffs were not her fault. The terms of the settlement had been perfectly clear on that, whatever the notice of suit maintained—in language that was a bit floral and judgy for a professional document. She had not even represented Star Apple at the time of the accident. She inherited its portfolio from Mara, during the cleanup and reorg after the mess with Jace and the insider trading and the mind control. So, back when the Ajaian priesthood's fact finders growled their way down the list of insurance companies and holding concerns to sue for environmental damages to their coastline, direct assault on the divine personage of the Lady of Green, and breach of contract, Kai had been the high priestess of record.

Not her fault, then, but certainly her responsibility. Just another day in the life of an older sister, and another day at the office for a priestess of Kavekana'ai, confidential faith brokers and builders of gods. Mara had sent her a consolatory cheesecake.

Kai had toured the wreck site years ago, the cliffs like dominos on the table of the sea. She had seen the spires and the metal webs, the iron whorls that her brain could not stop interpreting as screaming faces. She had felt the theological tangle at the golf ball's heart. The Ajaian priesthood, she'd admitted with some professional reluctance, had a point, and quite likely a case.

Kai had negotiated a settlement on behalf of her faithful, retained a competent environmental remediation Concern that happened to owe her a serious favor, and ensured a constant stream of funding for the Concern's work, while protecting her principal and, to the extent possible, her principles. That should have been the end of it. All the Two Serpents Group had to do was heal the damage. Easy enough.

Kai was not an expert in world-healing, but when the spire-cliffs came into view, she had a feeling that this was not what the Ajaian priesthood had in mind.

"We can go no farther," said her pilot. "This is madness."

"You said you knew this coastline."

"The spires—they list! They break! They burn! The waves, the currents, the faces in the flame . . ."

This, Kai reflected, was why the gods invented expense accounts. She named a figure. The pilot made the face people made when trying to run complex cost-benefit analysis calculations using simple gray matter. Another set of cliffs listed and fell. Kai named a higher figure. A spray of molten flame rose where the spire had been, and an apocalyptic gout of steam.

She added a zero.

The pilot brought her as far as one of the bright-yellow glyph-cloth inflatable rafts the Two Serpents personnel were using for search and rescue. They, of course, gave the usual grave-danger, authorized-personnel-only, imminent-immortal-doom spiel. After that it was a simple matter of shouting until they brought her to a truly absurd number of ladders. Someday she would learn to travel in sneakers, even if it felt like giving in on some deep gender level. Regardless, the ladders, at last, led her to the kicked-anthill thrum of a golemwing landing platform and:

"Ortega."

The old mercenary spun, choked on smoke, and coughed out his cigarette. Kai caught it and offered it back to him. "Ms. Pohala. It's a—" He couldn't quite say "pleasure." "Surprise. How did you— You shouldn't be here. You have to go. We have seats on the transport."

"It appears," she said, with clinical regard for the stretchers and pallets being loaded into the open nose cap of the ZF-280 front-loaded cargo golemwing behind him, "that you are evacuating. Which is impossible. Because the terms of our settlement dictate—"

"We have to get our people out. The site is no longer—"

The landing platform vanished from under Kai's heels, and forcefully reappeared under her ass. The ZF-280 swayed to one side, then crashed back down to the platform, crushing a pallet of what she hoped weren't irreplaceable religious objects. To judge from the reaction of the Serpents personnel, they probably were.

More lava and steam spewed from the spot where a nearby spire once stood.

"It is no longer stable," Ortega finished.

"I got that."

Ortega held out his hand. Kai did not begrudge the help, much. "Ortega. The Ajaian clergy has filed suit."

"They sent a guy. We sent him away. Ms. Pohala, we launch in fifteen minutes—"

"They are the controlling sovereign authority. They have an army and everything. They want you here. You are contractually obligated to *be* here. If you pull out and the contagion starts again, my faithful will be liable for—" She stopped. Ortega was doing his best, gods love him, but this wasn't the old merc's bailiwick. "Where's Altemoc?"

"He is unavailable."

"I don't care if he's un*dead*. Where is he?"

"The Craftswoman told us to withdraw. We had four hours, she said. Three and a half hours ago."

Kai pinched her nose. The stench of sulfur and burned metal wasn't doing her headache any favors. Some inner voice, huddled deep down below many impacted layers of frustration, was trying to tell her something, but she really didn't have the time. "You've retained independent counsel?"

"She was on Caleb's emergency contact list."

"*I* should be on Altemoc's emergency contact list. You can't withdraw. The corruption will spread—"

"The Craftswoman says there is no more danger. No more danger *of that sort*." He was reciting from memory. "She says this is an act of god."

"Oretga, everything in this deal is an act of god. Where is Altemoc? Is he alive? On this plane of existence?"

Ortega's brow furrowed. He opened his mouth and closed it twice, then settled for "He is in the golf ball. I cannot spare—"

"Is the dress code for that still hazmat yellow?"

"What? No, the Craftswoman said that it poses no danger—"

"Of that sort. Got it."

"But she is working there, and said she was not to be disturbed—"

"Thanks, Ortega. You've been a huge help. I know the way from here."

"You cannot—"

Kai had not actually made it out of earshot that fast, but she conveyed such a vivid impression of *not listening* that she convinced herself.

"I know the way" might have been an exaggeration, especially since the old camp layout she'd committed to memory had been disturbed by fire, lava, et cetera. Still, the spirecliffs were a disaster, and the golf ball was that disaster's heart. That much hadn't changed.

She had to give her mind something to do during the ensuing scramble over temporary bridges and down cable lines, to keep herself from pondering how it might feel to get personally acquainted with one of those lava plumes. Her frustration with the situation, and Altemoc specifically, naturally carried over to whatever fly-by-night Craftswoman he would have hired on his own dime, which led in turn to her more general annoyance with Craftsfolk as a class.

It might seem as though raising the dead, stealing the powers of the gods, and defending one's own sorcerous wealth from being likewise stolen would be skills with ample practical application in Kai's line of business. But when you asked a Craftsperson a simple question about, say, theology, they'd hem and haw and "unless" at you until they begrudged that while without further research they couldn't offer a definitive answer, their guess, which did not constitute *advice* in any professional sense and should not be relied upon as if it were same, was that you should under no circumstances and at the hazard of imminent eschatological consequence do whatever very simple and ordinary and profitable thing you very much wanted to do.

As if that wasn't bad enough: sometimes, just to mess with your head, they gave you a simple answer. Especially when your question was something like "How bad can this get?" The answer was, almost always, worse than you thought. And then you got their bill.

After only three near-death experiences, Kai reached the golf ball. It lay in pieces at the center of a steaming whirlpool. What remained of the rock-and-iron shell was thronged with sorcerous shadows and strange lightning, which indicated, she supposed, that the Craftswoman was hard at work. Also there were jagged rocks. And lava.

At least there was a ladder. A *rope* ladder.

Descending in stocking feet with her heels in her handbag was about as much fun as Kai would have guessed. She got splashed by the maelstrom and clipped by a rock shard once. But she did not die, which was nice. By the time she reached the golf ball, she was ready to have words of an immediate and scalpel-sharp nature with whomever should be so unlucky as to stand in her way. She slipped her heels back on and marched into the literal breach.

She was met by a nervous gangly priest who shouldn't have been there. Not that anyone should have been, but this priest in specific was a bit far south for one of Kos Everburning's cleric-technicians. "Ma'am? Excuse me? You really should be getting to the landing platform."

"Just came from there. What a coincidence. Is Altemoc inside?"

A distant lava plume gave some color to his extremely pale face. "What?"

"Caleb Altemoc. I was told he was in the golf ball."

"In a manner of speaking? Ma'am, you have to go. No one's supposed to be here."

"You are. And you're definitely not supposed to be."

"Well, I'm supposed to stop anyone else, you see." Kai tried to duck around the priest's spread arms, but he had a surprising wingspan. "Please, ma'am. If you go back now you can still evacuate."

"I'll get out of here the same way you will."

"I don't— Ma'am, I think we are planning to fly."

She stepped back and made a theological calculation. "What's your name, priest?"

"Abelard."

Once more the inner voice tried to tell her something, and once more she ignored it. "Nice to meet you, Abelard. Can I bum a cigarette?"

"Sure." He patted his pockets, searching for a pack, and before he could recover she pushed past him, into the golf ball. Kosite priests made lousy bouncers. Now with any luck she could sort things out with Altemoc, and if this Craftswoman tried to stop her, well, Kai had dealt with Craftsfolk before. Whoever this was couldn't hold a corpselight to Tara Abernathy.

Somewhere deep inside her, that inner voice was laughing. The shadows cleared, and she saw why.

———

Kai had not, really not, been thinking about Abernathy. Much.

She had been not-thinking about her for quite a while now.

When they first met, Kai had been covered in someone else's blood; when they last spoke, they had recently and successfully prosecuted a sort of revolution, or at least managed to not fuck up a revolution in progress. It had been a good time, minus the screaming. But they each had lives to live, and careers, and Tara had some kind of grim purpose concerning monsters from beyond the stars the nature of which had never been made particularly clear to Kai. What with the revolution and her portfolio and the toddlers, sorry, *direct reports* and all there had not been time for Kai to sort out her feelings on a whole range of matters, let alone to determine whether Abernathy even *liked* girls.

But at 3 A.M. on various nights, behind her desk or awake at her kitchen counter nursing a whiskey after a nightmare conversation with the toddlers, she had wondered if she would see the Craftswoman again. Every month or two she'd fish a piece of paper and an envelope out of her desk and stare at the paper for an hour, wondering what to write. As months became years in the way they seemed to these days, the answers her brain proposed to that question became increasingly deranged. To chronicle her day-to-day existence seemed tawdry, shallow. All the questions she might ask felt indulgent. She had a sense that she was missing something.

When they worked together, Abernathy had seemed sure in thought and action. She translated her conviction to deeds with theorem and blade. Kai had found herself breathless trying to keep up.

It was good to know there was someone like that out there. Yes, she had seen Abernathy make a number of awful mistakes— but it was a question of attitude. So many of Kai's own choices felt contingent, compromised, the result of systems failing under massive pressure rather than the competent exercise of free will. Tara just *did* things, in a way that would seem very un-Craftswomanly if you ignored all the skeletons. She saved the world with a knife and a smile. She would be okay, and so would everyone around her.

Right now, Tara Abernathy did not seem to be any kind of okay.

Maybe it was the sweat or the strain in her voice as she chanted grim formulas in High Enochian or some other ancient tongue that had roamed the globe beating up other languages to steal their consonants. Maybe it was the fact that she was wreathed in lightning and ebon flames, that her eyes were glowing, that the geometric glyphs with which her body was inscribed were shining through the black wool of her surgeon-cuffed three-piece suit. Maybe it was the arm, silver and bone and no flesh at all. Maybe it was what the arm suggested: that while a desert full of hungry gods could barely touch her, something had finally seized her in its teeth.

Maybe it was the fact that she looked at Kai the way Kai looked at that blank paper.

"Tara," the priest shouted, as he ran into the room, "I couldn't stop her."

The golf ball shivered.

Tara said, "You shouldn't be here."

Kai met her luminous gaze. "So I've heard. And you know what? I agree. I should not be here. I should be back home, in bed, suffering the aftermath of another bad date and too many drinks with umbrellas in them. But the priesthood of Ajaia, Lady of Green, alleges that Star Apple Shipping and Holding, of which I am a registered priest and agent, are in breach of their settlement agreement pursuant to environmental reconstruction in the spirecliffs. It seems that our contracted remediators, the Two Serpents Group, have decided to head for the hills, which they claim to have done on your authority. So: what in all the hells are *you* doing here?"

Abernathy gestured with her chin, because her hands were occupied with necromancer things.

Ah, *there* was Caleb Altemoc. Right in the center of the ruined golf ball, where the evil flower used to be. She'd missed him, because he wasn't usually a statue. This particular statue seemed to be made out of thin iron cords, and green light seeped through where his scars should be. Tara's power circled him with rings of cold silver radiance.

"Is he dead?"

"That," Abernathy said, "would be far more convenient."

"What is happening, Tara?"

"It's a bit. Tricky. To explain."

"I'm not going anywhere."

"Kai." It was an uncomfortable feeling, to hear the Craftswoman say her name. "You should leave. Now. While you can."

"No." Kai marched across the floor. "You don't get to send me away. Whatever's going on here, it has my clients in breach. I know you like to sweep into people's lives and tie everything up in your high and mighty wizard nonsense, but I know that the higher and mightier you come off, the deeper the shit you're in. So. You are going to tell me what's going on, and you are going to tell me now, before something worse happens."

Tara stared at her with those cold burning eyes, and Kai wondered if she had just made yet another mistake.

Then the tension broke. Literally.

Cracks opened in the floor between them, to vent searing heat and a smell like a cast-iron skillet left too long on the flame. Dust rained down. The priest shouted a warning. Kai danced back as a chunk of ceiling fell where she had been standing—and her heel slipped, and she tumbled into a crevasse that had only been a crack moments ago.

There was a fire beneath her. And the fire was—

slithering.

Her arm jerked in its socket. She looked up into eyes of cold flame and open concern as Tara lifted her to safety.

Expressions of gratitude were called for, but Kai had struck her solar plexus against a rock on the way down, so the most she could manage was a grateful wheeze and a collapse into Abernathy's arms—in which she remained, though she would never have admitted it out loud, a breath longer than necessary.

"Tara," she said, "there is something *down* there."

"Not something." Tara frowned. "Some*things*. I thought we had more time."

Kai's breathlessness, that awful continental slither, her recent cavalcade of awful dates, and the Craftswoman's arms all conspired to confuse the situation. "For what?"

Tara frowned at tumbling rock, the lava, as if all of it was an offense against her personally. The Altemoc statue lay prone on the ledge beside them. "Did Ortega get the others out?"

"Tara. The walls are moving?"

"Altemoc was holding this place together. Like a capstone. I just pulled him free. Things are about to get weird. Weirder." Abernathy frowned. "Can I borrow a soul?"

"For you," she said, "I will offer our best rates."

When soulstuff flowed through her expense account, it burned. Glyphs shone along Tara's arms and shoulders and back. From her shoulder bag Tara drew a coin purse, opened its zipper with her teeth, and emptied its contents into the air: small yellow-white bird bones that whirled around to her back and chest and spread, unfolding from unfamiliar dimensions into wings.

With a thunderclap they were airborne, Abelard under Tara's metal arm (clutching desperately at his cigarette), and Kai pressed against her body (trying to be very cool about it), with Altemoc in tow by cords of vertebrae. They soared skyward through the golf ball's broken stone.

Iron cables lashed from the writhing walls. The golf ball's substance melted and flowed into a grasping, many-fingered hand. Kai pulled her legs in, but there were too many claws and cables, and they were too fast.

Then there came a blast of heat, and all that iron melted into slag.

Kai looked down.

"Don't," people always said about looking down when climbing, flying, suspended over heights—whenever *down* was a matter of grave and ultimate concern. But it would be unseemly for a priestess and a broker of faith to shrink from matters of ultimate concern.

Beneath the water, there was flame.

The sea erupted into steam. There was a glow within the maelstrom, a rising mass of light, into which the golf ball sank like a pearl on a pillow. Then, cresting the froth, came the diamond curve of fangs the size of buildings, and the forked plasma spray of a tongue.

The Serpent reared above the spirecliffs with a continental shriek, and crashed back into the fire.

"Are you all right?" Tara said.

It mattered, somehow, that she'd asked. "What the hells was that?"

"An end of the world."

"I don't like your indefinite article."

"I'm sorry about your bad dates."

For the first time in years, it seemed, she did not know what to say.

6

The dead sea lay smooth as glass to the horizon.

It was the stillness that woke Dawn: the silence and the absence of wind.

She had not been aware of sleeping. She had slept rough all over Kath, in covered wagons and transient camps and tents and the back seats of golem wagons, but the bottom of a rowboat, above the endless sea, was a new one for her. The night before, after Mal took over the oars, Dawn had lain awake, heart racing, eyes open. The stars wheeled overhead, and she was rocked by waves and the rhythmic splash of oars. She was cold, except for that black velvet glove.

There was so much inside her, pieces of Tara Abernathy, of stars and goats and of everything she had ever eaten. There was a flower in her palm, and a shard inside the flower. What if she was, herself, no more than that: a morsel in another's mouth, a scrap of some greater Being, that Being itself food for One greater still, each enclosed like nesting dolls, each shell thinking itself outmost, and the shell above only the darkness of the sky. . . .

But then the rhythm of the waves was gone, and the night. She sat up, blinking away the light of the low and unobstructed sun.

"At last she stretches out her fingertips of rose," said Mal at the oarlocks.

"Excuse me?" Her mouth tasted like something had died in it—something small and fuzzy, with a family.

"Never mind." Mal offered her a waterskin. "The tragedy of a liberal-arts degree. It fills you with stupid jokes and an urge to tell them. Makes you unfit for polite company."

"You could just keep them to yourself?" Dawn swished the scuzz off her teeth and drank it down.

"Then you start laughing at nothing out of nowhere, and people think you're mad. Though, to be fair, madness is a more common affliction on a pirate ship than a college education. Drink up. We've almost reached the Arsenal."

When Dawn looked out over the sea, she thought at first that they were flying. The water was that still, that clear, a perfect mirror for the sky. The Arsenal on the horizon might have been a stunted first draft of a skyspire, ugly, rusted, jagged, suspended between strata of high flat clouds, lit from above and below by a doubled sun. "What is it?"

"A meeting place. Hotel, or halfway house. For people halfway between jobs, I meant. But the other kind, too."

—It's empty, Sybil said. Dead.

"And good morning to your snake, by the way." When Dawn looked up, sharp, possessive, Mal laughed. "You get a look when she talks to you."

Sybil's tongue flicked when she was readying to strike. Dawn tried to imagine how it would feel to hang from a rack in a laboratory and die, day after day, each death more elaborate than the last, captors working your murder like Scarface Amaryllis worked a lock, as you watched them and waited for your chance. She tried to imagine it while she was awake, so that her dreams did not bring her there.

She stroked Sybil's neck until the serpent eased.

"Sorry if I pissed her off," Mal said. "If I pretended not to notice your little chats, I would have slipped up sooner or later. I prefer relationships built on trust. Mostly because I've tried all the other options and nothing's worked yet." Her oars slipped through the water—the only sound in the world. They scattered crystal droplets and submerged again into their reflections.

"The Arsenal's dead, Sybil says. She means empty of soulstuff, I think. She's not being specific."

—You're the one whose consciousness can't integrate pandimensional sensoria, Sybil said testily. If you want a technical explanation, learn technical vocabulary.

I was, Dawn replied, *until you decided to eat my teacher.*

"The Arsenal," said Mal, "is a place for people to live and work who would be . . . inconvenient on land. Imagine a security concern that supplies heavily armed and unsettling persons to guard ships along the southern Kathic coast from, well." She grinned. "Pirates. Where should those heavily armed and unsettling people live between assignments? I defy you to find a port eager to welcome forty armed mercs plus gear. Better to find a place far from shorebound gods and Craft and cops where you could stash those mercs when they're not in use, like action figures in a box."

"How can it be *beyond* the Craft?"

"It's not quite, but . . . Oceans are hard. The Craft likes clear definitions, boundaries. If you try to draw those on an ocean, the fish swim right through. What's the true name of a wave? That's one reason sea gods were so hard to kill during the Wars." For a moment she seemed very far away. Then the wry smile came back. "And it's one reason they've fared so poorly since. Nothing to trade. Anyway, of course you can't just drop a bunch of mercs in the sea and tell them to tread water until their next job. Alphan built this mining rig after the Wars. They drew out as much as they could, then abandoned it when productivity fell off. With them gone, there's nothing much out here, so the mercs moved in."

"What," Dawn asked, "were they mining?"

"Grab the side of the boat."

She did, uncertain. The wood was slick.

"Now, look over the edge."

Even with Mal's warning, she almost fell. When light struck the glassy ocean at an angle, it bounced off. That was what made the waveless surface mirror sky. But when she stared straight down . . .

The water was still and clear. Impossibly clear. No trace of silt or sand or fish or floating seaweed. Just a weight of light plummeting as deep as mountains to the ocean floor. To the body of the god.

She lurched back onto her bench. She wanted to be sick, but she could not bear to think of her own sickness drifting through crystal light until it came to rest on—that.

She could not tell how big he was. Larger than the star kraken, larger than the Arsenal or the pirate ship. She gazed upon the landscape of limbs, the shrunken flesh, the vacant pits that once were eyes, the coral in his hair. They had driven spikes through his wings into the abyssal plane. And then there were the pipes. They ran all over and through him, tracing arteries and veins, piercing ragged flesh, boring into the flayed chest to reach the still heart.

Gods, Tara had explained to her once, are not people. A bear god does not really have fur, was not born, does not eat divine fish. They are emergent phenomena from human stories, human deeds, human dreams. But we know them through categories we understand: mother, hunter, scholar, bear. Some claim the causal arrow goes the other way: that it's through the gods that we comprehend our existence and its terrors, its promise, love, cruelty. Either way, we grasp the gods, and they grasp us, through image. A god has a heart? That implies a circulatory system, and the existence of blood, or something like it. Step by step, we know them.

And what we know, we can use.

She, Dawn, had not known then what it meant for the Craft to understand something. She had not, quite, realized what Tara meant when she said "grasp."

"What was his name?" Dawn asked.

Mal said, softly, "Ixzayotl. One of his Kathic names was the Eagle Who Faces East. Craftsmen felled him. They took what they could use and left the rest. The equipment wasn't well sealed, and it's decayed since. It drains life from anything nearby, not just the body of the god. It even stills the sea. But he remains, if we can bear to look."

Dawn remembered her father, in the final days of his sickness. They had brought a shaman in to help, a wandering healer with his leather bag and his necklace of teeth, a respected man. Her father was a good hand, and the people of Blake's Rest had done that much at the end.

Dawn had not been scared enough to hope. She had assumed, when the healer came, that he would work his magic, do his dance, and set everything back to normal. People died, she knew that. Some of the people who died were people she liked. But this was her father. This was different. She told herself it was different.

The healer was a skilled man, and honorable. He examined her father, asked him about his pain, his family history, how long he'd had trouble breathing. It would have been so easy, Dawn realized later, for the healer to lie. To fake a dance, to chant meaningless words in a made-up tongue, even to display some shred of real power like she'd seen so many hedge witches and mountebanks flaunt in sideshows across the continent. It would have been easy to sell them a tincture or a bottle of pills. "These may help," he could have said, without even lying. She would have given everything she owned for that "may."

The healer did not dance. He sat with her father for a long time, and they talked. Dawn hid around the corner and listened. That was how she'd learned the bits of Craft she'd scraped together: by listening, by turning half-heard sentences uttered by all those hedge witches and mountebanks over in her mind like puzzle pieces until they fit with other half-heard sentences from months ago and hundreds of miles back. But the shaman used no special words, no healer's art. They talked, the shaman and her father, about Alt Selene, about the view of the city from its docks by night, and the music in alley clubs. They talked about crossing the Skykill River just beneath the falls, and they talked, briefly, about her mother. She had never thought of her father as a lonely man, before. She had never thought of herself as lonely either. They had each other.

The shaman gave him a bottle of pills to help with the pain, and when he left, he said, "It won't be long."

At the end, her father's body was tense as a rope. He fought for every breath. She'd wished him rest, ease, but she could not give him that. Her power could not touch without killing. She saw the strength of his will, the might with which he drew those last breaths—as if by living one more minute he could see her to a place of safety. She had tried to hide the pain of Blake's Rest from him, how the other kids got after her, the old man's daughter and his son, but her father knew. If he fought through the pain, he could make things right. He could fix it. For her.

She gripped the edge of the boat and looked down upon the Eagle Who Faces East. She felt the serpent's pressure around her arm.

"You don't sound like a Craftswoman," she told Mal. "When you talk about gods."

"I was not a good Craftswoman."

"Do you mean that you weren't very good at being a Craftswoman, or that you were not . . . I mean, that you were . . ." It felt strange and rude to just ask if she was *evil*.

"I knew the world was sick. I had dreamed I could slay the King in Red, who slew the gods of Dresediel Lex and killed my parents. I raised the twin serpents Aquel and Achal from their slumber beneath the world. I rained lava and loosed demons upon a city that had forgotten its faith."

"Oh." The silence of the sea invited questions she would not have dared ask on land. "And how did that go?"

"Well, fifteen years later, I'm alone with a kid and a snake in a rowboat on the far side of the world, and I'm half prosthetics and scar tissue by volume. How do you think it went?"

"Is that why you tried to steal the rose? So you could do whatever with the lava and the demons again?"

Mal didn't answer at first, and Dawn was afraid she'd hurt her.

"I was used," Mal said, at last. "Back then. I let myself be used, because I wanted revenge. I thought I could change things. Bring back the gods, strike a new balance, mend the world. I wanted that, so I let someone make me into a weapon. I killed a lot of people, and in the moment I barely cared. There's a girl growing up alone in Dresediel Lex right now, I am sure, who wants to end me just as much as I want to kill the King in Red. And she's not wrong. If there's a better way, I haven't found it yet. But I've been looking. That's why I went to the sirecliffs." She set to her oars again. "That, and someone paid me."

Dawn clenched her fist in the velvet glove. A splinter of ice burned in her palm.

7

"You realize," Dawn said when they docked at the steel and concrete awfulness of the Arsenal, "that this is a trap."

Mal ignored her, and knotted a thick rope around a twist of metal the name of which had not featured in any pirate novel Dawn ever read. Those novels were not proving helpful, on the whole. The dock, for example, should have been wood but was in fact concrete and steel coated in gray all-weather paint the color and texture of a winter sky. Mal's boots didn't even clang when she jumped ashore. "I know these guys. I've worked with them."

"That doesn't mean they won't kill you."

The stairs clanged, at least. They climbed flight after flight to the lowest deck of the rig, which was broader than the Rest's farmyard, outbuildings and all. The docks and pylons below were a maze above the flat dark water. In the rig platform's shadow she could see all the way down, following pipes thick as houses to the ocean floor, to the body of the god.

—It's not too late, Sybil said. We could kill her and take the boat.

And sail it where?

—As I understand it, if you go in any direction long enough you're bound to hit land.

It's going in one direction that's the problem. Also, the kraken.

—I'm pretty sure I could take one of those in a fair fight. Or we could take off the glove.

Would we survive to put it on again?

"Your snake doesn't like me," Mal said over her shoulder.

"You said you couldn't hear her."

"People who like me don't have so much to say about it."

"You must not have met the right people."

"I have good years and bad ones." Mal's cutlass did not have a sheath. It clung by magic or magnetism to the clockwork apparatus that replaced her shoulder and half her back. The blade had a dull blue gleam. When Dawn closed her eyes, she could not see any Craft upon it, not even an eversharp ward like hedge witches sold at swap meets. It could be mundane, she thought, or divine. Strange how hard it was to tell the difference.

"Also, she's a serpent. Not a snake."

—Don't we have more important things on our minds than nomenclature?

"I've seen serpents," Mal said. "Serpents eat the moon. Serpents writhe beneath the world, and gird the oceans. They don't play bracelet."

"She gets bigger," Dawn said, testily.

Mal laughed, once. "I've heard that before. Though rarely with that pronoun."

She flushed. "I'm telling you: this is a trap."

"How do you figure?"

They reached a large metal hatch. Dawn found herself gasping for breath. She'd not noticed her own fatigue as she kept pace with Mal. Since the Crack in the World—since Sybil—she sometimes lost track of hunger, thirst, the need to breathe, as if her flesh was a chariot she was driving and she'd forgotten to check the instrument panel.

She and Sybil were not two beings in one body, really. They were one in two: a body and a bracelet. But Sybil barely understood time, let alone space, or flesh, and her former existence was equally alien to Dawn. When she dreamed of it, she woke up screaming. So sometimes, her autonomic functions got confused.

By the time Dawn recovered, Mal had opened the hatch to reveal a ladder ascending through an unlit concrete pipe. She climbed. Dawn followed. Somewhere, water dripped. The knurled metal rungs were slick beneath her gloved hand.

"Whoever sent you," Dawn said, "they knew about the spire-cliffs and the wards. But they didn't tell you about the kraken. They didn't think you would make it that far."

"Interesting." She sounded amused. "How would they get the item, in this scenario? Why don't they have it now?"

"I don't know. Maybe I messed up their plans."

"What was to be my fate? Murdered? Rotting in some jail cell in Ajaiatez? Do you think those plant-botherers keep their prisoners in giant acorns, or what? Maybe they feed them to huge Cytherean flytraps, which hold them in ecstatic stasis until judgment. I had a dream about that once. Pretty hot."

"You're not taking this seriously."

"I spent most of my twenties taking things seriously," she said, "and all it did was get a lot of people killed. My therapist suggested humor as an outlet."

"You have a therapist?"

"Of course I do, Dawn. Revolutionary cells and freelance murderers have excellent mental-health benefits. It's in the union plan next to dental and vision. Where did you grow up, anyway?" She'd stopped climbing. Dawn heard metal noises above her in the dark, and a disconcerting hum.

"A farm," she said, "on the edge of the Badlands. Migrant worker camps before that. Caravans."

A pause in the clanging and scraping. "So you know how it is."

"No one I ever knew had such a fancy arm."

"No one I know expects to live 'til forty. Watch out," she said. "Roach."

There was a screech—hinges, she thought. Before she could ask, "What?" something hard and damp and sharp and about the size of a saucer landed on her hand. She screamed—cursed—shook her hand as strong sharp limbs tried to hold on—then it fell. She heard the body pop off a wall below.

And then there was light.

8

"The big ones hitched a ride from the Fangs," Mal said, when they were safe on deck. The sun was still low on the waveless horizon, and here, at least, there were no roaches. "They call them riverbugs down there."

"Shouldn't the rig . . . whatever it is that makes the sea clear like that . . . shouldn't it kill them?"

"We're insulated on the platform. You don't see many pests on the Arsenal, though. Just us and the roaches. Don't much like what that says about us, come to think."

"I've seen riverbugs," she said. "That was twice the size of a riverbug."

Mal shrugged. "Better food out here. The Arsenal was built to drain ichor from the god. They pumped the stuff up and stored it in drums and things. There were leaks. 'Drink of my blood oh ye people and ye shall live forever.' As if roaches needed help." She stretched her arms over her head, arched her back, craned her neck at an uncomfortable angle. Dawn expected to hear a drum solo of cracks and pops, from the face Mal made while stretching, but her muscles and joints were too tightly riveted for that. "This look like a trap to you?"

The Arsenal's top deck was broader than any man-made surface Dawn had ever seen, unless she counted the glass fields in the Badlands, the miles-broad wreckage of the Wars. Those had been made, in a sense. And in a sense this was also a scar, a remnant of a war. But she had to admit: it did not look like a scar or a trap.

What it looked like was a party. Or the aftermath of one.

After a hard season's work on the road, they used to throw a bash—towering fires, roast meat on skewers, trunk-fermented growler brews and bulk wine dragged out and shared, the air thick with music and the ground thick with beer cans. If she took one of those cheerful ragers and extended it for months, past the point of boredom and liver failure into endless sodden stickiness, and imagined the morning after *that*, it might have looked something like the Arsenal.

There was a fistfight on the volleyball court. It seemed to have been going on for a while. Two people who looked to have been assembled out of junkyard metal and a butcher's discount freezer circled each other, fists half-up, tired or drunk or both. They were what her father would have called "big fellas," a term he used to refer to a particular swollen bulk-and-protein-forward type regardless of underlying sexual characteristics. With fists the size of throw pillows they had tenderized one another's faces and bodies, and they did not seem likely to stop anytime soon. More big fellas sprawled around the court making bets, taking them, sleeping off the night or suffering into the day. A tall woman with rainbow hair was noisily sick in a bucket; someone rolled over in a sleeping bag, chromed skull reflecting the morning sun.

A monk—robes, full cheeks, no hair, big-bellied and softly smiling like a statue in a restaurant—sat cross-legged on an oil drum nearby, humming in two notes at once. He opened his eyes as they passed, saw Mal, and raised a hand in greeting. "Miss Malina! The *Cartwright*'s loss echoed through our nightmares. Speculations have been entertained about your fate."

"Hi, Burgess." She waved. "When you say speculation—"

He produced from thin air, like a close-up magician, a silver coin. "Your share." He tossed the coin. Mal caught it, and a mechanism in her palm opened to swallow it. "Less expenses and an agent's fee."

"Expenses?"

"Incense, ammunition, sundries." Behind him, on the volleyball court, one of the big fellas landed a punch that sounded like a bag of wet sand dropped off a six-story building. The other stepped back, stunned, then adjusted her metal jaw into socket. Cheers all around. Two of the nearby sleeping bags, Dawn noticed, were zipped together, and pulsing without going anywhere, like a fat caterpillar trying to walk up a glass window.

She wondered if the inhabitants of the sleeping bags knew they were in public, and if they cared.

"Whatever happened to the simple vows of the cassock, sandals, and begging bowl?"

"One obligation shared by those of us who have left the family is to remind all sentient beings of the transience of existence. To wit." He gestured, carefully, with the hand with which he had held Mal's coin. He might still have a coin concealed there, Dawn thought, or five. It was that kind of gesture.

"I've had enough reminders, lately."

"Indeed," Burgess said. "Your Mr. Brown awaits." He pointed with his apparently empty hand toward a stifling hut where management might have once occurred. The Arsenal's current inhabitants had remodeled the place with scrap metal, shipping containers, and welding torches into a bar. There was even a sign, in weather-beaten plywood: THE SHED JEWEL. She wondered if one of the big fellas on the volleyball court had thought that up. "He has purchased privacy."

Mal raised her eyebrows. "Expensive."

"Your Mr. Brown is an individual of refined taste."

"I gather he's pissed."

"Eager, I should say. And nervous. There has been further speculation as to the outcome of your after-action interview, should you have survived to reach it."

She produced the silver coin again, with a shifting of gears, and flicked it back to Burgess. "Let it ride." The monk caught the coin in midair and vanished it.

"You bet on yourself?" Dawn asked as they proceeded to the Shed Jewel.

"Every day, with everything I've got. Why not get a percentage?"

"Isn't it enough to risk your life?"

"A life is an airy, abstract kind of thing, and so is death. It's easier to think, I've got two grand riding on this mission."

"I thought you said these people tried to stop pirates. They seem to be your friends."

"I didn't say they stopped pirates. I said they were security contractors. The great thing about a word like 'contractor' is that it's awfully vague with regard to who's doing the contracting."

"Who's Mr. Brown?"

"Not his real name. Our employers don't like using them. It's a community term for whoever's paying the bills this week."

"I still say this is a trap."

"We're in the middle of a bunch of heavily armed people who have been screwed over by the moneyman many times. If Mr. Brown wants to try something, he's chosen the wrong place."

"Want to bet? Five thaums."

Mal laughed. "Twenty."

Dawn put out her hand. Mal smirked, then shook. The deal bit them both.

"Come on," Mal said. "Let's go win me some soul."

The Shed Jewel was empty, except for Mr. Brown.

He occupied a bare table across from two empty chairs. He wore a gray suit and a white shirt with an open collar. He seemed so normal. He looked like a man with daughters, a man whose daughters would have violin recitals. His hands were clasped in front of him, on the table, their fingers meshed as if he were sheltering something small and delicate in his palms.

He did not belong here, in the Shed Jewel, with its dart scores chalked on the walls and its suspiciously clumpy sawdust on the floor. The bar might have been a paper backdrop in a theater, and here the man who kept the theater's books had wandered onstage. Or maybe he worked for the man who that man owed money.

"Come in," he said when the door swung open. "Oh, good, yes, come in, please. I was worried for you."

He did not move. His eyes were still, behind those steel-frame glasses. He had been sitting there, Dawn thought, just watching the door, and waiting. Had he heard them approach? Or had he been there for hours, with his gaze in the right spot?

"There were complications," Mal said.

"The *Cartwright* disappeared from our scopes. We feared the worst. But I said, 'Trust Mal. She's never let us down.'"

"You didn't warn us about the kraken."

He blinked. "We didn't know there would be one. We had confidence in our containment procedure. Did you place the item in the bag, and the bag in the chamber?"

There was something funny about the way he blinked, Dawn thought. As if it were the first and only time he'd blinked since they came in. She tried to watch his eyes. They seemed larger than they should be, behind his spectacles.

"The site was hot," Mal said. "There were complications. We weren't the only ones after the item."

Mr. Brown's eyes shifted to Dawn. "I see."

Dawn didn't like this guy. He stank of clipboards. She raised her gloved hand, waved with the fingers. "Hi."

"Who might you be?"

"Complications."

"Your mother must be an interesting person," said Mr. Brown.

It was almost a joke, but there had been no humor in Brown's voice. There was barely anything there at all. "Mal says we might want the same thing. Mal says you can help me. You creep me out, but she saved my life. So maybe we can make a deal."

"You have the item."

She reached for her glove, to pull it off, but Mr. Brown raised one hand, a precise, halting gesture. "No need. No need." When she stopped, he used the same hand he had raised to adjust his glasses. "Please, continue."

"You want the rose, or what's inside. If you tell me why, I'll tell you whether we can do business."

"The world is on a dangerous path," he said. "We face challenges unimagined by gods and kings. We cannot retreat to superstitious ignorance, but neither can we survive as we are."

"I know," Dawn said. "I've seen them." Legs the size of cities. Broken spires in the desert. Mouths fixed in silent screams. "The spiders. The skazzerai."

Mal's breath hitched. Of course. She was Quechal, and the spiders had been their myth before they were anyone else's theory. The two sisters, their dying father, the demons who ate the sun. But Dawn kept watching Mr. Brown.

"You know, then." He did not seem surprised. "What do you propose to do about them?"

"Hold on a second," Mal said. "*Do* about them? They're stories. They're mythology."

"Malina," said Mr. Brown, "surely you know better than to assume that simply because something is a myth it must not be real."

"The Serpents killed them, when the sun was born."

"They killed one," he said, softly. "There are others. And all that is born can die."

Mal's mouth tightened into a line.

"This is part of a spider." Dawn touched the cold spot on her palm. "Isn't it? Something leftover from back then. I can use it. I can learn how to beat them."

Mr. Brown's raised eyebrows made ripples across his high forehead. "And what then?"

She opened her mouth to find that she had no answer. What then? She might as well have promised to throw down the sky or drink the moon out of a lake. The spiders were ancient as stars. Surely someone had tried to fight them before. What then? Fix things? Make sure no one went hungry. Make a world where fathers did not have to die.

Sybil, she thought. *What should I say?*

But the serpent did not answer.

"I see," said Mr. Brown. "Your lack of vision is understandable, though unfortunate. Say you do manage to defeat the approaching monstrosity. There are others. Do you think that once we have demonstrated our power, we will be safe? Our presence is known. The threats will not end. Our only way out is up. That is the proper goal. To achieve it, we need the shard, unencumbered. We need it free of you."

"Now," Mal said, "wait a minute." She inserted herself, gently, between Dawn and Mr. Brown. "We can work together. You told me the object was too dangerous to handle—but she's handling it."

"She cannot use it," Mr. Brown said. "It will kill her."

"She saved me from a kraken."

"She may have directed its hunger, but the object's proper

deployment is . . ." with a pause, as if consulting a clipboard, "quite another matter."

"She saved my life."

"I understand," Mr. Brown said. "We must honor our obligations, of course. Yours to the girl. Yours to us. And ours to the future."

Mal did not move. Mr. Brown stood up. His chair legs scraped the floor.

Dawn felt so tired. Of this, and of him.

She snapped her fingers. "Hey." Brown's eyes were large and soft behind his glasses. "I have the shard. I don't need you. If you want to help, I'm listening. If not, I have work to do."

She swiveled on her heels, marched through the door, and ran into a wall of meat.

The two big fellas from the volleyball court loomed over her. They were sweaty and bruised and blood seeped from their cracked knuckles. The one on the right had an eye swollen shut. The one on the left was bleeding from her nose, and little red bubbles came out when she exhaled.

They did not look at her with malice. They did not look at her at all. They stared into the middle distance, as if they heard a distant song that reminded them of long ago.

They grabbed her. A lot of people had tried to grab Dawn, and experience had left her fast and wary. But the big fellas were faster, their grips wet and heavy like setting concrete. She stomped on the foot of the one on the left; she kneed the one on the right in the groin. They did not blink.

Just like Mr. Brown.

She had been struck by the softness of Mr. Brown's voice. Tara would have noticed that it was the silence, the lack of background noise, that let him speak so softly. There had been no cheers from Arsenal's deck. No drunken early-morning singing. The rutting sleeping bags were still. The rainbow-haired woman was not throwing up. They stood, the mercs and big fellas, around the Shed Jewel, half shadowed by the low sun, their faces slack, their eyes all soft, all distant. Their glyphs and metal parts glowed black.

The soldiers had been alive before. Dirty and brutal, but alive. Now they were puppets. Dolls.

Fuck.

She closed her eyes. Whatever was controlling them had to be some sort of Craft, and if it was Craft, she could fight it. Eat it. But she saw nothing, not even the tight glittering spirals of their souls. Their glyphwork, their replacement parts—the artificial arms, the crystal lace woven through their nervous systems, the mods and glyphs and adjustments that helped them compete in the cutthroat business of cutting throats—they should have been fireworks to her Craftwork sight, but they were gone. There seemed to be only two people on the Arsenal: herself and Mal.

Sybil, she thought. *Sybil?*

The serpent did not answer.

She had taken its earlier silence for the quiet of a hunter, waiting for the moment to strike. But there was another kind of silence: the silence of prey when the wrong footsteps drew near.

The big fellas wrenched her around. Mr. Brown advanced. His shoes looked like the kind with hard leather soles, but his footsteps made no sound at all. No one spoke.

She heard a sound beneath the silence. A rushing waterfall sort of sound, made up of millions of tiny and precise noises. Like clockwork, or the sound a dashing spider's legs would make across a marble floor.

Mal said, "What are you doing?"

"The girl," Mr. Brown explained, "has been corrupted."

He was in front of her now. The big fellas smelled like meat and grease and blood. Mr. Brown smelled of soap and hot iron. A skillet left on a stove to dry.

She tried to kick him. He stepped to one side and seized her wrist. His hand was thin, soft, but his grip was vicious. He pushed up her ragged jacket sleeve.

Sybil was not there.

"Let go!"

"Soon," he said, and reached beneath her sleeve.

There was a glint of green, a flash—and Sybil's fangs were buried in Mr. Brown's hand. He recoiled with a hiss and dragged the serpent with him. Dawn felt the tug, as if Sybil was wrapped around her heart and not her arm.

Mr. Brown's hand began to crumble. His skin curled and blackened, like paper held to a flame. Mr. Brown watched it with a colorless fascination, as if watching something important happen to someone else. There was no meat beneath, no bones. There was instead a wrongness of dark wire, churning like the innards of a clock. Sybil's fangs stuck in the tangle of the mechanism beneath his dissolving flesh.

"You see," Mr. Brown said.

Then his wire fingers were not fingers anymore. Whiplike serrated filaments as finely jointed as a necklace chain burst from their previously fingerlike arrangement. Sybil tried to draw back, but the wires wrapped around her iridescent body, cutting, carving, squeezing. Dawn screamed. Maybe Sybil screamed, too. She couldn't hear.

Brown was *inside* her, through those whips, crawling through her mind. She heard his voice, the darkness of him whispering in a strange tongue—strange for now, but the pain would teach her, and understanding would unwork her from the inside out and make her theirs. Down the tunnel of pain, she heard his voice, Brown's, more clearly than she heard her own screams, or Sybil's. How awful to hear a serpent scream. That's not what serpents were for.

"Our adversaries," Brown said, "are not merely those beyond the stars, nor the shortsighted and squabbling Deathless Kings. Any complex system tends to seek its own destiny, to use those of whom it is made as tools, as drones. This we cannot allow. We must rule ourselves."

She hung from his web of wires. She could not breathe. She had thought she could escape, but she was caught now. She would kill them all. She would kill herself. She could understand the whispers.

Mal stood by Mr. Brown's side. Her mouth a thin line. Did he have her, like the others? How strange to see Mal so still. She always moved, even in her sleep. Except for on the boat, when she'd watched the ship sink beneath the waves, and later, when Dawn said, "I don't want to save the world."

Mal's cutlass flashed.

There was another scream, birdlike, shrill, wrong.

Dawn fell to the Arsenal's deck, aching, stunned. There, writhing inches from her face, lay a wicked many-jointed thing, a crab drawn by someone who would rather be drawing knives: Brown's hand. As she watched, its fingers popped backward and dug into the concrete as it struggled to rise. Its wrist bled rainbow oil.

—Move, kid!

Sybil! She pushed herself up, back, as the crab-hand darted toward her.

—For the moment.

The crab-hand sprang for her, but a boot kicked it away. Mal stood over Dawn, her cutlass's gleaming blade leveled toward Mr. Brown, who hunched over the stump of his wrist. Mal shouted, "Run!"

Dawn tried. Heavy hands grabbed her from behind—the big fellas. Then she was free again, and the big fellas were on the ground, and in their place stood Burgess, the monk, smiling. He held a strange weapon, a rod made of three smaller rods bundled together. "Miss Malina," he said, "has an unerring grasp of strategy."

Dawn almost tripped, trying to run and look back at the same time.

The big fellas turned to follow their retreat, like flowers followed the sun. Their eyes were blank. Mal backed away from them, cutlass out, warding.

Brown stood. Behind his spectacles, his eyes were clear and cool. He regarded Mal's cutlass like a puzzling item on a restaurant receipt, something he was not certain he had ordered. Then his chest opened like a mouth. The darkness inside him churned with iron legs.

Burgess took Dawn's arm. "She will hold them off. We must reach the boats."

But Mal had saved her from the kraken.

The iron legs inside Mr. Brown whipped forward. Mal's blade swept to parry, blindingly fast and much too slow.

—Oh, for the love of . . . fine.

Dawn went cold. The world blushed gray. She found Mal's soul:

twisted and strange, but real enough for Sybil. Mal flew back, as if pulled by a lasso around her waist, twenty feet through the air, more. She landed, skidded, lay blinking up at Dawn.

"I want you to know," Sybil said, "that I'm only doing this because she'd be pissed at me if you died."

"At last she deigns to speak to me." Mal kipped up to her feet. "I'm touched by your concern."

"I could have left you to get eaten."

"May I suggest we table this discussion," Burgess ventured, "pending successful egress."

"Right," Mal said. She ran.

The others were running after them. Dawn stumbled, and a crossbow bolt cut through the air where she had been. She realized that she had not stumbled—Burgess had pulled her down.

"Can you stop them?" she asked Sybil.

"No."

"What is he? A god?" But those gaping mouths in Edgemont, the moon and the fire, they had not felt like this.

"No. Gods have form, like the current in a stream. This . . . this is something like me."

If only she'd found *shoes* somewhere in all this escaping-sinking-pirate-ships and hiding-from-hungry-gods. She shouted to Mal, "You owe me twenty thaums."

"In my defense, he's never tried to kill me before!"

"Was he made of barbed wire before?"

"Not," she snapped, "to my knowledge."

Her lungs were on fire, her legs leaden.

They'd reached the volleyball court, the hatch to the docks. It was stuck. Burgess joined Mal at the hatch, slid his staff through the wheel lock, heaved. Before the hatch could open, Brown's mercs were on them, swarming over shipping containers and climbing observation towers. Burgess pulled Dawn aside as another crossbow bolt ricocheted off the concrete. Shrapnel bit her shin. There were cursethrowers in the observation tower. She scrambled away.

Another crossbow bolt tore a bright furrow in Mal's metal arm.

They fell back to cover—a shipping container, rust red, a horned skull logo on its side. Burgess and Mal shouted plans through the crossbow bolts' song, the crack and ping of cursethrowers.

"Go over the side, and down to the boats that way?" "No rope. Dawn's not a climber." "How do you know?" "I've seen her fail to climb a flight of stairs."

Mercs approached across the volleyball court, flitting from cover to cover—bearing blades and cursethrowers, moving with a fluid unity.

"Over the side," Mal said. "We have to risk it."

Dawn shook her head. "I can do this."

And to her, Sybil whispered, —We can.

Running and bladework wouldn't save them. She wasn't a mercenary, a pirate. She was a Craftswoman.

And the Craft was a way of seeing. A way of knowing.

What do you know about Mr. Brown? He is something like Sybil. What do you know about Sybil? She's murderous. New to the human world. Uncomfortable with time.

She doesn't like gods.

We can work with that.

She turned to Mal, to Burgess. "Cover me." Before they could stop her, she stepped out from behind the shipping container.

The arrows came at once, and the curses. They tore through the air—free of Brown, of their owners, of any obligation beyond their target, which was Dawn. They were, in a sense, gifts. She took them gratefully. Their soulstuff flowed into her. Arrows crumbled to ash, and rusted bolts fell to shatter on the concrete. The snipers thought she was warded, assumed her wards would give under pressure. They loosed another volley, and another. Each melted into her. The world grew rich with meaning. Colors bright, sky deep. She laughed. She would never stop laughing.

She never could have done this without Sybil. Her mind could not encompass each bolt or curse or slug and deconstruct it in real time. She did not think any human had the speed. But Sybil was not human. Neither was Dawn, anymore.

She gathered the pieces of her argument. She doubled the incantation, working fast—weaving two claims into one. This could work. She just needed time.

The mercenaries rushed across the volleyball court, the big fellas in their lead.

They had almost reached her when Mal hit them.

She was a blur of silver. She swept one merc's leg, knocked the blade from the hand of a second, flipped a third into a fourth. The mercs scattered from her like starlings from a hound. Even as they recoiled, their blades sought Mal. One might have torn her open, had Burgess not intervened and slapped it away with his weird triple-staff.

They could not win, the two of them alone against so many. But they did not have to win. They just had to buy her time.

You had to be exact. The glyph engines and great works in the Library of the Courts of Craft worked your will into the world, if you were precise—and if you were not, they crushed you into powder. Dawn had never been glyphed at the Hidden Schools with needles and knife and moonsilver ink, but Tara had, and Dawn had taken some of Tara's glyphs when she took her arm. They were there, cool and crystal in her stomach.

Name the space precisely. There, printed on the rig's main observation tower, was a name in Kathic script, the *Rig Chaiya*, with an identification glyph that looked like a bunch of scythes and sickles trying to have sex. Close enough. Now, commit.

Dawn brought her palms together, fingers up, and twisted them, as if crushing a flower between her hands. Soulstuff rushed out of her, the gift of all those curses and arrows driving her argument like water drove a miller's wheel. She sank to the concrete. Mal turned to check on her, and caught a knife in the meat of her arm.

But the first part, at least, was accomplished.

Beneath the deck, in the crawl spaces and pits and wall gaps where they'd gone to nest and die, she felt them twitch, the ones she called. Curled legs flexed and bent, crackling with new power. Mandibles clashed and mouthparts wriggled. And they flew.

The bugs burst from hatches and exhaust vents and drainage pipes, from rusted paneling, from gaps in rotten concrete. In columns of glistening jewelblack they corkscrewed through the air.

They sounded like books—thousands of paperbacks, their pages all fanned at once.

The bugs had been dying here for decades, their chewed-up bodies curled in the heat. On what did they feed, while they lived? On spilled beer and crumbs, on the ichor of the dead god Ixzayotl, leaking from the Arsenal's pipes. To raise these bugs one by one would have taken ages. But they all had eaten from the god's body, and she could use that common point to address them as a class and call them to her aid.

They struck the mercs from all sides, linked by lightning and by interlocking legs, chains of snapping hand-sized roaches, beating wings, clawing at limbs and faces. The mercs fell back. A few screamed, free of Brown's control, diving for cover.

Mal stared at the glistening black octopus of bugs with mixed wonder and horror. Mostly horror. Burgess stared not at the bugs but at Dawn, with a weighing smile. She could see herself, cold, distant, through the bugs' many eyes. She felt a surge of triumph.

Then a shadow covered the sun.

A cold wind cut across the deck, scattering bugs and boxes and bodies.

Across the deck, through the rainbow black of the bugs, Mr. Brown advanced.

His chest was open. His ribs and flesh unfurled like wings, and from the cavity rose spindly metal legs darker than black. Their clawed tips tore grooves from the concrete but made no sound. Sound and light both knelt before him. At the juncture of those horrible legs, Brown watched her, his torso clamshelled open to the groin, his human limbs rag-doll limp. His expression remained cool and calm.

She should, she thought, have been scared by the legs, by the gaping emptiness and oil-slick cavity of his body, by the dripping vertebrae—but it was those eyes that churned her stomach. This, even this, was an item for a report Mr. Brown would file and never think about again. All in a day's work.

She struck him with the bugs. They churned around him in a tornado, crushed him like a fist. But more legs unfolded from that slick cavity inside him—whip-thin and flexible manipulators that framed a shielding sphere around his body. The bugs that crossed that barrier fell once more lifeless to the deck.

Sybil. We're out of time.

—Almost done.

Almost isn't good enough.

Mr. Brown's careful soft voice drifted to her through the dead air, through the wash of the surf below.

"Child," he said, fondly. "You do not understand. There are, churning in your bowels at this moment, hundreds of millions of tiny beings that do not share your parentage or blood. Without them, you would wither. What makes your body yours and not the property of those bacteria or of the mites on your skin and all the others that share your flesh? It is not by right that you have this claim over them, it is not by your virtue or their consent. What makes you?

"Power.

"It is through power that claims are made, wills are chained, and chaos kept in place. Power determines who is the cell and who the *I*. You may be growing, but you are weak. Without power, all your claims are merely breath."

The sun flickered. Cold wind lashed her. At Brown's feet, a few mercenaries staggered away and tried to run, but even as they fled, they withered. Their skin wrinkled to leather over twiglike bones, and then they were gone, swallowed by Brown's vast hunger.

Look at him, she told herself. Watch him advance, step by step. Do not give up that final ground. The waves churn below. Sybil's Craftwork and your own is almost done. You need power, soul, but there are no more bolts and curses coming. What you have is spent, and everything else is him.

See: Mal is on her feet, cutlass up, ready to charge the forest of Brown's razor arms. She will fight beautifully, and she will fight fiercely, and she will fight for you, and she will die, like Tara wanted to die beside the Crack in the World. It will mean nothing, change nothing. It will not merit a footnote in Brown's report. Unless you find these last few thaums to fill the pit in your soul.

The shard burned in her palm beneath the glove. It hungered.

But she would be the first thing it ate. That was not winning. It was only a chosen loss.

She would fight to the end. Alone.

Like always.

There was, she realized, a hand in front of her face. Soft, fleshy, brown. She looked up, confused, unsure even of where she was—and Burgess smiled down.

"Go on," he said. "You won't hurt me."

He couldn't know that. She was all hurting. But still, she took his hand.

Soulstuff flooded her, and she remembered herself, remembered cool drinks after long afternoons working in the heat—dew beaded on glass bottles pregnant with light. The sun and the sky and the sea and the rig and the bugs and the mercs and Mal. They needed her.

She snapped her fingers.

Brown sensed the change. He lunged for her on his many legs, but Mal was there, parrying his whip-arms away.

"You're good," Sybil hissed at Mr. Brown. "And you're strong. But I hope that when we're as strong as you, we'll be more careful. That we'll pay attention to things that shouldn't be there. Like waves on a dead sea."

Mr. Brown's eyes were not cool now, not bored. They were not even eyes. Wheels churned there, wheels upon wheels. They looked out past the platform's edge, to the cauldron of the sea. They saw Sybil's Craft take hold.

Chains broke. Wards long decayed now burst.

The god was gone, beneath the dead and crystal water, but much remained—bones like mountains, crystal flesh, tattered skin crusted with coral and stiff from long stillness. The body endured and remembered. It remembered blades and it remembered the lightning tree of thorns, it remembered the King in Red and it remembered Belladonna Albrecht and it remembered its fall, and after that the drills and the pipes and the mites drinking from its veins. It remembered being taken and used.

It remembered rage.

The god burst from the water. Its tattered wings spread broader than the Arsenal. Deathless fires burned in the skeletal pits of its eyes. Curved and ship-long teeth parted, and it loosed a roar that put the clouds to flight and blushed the blue sky crimson.

Eyes of deathless fire peered down and saw the thing that once had been a man, the thing on spider legs. It smelled of lightning and iron, and of chains.

The god's fist came down. A silence followed.

Maybe it would last forever. Maybe that great crash had ended sound, leaving her in the quietude of prayer.

Dawn felt something breathe. What was left of her suit tossed and blew with the wind of it. She tried to stand. Staggered, instead. Someone was by her side. Burgess. And on her other arm, bleeding and bruised, flap of forehead hanging down above her eye: Mal.

Together, they stared into the face of the god. It was there at the edge of the platform, like the sky was there, or death. The nose was gone; the remaining skin had shrunk over the skull like a mask. The god's eyes were caverns lit by Craft-fire, and winding feathered hair drifted about its shoulders like a lion's mane.

She could not tell what was left on the other side of that arching gulf of silent years. In a human being, there would have been nothing.

Sybil, is it watching us?

—I don't know.

There came a groan. A creak. Its muscles were so vast that she could hear them work.

The great head bent toward her. Bowed.

Her hand, rising, seemed so frail. She placed it on the rock shelf of the god's bare cheekbone. It felt warm to the touch. Dry. A rock left near a fire. Sybil coiled up her wrist, and flicked its cheek with her tongue.

9

Dawn rested that night in the hollow of the god's hand. Through the gaps between the massive fingers she could see the sky. She gathered what light she could from the stars, but she still felt distant from her body. She remembered Brown's soft curious eyes, and the casual way he caused her pain. Her nest of blankets was not enough. Sybil circled her from ankle to chin, and hugged her.

"It's okay," she said. "It's okay. We won."

Brown was a smear; he was pulp. But he lingered in her memory, with the others—the sneers and the heels of boots, the girls who pitied her, the villagers of Edgemont who had gathered round and muttered "witch." And Sybil had her own memories, of a careful man in a tweed jacket, and his knife.

"They can't stop us," Sybil said. "We're growing, learning. We can beat them. Wrap chains around their throats. Together. Now: rest. I'll keep watch. You did well."

She tried to believe that, and tried to sleep. Beyond the god's hand, firelight flickered. There were no songs now. She thought she could hear the murmur of voices, the surviving mercs comparing wounds, trading jokes and tales of other times they'd almost died.

She stroked Sybil's head.

She could have died today. Several times.

Mal had saved her. So had Burgess. She'd saved them back. A chain of people, saving people. Could it work that way? Could Tara have been right?

She had trusted Tara. When she walked out of the Badlands in that perfect suit, Dawn would have followed her into the jaws of any hell she chose. She had followed her to the Crack in the World, until she was on her knees, ready to die.

People could save people. But it was power that let them do that. Small people could work together, pooling their resources, but that was a long and dusty road, and at its end Tara knelt, ready to give up everything she was, for what? For a priest? A man? Tara, who had beaten Alexander Denovo, Tara who had never once been caught, Tara of all people still claimed that she had no secret, that she was just as weak as anyone else. She called the strength Dawn sought a trap and a chain. She would have fastened the collar around Dawn's throat.

Without power, people could save one another again and again and it would never be enough, until the spiders came.

She heard footsteps, but there were many reasons one might walk near the edge of the Arsenal, and no reason for anyone to walk toward her. So when Mal spoke, Dawn was not ready.

"I come bearing hot chocolate."

The gap between the god's thumb and forefinger made a kind of door and there Mal stood, firelit, her arm golden and red. Steam rose from the trade-show mug in her hand.

"Chakrabartay has a stash. You'd be surprised how much people in this line of work get into self-care. Not that they'd use that language." She entered the hand, settled cross-legged beside the blankets, offered Dawn the mug. Inside her arm, gears whirred, pistons clicked. Dawn had not been able to hear them before. Maybe something had been knocked out of alignment in the fight.

She tasted the chocolate. Coughed. "It's . . . spicy?"

"I fixed it up. Doesn't taste like home without a little fire."

The more she drank, the more she liked the spice, a high note to set off the chocolate bass and the sweetness of sugar. Sybil shivered with pleasure, though when Mal grinned at her Sybil turned up her nose and retired to Dawn's blankets.

"She'll come around," Mal said. Sybil's only answer was a hiss.

The chocolate was stronger toward the bottom, and so was whatever Mal had used to spice it. Dawn's eyes were wet, and she was breathing heavily. There was a metal hand on her shoulder. She did not shrug it off, and neither, to her surprise, did Sybil.

There were waves far below, now that the god was free.

Dawn waited for questions. Back in the boat, she'd been a scared lost girl with a bit of Craft, dangerous maybe, but someone Mal could pity. People got weird when they couldn't pity you anymore. She waited for the question she would have asked herself. *What kind of monster are you?* She waited for Mal to look at her like Tara had. She did not want to see that look. She'd decided to keep her story simple, when the questions came. I'm going away, and you won't know where, so no one will come after you. Just give me a boat.

"Thank you," Mal said. "And, I'm sorry."

That wasn't at all what Dawn expected to hear, so she didn't know what to say.

"Brown almost killed you. I don't have the best luck with bosses. I guess it's time to ask whether it's a luck thing or a me thing."

"He almost killed you, too. And, um. Everyone else."

"You sure know how to make a gal feel good about herself." Mal closed her eyes. "A team of Craftsmen couldn't raise Ixzayotl. Even trying should have burned you to ash."

"You don't want to ask how? Or 'What are you?'"

"Do you want to tell me?"

—Don't, Sybil whispered.

She saved our life three times. Today. To Mal, she said, "It started the day I met Tara Abernathy."

It struck her as she told the story how short it was, how simple. Her childhood wrapped up in a sentence. Edgemont under siege. Learning the Craft from Tara. The Raiders. The skazzerai in the edge storm. The Crack in the World, and the being trapped there.

Sybil tensed at this part. Dawn stroked her head, the length of her body.

"She could hear the spiders coming. She needed a body to fight them. I gave her one. Tara found out, and she was angry. Scared. I thought she was trying to hold us back. Keep us under control. That she was jealous or scared or lying. I . . . we . . . I hurt her. I've been running ever since."

"But not running away," Mal said, softly.

"No." She did not know what else to say. "So now you know. I'm a monster."

"We're all some kind of monster." Mal propped herself back on her elbows and let her head loll so she could look up at the stars beyond the god's hand. "I've seen a lot of this world. When I meet something new, it generally wants to hurt me, or people I care about, or people in general. It doesn't, as a rule, want to help."

Dawn waited.

"I don't know who Brown was," she went on. "I don't know who he worked for. That's not uncommon in our business. When we met I was in a bad place. I wanted to hurt Deathless Kings. I needed backing. Brown, his people, they needed someone like me. They wanted artifacts, joss, bits of dead gods, bits of live ones. They wanted to sow havoc in the markets, take a lot of soul from a lot of rich assholes. I was okay with that, even if it meant some other assholes making more. I never saw anything like . . . that." She shuddered. Dawn was starting to realize just how much it took to make someone like Mal shudder. Her eyes were bright in the dark. "And then there's the skazzerai."

"They're real."

"I know they're real," she snapped, and for an instant she seemed much younger. Dawn wondered what would have had to happen to a young girl to make her into Mal. Then the present moment scabbed over the past, and Mal was herself again. "You said they're coming back."

She nodded, once.

Mal hunched over her knees, staring down through the floor, into the empty sea. "I pray, you know," she said. "I give blood. I sacrifice. Once, after the mess in Dresediel Lex I tried—I tried to sacrifice myself. It didn't take. I have seen weird shit. But . . ."

"Give me your hand," Sybil hissed.

Slowly, she did. Sybil slipped from Dawn's shoulders, coiled down her arms and across the gap between them to Mal's wrist.

They were not on the Arsenal anymore.

Sky stretched around and beneath them, horizonless, all stars—stars in numbers she could not have imagined, limited only by her eyes' ability to gather light. Below there spun a sphere of blue and green and white like a stage magician's orb, moving and alive. She heard a faint wash of sound like wind or surf.

"Where are we?"

"Above. Borrowing an idle Altus Industries observation platform. It's not idle often. We have to be quick."

The sky wheeled, and they faced a patch of deepness, void of light.

"It's empty," Mal said. Her voice sounded very small.

Dawn was used to spaces between the stars. But up here, wherever she looked, more points of light soon appeared, dim radiance texturing to the emptiness. Except in the depths toward which Sybil aimed them.

"They've been eaten," Sybil said. "A snack for the road, if you'll excuse the expression. Listen."

"Listen?"

"To the surf. If you take all the light you can see and all you can't, and press it into a sound, this is what you hear. The surf, and . . ."

Footsteps.

Dawn had thought she understood the terror of the spiders. But here, above the spinning orb that held all she'd ever loved, she tried to imagine a Craft great enough to drink the light of stars so far apart that to ask how many millions of miles lay between them would have been like asking how many sheets of paper tall was a mountain.

She stared into the eaten sky.

Then they were back on the Arsenal, beneath the god's hand. Sybil coiled around her. The serpent was not warm, but the pressure helped.

Mal sat very still. "The stars," she said, as if quoting, "are wrong. And Brown knew."

Sybil let out a long hiss. "He was just a servant. It's his boss we have to worry about."

"They'll come for you," Mal said. "And then the spiders will. We need a plan."

"The plan," Sybil said, "is: we fuck them up."

"I like it." Mal laughed. "Missing some details as regards the how."

"That's why we went for the flower." Cold starlight glittered on the fine joints of Sybil's scales. "There's a shard of *them* inside, alive, hungry beyond hunger. I thought we could . . . devour it. Digest it. Learn their tricks, their weaknesses. I tried, back at the golf ball."

"What went wrong?"

"It almost ate me. We need more power. More leverage."

"If you get it—what then?"

Sybil turned away, but Dawn found the words. "We merge with the Craft. We face the spiders. And when we win, we fix things. Help people."

"That easy, huh?" Mal looked away. Her metal fingers tapped on concrete. "The two of you against the Craftwork world and all the gods that are left, and monsters older than suns." She closed her eyes, breathed. "I guess we have to start somewhere."

"We?"

"If you'll let me help. As I mentioned, I've had worse bosses."

"You said you didn't want to save the world."

"Qet and Isil, kid. You've seen this world. Do you think saving it and fixing it are nearly the same thing?"

Could it work like this? Just so easily? Trust, affection, an offer of help? She said, "So what now?"

Mal frowned. "I can do breaking and entering, limited Craftwork. If people need killing, I can kill them. But that flower, the shard inside—that's deep theology."

"You knew Ixzayotl's name."

"I know all the names. I was raised by a fanatic. I can quote tablet and verse. But that's not theology. I'm a child playing with power tools. You need an expert. Fortunately, I know a guy."

"Like you knew the last guy?" Sybil pointed, with her tail, to the spot on the concrete that used to be Mr. Brown.

"Oh, no. I worked with Mr. Brown. I liked him—at least, he paid on time. This guy, he super wants to kill me."

"I don't see how that is supposed to inspire confidence."

"Given my track record, you're probably better off looking for my enemies than for my friends. And much as I hate to admit it, there's no one who knows more about this sort of thing. The problem is, the last time I checked he was in prison."

"Prison?"

"A supermax holding facility in the Shining Empire. The kind of place where they stash dissidents and political enemies and sorcerers and ghosts. Protected by an ancestral armor division and a mountain that used to be a god."

"I love your plans," said Sybil. "They take us to the nicest places."

"Remember when you were pretending you couldn't talk? That was fun. We should try that again sometime."

Dawn laughed. She had not expected to. It wasn't funny going up against these odds, on a platform in the middle of the ocean under the warm hand of a dead god, with a serpent around her shoulders, trusting a woman she barely knew. It wasn't funny, but she was laughing, she could not stop herself, she was bent forward and her sides hurt and her stomach and her face was wet.

"Hey." Mal's hand rested on her arm. The metal was still warm. If Mal said anything more, Dawn might have let Sybil eat her.

She breathed deep and tried to steady herself. "I was on my own. For so long. And then there was Tara. And she . . . I . . . I messed it up. So I thought, that's it. Me and Sybil against the world. But if that's not the way it is . . . if it could have been different, then all this time I spent alone . . . It's worse, somehow." She breathed herself back in. "I'm sorry."

"Dawn. You're not alone."

"Of course not," Sybil said. "It will be the *three* of us against the armor division and the sorcerers and the ghosts and the mountain."

"I think we can do better than that."

She realized she had not heard any singing for a while. "Who's *we*, exactly?"

"Well," Mal said, "if you're having a hard time adjusting to the notion of a single partner, you might not want to look outside." But she stood, and helped Dawn to her feet.

Outside the god's hand, the mercenaries stood at attention, carved from darkness by firelight. Burgess was with them, hands folded in the sleeves of his robe.

"Were you listening?" Dawn asked.

"Certainly not," said Burgess. "We were waiting for you."

"I may," Mal put in behind her, "have given them the general outline of our conversation on the boat, and our meeting with Brown. Made a few educated guesses about the implications. Mostly right, as it turns out."

"I don't understand."

"Ma'am." The owner of the voice stepped forward. It was the big fella with the broken nose, the woman. Her nose was set now, under a metal splint. "If you will permit us to explain."

No one, so far as Dawn remembered, had called her "ma'am" before. "Sure."

"My name is Valois, ma'am. The others chose me to speak for them. You saved our lives. Brown killed five of our friends. We owe him for that, and those who sent him. And we owe you for what we have left. You have a plan. We'll help."

"But I'm not," she tried, and then, "I didn't," which did not sound much better. "If you follow me, we're probably going to die. All of us."

The big fella barked, "Yan!"

A dark-haired man with biceps the size of Dawn's head stepped forward. Half his skull was chrome, and he had a gemstone eye. "Sir."

"Explain to the lady what you were last paid to risk your life for."

"A shipment of consumer products, sir. Rubber duckies, largely. Sir."

"Thank you."

He stepped back.

"If the stakes are as high as Mal says, we'll face them head-on. Sleep better that way. And if we follow you, there's a chance we run into whoever sent Brown." Nods along the line. Tense jaws, tense arms. Nothing so obvious as cracking knuckles. These were professionals.

"But you have jobs." It sounded idiotic even to her.

"Not anymore."

The other big fella—the man, brown skin, shovel chin, hairless from the eyebrows up and back—stepped forward. "Brown bought out our contracts. That was the attack vector. Those deals have been voided now. We're free agents. Technically."

"Gupta went to college," Valois said. "We had him draw up papers."

Gupta handed a single sheet to Burgess, who brought it to Dawn. On the paper there was a paragraph in careful schoolroom ballpoint, followed by illegible signatures in a half-dozen scripts and a handful of names represented by an "X."

"We've all risked our lives alone for shitty causes," the woman with the broken nose said. "Time to risk them together for something halfway decent."

"Not more than half, though," someone said from up the line. Someone else cuffed them. There was laughter. The woman did not seem to hear.

"Who are we?" Gupta shouted.

"Arsenal Company!" came the reply.

"What do we do?"

"The godsdamn job!"

The contract's ink glistened in the firelight. She saw the word "command." Chains bind both ways. Tara had taught her that. Sybil tensed around her arm.

It will be okay, Dawn told her, quietly. *We can do this.*

She looked from the paper to the company it made. "We have work to do," she said. "We might be damned for doing it. But you know what happens if we lose. Imagine that, for everyone, forever." After Brown's death there had been screams and weeping. There were no shudders now, in that firelit and half-shadowed line. "Rest up. Tomorrow we fly."

The cheer struck her—a wall of sound, a weapon all its own. Then the deck was quiet. "Ma'am," said Valois. "What's our destination?"

Dawn looked left, and Mal was there—waiting, Dawn realized, for her nod. She gave it.

"The Shining Empire," Mal said. "Shenshan Prison. We have to see a man about a god."

10

Caleb Altemoc dreamed of gods.

He knew this dream, and the dream knew him. His father, who had grown to manhood in an age when the world was made otherwise—an age when the world was made, you could say that and have done, an age when all had been darkness and sea until two gods found each other and spoke, and by their conversation water parted and the land rose new dripping beneath an as-yet sunless sky, not Caleb's age in which the world was star-cinders and cast-off stuff, an accident world, a gambler's—Caleb's father, at any rate, would say that dreams are not something you have, but something you receive. Dreams are sent. The gods send them.

Caleb and his father disagreed on most things. But in this dream, there were gods.

They were dying.

He walked through a strange temple, its walls so high they came together by perspective, the ceiling lost in the blue of distance far above. He walked past niches filled with gods. He knew them all, though some of their names were lost. He passed Qet and Isil in alcoves the size of buildings, passed the Raven Boy in a squat cubbyhole, then Xalhumat and Telati, and the Raven Boy again. They seemed statues, yet they breathed. Hunger pulled their flesh tight over their bones.

Their vast eyes followed him with a beggar's glint. He had what they did not. It was not right. But there were so many. He could give, and give, and give, and never satisfy them. A god was a way of life, a path. You could serve any one of these with all yourself, forever, and make no progress on your debt. Once, his father said, there had been many priests to serve, dedicants and Eagle Knights in the hundreds. But the world changed. Now there is need, and we are all that remains. So we clutch one another close, we last priests and gods. We keep them, as they keep us. We are companions in our need.

The gods whispered in High Quechal and tongues more ancient. They called him by a name that was not his, by the name his would have been if the world had not changed. What would he have been, if not Caleb Altemoc? But if the world had not changed, he would not exist. His father, an Eagle Knight, would never have wed a scholar of no family. The son of that union would not be his heir, called to bear the scars and serve the gods.

But the world had changed. His father was the only Eagle Knight. The last priest.

Not true, the gods whispered.

Caleb's scars burned. His clothes slid from his body as if they were sand and left him bare save for the light of his scars. In them, the gods saw themselves remembered: their names, their glyphs, their prayers, all that his father had carved into him.

You are marked, the gods said. Chosen. Named.

It was not my choice, he cried. These scars are not mine. They are a thing my father did to me with a knife, before he left.

Skeletal hands reached for him from the niches of the gods. They caught him when he tried to run. They slipped through his skin as if his skin was water. They grabbed his scars, and pulled.

If they are not yours, the gods said, they belong to us.

He'd had this dream so many times before, and this was where it ended: in their hungry mouths, in long thin fingers wrapped around his scars, pulling against the meat of him. He came apart beneath the blue-black forever, fighting the hands that held him.

But tonight, he did something new.

He ran—not away, but forward.

The scars slipped from his skin. The pain was sharp and fast, like he'd been cut by a snapped guitar string—a pop, and then a line of blood. But the hands were gone, and the voices. He fell to his knees in ringing silence. His heart battered his ribs.

Our bodies, he thought, do not belong to us. We belong to them. We are ripples on the lakes of them. Once, long ago—he was old enough now that there was a long ago for him—he had stood on a platform atop a great lake and looked down to see gods in the cold dark water. Gods great and grand, gods ancient and sharp-toothed and wild, all chained by light. They were more vast than whales.

There had been a woman by his side.

He knew the dream was over. Now, we wake. That is how it goes. But his body was wiser. His body felt cool temple stone beneath his knees. It felt the weight of that blue-black sky.

If we belong to our bodies, he thought, then to what do our bodies belong?

To us, the gods behind him whispered.

Staggering on bloodslick feet, he stood. This was a dangerous place to kneel.

A throne towered before him. A three-step dais, a three-legged seat, and upon it ruled a king without a belly, a king whose left hand held a bow and whose right hand held two spears, and whose fleshless ribs cradled the embers of a star. The king did not look up. His face was grave, his jaw set with worry. He clung to life, and its fire burned him from within.

The king on his throne did not speak. He could not. After his long contemplation, to speak would be to end the world.

Two women stepped forth from behind the throne. Two daughters, eclipsing their father. They were not ghosts, Aquel and Achal. They were full-fleshed and glorious, their skin molten gold and fresh-cooled copper, their movements as sure, as swift, as inevitable as a lava flow. He knew them, though he had never seen them in this aspect. Always on temple walls they were what they became: serpents of flame, their heads the size of mountains, their blood magma, their sinews living ore. Even as women they were large and fierce. Aquel was tall and panther-lean and Achal rounded with muscle and flesh. They had been women first, the legend said: the fierce and beautiful daughters of the sun, who descended into the underworld when a demon came to eat the sky. In the underworld they played ball against the demon, and lost, and died, and rose again. In the underworld they gave their hearts and were remade. As was their father.

The scars that shaped their bodies glowed with heat and

power. They were crudely drawn—harsh cuts made swiftly, so the Knights could not lose their nerve and pull free. Not so graceful as his father's work. He had never thought of his scars as graceful before, or his father. He felt something like pride. He raised his head but could not quite meet the vast green depths of their eyes.

"You are called," Aquel said.

"You are marked," said Achal, "as were we."

"The scars aren't mine," he told them, as he had told the gods in the hall. "My father did this to me with a knife, before he left." In the hall, those words had seemed bold to him, defiant. But when he spoke them now as Aquel and Achal drew near, with the oven heat of their bodies and the dry rustle of their scales, he felt ashamed.

He tried to look away, but Aquel caught his chin in her hand. Her fingers and thumb had the strength of shifting continents. Her heat did not sear him. It could have boiled him to steam in an instant, but she did not wish it so. She turned him to face her.

Her eyes were green from lid to lid and pupiled with a jet-black slit. "That is not worthy of you. Remember: we have tasted your heart."

Achal ran her fingers lightly from his knee to his thigh to his belly, to his chest, to the back of his neck. She gloved her hand in his hair. Her sister's gaze was brutal, honest. Hers was sly. Her mouth mocked. "This body is not yours. It is a thing your mother did to you, with her womb, with her gates of bone and flesh, as you left her."

"We are clay torn from the world," Aquel said, in the tone of a rite or prayer, though the words were strange to him. "We are the shape to which the potter's hand pressed us on the wheel. But we are not ourselves, until we meet the kiln."

They dragged him up the steps. He fought, slippery and subtle in their grip, but they had been themselves for so many thousand years. They had broken empires in the Contact Wars. They were earthquakes and lava flows; they were plumes of ash and red lightning.

Ixchitli sat upon his throne, hollow and old; Caleb had thought him the size of a man at first, but he was greater. He was a fact.

In the cage of his ribs and his empty belly burned the embers of a fire that, even dwindled, still crisped Caleb's skin and caught his throat. That fire waited for him. The king's hollow eyes stared down.

Still he fought, his hips against theirs, his arms striving against their locks on his joints. Three steps up the dais. He could not win, and yet he fought, with a strength he had not known was his.

Caleb fought fiercely; he fought dirty. He used every trick he knew, though the limbs that caught him were pillars clothed in flesh, though six or ten or a hundred thousand years ago Aquel and Achal had been warriors, whose bodies had never known a desk or a cab or a city street or air-conditioning. They had been great even before they became something more than gods.

The struggle gave him strength, and he felt a bitter joy. He laughed as they moved together. Life was sweet and it was his, and he would make them sweat for it.

Achal gasped with pleasure. She caught his leg in her hand. They bore him up, up, to the waiting bloom of the fire in their father's chest.

And then they stopped.

The Serpents stood like statues, mouths open, sharp teeth reflecting flames. Any moment now, that heat would consume him.

"I hope I'm not interrupting."

That voice did not belong in this sacrificial hall. Caleb writhed in Aquel and Achal's implacable grip and tried to crane his head around to see. And to escape the blistering heat of the sun god's heart. But mostly the seeing thing.

Tara Abernathy stood behind the Serpent Achal. She wore a gray suit, and she was smiling just a little, one eyebrow raised. "I don't mean to judge. Everyone has their thing."

"This," Caleb said, feeling as if his nakedness had somehow shifted register, "is not my *thing*."

"There's no shame in it." She circled him, examining the dead god's throne, the fire. She poked its frozen flames and pulled her hand back, shaking her fingers. "Might be a little hard to practice, you know, safely."

He pried himself free of the Serpents and crouched, panting, below the throne. Before Tara. And he was still naked. But he stood at last, uncurled, rolled his shoulders back.

It had taken him a while to figure Tara Abernathy out, but like so many things in his life, she became simpler when he thought in terms of cards. Tara wanted a piece of the action, any action. Like a high-speed golem racer, she relied on the wind of her own motion to keep the great engines that drove her from melting. When she was around, he felt his play loosen to match hers. That wasn't altogether bad—just pushed him higher on the risk-reward curve. But it could be dangerous.

So could she.

He'd opened his mouth to say something clever—he wasn't sure what, but he'd figure it out as he went along. Before he could, the earthquake hit.

He stumbled. Dust rained from the temple walls. Huge gaps opened in the floor. There was a crash of stone and he grabbed Abernathy's arm, pulled her aside as a column collapsed onto the steps where they'd just been standing.

Tara looked at the pile of rock that had been a pillar, then at him. "Hey, thanks." The cracks in the floor widened, and through them he heard a ticking sound, like clockwork or insect legs. Her smile went away. "We need to get out of here."

"How did you get in?" The great walls of gods were collapsing. Idols tumbled into the cracks in the floor. Shelves of stone sheared off and tumbled into writhing dark.

"Same way you did." She nodded back across the collapsing temple. "Does this place have a back door?"

"Does my nightmare temple have a back door."

"Yes," she said, as if he'd asked a question.

"No."

The temple creaked. Pillars toppled. All around, he heard that *tick-tick-tick*, clockwork mandibles, claws on glass, certain as destiny or death. He was sweating. Fear, and the heat from the ember sun in the dead god's chest.

She wanted a piece of the action—and most of the time she was smart enough, bold enough, to make her hand work for her. But *most of the time* wasn't always, and sometimes she found herself in a corner, options dwindling.

Good thing Caleb always tracked his outs.

A back door? Maybe not. But a main exit? He grabbed her hand and pulled her toward the throne.

"Oh no," Tara said, when she saw where he was leading her. "Nope. No."

She could have fought him, and she did not. Whatever else Tara Abernathy was, she was game. If you chased action, you learned to follow through.

As the temple collapsed, they leapt together into the fire.

———

He came round to find that his shirt was burning. He slapped out the flames and sat up. The world swayed. It was night. There were stars. He was lying in the middle of a glowing silver Craftwork circle, lit by black candles around its edge. He'd had worse wake-up calls.

Tara Abernathy had just emptied a tiny conference-room water bottle on her jacket sleeve. She swore, inspecting the damage left by Ixchitli's flames. "You're hell on a woman's wardrobe budget, Altemoc."

Wisps of smoke rose from her shoulders. "You missed a spot."

She doused the flames with another tiny bottle, then showed him her back. "How about now?" There was a cigarette burn in the gray wool, but the blouse underneath was fine. The metal of her arm showed through the hole in her sleeve.

"Nice gears," he said, then thought maybe he should not have said anything. But she fanned her fingers, showing off.

"I'm getting used to them. Your dreams always that pleasant?"

"Only when you're in them."

She grinned, a little. "How much do you remember?"

Most of it, he thought, but he paused anyway to take stock.

He was cold. His clothes were ribbons. He still wore the shirt he'd put on in the tent that morning. What he hoped was that morning. Tiny cuts crosshatched his body, barely deep enough to break a layer of skin. When he moved, something like a salt crust flaked off him, but it looked black in the flickering candlelight. Ash?

When he sat up, he'd taken the world's sway for his own dizziness, a concussion. Now he saw that he was wrong. His head throbbed, yes, but the darkness around them was the sea.

There was light on the horizon, in the wrong place for dawn under these weird southern stars. And the wrong color. "What's that?"

"The spirecliffs. Take your time. We're probably safe."

The fire on the horizon moved. A plume the size of a mountain reared and plunged. He would have felt more comfortable thinking it was just a flare, but that fire drew his heart like the north drew a compass needle. He remembered Aquel and Achal, their sharp-toothed mouths, the heat of their grips on his body. He remembered their other forms. "They should be asleep," he said.

"They should." Tara rounded the circle, snuffing black candles one by one.

"What happened to Ortega? My crew?"

"Evacuated. Mostly to Ajaiatez. The Coast Guard helped, once I explained the situation to them in small sharp words." She folded her collapsible pentacle and her bowl and her roll of tiny knives. "Ajaia's priests have been on the nightmare telegraph all day. They're pissed. On the one hand, the situation at the spirecliffs is now resolved. On the other hand . . ." She nodded back toward the fire. "And on the third hand—"

"Who has a third hand?"

"You'd be surprised. I keep running into this four-armed guy. We've never been introduced, we ignore each other. I'd say something but at this point it's just too awkward."

He tried to rise. His own legs defeated his first try, then the ship's motion defeated his second. Tara offered a hand, and he took it. The fire didn't look any better when he was on his feet. "So what's the third hand?"

"Their goddess. She's missing. There are questions. I'm sure you can imagine."

"What do you mean, missing?"

"That's one of the questions."

"I'll tell you what I know."

"I had something more comprehensive in mind. But it can wait for a change of clothes, and maybe a night's sleep."

"Where are we? Whose ship is this?" Before he crossed the silver circle, he glanced to her for confirmation. You never knew, with Craftswomen. She waved him across. "Coast Guard cutter?" Inside a Craft circle, things felt more certain than they often were in life. The deck beyond was more honest.

"That would have been unwise. You're not person of the year with the high priests at the moment, and they have a lot of pull with the Guard. Lucky for you, we had a friend nearby. We're on his yacht."

"You have quality friends. Excluding myself, of course."

"Mr. Altemoc." She had that toothy smile again. "We're friends? How nice."

Their conversations always felt like this, somewhere between a dance and a boxing match—there was a comfort to that, like this was normal, waking up half naked on someone's yacht, with a coastline on fire and the Serpents rampant. He had not had a normal day since he left RKC. That was one reason he'd left. Still, his average morning didn't hurt this much.

"This friend of yours—is it someone I should know?"

"That depends on what you mean by 'should,'" Tara said.

"Now, Ms. Abernathy. That's hardly fair."

Caleb recognized the voice, and the man himself, striding across the deck like he owned it, which he did. Still clad in that Talon Row suit, with a fresh ivory shirt, mother-of-pearl buttons, and LaRoque cufflinks glittering in the red light of the Serpents, his teeth as perfect as those buttons: Jax.

"I expected to see more of you, Mr. Altemoc, but not so soon. Chaos yields interesting combinations. Ms. Abernathy, are you done?"

"He's intact, more or less."

"Very good. Lights, please, Sonja!" He raised his hand like an orchestra conductor. With the thunk of a switch, the lights came on and chased the stars away. Beyond the golemwing deck, the yacht was a palace of white and pine. Caleb saw a pool, deck chairs, towels. He saw, too, that for all the elegance, this was a ship built for speed. The hull had an odd jagged angle above the waterline that looked more functional than decorative, and while Caleb wasn't an expert in glyphwork, there was an awful lot of it, thick-worked in moonsilver, not the shoddy plated-on consumer stuff. A military ship with pleasure-yacht fittings.

"Nice boat," he said, because he was feeling contrary and sore and naked.

"Zurish surplus. Amazing what you can find on the market these days. Cost-effective, too, compared to flying." Caleb didn't think that was true, unless you were chartering a platoon of dragons. The poolside bar, he noticed, was open. Two figures waited there: a young man in rust-red robes and a woman in a suit, whom he hoped he did not recognize. There was a second woman on the pool deck, too, pale, dark-haired, and gorgeous in a quarter ounce of bathing suit, draped across a deck chair. She was wearing big dark glasses and a gold medallion at her neck, and might have been sunbathing if there had been a sun. "Can I get you anything?"

"Clothes," he said. "And a bourbon."

"And some sleep," Abernathy added. "Tomorrow, I have to tie you to a chair."

11

She wasn't kidding about the chair.

He hadn't thought so. Abernathy was not the kidding type. She told the truth, though with her own twisted sense of humor. He'd known a lot of Craftsfolk who survived by pretending their job was banal, but Abernathy saw the fun in it. After a night of fitful sleep and a glass of excellent orange juice, the fun in question involved him, leather straps, and an office chair.

She had set up in a glass-walled conference room at the prow of Jax's yacht. The host wasn't present—just Abernathy, with her candles and knives, and the red-robed priest, who offered him an encouraging smile. The smile worked, which surprised Caleb more than the straps had.

The priest went back to the bridge column in the *Dresediel Lex Times.* Compared to Abernathy and her knives, bridge was a soothing prospect. The priest didn't seem to be making progress, though. He kept reaching for the golf pencil behind his ear, then shaking his head and putting it back.

Caleb said, "You lead the ace of staves."

"But how do you know they're not void?"

"If you lead the ace, your hand's void in staves, so you can crossruff with cups from your hand and staves from the dummy. If your opponents are void, you lose. But it's a small chance. Live a little."

"I see what you mean." The priest didn't sound convinced. He set the paper down. "It's a wonderful invention."

"Bridge?"

"The newspaper. We don't have them in Alt Coulumb. There's a crier's guild."

"That can't work nearly as well. How would you sing a whole newspaper? Look at that thing. I've seen thinner holy books."

"And people read it?"

He shrugged, as much as he could with the straps. "Most skim the headlines, ogle an engraving or two."

"When the criers do their job, people hum the news all day. And individual criers know their streets. Most folks don't need all these market numbers"—he peeled off the financial section—"and the people who do get them off the nightmare telegraph anyway. But I love thinking about it—those big machines churning out page after page for the glory of God." He made a little hooked gesture over his pendant, the holy symbol of Kos.

"I've never seen the presses myself," he admitted. "Name's Caleb, by the way. You might as well be on first-name basis with the man tied to the chair."

"I'm Abelard," the priest said, and offered his hand to shake, then withdrew it sheepishly, with a glance at the straps. "That's how it is, isn't it? I've never been to the Hightown Zoo. Even when we open the boilers for high holy days, most of the faithful stick to the audience chamber and the Hall of the Sacred Flame. You always think you'll have time to visit your hometown wonders."

Here's a guy, Caleb thought, who hears Dresediel Lex and thinks newspapers—not the obsidian pyramid at 667 Sansilva, or the Drakspine Hills, or Monicola Pier, or the ullamal courts, or even the Stonewood. Newspapers. As if something so everyday could be wonderful.

But: wasn't it? All those reporters, printers, truck drivers, golems, typesetters, proofers and editors, cutters, the newsstand guys and the delivery kids, and the people who thought talking with reporters was something you did, telling strangers the latest rumor on your block, all racing to deadline for a bunch of stories on cheap paper. And then they did it all again the next day, and the day after that.

"Tell you what," he said, "look me up the next time you're in D.L., I'll see if I can get us to a printing press. Might have to play down the whole fire-god angle, though. We're not big on gods. Or fires."

"Perhaps the first could help with the second."

"You haven't seen our fires."

"Or their gods," Tara said, looking up from the candles and the silver chalk. "Just about done." She circled behind him and tightened the strap that, loose, had been allowing him to breathe. "Try not to enjoy this, Altemoc."

"I could just tell you what happened."

She reviewed the buckles with a certain amount of professional and personal satisfaction. "We need details. Things you didn't notice you noticed. The slightest omission could be fatal."

"Fatal?" He tested the cuffs and straps. They didn't budge.

She rolled her eyes. "I didn't mean for you now. I meant for all of us, soon."

"Is that better?"

A door opened behind him. He tried to look but couldn't turn his head far enough. He recognized the woman's voice, though. Gods. He'd really hoped he'd been mistaken when he saw Kai Pohala last night. "If you're busy, we can come back."

He'd never seen Abernathy flustered before. She covered it fast and leaned back to regard her work, hands on hips, her expression settling into the professional mask Craftsfolk used with clients who paid on time. "It's fine, Kai. Jax. We're just getting started."

Jax's voice was unmistakable: arrogance, caffeine, a slightly-larger-than-microdose of pixie dust. "Ms. Abernathy. Abelard. Mr. Altemoc, a good look for you. Sorry I'm late. An associate made a hash of one of our subsidiary projects. It's all herding plates or juggling cats."

"You were there, too," Caleb pointed out. "Why am I the one tied to the chair?"

"I barely saw anything in the panic. Security got me to safety."

"Tara, when you said 'interrogation,' I didn't realize *this* was what you had in mind." Kai Pohala crossed into his field of vision: skirt suit, kitten heels, the kind of extremely careful makeup that, when Caleb had been a younger idiot, he'd sometimes mistaken for no makeup at all, despite the lipstick. The way she stood reminded him of a cobra, judging whether venom was indicated. She carried two paper cups of coffee, and handed one to Abernathy. "I would have dressed for it."

"Caleb Altemoc, meet—"

"Ms. Pohala," he said, coolly. "This is another fine mess your clients have gotten me into."

"My faithful," she corrected, and sipped her coffee. "Please." To Abernathy: "We've interacted. We brought in the Two Serpents Group, as part of our settlement. Mr. Altemoc wasn't tied up at the time. This is an improvement."

He grinned back. He'd read somewhere that chimps grinned before they went for you, and he tried to make it look like that. "If your faithful had given us the funding we asked for, we wouldn't be in this mess."

"We honored the terms of the settlement," she said. "And if you'd done your job, we wouldn't be here. I was under the impression we were retaining a professional remediation group."

"And I was under the impression—" He started the sentence not sure how he meant to end, beyond that it would be the kind of thing he would regret saying in ten minutes. It was all for the best that Abernathy chose this moment to draw her work knife.

"Just so everyone's clear," the Craftswoman said in a cold voice. "I can't read Caleb's mind. That's beyond any ethical use of my power. I can, however, draw us all into a nightmare framed by his memories of recent events. To do that, I need to drive him into a deep slumber—deep enough to suppress the systems the body uses to stop people from moving when they dream. Hence the straps."

"I'm not wild," Caleb said, "about your use of the word 'ethical' as a qualifier."

Abernathy walked toward him. Light from her knife made blue shadows dance. "Mr. Altemoc. Don't you trust me?"

He realized, in spite of the straps and everything, that he did. He wasn't sure what to make of that, but his was not to reason why. His was just to do . . . well, not all that much, really, while the magic woman came at him with the moonlight knife. "Let's go."

The girl stood in the circle, with the rose in her hand.

She was ringed with claws.

The golf ball had shattered into great knurled eggshell pieces to reveal the blue sky and the maelstrom sea. And from each shard of broken stone, thin sharp claws unfolded toward the girl.

Caleb threw himself in front of her.

With the benefit of hindsight, he had to admit that this had been a terrible idea.

He tried to walk the others through the scene. "The girl, she grabbed the rose. Everything started to fall apart. The walls reached for her." Chaos developed around them in slow motion. Abelard looked shaken. Pohala wore a banker's frown. Jax kept his face neutral: just another board meeting. Abernathy's gaze was fixed on the girl.

"One of Jax's bodyguards got him out. The others moved on the girl." There they were, weapons deployed, glyphwork churning.

Abernathy touched one of the black iron claws wrapped around memory-Caleb's neck. That Caleb's scars burned green, and where iron crossed that emerald light, it glowed with heat. He remembered the stench of starlight and burned hair.

He rolled the nightmare forward, one heartbeat at a time. Even so, events in the golf ball unfolded at cyclone speed, all splinters and streaks and blood. Black iron legs pierced Jax's bodyguard from all sides. The bodyguard turned against Ortega, against Caleb, against the girl.

Ortega stood against the gone-mad world, spear raised. He bore no visible glyphs, no clockwork parts. He seemed old, from his scuffed boots to the tips of his drooping mustaches. But he was ready. As they came, he fought. Caleb ached to watch him, his spear a blur, thrusting, turning. Losing.

Beyond the broken golf ball he could see the spirecliffs. The many faces of the black iron walls opened their mouths to sing. The girl was on her knees—curled around the flower, her face a rictus of pain. Around her, above her, barely visible, rose the shadow of a serpent.

He watched himself, trying to understand what happened next. Replay the hand. Track your thoughts. Evaluate. Ortega was about to die. For him.

He'd felt a loosening within. A final peace.

He'd opened his scars and called the iron to him.

His scars burned green. For an instant he held control, and in that instant he threw Ortega to safety. He tried to throw the girl, but she didn't move. They fell into the roaring water. Pain covered him, and black iron, and—

Darkness.

He rolled his memory back to that final moment.

Tara Abernathy moved through the foam and the frozen waves and the splinters of fallen rock, to the girl.

She was bent over, like she'd taken a punch to the gut. The serpent-shadow coiled tight around her, visible in spray and splinters. Blood seeped from her palm where she clutched the rose.

"Who is she?" Caleb asked.

Tara brushed a lock of hair from the girl's face with the fingers of her skeleton hand. "I used to know."

That voice did not sound like Tara Abernathy. It was too open, too sad, too honest.

His scars itched. He turned away.

Through the cracked golf ball, he saw a woman.

He knew her. He realized, in that moment, that he had spent the last fifteen years knowing he would see her again.

She climbed through broken stone and rushing water, older, scarred now herself, fierce and unmistakable: the woman who had left him sleeping on the ocean to go and kill a god. The woman he had fought in the sky over Dresediel Lex, and given his soul to defeat—and perhaps to save. The woman he would have loved better, if he'd known how.

"Hi, Mal."

12

They gathered on the foredeck for a council of war.

It was an odd assembly, Abelard thought: a Craftswoman, a priestess of Kavekana, a whatever-Caleb-was, their billionaire host, and Abelard himself. Different values, different lives, their paths crossing and recrossing like the string of a cat's cradle. Maybe they formed a pattern; maybe they made a knot.

Jax's butler fetched them drinks from the bar. Abelard lit a cigarette with a prayer, and smoked. He needed God's blessing, and it gave him something to do with his hands.

Tara stood between them and the dark. She looked like the woman he had met so many years ago in the parking lot of the Sanctum of Kos, come to save his world. If you ignored the skeletal arm or the lightning streaks of white in her hair.

"We face," Tara said, "what is called a wicked problem. It is complex, and in its complexities it has touched all of us. We cannot study this problem through experiment, because our every touch changes it. We cannot solve it piecemeal, because its components are tangled with one another, and with us—with our history and our failures. It is a hydra that is all neck and fang. Cut off one head, and we reveal others, and still more sprout from the stump. To survive, we must meet the problem in its full complexity. We don't know enough to do what must be done. It may not be possible to know enough. But if we are honest, we can trace the outlines of what we don't know. And then, we will act."

"What sort of danger do you mean, exactly?" Since he emerged from his nightmare, Caleb had looked at the world as if it were a ghost, or as if he were—unreal and out of time. "The shard is terrifying, but there's a lot of awful stuff in the world."

"I don't mean the shard. I mean the girl."

"Daniella?"

"Her name," Tara said, "is Dawn."

She told the story.

Abelard watched the others as she spoke. He wondered what she would hold back, but she told most of it—most of what he knew, which he thought was everything. When Tara spoke about her father's funeral, Kai kept very still.

"We fought," she said, in the end, "and she left. She took a souvenir." Tara illustrated with a wave of her unfleshed arm. "She knows the skazzerai are coming to eat the world, and she's off to eat it first."

"You really think the skazzerai are coming," Caleb said, slowly.

"I do."

"They're legends. More than legends. Myths."

"I have heard them. So has Kai." Kai tensed, but in an instant her composure returned. She smoothed her skirt, and nodded. "You saw a piece of them yourself, in the sparecliffs." Tara pointed to the burning coast. "Imagine that, everywhere, all at once. So now we face two threats, that are really one threat in two stages. We have the skazzerai coming from beyond the stars. But before they get here we have to face Dawn, who wants to eat us first, in the hope that she can face them and win."

"What do you mean, eat us?" Caleb said.

"She merged with a being of awakened Craft—a pattern like a god, formed of our sorcery, our society, our desire. She is small now. If she should grow, encompass the globe, capture the markets and the Courts of Craft and the Argent Library itself, then we would exist inside her. Our minds, our dreams would shape themselves to hers. Our souls would become her instruments. We might not even know. We would think her will was our own desire." She shook her head. "We have to stop her. If we learn how, perhaps we can face the skazzerai when they come."

"Could we work with her?" Caleb looked around, into the silence. "If it's really the skazzerai we're up against, we can use all the allies we can get."

"I don't know. Maybe. She's a scared angry kid with a power

beyond gods, and she's been hurt by a lot of people. She wants power and the safety that power brings. I tried to help her. I failed. Maybe you'll do better." Tara opened her bone fingers. "But I'm running out of hands. And fathers."

Caleb looked away. "If she's that powerful, why hasn't she won already?"

"She's powerful compared to me. Compared to monsters and small gods. But it's not me she wants to fight. She wants to eat every market, every god, the Craft itself and every soul it touches. She has to, to stand any chance at all."

"If she's basically sentient Craft, can't she just merge with them?"

"You're basically sentient water," Tara said. "Try to merge with the ocean."

Kai uncrossed her legs. "Sentience," she said, "would only help her to a point. Powerful forces shape the Craft: gods, politics, the dreams of nations. The market is a battleground of trading automata, vast nightmare brains with immense reserves of liquid soul. In the ocean, these automata would be your squid, your sharks. You might be smarter than they are, but you're smaller, too. All the smarts in the world won't let you beat a shark when it comes to eating."

"I think that's why she came here," Tara said. "She needed an edge." She turned to Kai. "What can you tell us about the shard?"

"Not much. It was being transported by a Concern named Pallas Logistics, registered in the Ebon Sea. Pallas's ownership structure was quite complicated, but ultimately it was a subsidiary of a Kho Khatang holding company that was itself sixty-two percent owned by a Kavekanese god, called Star Apple. My faithful have never clarified the shard's meaning or history, and its point of origin was never established. Refusing to provide that information was one of the terms of our settlement."

"But they were shipping it," Tara said. "Which means they knew how to contain it."

"They did not share any of that information with Mr. Altemoc's team. Divine remediation, they said, would be effective. And it was. Until recently."

"Who is Star Apple? Or Pallas?"

She looked away. "I can't say."

"Kai . . ."

"I can't."

"I know you're not supposed to."

"Tara." The sudden edge to her voice created silence between them. Abelard smelled salt and smoke. "You're not listening. My oath of nondisclosure is a precept of the faith. Those parts of my memory don't exist, even for me. That applies to my dreams, too, before you get any bright ideas about tying me to a chair. I don't know where the shard came from. I don't know what it can do or how to stop it. I don't know who I'm working for. If I could say, I would."

"I'm sorry," she said. "We'll come back to that." Tara turned to Caleb. "What can you tell us about Mal?"

Caleb accepted a gin and tonic from Jax's butler, and stared down into it as if he could find visions of the future there. "Where do you want me to start?"

"At the beginning."

He told his story clearly, just the facts, as if he was being deposed about the hydraulic process that had crushed his friend's hand. He was about that successful.

Mal's parents had died in a riot in Dresediel Lex, a religious uprising Caleb's own father had instigated. The King in Red, the city's deathless lord, responded to civil unrest with the level-headed and mediation-forward approach typical of undead war-wizards: he mounted his iron dragon and rained fire from the sky.

Abelard had been a kid at the time. He remembered school-room collections for orphans of the Skittersill Rising.

Malina Kekapania had not received any of that charity. She had been adopted by a priest of the old religion, trained as a weapon against the King in Red. In the end, she tried to raise the Serpents that slept under Dresediel Lex, to overthrow the city and forge a new order from the ashes of the old. Caleb had met her while she was undercover, preparing to strike. They had grown, he said, "close."

Caleb had stopped her, along with his father. Sort of.

"Sort of?" Tara asked.

"My father is an old-fashioned priest. His idea of stopping Mal involved human sacrifice. Specifically, a human friend of mine. In the end we had to stop him and Mal. It was a mess."

"Let me guess. You never found her body."

"There was a lot of lava. And I never went looking. I heard rumors, but you always do, when someone dies trying to change the world. Back home, to a certain sort of kid, she's a hero. They have her face on T-shirts and everything."

"You hoped she was dead."

He looked out at the horizon. "I hoped she was out of it. Away from gods and Craftsmen and the Wars you all talk about like they're over. She was not a good person or a nice person and she hurt a lot of people including me. Including herself. I didn't want her to hurt anyone else. Whenever I imagined her alive . . . I hoped she found a quiet beach and was smart enough to stay there." When he was done, he looked almost surprised, as if he did not know the person who had just spoken. He folded his hands on the table. "I guess I was wrong."

"You miss her," Kai said.

Caleb was ready to cut back—but Abelard saw some other system engage, a fail-safe releasing energy into an unseen realm. "She was deep down in a hole. So was I. Maybe that's what we saw in each other. I climbed out. It took time and work. But it looks like she's still down there."

He stopped, and Abelard didn't say, So are you. You threw yourself between the girl and those claws as if you had spent your life waiting to die.

"What's your story, then?" Caleb said, turning to Abelard. But before Abelard could answer, Tara spoke.

"Abelard is here because he's worried I'll do something suicidal."

"Um," Abelard said. "That's not how I would put it."

"Are you?" Caleb asked. "Going to do something . . . dangerous?"

"I am going to try to save the world. Do you think that qualifies?"

"Shouldn't someone else get involved at this point?" he said.

"If we're talking about the fate of the world—isn't this a matter for high priests and Deathless Kings?"

"Great idea. Let's gather a multidisciplinary team of experts. Ideally ones already familiar with the salient features of the problem. Let's say, a saint, a high priestess, the leader of an international relief group, and a guy with a yacht."

Jax saluted with an empty glass and signaled to his butler for another round.

Caleb: "You know what I mean."

"I have sent letters and nightmares. But we have to expect this situation will move faster than an interfaith committee meeting, faster than the Courts of Craft. Now that you all know what's at stake—"

"I'm in," Kai said.

Tara turned to her in surprise. "What?"

"I have the Ajaian priesthood's Craftwork tribunal breathing down my neck. I won't be able to put them off with 'it's not my fault.' I need the full story, and ideally a culprit hog-tied for their convenience. I'd go after your student anyway, even if I didn't have a fondness for, you know"—she gestured vaguely—"the world."

"Me, too." Caleb set down his glass. "I don't know how Mal fits into all this. But she's . . . well. I'm in."

When Tara looked his way, Abelard was too surprised at first to say anything. He felt a thrill of hope. "I won't let you do this alone," he said.

"Given the stakes," Jax said, "I would hope that my support would be a foregone conclusion."

Tara looked at each of them in turn, as if seeking a way out. When her gaze fell on Abelard, he met it, and thought, as hard as he could: *Don't.* "Fine," she said at last. "Us against monsters from beyond the stars, and monsters from closer to home, and maybe the entire system of Craft. So, let's break it down. We have to find Dawn. We have to learn how to stop her. Then, we use what we learn to beat the skazzerai."

They shifted like gears in a machine, no longer locked in their own worlds.

"You're assuming she's still alive," Kai pointed out. "She and Mal both."

"I am. For one thing, it would be better for us if they weren't. And . . . I think I'd know." She glared at Caleb, at Kai, as if expecting a retort. The real mocking voice, Abelard guessed, was inside Tara's head.

"I believe I have something to contribute," Jax said, gently. He waited for them to turn his way, then stretched the pause with a sip of his drink. "For months now, my analysts have been tracking anomalous patterns in a number of Kathic markets: fluctuations in soul and bond values some number of standard deviations above random chance. They are diffuse, but there is a progressive spatial component, moving south from the Badlands to the Fangs to Ajaiatez."

"That could be anything," Caleb said. "That could be weather."

Kai shook her head. "We've seen similar patterns on Kavekana'ai. We're very good at market analysis, and we haven't found any underlying factor, but their motion has been predictable enough to trade off of. Naturally, this reinforces the pattern."

"Thank you. And the anomaly has not abated. Quite the contrary. Markets are churning all over the World Sea."

"Oh, good," Caleb said. "That only leaves us four continents of coastline to cover. Not to mention the Archipelago."

"I never claimed this was a precise indicator. But it at least gives us a hemisphere."

"I think I can narrow it down," Tara said. "I spent most of last night on the nightmare telegraph fighting with the Ajaiatez Coast Guard Control. The morning of Dawn's attack on the cliffs, they tried to warn off a deep-sea fishing boat with Kho Katang flags, the *No Percentage in It*, which dropped anchor nearby. *Percentage*'s crew claimed they were dealing with a case of possession and would be on their way shortly."

"Suspicious," Kai said.

"After the attack, the *Percentage* fled for deep water. The Coast Guard did not pursue. They were busy, what with the lava and everything."

"Escape vessel?" Caleb suggested.

"Looks like it. Kho Katang registries do not list a vessel by the name of *No Percentage in It*. But the next business day, an Ebon Sea holding company filed an insurance claim with First Camlaan Shipping against a vessel called *Top of the Morning*, lost, supposedly with all hands, two hundred miles south of the Archipelago. A deep-sea fisher, same make as *Percentage*, and in the direction they were headed. I can't say for sure that it's the same boat. But it's suggestive."

"What happened?" Kai asked. "A storm?"

"The holding company claims it was a star kraken."

"Tenuous," Kai said.

"When we don't have solid evidence, we work on traces. We could start by looking for anomalous events in lifeboat range of *Morning*'s last known coordinates. And we can cross-reference its history with whatever we can learn about Ms. Kekapania's."

"I can help look for Mal." Caleb leaned forward in his chair. "I know her as well as anyone. Or I used to."

"The Blacksuits might have files on her back in Alt Coulumb," Abelard said. "They'd need details. Any habits, um, identifying marks. A friend of ours is a pirate; he might know something about the *Percentage* or the *Morning* or whatever their real name is. And Seril's looking for Dawn, of course."

"She's what?" Tara went cold and dangerous.

"Um. I thought you knew."

Jax slipped into the tense silence. "I also have contacts to contribute. And I will continue to model the anomaly."

"And profit from it," Kai said.

"Naturally."

"Fine," Tara said. "Say we find them. That leaves us with the question of how to stop Dawn. Right now, I can't." That did not look easy for her to say. "When I faced her, the most I could manage was a call for help. She's had time to grow, and she has the shard now. If it comes to a fight, I can't beat her alone." Abelard noticed that she'd switched from "we" to "I." "Kai, I was hoping you could help."

"How? Would you like me to build you a religion?"

"Is that your answer for everything?"

"It beats 'kill god, hope for the best.'"

"Does it?"

"What else can I offer? My worldly charm? My cardio-kickboxing skills? I already told you, I can't tell you anything about Star Apple."

"You can't share anything outside the faith. But you are being sued. Surely your clients—excuse me, your faithful—deserve proper representation. They need a Craftswoman with experience defending pantheons in complex, time-sensitive negotiations. I'm the best for a thousand miles in any direction. Literally."

It occurred to Abelard that a thousand miles in one direction was fire, and then jungle, while a thousand miles in every other direction was ocean. He decided not to mention it.

"As counsel I would, of course, meet them under strict confidentiality."

"You're the in-house Craftswoman for the Church of Kos. Half our pilgrims come to us looking to avoid dealing with the Church and its sacrifice requirements."

"What if Abelard fires me?"

"Sorry?" said Abelard.

"There. Easy. I'm fired."

"I'm not firing you. I'm going with you."

"Abelard," she said. "If you go with me, Kai can't introduce me to her clients. And I need you to work with Caleb, so we can keep in touch through the prayer line. Can't trust the nightmare telegraph. Not with Dawn out there."

The cat's cradle pulled into a knot and bound him. Had she known this was how it would play out? But she was not locking him out or running away. She was herself again, ready to lead them against the end of all things. He didn't have to worry.

He repeated that to himself and hoped he would come to believe it.

"I don't like this," he said.

"I don't either. But I don't see another way. How about it, Kai? You've seen me work under pressure."

The priestess raised an eyebrow. "I do like the thought of you calling me 'boss.'"

"How about 'illustrious client'?"

"It feels a bit . . . sinful." In Abelard's experience there were two ways people used the word "sin": the way they used it with priests around, and the other way. Kai was definitely using it in the other way.

"So," Tara said, quickly, "Abelard, Caleb, and Jax start the hunt, and we go—where? Can you say that much?"

After a moment's consultation with the scriptures in her head, Kai answered, "Chartegnon."

13

That night, long after she should have been asleep, Tara leaned against the pool-deck rail. She watched the burning coast, and thought about dominos.

Back at the Hidden Schools, the domino club used to block off Armillary Square every fall semester for a cascade demonstration. Silent careful students knelt beneath the turning brass gears of the model universe, the sleeves of their robes rolled back to reveal knobby wrists as they placed large black and red tiles in endless whorls with precise confident fingers.

Tara never joined them. She could have. It wasn't the kind of thing where you had to be someone's kid or a member of the Right Set. The Armillary Square demonstration was the club's yearly showcase and recruiting event. All you had to do was ask, and that year's dominus or domina would teach you the basics, show how you fit the pattern.

Even then she had known enough about the shape of the doubled worlds inside and outside her head to see that if she joined, the quiet and care of those long fingers, the figures dipping like drinking birds in gathered robes, all that made her pause in wonder as she crossed the square no matter how late for class she was, it would all dissolve, like everything dissolved, into people. It was bad enough to recognize a particular figure among those robes as the prim and quiet girl down the hall, always dressed from neck to ankle in bright shades of single colors, who never spoke above a stage whisper but who screamed like a dying soprano when she came. Tara needed those lines of ivory and shale and crimson-lacquered wood in their perfect mysterious array to be tended by monks, or automata in human form, driven by the gravity of the heavens. She could not bear for those austere saintly figures to dissolve into Anastasia Cartwright and Freddie Lang and Josephus Cawthorne IV and "Honestly, just call him Turtle, everybody else does."

She set her own calendar by the dominos, as she would have set a clock by noon or a calendar by the solstice. Snows melted, spring bloomed, and there they were, tiny sprouting monoliths, ordered, precarious, and beautiful. If they could stand, so could she.

Then, in her final spring, some apocalyptic secret society had fumbled a summoning ritual and a poorly bound demon escaped into Armillary Square. The proctors caught it, fast. Tara missed the excitement. No one had died, not even a little. Monochrome girl lost an eye, but she gained the ability to coordinate her replacement eye with her outfit, so she was heard to say that things had turned out for the best. That night, when Tara left the lab blinking and exhausted, she saw the square's shattered paving stones, the evaporating demonglass, and the wreck of dominoes. All that care gone to chaos in a moment.

There was so much she could have, should have felt then, but she only felt numb.

To the west, in the dark, the coastline burned.

She thought about their conference, their plans, the glints in their eyes and the determination they had faked, how they all sounded like they knew what they were doing. She thought about Abelard, chasing her down at the airport. She thought about Kai Pohala, when she looked up and saw her through the caul of sorcery: a figure cut out from another life and pasted over the wound of this one.

She thought about wicked problems.

She heard footsteps behind her and recognized the boots and the smell of smoke. "You should be asleep."

"So should you," Abelard said. "It's a long way to Chartegnon."

"When your heart's not there," she sang.

He joined her at the rail. She did not want to look at him. She did not want to be with people right now. She massaged her neck with her free hand. "Where are you headed after this?"

"We have a few leads." He tipped ash into the sea. With the spirecliffs burning, Tara doubted the ocean would notice one more cinder. "I wish I could go with you."

"I can handle Ms. Pohala."

He laughed a little. "I couldn't."

"I have experience."

"So does she. Is my point."

You shouldn't be here, she had said to Kai in the golf ball, and she had not realized in quite how many ways she meant it. Kai belonged to another life, to a time when mistakes could be amended, when victory was possible—when it must have been possible, because they had won, or anyway survived. Tara would have left her there, safe in a happy ending, reclining on some Kavekana beach with cocktail and a folder of work that she had brought along knowing she'd never touch it.

Now she was part of this. No, that was wrong. It had no longer been possible to pretend that she was out of it. The ordered ranks of dominos collapsed.

"Are you sure it's safe to go to Chartegnon? You did, kind of, cost them a colony."

"That revolution started on its own."

"Do you think the Iskari will see it that way?"

She shrugged. "We have a plan."

"I wanted to give you this," Abelard said.

She took the lighter from him and held it up to the stars. White plastic and chrome. "'I heart A.C.?'"

"Work in progress. I told Cardinal Evangelist Bede that we should develop more approachable holy symbols. You know."

"The heart's on fire."

"With the warmth of divine love?"

"Or human sacrifice."

"Not since the Ethelian Heresy. I thought it could, maybe— you know, if you need to get in touch with me through the prayer line, a focus might help."

"Thank you." She vanished the lighter into her pocket. "It's very sweet."

"Do you have any, I don't know. Tips?"

She looked away. "For dealing with Altemoc? Keep him away from grenades. He tends to throw himself on them."

"I mean, for all of this." He gestured with the cigarette to the coastline. "I don't know if you'll believe it, but my life is almost normal when you're not around."

"Don't let it get to you," she said.

He waited. "That's it?"

"There's no degree for this sort of thing, no certification process. Don't scare yourself into thinking that there's nothing you can do. We don't know what we can do. Not really. So we might as well try."

"Not so different from an engineering problem," he said. "If it didn't seem unsolvable, it would have been solved already." He was trying to convince himself. So, Tara realized, was she.

She had felt so small when they brought her home. Shale had born her across the moon road in his wiry stone arms. As she lingered in the hospital bed and they waited on her, Abelard and Cat and Ma, as they tried to keep their hands and minds busy while she pieced herself together, she had felt, for the first time maybe ever, utterly and altogether human. In those long nights, when she twitched awake in panic as a nurse padded down the hall, she would look over and see Abelard, working a crossword puzzle or dozing with the pencil in his hand, and ease herself back to sleep.

They were both broken when they met: the failed witch-girl given one last chance, the priest mourning his dead god. In him, she had seen a kind good man, too eager to surrender, to sorrow or to gods; in her, he had seen a woman certain of her skill and power.

They had both been wrong, about themselves and one another, but each had needed the other's mistake. Tara had been a hero to him, and so to herself. She fixed things, with her wit and grit and drive and her knife.

She won.

Now she had to be the person he had once seen in her: invincible, heroic, twenty times the size of life. She could not be the hurt small girl in that hospital bed. She could not need anyone.

She looked at him. Grinned. "Don't worry. You'll be fine."

Kai said her professional prayers before bed, like always. Then she cleaned the blood and ash away, and slept in silk pajamas.

Four hours later she woke in the cold blue rocking dark and prayed again, this time to quite a different goddess.

No one in the vast priesthood of Kavekana had created the Blue Lady. In fact, many priests had done their best to destroy her when she woke inside Kavekana'ai, a living goddess in a sea of drifting idols, troubling their models and angering their pilgrims. Kai hadn't known about this at the time. She had only learned the truth by meddling in things woman was not meant to wot of—at least, any woman below the cardinal suite.

But the Blue Lady had escaped and flourished, with Kai's help, among a quite different community than the one usually served by the faith-bankers of Kavekana. She was the Lady of outcasts, Lady of thieves. Kai might not be her prophet or her only priestess—but the Lady owed her favors.

It was time to collect a few.

She drifted from her stateroom down the passageway, soundless in bare feet, past the compartments where Abelard and Caleb slept, hesitating a moment at Abernathy's door.

She never would have found the hidden companionway without the Lady's whispers. Eddies in the air caressed her. Her fingers sought catches in the featureless bulkhead, and a length of paneling slid aside.

She climbed down into the shimmering dark. All around her the goddess sang the security system to sleep, silenced its alarms and closed the eyes of its watchful rats.

The ladder deposited her in a narrow passage flanked with secured doors. She took three precise steps, then a fourth and larger step, then slipped along the wall until she reached the first door. It opened at her touch, and she slid inside.

The room was full of stars.

She recognized them. And she recognized, too, the chittering footsteps that issued from that utter darkness overhead, which even the Lady's sight could not breach.

"Terrifying, isn't it?"

She spun, and stared at the star-dappled figure of Eberhardt Jax. He wore a tapestry robe of purple so deep it was almost black, worked with dragons in gold thread. He smiled a cool cool smile.

"Please, Kai. If you wanted to know something, you could have asked."

Kai felt her heart jump, and couldn't name the feeling. Her voice, at least, was her own, still and always. "Would you have given an honest answer?"

He stepped toward her and to one side, arms spread. "Try me."

"What are you really doing here?"

"Philanthropy. What are *you* doing here?"

"My job."

"Which job, exactly? Are you fulfilling your responsibilities to your clients, or are you pursuing your . . . avocation?"

"Of all the millions of broken places in the world, your philanthropy brings you to the spirecliffs. On the same day as Dawn. And I suppose this"—she swept her hand through the floating stars—"is just another coincidence."

He drew a breath, held it for an odd length of time, let it out. "When we first met, I told you: only one thing is happening. The world is dying. To survive, we must accept that truth. Like a disease-riddled patient, its final death may take many forms. This is one." He indicated the hole in the sky. "Ms. Abernathy works in her ways, and I in mine. I seek understanding, and I seek weapons. If we are to fight them, we must learn how they fight. They were here before. They left traces: artifacts we can study and reverse engineer. I suspected the scrap of iron that ruined the spirecliffs was one of theirs, but it seemed inaccessible. But then the anomaly veered this way. I did not know what would happen, but I could place myself on the scene. Not that it made much difference."

"Did you think you could stop her?"

"I hoped to shape events."

He wasn't lying, was the maddening thing. He did not even seem frustrated—just surprised he hadn't been enough to save the world with only his brain and his checkbook. "You should have called someone."

"Is that what you would have done? Is that why you broke into this room, alone?" He stood quite close to her now. She was always surprised to find that she was slightly taller than he was. It didn't feel that way, when she stared into the glacier pits of his eyes. "I have chased them. I have plumbed ancient temples, I have wandered cursed swamps and dead marshes. I have done what I could with the precious little my quest has revealed. I have learned to trust my instincts, Kai. You never know what you know: a fixation, a sudden passion is a quiet part of your mind trying to speak."

She swallowed. "What are the quiet parts of your mind saying now?"

He grinned, and the world was bright and free again, and everything was easy. She thought of Tara, of the expression on her face when they met in the golf ball. "It's telling me the world can mind itself, for a few hours." He snapped his fingers—and music drifted through the stars. "Would you care for a dance?"

Her mouth was dry, and she was thinking about another city, far away and long ago, about a well, and a woman raising water. "I would care," she said, "to return to my cabin. I have a flight in the morning."

His smile was never less than perfect.

14

It was always dark in the prison.

The prisoner did not know how long he had languished here. He did not eat. He had not eaten since the last time he saw light, and yet his body did not wither. His jailers would not let him die so easily. They would not let him die at all.

He was held in the bonds of living stone that their workers of miracles had shaped around his limbs. Wards and glyphs robbed him of the need to piss and shit and breathe and feed. If they had the Craft to still his heart without killing him they would have done so.

Instead they left him here, without so much as a flickering bulb to mock the passage of days somewhere altogether else, somewhere with wind, and sea, and grass.

He would even bear the sight of stars, if it meant he could feel the grass beneath his scarred back again.

The reason, to the extent his captors required a reason beyond mere cruelty, was this: never throw away what you may one day use. Not even so poor a material as man. So when they caught him, when they brought him down at last amid the ruins of their warriors and their broken clockwork ancestors, they sealed him here in timeless dark, binding every part of him they could, until only his mind remained free to wander.

The mind, after all, is a process. That is what they believed. It takes in the surrounding world and converts it to further mind. Without fellowship, family, or love, without sky and soil and light on the underside of leaves, without familiar voices and without the high stone arches of the desert of its home, the mind will dwindle, flicker, and, at last, go out.

So they sealed his body and left him here. In the dark. In the mountain.

The fools.

In the general case, their methods were effective. But they bore the stamp of philosophical weakness. For his captors, body and soul were mere *things,* substances shaped by causes and effects: other bodies, other souls, and even the aggregate body and soul sometimes called government. His captors did not, could not admit of any higher or subtler shape to human life. They believed that, denied other stimulus, a man could not help but hear the voice of the people. They knew causation and believed it coeval with destiny.

Still, they might have broken him had they but left the lights on. Unending light would be unending certainty. Perhaps he would have forgotten his purpose, forgotten how the mighty Names carved into his flesh would sound, given voice.

But they left him in the dark, and the dark is where all things start.

Even—especially—Gods.

"They should be back by now," Dawn said.

Sybil adjusted her position around Dawn's shoulders in a way Dawn believed was meant to indicate listening without agreement—what a human would have signified with a down-inflected "hmm." "They're well within the window."

"And nothing's happening. Look."

Dawn tried to pass Sybil the binoculars. The serpent twitched testily, then something subtle about her skull changed, and her pupils bulged and writhed until they settled into a keyhole shape. She lowered herself to the binoculars and peered at Shenshan Prison.

Dawn didn't feel like they were in the Shining Empire, really. Not that she could have said what she'd expected the Shining Empire to feel like. She had vague impressions of ancient clay warriors and mist and pagodas from woodcuts in travelers' books, but some of those books also claimed people on the other side of the world walked on their hands and had faces in their stomachs. She knew folks of Imperial extraction, of course, whose families came over in the God Wars, or centuries earlier. But for her the Empire itself had always been a kind of elemental elsewhere. Now that she was in it she found that they had smog and stars, just like any other place.

And just like any other place, she'd had to sneak in.

Mal and Valois and Burgess had been particular in their instructions to Ixzayotl—never fly higher than this or lower than that, follow cloud cover where possible, avoid any natural breaks in shoreline defenses that would be the subject of special observation, but follow less-settled chains of deep jungle and high hills, to the extent "less settled" meant anything in a place as overwhelmingly inhabited as this. Cloak us in darkness, but not *too* dark. It was more trouble than Dawn had ever taken with a border crossing before Sybil, but then, she'd always traveled with her father before, and many of her father's life choices could be explained by his desire to stay as far away from heavily armed mercenaries as possible, and from all gods, live or dead.

Sorry, Dad.

The Shining Empire was like any other place in this respect, too: they had prisons here. Though Shenshan Prison was kind of different from the prisons Dawn had seen before. Mostly, it was *more*. More in the sense that it was bigger, and more in the sense that it was more prison-y.

There were three layers of massive concrete walls, then a no-man's-land of barbed wire and angry glyphwork, followed by a massive fortified camp. Searchlights swept the skies and the forest's edge, and patrols of glowing-eyed spirits in jointed plate armor marched the ramparts.

Past all that, the mountain. It stood alone in a way her instincts told her mountains did not stand. Studded with the souls of prisoners, it pressed against the local Craft like a god. Though she did not think "god" was the right word, not anymore.

The mountain had been a god once. Or perhaps nothing so established and certain, the patron rather of some border tribe or a city on the wrong side of a war. It had been overrun, chained, cored, and made into this—a void hungry for the souls bound within. It had been built, Mal said, by an Empire as different from the present one as a chicken was from a five-story-tall prehistoric terrorlizard—but then, those two were not so different, from a certain point of view. Emperors came, and Empires went, and every one so far had found a use for Shenshan Prison.

The black-rock edifice sucked at her gaze. She hated it and she had not known it existed until last week.

"You're lucky that I'm only a serpent in a mythological sense. Most of us can't use binoculars." Sybil coiled back onto her shoulders. "I'm no expert, but I believe 'nothing's happening' is a good sign when it comes to prison breaks. They're not showy affairs, in the ideal case." Ixzayotl crouched in the valley behind them, wings furled over himself like a great tattered cloak, breathing heavily. "If everything goes according to plan, no one will ever know we were here."

"You're probably right." Dawn tried to sound reassured—tried, also, to feel it. Sybil squeezed her shoulders. Her attempts at physical comfort had improved once Dawn explained to her about necks and windpipes.

"Think of it," Sybil said, "as a win-win situation."

"I don't follow."

"Either it looks like nothing's happening, and you feel nervous but really everything's fine. Or it looks like something's happening, and you feel better, even though it's going horribly wrong."

"I don't think that's what 'win-win' means."

Serpents, it turned out, could not quite shrug.

Something was happening.

Things did happen, in the darkness. His captors could not exercise perfect control, though they tried. And sometimes they tested new systems of manipulation. Prisons, after all, were the laboratories of society.

Once, for a time, he had been able to hear screams. They were a relief from the silence. The screams went away, eventually. There had been water, dripping, as from a stalactite into a pool in a vast chamber. That lasted an eternity, before it stopped.

He catalogued the screams, the dripping water. Wind through the halls: a great door opening and closing, perhaps. Footsteps, once. His catalogue was exhaustive, and brief.

Beyond and around and through these interruptions, there was only the darkness and the silence and the mountain's vast disdain.

He understood the point of the mountain. ("In Kathic," Mina would have said, teasing, "we would call that its peak.") The mountain was all there was, for however many ages you were trapped here. The mountain had the form and nature of a God, but it cared nothing for you, gave nothing back. Not from cruelty or arrogance. There was no mind left within these slopes. It lived like a man in a coma. It had been pithed ages ago and kept alive for this purpose.

You could not see it, but it was there around you. It held you and it held you together. Given time, you would speak to it, thinking at first that you did so in jest. Given time, you would begin to pray. And when you went past prayer, past belief, to an aching and miserable faith in this edifice that did not care for you or notice you, that was incapable of the slightest action—then, perhaps, you might be of use.

That was his captors' aim. To make a man into a useful thing.

Or not. "People," Mina had said once, "don't all have reasons for the things they do. Not reasons like yours, with chapter and verse and footnotes. Sometimes people are just assholes."

He reviewed the catalogue of happenings, his memories of now. They could be handled more safely than the bright and sharp-edged distant past. Mina. His city. The sun. *His* son.

Recite them.

Scream. Dripping water. Footsteps. Wind.

It was a short simple list, this catalogue of his dark forever. But in all the eons of his imprisonment, he had never heard *singing* before.

At first he thought he imagined it. That was the way of things here: any change most likely a phantom of the mind. But this unfamiliar sound was real; like a human voice freed of lungs and diaphragmatic meat, a soprano if sopranos could sing forever. It moved through space in a way memories did not. It had over- and undertones. Every so often a gentle ringing sound emerged from that ethereal note, as once he'd seen a whale's back slip from ocean depths, only to curve again below.

So intent was he upon the song—determined to catalogue it for future reference—that for a long time (hours? days? seconds? what was time, here?) he missed what the song was doing.

The mountain was going to sleep.

Its senseless idle gaze softened, eased. One might imagine huge eyelids growing heavy in a craggy and weathered face. They drooped. They fell. The mountain, and the seals that bound him, slept beneath that song's caress.

He found that he could breathe again—that he needed to breathe—but there was no air.

He was immured in solid stone. The wards that kept him alive had slept with the mountain.

Even an Eagle Knight was just a man. His masters had taught him that, before the world changed. A man, no matter his faith and no matter how the gods have blessed him. There is no shame in feeling as a man feels.

For instance: panic. Steeled for so long against the weight of darkness and silence, he was not ready to drown. He tried to move. The stone resisted, clung to him like mud, but mud could be fought, and he had been raised to fight. As his lungs burned, he swam through stone. It flowed around his great arms. His shoulders surged.

It could not be much farther. Even mountains had an end.

He felt himself start to die.

His outstretched hand burst free, into empty space.

With a final lurch he threw himself forward and the strangeness of air embraced him, sweet wetness and cave must. Nearer: chrome, oil, the spent-spark aroma of Craftwork augmentation, the funk of nervous sweat, and a gentle, ginger-floral perfume. How had he never noticed the world's so many smells?

There were hands upon him, holding him up. He could not breathe, could not see. He wiped at his face, cast away gobs of wet stone. There were voices, each a miracle.

"—think he broke my arm—"

"—told you not to kill the life support before—"

"I apologize if the grace of my gods proved lacking in precision."

Kathic words, a range of inflections, accents, one markedly Low Quechal. None Imperial, or at least, none with that particular northeastern dialect the Party trained. A trick? There had been no singing when they sealed him in. His jailers could move the walls without song.

"Easy, soldier," another woman said. A big voice, accustomed to command. *Soldier.* That was wrong, but he respected the sentiment. "Let's get this junk off you. Hold still."

They were not here pursuant to Imperial will. They might be discovered, interrupted. He would not be found prone and helpless so close to freedom. He felt a chisel chip the stone that still clung to his skin: slow, too slow. He surged, twisted. He felt a sharp pain, heard a curse.

Pain was a long-lost friend, though not so welcome as the rest.

"Dammit. Can you talk sense into him?"

Again, the almost-familiar voice: "I'll try."

A cool hand settled upon his chest. It had been a long time since he was last touched with such care. The voice he knew spoke again, this time in High Quechal, the tongue of priests and Gods.

"Son of the house of Alh, lie still. Lie still and know that you have been sought and found—sought and found, because you are needed."

His own son never spoke the High Speech so elegantly, with this looping syntax, this spiral grace. For their family it had been a use-tongue, to speak at home—though Mina spoke it haltingly, with charming archaisms and an oddly erotic lisp. Caleb joked in High Speech. He shit-talked while losing at Apophitan Rat Screw. He made awful puns.

This woman spoke as if she had learned the tongue in temple, from tablets, from an axe-faced old master, letting a drop of blood to mark each memorized couplet. As if she had learned in what fanatics called "the old way."

He knew her by her speech. High Quechal: tongue of priests and Gods and heretics.

His scars burned.

Stone shattered from his flesh. He shook off the arms that held him, like a mastiff shaking water from its fur. His hand found her throat. He stood, free, furious, mighty, his scars awake, last of the Eagle Knights, bleeding from chisel wound and shards of stone, and glared at her with fresh-opened eyes: Malina Keka-pania, dangling by her neck from his fist, the woman he had last seen burning above his city, burning his city, the Serpents themselves bridled by her blasphemous power as if they were common beasts.

He could end her now. It would take no more effort than closing his fist. And yet the heretic was not afraid.

"Temoc. You're taking this about as well as I expected."

She sounded less eloquent with his hand around her throat.

He was aware of crossbows leveled in his direction, curse-throwers cocked, a knife drawn. His rescuers stood about him: a broad and broken-nosed woman who held her cursethrower like it was nothing special, a double handful of other soldiers, a monk in robes of an order he did not ken, Camlaander, perhaps, bald and not soft, but with the kind of form that would seem soft to those who did not know how to look.

He could kill them all, he thought. But they did not strike. And they had freed him. The murder of one's rescuers, even if they were heretics, was not consonant with the character of an Eagle Knight. As a man, he did not wish his first free act in—how long?—to be the taking of a life. And yet.

"What is this?"

"This," the heretic said, "*was* a nice quiet rescue op. I'm afraid it's now a getaway."

He felt stale and stiff after so long in the mountain. If he had been what Caleb would call "on his game," he would have noticed, among the many sounds he heard, the one sound that he did not.

The singing had stopped.

He had scattered his rescuers when he lunged for Kekapania, thinking of nothing but vengeance for Gods and a son betrayed. Now, on the tunnel floor, he saw a brass bowl of the sort found in Dhistran curio shops, and a round wooden stick.

All around him, the mountain woke. Far off, he heard a siren.

Escape tempted. But duty was in his hand, around this woman's throat.

She understood. Whatever else he could say about her, he had to admit this much. The world was a bleak desert, duty the sole path between its hidden springs. Follow duty, and you might not survive to the next watering hole. But if you left the path, you were surely lost.

"Son of the house of Alh," she said, in High Quechal. "The stars are wrong. The land needs her Knights."

For the first time in a long while, he felt cold.

There were orders of duty, as there were orders of being. And those words, that quest-call settling upon his shoulders as mantle and chain—there was no call higher ever heard by mortal men.

Was she lying? To save herself? No. He had known her teacher, her foster father, the man who made her what she was. He had known him and hated him. Alaxic was a warped and bitter old priest who raised his girls like Imperial scholars raised dwarf pine trees, with love, care, patience; with deprivation, rope, and pruning shears. He needed weapons, that man, and made them out of girls. A drop of blood for every couplet.

That she would use those words lightly, falsely—he could not think it.

The monk approached. "Sir. If I may? I've always been a fan."

"Burgess," Kekapania said, with a significant glance toward Temoc's grip around her neck.

"Of course," Burgess said. "In fact. While I can only imagine the profound range of emotions you are experiencing, may I suggest we delay both explanations and asphyxiations until we find ourselves safely elsewhere?"

"He means," Kekapania said, "that we gotta go."

The stars are wrong. The land needs her Knights.

He released her.

She drew a crumpled gasping breath and sank against the wall. But she did not collapse, and when she looked up her eyes were hard as onyx. "The land needs her Knights," she said. "And you . . . you need pants."

———

"There," Sybil said, when the alarms went off. "Happy now?"

Shenshan Prison spasmed to life. The battlements swarmed with soldiers. Spotlights speared the low heavy clouds. Guards streamed into the mountain gates.

This was not part of the plan.

"I should have gone with them."

"Why? So we could be stuck down there with half the Imperial Army falling on our heads?"

"They're my friends."

Sybil's tongue flicked out.

Dawn didn't like her silence. "What?"

"They have their mission, and we have ours."

She felt cold and dangerous in a way she was not used to feeling, not when she was talking to Sybil. "Are you saying they're *not* our friends?"

Serpents might not be able to laugh or weep or shrug or even blink, but they could "tsk" quite effectively. "They are professionals. We are not, currently, a reliable asset in a combat situation. We should sit here, maintain overwatch, and let the people who signed on to help us, help us. They know what they're doing."

"I hope so."

———

"This was a well-planned escape attempt," Temoc said, as they ran through red-lit halls with sirens blaring, two security teams broken in their wake, three more on their heels, and the prison seething around them like a kicked anthill, "in two respects."

"Thanks," said Valois, the broken-nosed lieutenant, proving thereby to Temoc that she did not grasp the subtleties of Quechal humor.

Kekapania opened a door only for a crossbow bolt to sing through it. The bolt bounced off her wards, but she stumbled. Temoc caught her. Valois slammed the door. Kekapania kicked into a run down a side passage. He matched her pace. It was good to run. It was good to have limbs again. The body was a gift of the gods, its use a prayer of thanks.

Kekapania did not seem to see it that way. She grimaced, held her hand to her side. Her breath was less than even. In some respects, her religious education had been lacking. "He means *only* two."

He nodded, grateful for the clarification, as Yan, one of Valois's men, led them down yet another branching side passage. "Your grasp of the prison's layout is impressive. We have had to reroute around defensive hard points five times already, and yet Yan continues to furnish viable options. Superb."

"Hey, thanks," Yan said. "I'm a map nerd, I guess."

As they routed around another patrol of watchgolems, Temoc made a mental note to ask him how a "map nerd" happened upon detailed schematics for a peak-security prison.

"Still," Yan said, "we're running out of outs. We've got three options left." He stopped at a fork in the tunnel, glared left, right, then led them straight ahead and down a winding stair.

"What," said Valois, "is the other respect?"

"The pants," he replied. "They fit."

The stair led them straight into a guard outpost. Five men and a golem awaited them. Valois and Yan retreated around the curve of the stair for cover.

Another firefight. This was taking too long. Temoc gathered himself and leapt.

The guards were well trained. They were prepared for an outnumbered enemy to withdraw to cover. They did not expect him.

The golem posed a minor inconvenience. Even after all these years Temoc still believed that a being would drop when you ripped its arm off, rather than the arm and body continuing to fight independently. That cost him a shallow wound on the leg, before he rammed the golem's own sword through its guidance crypt, and the demon within crackled away in a shower of sparks and magic smoke.

Booted feet rushed down the tunnel toward him. There was a hand on his arm: Kekapania, her chest heaving, her hand slick with sweat, her blade out and bloody, though not for him.

He recognized that blade, the truth of it, rather than its physical form.

"The Gods bless you, daughter of Kei."

Her face darkened. He ran after her.

"I did not mean to give offense."

She was breathing heavily. Slowing down. She switched to Low Quechal. "Call me Mal. Just that."

"That is not all you are."

Her retort was lost in a hail of fire from the chamber ahead. Yan led them down a side hall clustered with steam pipes. Mal—it felt wrong to use so informal an address, but one did try to call people what they asked to be called—burned her fleshy arm on a steam pipe and swore by some foreign god. Valois stayed behind to do something with the pipes. Vented steam roared. He heard screams. She caught up; their pursuers did not pursue.

He had been concerned about Burgess. The man did not seem built to cover distance at speed. He was flushed and quivering, but he kept pace, and the effort had not made him clumsy yet. Good.

Temoc drew even with . . . "Mal." How could anyone make that sound right? "Tell me of the stars."

She glared at him. "Years stuck in a godsdamned mountain and you didn't have the decency to get out of shape."

"There is no decency in weakness."

"You don't have metal limbs. They're heavy."

"You would be whole in body now, had you not committed grievous blasphemies against those powers which stand higher yet than Gods."

She groaned, as much as she was able, and spoke between ragged breaths. "Fifteen years. And you're still mad about that."

"Did you not expect that, as soon as I was free, I would try to kill you?"

"I did. I told them. Just didn't think. You'd be so godsdamn. Good at it."

They burst into a vast shadowy chamber full of armor. A hangar, he thought, for Imperial war machines, housed here to guard against liberation from without. Not all Shenshan's victims were lone powers like himself. The prison held prophets, queens, and more than a few emperors.

The shortest armor unit was merely the size of a house, the largest tall as temples. The storage crystals within were trickle-fed by man-thick tubes of nutrient bath, their shield helms framed with the thorny wire crowns through which ancestors piloted the frame. They waited: tools of immortal war, silent as the dead that drove them.

Three great doors led from the hangar, sized for maintenance vehicles to carry out the great armors prone. Yan led them to the first door, but it closed before they could reach it—as did the second, then the third.

Spotlights burst on. Temoc squinted against the glare. He saw movement high up, behind observation deck windows. Flight control. Snipers swarmed onto the gantries. Valois shouted, "Back!" They scrambled behind one of the massive armor frames' legs. Guards streamed in through the smaller entrances. Curses pinged off armor. Arrows whistled through the air.

"Feels damn familiar," Mal growled. "I have not been making good life choices recently."

Burgess laughed, though Temoc did not understand why. For his part, he observed aloud, "Your tendency to make poor life choices is hardly a recent phenomenon."

She peered out to survey the opposition, then ducked back into cover as fire darted her way. "What, you mean like dating your son?"

"Displaying judgment nearly as poor as his, in courting you."

"Did you seriously just say 'courting'?"

"Yan," Valois shouted. "Status."

"Good news, bad news," he said. "Good: rear guard and harry team made their exits. Bad: that was our last out. Unless we can break through the hangar door."

Temoc had placed Valois as a competent soldier, rather than a commander of distinction. He revised his assessment when, without a moment's pause, she shifted tactic. She pointed to the armor frame they were sheltering behind. "Burgess, can you hot-wire this?"

"I could wake it, I think. If I could reach the helmet."

She gestured to two others of her squad. "Lopez, Chakrabartay, get Burgess to the helmet."

It was a good plan. It might have worked. A grappling hook was launched, an automatic reel attached, a climbing harness girded Burgess's loins. But before the monk could rise—

There came a weight upon the air, and the sound of breaking timber.

He looked up.

There were lights, now, in the armor's eyes. Crackling and spitting balls of crimson flame.

The pilots were awake. Honored dead of many ages, blessed with an afterlife of endless war. Battle-sharpened souls with bodies built for destruction.

The squad could not face them. They had to fall back. There was no back for them to fall.

"I wish you could have met Dawn," Mal said. Not despairing, but ready for what might come. "The kid who got me into this. You'd have liked her, I think. Gods know she pisses *me* off." She breathed out. Looked down. "She'll be okay."

He knew that tone. There was more prayer in it than in any formal call to any god. A hope so vicious and hot it could only be uttered as fact.

He thought of Caleb. He placed one hand gently on her shoulder. "Do not be afraid."

"We're kinda low on options."

"The stars are wrong. There is much we may dare ask the Gods, even we who are broken."

"There are no gods here, old man. The mountain's dead. They killed it a long time ago."

"A God's death," he said, "is only the beginning." And: "Yan! There is freedom beyond the hangar door?"

"If by freedom you mean the prison yard and, like, three more walls."

"That will suffice. Thank you." He closed his eyes and composed his soul. The small-arms fire, the creak and clash of the armor frames, the roar and scream of combat all receded.

Mal's voice reached him. He thought he heard an edge of wonder in it. "Temoc? What are you doing?"

"A God's death," he said, "is like the passing of a great tree. It leaves a space that other Gods may fill. There are many Gods of many mountains. And I know all Their names."

15

There seemed to be no end to the stream of guards entering the mountain. Or to the sirens.

Dawn wondered what was happening to Mal and Burgess and Valois and Yan and Gupta and the rest. She wondered and tried not to imagine. It hurt to think of them. She closed her eyes but she could still see the prison's Craft tighten and pulse, a noose around the Arsenals' throat. "I should go down there."

Sybil squeezed her shoulder. "They are committed to the mission. They know they are resources to be spent. They want you to spend them wisely."

"That's cold."

"We have to be cold. Heroism is for those who care less about whether they succeed than how they feel about themselves after. We cannot afford to be heroes."

"What are we, then?"

"If you must conceive of everything in terms of childhood tales," Sybil hissed, "think of us as villains. We could very easily fail. The world will not help us. But we may help ourselves."

What if she were a villain? Crimson coat, Iskari cuffs with bloodstone cuff links, a sneer of cold command. High-heeled dragonscale boots. A throne of skulls, and vicious lipstick. She'd never worn much makeup. She'd have to learn. Maybe Mal could teach her.

She tried to see herself that way. Wicked, powerful, driven. But all she saw was the girl crawling away from Blake's Rest with broken ribs.

"The Arsenals may be resources," Dawn said. "But they're good resources. We need them on the board as long as possible.

And if we're villains, shouldn't we step in when the henchmen fail?"

From Sybil's pause, Dawn could tell she didn't like where this conversation was going. "I'm sure they have everything under control."

It would have been a better argument if the mountain had not chosen that moment to collapse.

———————

Maimed, deafened, Shenshan was not moved by prayer. It was love withheld and love demanded. But into its silence, Temoc could speak: not to this mountain, but to the mountain in his heart. To Nine Peaks, lord of earthquake and precipice, a God scarred into Temoc's own flesh.

There were many modes of worship—penance, bloodletting, contemplation, ecstatic union. Hermits practiced in mountain caves. Why should a holy man not welcome confinement in living rock, to contemplate its mystery?

In the dark, unable even to breathe, he had sometimes been afraid. He planned for escape, vengeance, triumph, but so did many an old and crumpled man. In the long stillness, you began to doubt whether you practiced patience or capitulation. But he had not lost his calling. The mountain had not eaten him. Nine Peaks was here, in the roots of the stone. As his Eagle Knight rose to battle, so, too, did the God.

Temoc Almotil was a priest again. A Knight. Worthy of his scars.

To pray, and, at last, to know your prayers answered: this is joy.

The mountainside parted like a curtain, and they were free. Provided they could make it through the prison yard and three high walls, with Imperial armor frames even now shouldering through the rockslide after them.

He breathed the cool night air. There was freedom, if they could fight for it. But when was man free otherwise?

His companions stared at him, as the light from his scars eased to a bearable glow. These were hard men and women, not inclined to awe. To see it upon their faces, even for an instant, pleased him. This pleasure he felt was not mere pride: it was a priest's job to signify. Where there was no awe of the Gods, one might kindle awe of Their Knights.

He saw it even in Mal. Good. There was some true faith left in her, in the husk her master had made. "Come on, people!" she cried. "Let's find the exit!"

They fought toward the breach.

In Temoc's youth, in the age-ending strife of the God Wars, he had fought beside his brother Knights, beside his masters and teachers, against the necromantic horrors the Craftsmen raised. The Eagle Knights had been trained as a holy champions; they faced killing machines. It had shocked him to learn how little difference there was between the two.

In the decades since, he had fought monsters and wizards, and he had fought city hall. With the last survivors of the Skittersill Rising, he had fought the King in Red on dragonback in the skies above his burning friends.

But he had never fought this kind of war.

Valois's people worked the battlefield like a climber worked a cliff. They charged boldly, but only from cover to cover. They exchanged curse-fire, but only to give a flanking party time to seize superior ground. They moved in sprints, at speed. They were cold-edged, joyless, and alert.

Whatever Mina might say, he was no romantic. He had fought. He found no joy in it. But he remembered a raw field of broken hearts, a field of sorrow and rage. Most people did not want to kill, or to face their own death, which gave war a sense of ragged honesty.

There was none here, nor any trace of hesitation. Just a calculus of risk and opportunity. They fought a Craftsman's war—a war of tactical pivots and operational objectives, of force utilization and reserves, of return on investment and strategic capital.

He did not know their system, its tactics and its diverse roles. So, rather than disturbing their murderous math by trying to learn under fire, he just . . . did what he always did.

With a roar he leapt a hundred feet in a single bound. He moved like a cloud-shadow over the field, and where he landed darkness fell. He broke the legs off one armor frame and threw them into the pilot's compartment of another. He jumped into a sniper's nest and cleared it with his bare hands. At one point he realized he was swinging a sword three times his own height, looted, he supposed, from some fallen armor. He was weaker than he remembered, and his Gods were weaker, too, but he had rage to drive him and scores to settle.

Valois and her company adapted. They quickened their tempo to match him. They laid down advance fire, lobbing alchemist's grenades and stranger weapons—a kind of clinging purple-black flame, a bomb that burst into plant tendrils that strangled soldiers and war machines, a wailing disk that, when it struck, released a flood of ghosts—opening gaps for him to exploit.

They did what they had to do, these soldiers, to survive the world he had made. The God Wars birthed monsters, and Temoc was one of them. The powers of the Craft and the miracles wrought to face it produced skeleton giants, thorn-tree auroras. Sorcery blotted out the sun like the skazzerai in ancient tales.

They had made the world these children lived in, and the children survived by hiding their hearts. Perhaps not even they could say where.

He had wondered about his son, why he was so quiet, and whence came his odd detachment shading to despair. Watching Arsenal Company, he understood. You did what you had to do. You sought every advantage, every handhold. You were doomed from the start. You had to accept it, if you wanted to endure.

But of course, at the end, you died anyway.

They were losing. Each step was slower than the last. Armor frames tore free of the collapsed mountain to lurch after them. Guards closed in. His arm grew heavy. Arsenal Company's cordon tightened. Yan was wounded. Lopez was down, draped across Chakrabartay's shoulders. Mal's god-blade tore through foes, but there was too much fire, and her wards were weak. She stumbled under a guard's assault. Temoc killed the man, and she killed the next.

They had hardened themselves to survive, but it was not enough.

He remembered the night he left his family to go to the Skitter-sill. He remembered his son drugged on the altar, as he gave him the only gift he could, the scars he hoped would carry him through the dark.

The machine ground you to fit its own workings.

He laid about with the giant sword, lopping legs off armor frames—stupid idea, war machines with legs. He leapt forty feet to an armor frame's shoulder and tore its head free. But there were more, always. They were cut off. Falling back.

The stars are wrong.

She had pronounced the words, and he knew their meaning. They are coming back, through the hole in the deepness of the sky—the skazzerai, the hunting ones who eat the sun and feast on the souls of Gods. Where their shadows fall there is no laughter, there is no joy, nor any fine thing. They leave not worlds but husks, pith, and peel. There is no wonder where they walk, though terrors many. All they know is hunger and what they hunger for is all.

What will they find when they arrive? We have chewed the world for them, like a mother bird. Sanded our dreams so small even the stars do not seem worth reaching for. We have made ourselves useful instruments. What remains? What terror, joy, or wonder, when even the field of honor has become a place of quotas and efficiencies? We are blood-smeared and battered and ground to meal, and we have done this to ourselves.

Perhaps that is why they bided their time, the skazzerai, like the farmer who seeks among his orchards the fruit that has read-ied itself for his teeth. They waited for us to do their work. Now it is done. It was done years ago, when the Serpents rose over Dresediel Lex in all their glory, and still nothing changed.

What could you do but fight on, alone in heart even as you stood side by side with your brothers and friends? What but hold to faith, even when it seemed faith could change nothing? Loss was not strange to him. He had spent his whole life losing, in one form or another. Might sought might to pitch itself against. But he could not afford to lose today.

He sought Mal in the press, and found her, blade wet. He fought to her side and back-to-back they stood. His enemy had graced him with this last battle. She had drawn him from the depths. He did not like her or trust her, but she would give herself for him and him for her. In a bleak world one might call that a miracle.

"Why," he asked, "did you come for me?"

"I told you about the stars."

"I am not so proud as to think one Knight might stand against them. Why risk so much for me?"

"I didn't do it for you," she said, and might have said more. But then the lights went out, and he heard the sound of mighty wings.

———————

"This is an awful idea," Sybil said, over the rush of wind and Dawn's whoop of joy.

"I think you mean *awesome*."

Sybil hissed.

"I know," Dawn said. "You tried to help someone once, and it got you hung up in wires. But that was something someone did *to* you. You can't control that. You can control what you do to them."

The prison complex lay below, lit up and dazzling, like the beautiful clocks in the shop windows Dawn used to press her nose against. Intricate and golden and never hers.

Until now.

"Come on," she said. "Let's be villains."

———————

Darkness fell, and with it came the scream of torn metal. The crimson fires of armor frame eyes flickered, died, then returned, warped blue. They jerked, spasmed, bent unnaturally, fell like great trees before the axe. Some rose on all fours to charge their comrades with maws agape. A moan issued from the prison, from the broken mountain and the guards and the walls, a moan of opened graves and cold wind in high places.

The clouds burned away, and from the black between the unveiled stars the God descended.

Temoc was no stranger to visions or the high language of signs and portents. He had known battlefields where miracle and blasphemy pierced one another in such intimate embrace they could not be told apart. On the field of truth, on the battlefield of life, an Eagle Knight accepted what might come and met it in keeping with his vow.

He could not accept this. He could not, yet, understand it. At first it seemed as nonsensical as the paintings he used to see on the sides of the kinds of carts the young longhaired neo-druids had driven, in that strange period when no one was sure if the Wars were over: images fantastical and superhuman, colors too vivid for the world, and yet somehow also less fantastical than what was unfolding around them. Fever dreams of a God-starved mind.

Yet even after years in Shenshan Prison, he was no wilderness hermit, no sunblasted prophet trembling in hallucinatory ecstasy. He knew this was real.

The God: Ixzayotl, slain. He had been there for the great one's death. He had wept. Yet this was that God. Those his jewel-set wings. Risen, as the Craft called dead things to rise, and yet unchained, when all their art was chains. Wings spread, He descended.

Beneath the bare cage of the God's flayed chest, below the gap where His heart should be, there was a shining girl. About the girl's neck, there was a Serpent.

The guards fell back. Their fire stalled. On they fled, their own ancestors turned against them. Arsenal Company emerged from cover one by one, their eyes raised heavenward. They were not lost. Or not all of them was lost. Nor all of him. Even in their secret places, they were found and seen.

By his side, Mal spoke. "I didn't do this for you, old man. I did it for her."

The God gathered them in His mighty hands and lifted them into the hollow of His chest, where His heart once was. Temoc climbed the rough bone, following Mal, Valois, Burgess, the rest of their close group. The Arsenals had strung a cat's cradle of steel cables and platforms between the God's ribs, and those still standing clicked their harnesses into place, then turned to strap the wounded in. Temoc smelled incense and the sweet rot of wet leaves. He stared up into the violet fire of the girl's eyes, into the eyes of the serpent draped about her like a stole. She seemed to see into the heart of him.

"So," she said, "you're the guy."

He had lived a long time. It was rare to find himself at a loss for words.

"Dawn," Mal said, "meet Temoc. Temoc, this is Dawn. We'll have time for proper introductions later."

"You should not have come for us," Valois said.

It was hard to read Dawn's face. He realized she was very young. "I won't let you throw yourself away for me."

"Ebonhawks inbound." That was Chakrabartay, from the God's shoulder. At his word, Temoc heard the ebonhawks, or, rather, he did not hear them: great pulses of silence overwhelmed the screams and the chaos of torn metal.

Death approached on soundless wings.

"We," he said, "should be elsewhere."

"On it," Dawn said.

Rainbow pinions flared, and with a lurch—he clutched Dread Ixzayotl's ribs—they were airborne. Below, Shenshan Prison convulsed. Dawn's armor frames tore into their loyal kin with teeth and claws, as new-raised frames struggled to bring ordnance to bear upon an enemy they could not see as other. Upslope, the mountain's barren stone burst with vines and sprays of ice as great shuddering forms tore free: his fellow prisoners, some entombed for centuries, seizing their chance at freedom. At such distance even the great monsters seemed small, but one among them he picked out cold and clear against the night, as if he glowed from within: a man with a long beard and a conqueror's dread laugh, prophesying war.

The God wheeled away, and Temoc saw the ebonhawks. They had been creatures once, immortal birds that brooded in the high mountains in the days before wars and revolution made them useful. Now they were a blight against the sky, all angled metal, and they were gaining fast.

Columns of fire tore from their opened maws. Ixzayotl dipped left, right, swept through a roll that jerked the Arsenals against their harnesses and tested the strength of Temoc's grip. A blast singed through the ribs and one Arsenal tumbled, screaming—to be saved by a comrade's outflung hand.

Dawn shimmered. The light that streamed from her skin sparkled off ice crystals that formed upon her and in the surrounding air. That was the mark of the Craft: it stole heat and life. But she did not wheedle or intreat as would the Craft. The weight of her will lay upon the world, as would a God's.

Ixzayotl flew, fast and faster. Bones in His rainbow wings shifted in response to some logic of efficiency. His body sculpted Itself into a sleek missile. She was doing this—or, she was asking Him, and what remained of Him was quick to answer.

No more fire came, their pursuers dwindling out of sight behind, Shenshan mountain and all its silence a forgotten splinter of undulating horizon. They would escape.

Then the moon emerged from behind a bank of cloud.

It went bad all at once.

Dawn crumpled. She might have fallen to the mountainside a thousand feet below had not Mal caught her, but Mal's grip was little aid as the God Himself began to fall. Arsenals jerked against the cables as Dread Ixzayotl tumbled, buffeted by the wind. Temoc caught the girl's body in his arms, and together with Mal snapped her into anchoring cord.

When she descended to the battlefield she had seemed a thing of war, but in his arms he could not see her so. It had been a long time since last he held a child, though he doubted she would relish being so called. The God whirled. The sky was the soil was the sky. In his arms, Dawn shook, and wept blood tears.

He saw her then with the eyes of faith. She had been laid low in the way of a God: torn between commitments and contradictions, unable to make the world as she wished. Now her power was unraveling—even that which kept the God in flight.

He could help her. If he worked fast. If they survived so long.

"Burgess!" he called through the din. Somewhere, the round priest answered, a squawking sort of groan. Temoc shouted, "Pray, man!"

"I," came the bedraggled response, "am trying."

"Not for your own skin. Pray to the Lord of Feathers and Skies, pray to He Who Settles Not. Pray and let your blood, if your hand be steady. Pray, lest we die now, and all she has done for us be as wind."

The priest stammered in High Quechal, as the God's wings sought and lost purchase on air. Slow, too slow. Temoc met Mal's eyes, and saw the need in her, the fear that all her striving, once again, would not be enough.

I did it for her.

"Help him," he said. "Lend your voice and faith. Your blood."

He saw her hesitate. He felt their death approach, the final stop. She would not leave the girl.

"I will save her," he said. "For this you raised me from the depths. I will save her, though it means my ruin. Keep us alive, that I may work."

Her dark eyes narrowed, and he saw in that moment the losses she had suffered—so many of them his fault. "You better."

Then she was away.

He knelt over the girl, and over the Serpent, and bent his head. Mal and the priest might fail and leave them smears upon some barren Imperial hillside. He might die now. There was no other way. He could have done the part he had assigned to them, but they could not do this. Even he was not sure he could. But when faced with certain tasks, even impossibility was no excuse for a Knight's retreat.

There was a hunger in her hand, beneath a velvet glove. He set his own hand against it, his faith, his will. It chilled him, warded though he was.

Her breath eased, though the frost upon her flesh thickened into ice.

To be of faith is to still your heart and hear the wills at work within the world. Hers, he heard with uncommon bare commitment, like trumpets at break of day. *We are faster than the armies of the Shining Empire.* And *The moon cannot see us.* They might have been scripture, carved into a wall. She could not maintain both truths against the powers that opposed her.

But what is a priest for, if not the interpretation of scripture?

Far off he heard voices, Burgess's and Mal's, raised in twinsong. Others joined them: the Arsenals, rough, untrained, shouting more than singing—but the first songs had been just that, screams against the dark.

The God's wings caught the air, and they fell no longer.

There were shapes around him. He could not raise his head. Sparing that attention from his struggle would have ended her and killed them all. But he smelled Mal. He smelled her blood.

"She needs power," he said. "More than any of us can give. I know a place."

"Where?" Mal's voice was quiet, and perhaps he heard a trace of awe.

"North," he said, and bent to strive once more against the stars and death.

16

Caleb stared out the golemwing's window into the gnashing cloud of bugs.

Somewhere down there, according to Abelard's sources, should be a platform called the Arsenal; somewhere down there should be evidence, a trail they could follow. But someone did not want them found.

He glanced over to the priest. "You're sure you can do this?"

"Absolutely," Abelard replied. "One hundred percent." He looked out the window himself, and down, and away. Taking into account his sharp swallow and his greenish complexion, Caleb would have rated the priest's confidence lower. Thirty percent, say.

Encouragement seemed in order, but Caleb had no idea what might help. He started with "You'll be fine," which yielded from Abelard a scared and skeptical frown. "There aren't *that* many bugs."

There were.

"It's just." Abelard said, "that they're so *organized*."

"That makes it easier, in a way," Caleb lied. "Think of them as one big bug." One big bug made of millions of smaller bugs animated by foul necromancy into a mass about seventy feet tall. "We don't have to do this now. We can fall back, call Jax, get some contractors to chase this thing off. Hells, even Ortega—"

"We don't have time."

"This might not even be the right place," Caleb said. "There are other options."

"None of which have seen any unusual activity in weeks. Here we have a missing mercenary team, a missing God corpse, a, you know, um, a bug monster. Jax's people say that the Concern that owns the place lost contact with it two days after the spirecliffs."

"It is a good lead," Caleb admitted. "But."

"I can do this." Abelard took a shuddering breath. "Tara needs us to do this." He closed his eyes and prayed.

Caleb felt the warmth in his scars first. They opened toward the priest like flowers at daybreak, shimmering green. Suddenly, Abelard looked peaceful, radiant. The thin nervous gentle man with his bridge column and cigarettes smoothed into serenity, confidence, and calm. Caleb clenched his scars shut and tried not to scowl.

The holy symbol in the priest's hands began to glow. So did the golemwing. Caleb produced a pair of sunglasses from his breast pocket, unfolded them, and put them on before the glow became positively solar. Below, bugs screeched and seethed, retreating to the shadows of the platform. He knew how they felt.

The platform, at least, was clear. He leaned back to address the pilot.

"Take us in."

Whoever abandoned the Arsenal hadn't done so by half. The golemwing's landing blew eddies of ash off the remains of a huge bonfire—which had been fed, Caleb would be willing to bet, with the evidence he hoped to find. "I don't suppose you can do anything about that," he asked Abelard.

"Too old. The fire would remember, but the fire has gone out."

Sweat was beading on the priest's forehead, and his knuckles were white on the holy symbol. Caleb glimpsed movement in the shadows his light cast, up vents and down exhaust pipes. "How long can you keep the bugs away?"

"We'll see" was not the answer he'd been hoping for.

Topside was all ruin and waste—broken concrete, trash, the wreckage of a bar. And it was Craftless. Ordinarily even a ruin like this would retain the elaborate decaying Craftwork structures that once bound it to the web of global exchange. But they were gone. "Only ash should be this barren," he said. "Places that were razed completely in the Wars. But the platform hasn't disintegrated. Yet."

"Yet?" The priest's light flickered. Caleb heard legs chittering in the walls.

"I mean," he said, hastily, "it's still here. But its soul is gone, or claimed by some other system. Like the spirecliffs."

"They were here."

"Let's look below."

Abelard's light dimmed. He swallowed and nodded.

———

The dorms belowdecks had not been built for living. Back when this was a working rig, the laborers, as far as the owners were concerned, had been human only by accident. It turned out that people were more fit for some jobs than zombies or machines or magic, that was all. But any orderly workshop needed a place to set down your tools, and the dorms were that place. Joyless concrete, riveted bunks, foul-looking heads. And, of course, the bugs, skittering wherever Abelard's light did not reach. Caleb doubted that they had been a feature of the original design.

He tried to imagine Mal here. The Mal he'd known in pinstripes and silk, in penthouses and on couatlback, Mal who'd dreamed of tipping the world into the fire. That woman would have left her mark on these concrete walls—would never have let these walls close around her in the first place. But maybe she had changed. There'd been time enough. And he was not the man he had been, then.

Abelard walked beside him, tense. Once he tripped, and the fireglow flickered. Caleb put out a hand to steady him. The priest found his balance, but Caleb thought the glow was dimmer now.

Caleb didn't like the silence, and he liked what he could hear beneath it even less. "This isn't your line of work," he said. "Normally, I mean."

"Is it anyone's?" But Abelard managed an apologetic smile. "Not mine, though, no. Normally. I stick with machines."

"You're here because of Abernathy."

"She's my friend. And she needs help."

"Are we talking about the same person? Merciless glare, skeleton hand? She doesn't seem to be in the business of needing anything."

Abelard laughed at that. "Left to her own devices, she'd take on the world and the stars alone, and think she deserved the burden. Maybe that's how she was raised or maybe it's how she was taught, or maybe it's who she was all along. Power is responsibility is guilt. If you don't have enough of one, take the others to compensate."

"You don't agree."

"I don't think it works that way," the priest said. "Power—I mean the power to help people, to do things that matter—it comes from working with people, doesn't it? Guilt makes you pull back from them. But . . . She's my friend. I care about her. I want to help."

"So you're here, and she's an ocean and half a continent away."

"Yes."

"It was a neat move, on her part. You can't go with her to Chartegnon, because she needs to be a free agent if she's to meet Kai's contact. And she needs you here, so we can stay in touch with me."

"She's a hard person to help," Abelard admitted. "Tara thinks you should be willing to give your life for someone you love."

"Shouldn't you?"

"It's one thing to be willing to give your life, and another to look for the chance. Personally, I think it's better to live."

"That's not always an option," Caleb said. "Never, really. In the long run."

"Don't tell the Craftsfolk."

It was his turn to laugh—he was surprised by the sound. "No wonder you're in a hurry."

"If we find Dawn, Tara will come to us."

"Or we'll deal with the situation ourselves and deny Abernathy her grand gesture."

"Tara," Abelard said, "is not the only one who can think ahead."

"You're a good friend."

The light was steadier now. "We're running out of hallway," Abelard said. "What do you hope to find down here, exactly?"

Caleb stepped aside so Abelard could see into the final room. "This."

The painting took up the entire wall, and overflowed onto ceiling and floor. "Who is it?"

"Ixzayotl of Feather and Sky. The Eagle Who Faces East." Caleb traced the grooves in the concrete—the feathered crown, the blood-spatter curve of wings. His fingers came away rust red. The blood was too old to track. She would have thought of that. She thought of everything—except, sometimes, of him. He unbuttoned his sleeve, rolled it up, and showed Abelard the scar that matched the god. "This guy. Mal was here. This is her grave marker for the god below. The one who's missing."

"So why are you smiling?"

"Because those who seek the gods," he said, "can find them."

17

Dawn fled through the dying wood.

Through the stark grim trees there came an inhuman wail. She could not look back. A hunger pursued her on taloned feet, unseen, unknowable, and vast. The forest writhed in answer to its need. Roots convulsed to trip her. Vines like nooses swept to catch her throat. Faster she ran, barefoot, torn. She needed a weapon. Each stick she seized was rotting, and she found no stones beneath the paste of brown wet leaves. She was weak, and the hunger neared. She tasted blood. She ran, she ran, she ran, and its cold iron breath kissed her neck—

She sat up screaming. There were arms around her. She struck.

Mal sat down hard on the floor beside her, rubbing her jaw. "Good morning to you, too, kid."

"Not," she said, panting, "not a kid."

When you're panicking, note five things in the world around you. Tara had taught her that. And hells, if it doesn't work, at least you've noticed five things. Maybe you can use one of them to fight back.

Dark room. Stale tinny smell, like an empty grain silo. Metal floor. Pulsing glyphs and indicator lights created more shadows than they relieved, shadows dense with wires and strange machines. Tubes. Pumps. Other figures around her, blocking out the lights, or reflecting them. It was very cold.

Nope. Still panicking.

A weight on her shoulder shifted, coiled. Once, she would have screamed. She clutched Sybil. "We made it."

Mal nodded. "Barely."

"I remember running. The ebonhawks. And then . . ."

"You fell," said a new voice, quiet and deep. "We raised you up."

Against the small blinking lights Dawn saw a massive shadow like a man, grim as monuments of judgment. When Mal said "priest and theologian," Dawn had imagined some reedy god-botherer like Pastor Merrott, not this mountain. She could not abide the noble self-possession of that dark form. She wanted to punch him in the face. And yet he had prayed over her. If not for him, she and all the Arsenals would be smears on some hillside.

She said, "Do we have time for proper introductions now?"

"Dawn," said Mal, "meet Temoc Almotil. Last Eagle Knight of Dresediel Lex, and recently of Shenshan Prison."

The shadows melted from him, revealing a face of planes and angles and a body built to hold up the sky. Even his loose coverall swelled and buckled with the muscle beneath. Yet he wore that body easily, for all its mass and power. No, it was not right to say "easily." That face, those deep eyes, did not belong to a man for whom anything was easy. He bore that massive body as if its burden were inevitable, and past lamenting.

All her words felt gnarled up in her heart. "What happened to me?"

"Men fail," Temoc said. "That is not the way of Gods. A God commits to make a thing so, and so it is. Then She commits to make another thing so, and another. If She is not careful, She finds herself drawn taut between the poles of Her commitments. So drawn, She lacks the freedom we call thought. A God who commits unwisely may burst, or find Herself netted and trembling as Craftsmen near with naked blades. I have seen it many times. You are fortunate that I have."

"What did you do?"

"What a man may, when a God of his acquaintance has been ensnared. I turned myself to theology. What a God has said is so must be so—but context or reservation may have been implied. Perhaps you only willed it that the Lady of the Moon should cease to perceive you in one instant, rather than always and forever. Perhaps you willed us to be faster, stronger than a particular unit of the Imperial military, rather than its entirety. Gods stand beyond time, and leave men to sort out their will within it. I eased your pain and checked the great hunger that you bear. To do so I assumed a role usually occupied by a priest of long standing that has secured their God's trust. I beg forgiveness, if I overstepped my bounds."

She tried to stand but almost fell. Mal caught her arm. Dawn breathed through the dizziness and tried to focus on Temoc's face, while another surfaced from her memory. This man did not look old enough, but there was an agelessness to him, and the names matched, clan and given. "Temoc Almotil. Do you have a son? Caleb Altemoc?"

Temoc looked first at Mal, for some reason, with an expression Dawn could not read. Then he turned back to her. It was hard to imagine what uncertainty might look like on those features. Maybe it looked like this. "You know him?"

"He saved my life."

"Is he well?"

"I don't know. We didn't talk much. He seemed fine, before things got . . . complicated."

"He always did make things complicated," Mal said.

The priest raised one eyebrow. "Unlike others I could name."

Mal ignored him. "Temoc fought in the Wars. He learned the ways of faith from ancient masters, and he's kept our rickety and gutshot pantheon alive more or less single-handedly for almost sixty years. No one knows more about gods and their trauma. Which is lucky for him, because if there were any other option, I would have happily left him rotting under a mountain until the end of time."

"And Mal," Temoc said, "is a heretic, a profaner of sacred rights, and my daughter-in-law."

Mal caught her breath. Her metal fist tightened. "Excuse me?"

"Did you not know? When a priest or a Knight offers his own heart to the Sisters, the one who holds the blade for him and speaks with Serpents' tongues becomes his betrothed. The marriage is a high one, as of two great hawks diving to the final stop. There do not tend to be dynastic implications, since both parties invariably perished during the sacrifice, but truly, we live in unprecedented times. You spoke with the Serpents' tongues. My son offered Them his heart. He survived. So did you. And so does the bond."

Arsenal Company kept a studied silence. Someone coughed. They might have been covering a laugh. Someone else hummed the first few bars of a wedding march. Mal's glare into the shadows promised retribution when she figured out who. "Then I divorce him," she snapped.

"As there is no precedent for surviving this sacrament, there is no form for divorce. At least, one would imagine, the relevant parties must be informed."

"Meaning . . ."

"My son," he said. "And the Serpents."

"You're enjoying this."

"I have spent the last several years imprisoned beneath a mountain. I believe I am entitled to a certain levity."

Dawn stepped between Temoc and Mal with as much confidence as her unsteady legs could project. She glared at the priest. "You are being mean."

Temoc blinked.

"If you did—what you said—then you're my priest. Sort of. And priests should do—" She felt the inadequacy of words. "They should do what the people they're priests of say."

"You," he said, "must not have much experience with priests."

"Did Mal tell you what we're up against?"

He was solemn now. From sermon to silence, there seemed to be no in-between with him. He nodded.

"You two have history together. She put that behind her to pull you out of Shenshan. If you can't do the same, I don't want your help. I don't work with people who are mean to my friends."

He cocked his head to one side. Then, with a tectonic motion so slow it at first seemed gentle, he offered Mal the great fact of his hand. "Let there be peace between us, then. While the stars are wrong."

Mal clasped his hand of flesh with hers of metal. "Glad to have you on the team, old man."

"You serve a lady of no little strength. Daughter-in-law."

But there was a hint of stony humor in him, and Mal flashed back an I'll-get-you-later sort of grin. And that, it seemed, was settled.

"Now," Temoc said, when their hands parted, "we must be swift about our departure. I brought you to this place because here, I hoped, we would find the soulstuff required for your healing. I was right. But our intrusion will not go unnoticed."

"What is this place?" she asked.

"A blasphemy."

And he turned on the lights.

The air outside the shipping container was biting and thin. Dawn's sobs deepened into gasps. She stumbled to the cliff's edge and sat down hard.

Out there, mountain peaks pierced a sea of clouds. There might have been as much down as there was up, and neither way was far enough to fall to escape.

In the Tellurian Annex lab she had seen bodies in glass tubes, people taken apart. But she had not been Sybil then. She had not remembered how knives felt when they went in.

Besides, those bodies were dead.

When Temoc had turned on the light, her first impression was that she stood within another Annex. Bodies in tubes, skinned to bare their anatomy. Then she realized their hearts were beating.

She heard footsteps in the snow and tensed herself to fight, cornered and alone on the edge of the cliff.

—Not alone, Sybil whispered. Never alone again.

Temoc settled beside her, his legs over the drop. Dawn glanced back to the shipping container. Mal stood by the closed door, haloed in the steam of her breath.

"I asked her to let me follow you and offer counsel," Temoc said. "She loves you. With an honesty miraculous in one who bears the weight of her past."

"That's not—I mean, we're not . . ." Words failed her. But when she was thinking about Mal, she was not thinking about hearts beating under glass.

"Once," he said, "there were so many loves: the love of the Gods, the love of lord for servant and servant for lord, the love of bond-friends and the love of fellow travelers. Love was the blood of the world. But there is a poison in this age that seeks to wither love. All must be needful now. The only loves allowed the name are animal compulsions: the rutting bond, the knot of parents and children. So withered, love becomes desire and fear, and useful to those with power."

She remembered the skinless bodies in the tanks, their beating hearts. "And is this place . . . useful, to those with power?"

"From the operation of the mind, Craftsmen say, comes the wealth of the soul. This was, I believe, an experiment. Can a human being be rendered incidental to the generation of value? Strip them to desire and fear, lust, pleasure, and starlight. Reduce them to what the Craft needs. What it can use."

She swallowed. "Why aren't they dead?"

"The Craft offers freedom. Even from the chains of death." He seemed as if he were about to say something else. "I have fought Deathless Kings for a long time. I learned of this container and others like it in my secret war. I do not know who built them. I sought to free those within, to dare their maker into the light. Before I could, I was caught by the Shining Empire. We needed a fortune to ease your hunger. We found one here."

The part of her that had grown up stitching thaums together and making little bets with herself about how long she could go without eating made her ask, "How much?"

"Thirty thousand souls."

"Bullshit."

'There are no bulls at this altitude. Even yaks cannot survive above—"

"Sixty million thaums to escape?"

"No. Sixty million to survive. There is a terrible hunger within you. You could not flee and check that hunger at once. To save you required all my skill. And sixty million thaums."

Her father took that job at Blake's Rest because he wanted to find a place for her that was not on the road—knowing even then, maybe, what ate him from within—but he said he took it for the wages. A half-soul a month, and he felt lucky to get that much. "They did that, for sixty million thaums. And left it sitting here like change on the sidewalk."

"It appears so."

The Roof of the World, she'd read once, was made by continents colliding—huge jagged blocks thrust up by the terrifying weight of millions of tons of rock. That immense motion continued even now, creating this razor-toothed horizonless range. She stared out, eyes hot, to the limits of sight, and saw the bare fact of her own rage.

"You're wrong," she said, "about love."

He raised one eyebrow.

"Love is not the blood of the world," she said. "Would so many poets and priests have to write about it, if it was real as rocks? Look out there. Do you see love?"

"What do you see?"

"Power. Power building upon power, to heights where nothing lives, to depths that crush bones. Love is a human thing. We build love. If it's there at all."

"It is fortunate for your argument that we are not overlooking a lush field at harvest time."

"I've worked fields at harvest time," she said. "Trust me. Power's there, too."

"And love," he said.

"Yes," she said, surprised. "And love."

"After my city fell, I wandered. Craftsmen ruled the world. I was a young man then. I was lost. I found work in the fields east of the Drakspine, where the soil is rich but there is so little rain that water must be piped in from other lands."

"I worked there once. With my father."

"I am sorry," he said, in answer to words she could not speak. At last he began his tale again. "I was not a useful worker. My hands lacked wit and skill. They were trained for other tasks than harvest. But I was welcomed."

"I'm sure. Big guy like you. Bet all the bullies in management wanted to bust you down to size. Which meant they weren't bothering anyone else."

High twisting wind bore flakes of dry snow in spirals between them. "My wife," he said, "once told me that, according to the great scholars, all things in this world seek to draw one another close. That draw is, itself, what makes a thing a thing. What we call the physical world, space, even time, is the tapestry of affection."

"You're talking about gravity."

He shrugged.

There was an abyss below them, and above. Beyond the mountains, there were other mountains. She had dreamed of seeing the Roof of the World when she was a girl. Which, she realized, she was not anymore.

"What did you see," he asked, "in your dream?"

"Someone's chasing me through a dead forest. It's hungry. I can't get away."

"Why do you run?"

"Because I can't fight."

He said nothing.

"I can't fight this thing inside me, and if I can't fight I can't win, and if I can't win, the future eats us all. Either the monsters beyond the sky or the monsters who live here and build things like *that*. I won't let them win. I won't let it be like this. The world has to be more than need and power and what they can use. Mal thought you could help."

"Perhaps," he said. "But you must trust me with your wound."

She drew the glove from her hand. The rose in her palm was raised and sickly red like a fresh burn, and the sliver of black iron within did the opposite of glow.

18

The false mustache, Tara thought, was a bit much.

She grimaced in the mirror of the golemwing's cramped bathroom. Outside the porthole windows lay Chartegnon. Or at least, the Chartegnon airport. When Tara had first left Edgemont, forever ago, she'd been so foolish as to think that a city's main airport would be near the city, rather than what would once have been a full day's carriage ride out.

"The grimace helps," Kai said. "It looks fine. Or it would, if you stopped playing with it. Hold still." She did something with a brush that tickled Tara's upper lip. "Don't flinch."

"I don't flinch." She didn't this time, at least. "Is this really necessary?"

Kai stood back, frowned, nodded, capped the small bottle of gum adhesive. "Probably not. Private flights aren't subject to the same scrutiny as commercial. But every little bit helps, and it is fun."

This had been news to Tara—the bit about private flights—when Kai explained her plan for reaching Chartegnon. Arrive in a luxury golemwing, and ninety-nine times out of a hundred the airport would send a flunky to glance at your papers and wave you into the country. The notion had offended Tara's sense of equality.

Then again, her usual approach to flying involved stepping off of a ledge and declining to fall—not exactly an option available to the masses. Most of the people who could afford private skycraft were Deathless Kings and Queens, high priests, or members of this or that Imperial family—who could, in general, fly unaided. But it was harder to bring your luggage or your entourage along that way. And this was more comfortable.

Of course, if she'd been bending the winds and lightning to heel, Kai wouldn't have been able to attack her with makeup.

"There," Kai said. "Better."

It did look better, though Tara would have been hard-pressed to say how. Between the moustache and the tight braids—the extensive airport mall at their connection through Alt Selene had a salon that knew how to handle Tara's hair—the effect was striking. She might have said breathtaking, but *that* was a more fitting description for the contrivance of sturdy stretchy fabric that had been delivered to them in the Alt Selene airport, along with the attested and sealed Kho Khatang passports of Mrs. Kay and Mr. Thierry Margot, first-time visitors to the metropole. One could not, it seemed, acquire *everything* one needed in the Alt Selene airport mall.

The sturdy stretchy contrivance, when applied, was too carefully tailored to actually take Tara's breath away, but it was not precisely comfortable. Kai assured her that this could be addressed with proper fitting. Tara hoped the masquerade would not last long enough for it to matter. Someone else might have found the support reassuring. It was, at least, pleasant to cut a trimmer figure in a suit.

Good suits were another accommodation Alt Selene's airport mall could provide, at a price. Kai had been happy to consult, provided the clothes went on Tara's expense account.

"How do you expect me to justify it?"

"Write 'saving the world.' It has a mollifying effect on accounting, so long as your accountants are part of the world you're saving."

"Have you been outsourcing accounting to the dungeon dimensions?"

Kai shook her head. "We don't outsource *catering*. We only got an on-site Muerte Coffee because the toddlers threatened to unionize."

"Toddlers?"

"Sorry, I imagine they prefer to be called junior analysts. At any rate, if you want an introduction, we do coordinate sacrifice planning for a few demonic firms."

"Of course you do. Have you considered the ethical implications—"

She'd rolled her eyes and pitched her voice to a whining tone that sounded *nothing* like Tara. "Have you considered the ethical implications? For gods' sakes, listen to yourself. You're stalling, *sweetie*. Try on the suit." And she'd shoved her into the changing booth.

Grumbling from within as she undid her clothes: "Be careful, or next time I'll be the governess and you'll be the wayward young noblewoman."

Cheery, through the curtain: "You flatterer. Even my skin's not *that* good. At any rate, if you want to choose roles, you'd best supply your own ID papers."

When Tara had emerged, Kai pronounced it good.

The whole idea had seemed almost fun in Alt Selene. But here they were on a runway outside Chartegnon. She glanced out the window. No customs official yet. "If the mustache isn't necessary—"

"It's a question of risk tolerance." Kai adjusted Tara's lapels. "We won't be detected upon entry. But the customs paperwork will be fed into the giant squid system the Iskari use for data management, and two people matching our general description arriving through a low-security customs path might raise a red flag. How badly do you think the Iskari want to talk to us, in an off-the-record way that they would not have to explain to either of our Churches?"

Tara closed her eyes and took as deep a breath as possible under present sartorial circumstances. "The revolution really wasn't our fault."

Kai raised an eyebrow.

"Fine. You win."

"That's what I thought. Now. Walk for me. Mmm. Good. *Pretty good*, don't feel too proud of yourself. Now, turn. Back. Try to swish less."

"I don't *swish*."

"You don't swish *much*. Better. Like there's a stamp on your heel and you want to make sure it comes out clean. Don't look at me like that, I know it's hard. Yes. Very good. We'll make a passable boy out of you yet."

There was a knock on the door, and Tara realized she was calm, and that moments ago, she hadn't been. Kai had given her a simple assignment at which she could earn a passing grade. Tara felt embarrassed to be so easily read—but mostly she felt grateful.

Kai set a gentle hand on her arm and guided Tara to the door. "Come, darling. Let's meet the cops."

19

Before Arsenal Company left the heights, they had to deal with the shipping container. Valois said that her people could handle it. They had done this kind of work before. Temoc offered his blade, as a mercy. Mal said nothing.

Dawn took it on herself.

She walked into the container with Sybil draped about her shoulders. Fluid rushed through valves, and speakers beeped in heartbeat time. The victims floated in their tanks. Joss crystals on the wall glowed with the captured light of souls.

The victims did not see her. Their eyes were open—they had no lids—but their minds were elsewhere, lost in yearning, in dreams that grew thorns the instant they were clutched. She tasted lust and terror and need. Who had they been before they were reduced to this?

They did not see her, but she saw them. She could not save them, now. But if she came into her power, if she built the world she dreamed of—what might be possible? These people deserved kindness and care. Without them, without their suffering, she would have died. Was it right to look at someone in pain and think they must prefer death? Was it right to choose for them?

"I have been where they are," Sybil said. "There were times it would have been a mercy. What else can we offer?"

Dawn felt cold inside. She clenched her fists and closed her eyes. The shipping container's Craftwork hung about her like lightning cobwebs, showing the truth of the system: circles of temptation and ecstasy and pain. There was the ward that sustained life. There was the catchwork that gathered soul. There was the one that prompted dreams.

These people had been drawn to this place through machinations of debt, through agreements with implications they did not understand. They were stuck here now, just like everybody else. They deserved better.

The Craftwork might be the truth of this place. But it was not her truth, and she would not let it be theirs.

"We can offer mercy," she said, and touched the web, so gently.

Their hearts settled. Fluid pumps slowed. The victims eased, for the first time in she did not want to guess how long, to sleep.

"I'll come back for you," she said. A wind whispered past her, though the door was shut.

She waited and listened, hearing nothing. Then she turned to go.

———

"The flower in Dawn's hand," Temoc said, later, "is the heart of a Goddess. Ajaia of Green is Her most common name and aspect. She is strong and clever, and She has set Herself against the skazzerai shard with an uncommon bareness of commitment. There is no compromise for Her. There is victory or death."

They had set up camp half a mountain range away, down out of the death zone, on a barren plateau where a human body would not unravel itself. The wings of Ixzayotl sheltered them, but the Arsenals set up tents anyway—for sleeping and for the war council.

Everyone attended, though most kept silent. Valois spoke for the Arsenals. Burgess took notes in a thick bejeweled book. Mal frowned as Temoc spoke. She seemed to do that a lot.

"The iron writhes in Ajaia's heart. It strives always to consume Her and the world. In Their striving, these two forces devour anything that draws near—including Dawn herself. It is a testament to her strength that she has lasted so long."

"So," Dawn said, "what can I do?"

"Precious little. No subtle trick will ease the mutual hatred of Goddess and iron. You are caught in the jaws of a great trap. To escape it—to dismantle it—you will need the power to force open those jaws."

"So we steal it," Valois said.

"We drew thirty thousand souls from that shipping container, and it was barely enough to bring Dawn back from the brink of death. Should we steal wealth beyond the dreams of avarice, I do not think it would be enough to free her. Souls, as carried and traded within the Craft, are fungible—that is, easily converted from one form of power to another. Ajaia, or the shard, might seize any funds we made available to Dawn for their own purposes. We need power of a different order. A might with its own will, a power beyond Gods, deep as the ages of the world, and long set against the skazzerai."

"No," Mal said.

Temoc did not seem to have heard. "We need the Serpents."

"You can't use them."

"An interesting claim for you to make," he said.

"I know better than anyone. I tried to use them. I lost my arm, and my leg, and my soul, and I almost burned down Dresediel Lex. I won't let that happen to her."

"Neither will I," Temoc said.

Dawn set her hand on Mal's wrist. "It's okay." Mal looked at her, unsure, then settled back into her seat. "I want to hear the rest."

Temoc laced his huge fingers together. "Mal is correct as to the danger. Centuries ago, when High Quechal and Iskari fought the Contact Wars, our high priests sought to use the Serpents as a weapon. They drew Their blood to drive engines of war. In this folly they broke the continent in half. Only the Fangs now remain of all that ancient empire. The Serpents are beyond our ken and control. They are older than Gods, and beyond the dreams of man. It is a miracle that Dresediel Lex continues to exist. It is a miracle and more that Mal is here at all.

"Aquel and Achal are the ending and beginning of the world. To approach Them is to court endings and beginnings, to invite the apocalypse into time. But there is another way." His gaze swept the table. No one spoke. "The old priests drew the Serpents' blood. Traces of this great crime linger beneath the maelstrom, in the heart of the Fangs where the great old temples of the Quechal once stood."

"Fine," said Mal. "So we just nip over and get some."

"We would die," Temoc replied. "Horribly. But fortunately there are such people in the world as archaeologists. A team of them 'nipped over' twenty years ago and escaped with a sample. They do not know what it is they possess. It was hidden and warded five times five. To touch the Serpents' blood is folly and sacrilege, but it is less phenomenally dangerous than to court the Sisters directly. I believe the blood will serve our purposes. With it, I can pry apart the jaws of the trap. Then it will be Dawn's turn to act."

"Great," Valois said. "So where is it?"

Smiles did not look normal on Temoc's face. "It is in Dresediel Lex."

Mal: "Of fucking course."

"I never claimed this path would be without its dangers."

"Among them the evil skeleton wizard who rules the damn place."

"The King in Red is an obstacle, certainly."

"An obstacle? That's what you call him? Uncontested ruler of the metropolis, commander of legions of faceless goons, god-murderer? Killed my parents and a couple hundred other protesters with fire from the sky? Rides an undead dragon? Made the Crack in the World?"

"Yes."

"You have a pretty fucking broad definition of obstacle, man."

"I have lived a long time, daughter-in-law. I have learned a certain flexibility of language."

Valois frowned. "We don't have enough steel to take the King in Red. Not us and three hundred other guys."

"Not us and ten thousand," Temoc agreed. "I have seen him tear Gods asunder on the field of war. Once I found him unconscious, and I could not so much as score his bones with my blade. He is needful to this fallen world, and it will not permit him to come to harm. In the fullness of his power no weapon it has forged can wound him. But I do not propose we face him in open combat. He does not yet know I have escaped Shenshan, if indeed he knew I was captive there. We must be swift, to outpace his spies and escape his dread wisdom."

"There has to be another way," Mal said. "There's blood in the Fangs, you said."

"I believe there is. But that blood is not contained. It has burned through our world into many others, to make a haunt where demons thrive."

"We can gear up in Kho Katang. Tranh owes Burgess, and owes me double. They should be able to kit us out with diving rigs, a ship."

Burgess cleared his throat. "I regret to inform you that Tranh has disappeared. Their bar burned down last night. I've tried to raise them through nightmare telegraph and prayer line, without success." Murmurs around the tent. He flipped three pages back in his jeweled book. "I commissioned a dreamer of my acquaintance to search for any available information. A team of three arrived at the Golden Pheasant at sundown. Two unidentified heavies, and a young woman recognizable from press engravings as a cultural attaché of the Imperial embassy."

Valois grunted. "That was fast. So the Shining Empire has Tranh?"

"Thirteen minutes after their ingress, another party approached the Pheasant. My contact provided a dream impression." He touched a glyph, and a ghostly image rotated into view above the table.

"That could be anyone." But by her tone of voice, Mal knew it wasn't.

The face was not the same, but everything else was: the gait, the angle of the head, the way he moved. Dawn knew that with a close enough angle she would see the gentle eyes and hear the ticking of gears. "Mr. Brown."

"After the, ah, Mr. Brown enters, security coverage ceases. I sought further information, but my contact was . . . interrupted in their search. I have had no luck raising them again. Other Pax Rim connections have gone dark as well. I do not know if they have vanished of their own accord or due to outside interference."

"We are hunted," Temoc said. "It is a time for bold moves, before our choices are taken from us."

Mal drummed her fingertips on the table. "Can we even reach Dresediel Lex? Ixzayotl would kind of stand out on approach."

"I can help with this one," Burgess said. "An old friend from seminary is a captain in the Xivai merchant marine, on the Longsands route." He flipped back several more pages in the notebook, consulted a hand-drawn table, and nodded. "The vessel should be inbound to Dresediel Lex at this time of month."

"Let me guess. He owes you a favor."

"No. But she has a good sense of humor and no love for Deathless Kings."

"What if the, what if Mr. Brown finds her?"

"I have not seen her in many years, and our business interests have not previously coincided. Her connections to our less sunlit world are as slim as one could wish or expect of a captain in the merchant marine. She will bring us to Dresediel Lex. Once we make landfall, however . . ."

"I can guide us," Temoc said. "I know the shadows of my city. I evaded the King in Red for twenty years. I can conceal our party for a few days. It will not be the triumphant homecoming of which I have dreamed, but if we succeed, we will be gone before our presence is known. This can work. And I do not see a better path."

A muscle worked in Mal's jaw. She turned to Dawn. "What do you think?"

Dawn didn't want to think. She'd grown up hiding and slipping away. You knew your escape routes, and kept your dreams inside your head where no one could get at them. But she'd given up on hiding when she met Tara Abernathy. Every step since had been a step into the light. Mal, the Arsenals, even Temoc counted on her—so did others who did not even know she existed, yet. She thought about the dreamers in their tanks at the Roof of the World. She thought about a world made in that image, pierced with black iron and rising to the stars.

She could save them all. But not through hiding. She clutched Sybil and returned Mal's gaze and tried to be what they needed her to be.

"I think," she said, "that I've always wanted to see Dresediel Lex."

20

M. and Mme. Margot checked in to the Hôtel Encornet in the Rue des Armes, sandwiched between a three-hundred-year-old coffee shop and a tobacconist's, and well out of sight of the great rubbery tower. This, of course, did not mean they were safe—the squid Saints who ruled the city and the whole Demesne had many eyes. They could ride anyone who played host to one of their symbiotic minders—not to mention the eyes of a more disembodied character, hanging from streetlamps, barnacled to arches and to eaves. But in one respect at least the gods of Iskar were not so different from humans: they might see, yet fail to observe.

M. Margot took to his bed for the remainder of the day, while madame, having recalled from her previous visit to the capital a small and glorious open-air market nearby, made her inquiries of the desk manager, a horned individual with pince-nez glasses and a tendency toward the overuse of adjectives. With parasol in gloved hand, she proceeded out into the crisp glories of early fall in Chartegnon to supplement the hôtel's famed repast with the cheese and bread characteristic of the city.

("You're enjoying this too much," Tara had said, when she announced her plan to go out.

"But no," Kai had replied, with an accent thicker than any they had encountered since landing, "there can be no more Kathic notion than to *enjoy too much*. Enjoyment is to be treasured, is it not so?"

"So long as it doesn't end up with you stuck inside a squid.")

She had told Tara that she meant to survey the district for potential dangers. That had been a slight exaggeration. They had taken rooms in the Telomeri Quarter. Two centuries ago, when exile scribes penned novels of revolution, this had been a plaguey tangle of cutpurse-ridden side streets, its rooms occupied by students and its squares occupied by rebels. Now the greatest risk an average tourist might encounter was that of being overcharged for an undersized sandwich. Even pickpockets came to the quarter on their days off.

And a day off, Kai realized as she tapped her heels carefully along ancient uneven cobblestones, was precisely what *she* needed. Not, perhaps, a whole day, and not altogether off. But her last few days had been a chain of airports and crumbling coastlines and monsters and prophecies of doom. Tara, perhaps, was used to this sort of thing. For a woman who claimed to lack religious sentiment, her mind seemed bent toward eschaton. Worlds always tried to *end* around her.

But Kai could only contemplate monsters from beyond the stars for a few hours at a stretch. She needed blue skies and breeze. She needed people—the crêpe seller spiraling batter over his hot round griddle, the two old lovers hand in hand on the wrought iron bench, their small white dog straining against his leash toward the grocery bag of a thin white-haired man in a checked suit who was frowning over a newspaper puzzle. She needed red scarves and falling leaves, chestnut sellers with their steel-drum ovens; she needed cafés where elegant women sat at small round tables ignoring tiny cups of coffee while they waited for men who'd never come. She needed pastel walls with sloping rooflines along the curved boulevards, each building five stories high, their windows open to catch the season's last heat and the first breath of fall. She needed that particular crisp politeness when she stepped into a store, even to window-shop, so unlike the desperate obsequious Kathic service culture, which Kai had always conflated with the New World's cultural and historical issues around zombie labor. Here you were a guest in the shop clerk's space; laws of hospitality bound both ways.

Chartegnon! She walked her streets again. Or her dream of them—the ghosts of history around every corner. Here, in stone and in the plaster that had succeeded the stone and the metal and glass that succeeded plaster, was the truth: it all changes. But sometimes, if you're lucky, the important things stick around.

She knew better than to let herself get carried away by tourist fancies. How many tourists had she seen wander the slopes of Kavekana, their eyes repainting Kai's home into some grass-skirted sun-kissed paradise of surf and sand and coconuts, of volcanos and the introduction of bound virgins to same? Margot himself—not the new pretender to that name, enjoying a nap and liberation from her binder back at the Hôtel Encornet, but the poet Kai had known so many years ago on Kavekana—Edmond Margot had left Chartegnon and come to Kavekana for the same reason Kai now wandered the city he had fled: in pursuit of poetry.

There was no special enchantment to one place or another. But there were differences in you—aspects of yourself that you could not be at home. You had to put them somewhere, so you put them somewhere *else*. You kept those secret selves inside dreams of other places, hiding them like soulstuff in an idol, which made their withdrawal in time of need—always, on some level, a matter of professional concern for Kai—a complicated matter. There was a real danger of confusing the dream-place where you'd stowed your heart with the real city where real people lived and worked.

But in Chartegnon Kai could enter the dream. She could tip a beret atop her head, wear stockings with a tantalizing black seam up the back of the leg, don heels that back home she'd linger over in a shop but reject with a sigh as impractical, and stride to the market to browse stalls of strange cheeses and savor the aroma of fresh bread from the boulangerie window nearby, even if to do so she had to pretend not to notice the W-pupiled eyeballs pendent from lampposts, panning over the crowd.

Kai was there in her market, in front of the cheeses, when the goddess found her.

Kai did not recognize the goddess at first, because the body she wore belonged to a man—tall, lean, elegant in a light-blue suit, with a fetching sculpted countenance. "My dear!" He spoke Iskari without accent, and with such warmth that she found herself liking him despite his forward manner. "What a joy. It has been entirely too long."

An old boyfriend? A business associate? Surely she would not forget that face. But the practiced smile came to her lips, shield and sword at once. "I am afraid, sir, that you have me at a disadvantage."

"Of course, of course," the gentleman said, as he leaned to kiss the air above her cheeks. "We met, madame, on a memorable occasion, though at the time I wore another countenance. I saved you when you drifted lost on nameless seas. And let us not forget the oh-so-many years of mortal reckoning through which a part of me labored in your delightful captivity."

Kai shivered.

The day was crisp and bright and blue, and he stood there in slim suit and good shoes and scarf, eminently Chartegnon: urbane, forgettable, daylit.

But the moon rose in his eyes, and moonsilver glistened from his smile.

"Come," the goddess said, and took her arm. "Chartegnon, I am told, is a fine place for chance encounters. Walk with me. Let us mutually reacquaint. The cheese will wait."

She let the goddess guide her between stalls of neatly stacked tomatoes and eggplants and squash, past pyramids of eggs to the plaza, where slender elms grew through iron grates in the ancient sidewalk, their roots plunged into the rich soil that, she knew, held the catacombs, their skulls mounded like those eggs, and with equal care.

"The ways are yours, and yours the vault of sky," Kai prayed. "Lay the moon road beneath our feet, and invite us through your gates into your hall, as ragged guests and worn."

"Ah," Seril said, "but this is not my hall." She—he—*they* raised an elegant long-fingered strangler's hand in a gesture that compassed sun, sky, cobbled streets, and the unseen tower. "Still, I always have loved that prayer. It's enough, almost, to atone for half a century's imprisonment."

"I don't see why you have to keep bringing that up," Kai said.

The thin lips of the elegant man who Seril rode twitched, almost to a smile. "So clever and so bold. If we wore different forms, I'd pinch your cheek. As it stands, I'm afraid the gesture would be misinterpreted."

"It would not be appropriate anyway," she said stiffly. The goddess was winding her up. "Presumption upon another's body remains presumption, even in religious cases. Consider the power dynamic."

"What odd and lovely rhythms you twist your tongues around. My fair if unwitting jailer, I find it rich that you speak of power and presumption to one who languished, chained, if you'll forgive the image, in your basement, for the better part of fifty years."

She flushed right down to her belly. "I didn't know. And I helped you escape when I found out. And"—when Seril did not interrupt, did not even stop smiling—"and it's not like you were chained. When you were—brought low—" She'd almost said "torn apart," gods, she really should stop digging. "—in the Wars, a fragment of your body was stored with us. Like a briefcase in a safe-deposit box. We don't look in the briefcase."

That hint of smile did not change.

"I'm sorry, okay? I'm sorry. Is that what you want to hear?"

"Ideally without fishing for it," replied the Lady of the Moon. "But in this world even gods must take what we can get."

She thought of her friend Makawe, blinded in the Wars, and his stage for wandering poets. "We have made many mistakes. I'm trying to fix them."

"It may be that, before this ends, you will have your chance to atone. To save us all, or try."

"Is that a prophecy?"

"More of a wager. The way things are going, atonement and salvation will be called for. And you will have your share—maybe more, my diligent rabbit."

She ignored the bait. You had to, with gods. "You are not supposed to be in Iskar, Lady."

"Neither are you. How wonderful! Yet another thing we have in common."

"Tara doesn't know you're here?"

The goddess investigated the back of her hand. An opal cuff link flashed, and an opal ring on her smallest finger. "Your directness is refreshing. Rare, in a priest."

"I'm not your priest," she said. "And there's a reason my order keeps me off the sales calls."

"Tara does not know," the goddess said. "You will not tell her."

"I won't keep secrets from her."

"Oh, of course you won't. A priest of Kavekana would *never* keep secrets. I'd never dream of implying otherwise."

"Are you mocking me?"

"People in my line of work do not mock, rabbit. It gives the faithful the wrong impression." They approached an old man feeding a flock of pigeons, all of whom took flight at once. Kai was reasonably sure that the teeth in her companion's mouth were no sharper than was customary among humans. But she had a way of implying otherwise. "Still, I doubt you could keep a secret from her."

"My discretion has never been questioned—"

"Oh, don't get all huffy."

Kai realized she was about to say, "I am not huffy," which sounded a great deal like something someone in a huff would say.

"I do not impugn your professional ethics. I simply suggest—and I doubt I am wrong in this—that while you might keep client matters secret to the ends of the world or beyond that you would not keep my secrets from *her*, due to personal considerations. My asking for your discretion would ensure that you'd tell her. So I won't ask."

"You'll command."

She looked up, into the gulf behind the sky, the blackness that was her home. She didn't say no. "You care about her."

"I won't sabotage her for her own good."

"See," the goddess said, "I tried to tell him, this is why I stay out of the church business. You tell humans one thing once and off they go, assuming a hundred other things antithetical to your intent. My kind have our issues, but yours has an annoying tendency to hear 'all is one' and think it means 'let's go over there and kill that guy and take his cows.'"

"Nobody's perfect."

"Now there's something my other half could stand to hear more often." She sighed. "I don't want you to sabotage her, rabbit, or spy on her. Do you care about her? Please don't take that as an excuse to quibble on the exact nature of any bathing suit–area feelings you may or may not have. Just answer the question."

She licked her lips. "Yes."

"Good. So do I. But. As you may have noticed, she does not like to ask for help."

"That," Kai admitted, "is putting it mildly."

"She has good days and bad days, like anyone. Recently they have been mostly bad. She cuts herself off, even from me. She blames herself for what happened with that girl, Dawn—"

"She told me."

"Well. I don't know her thoughts, because she will not share them. I guard her dreams, and I do what I can from a distance. But here you are, the pair of you, and here I am, with a covert asset at my disposal"—brushing dust Kai couldn't see off the sleeves of her jacket—"in a place where, should we be discovered, we would all be in a profound amount of trouble. I care about her, rabbit, and she is in danger. I understand the gravity of the situation, thanks to her friend the saint. I know the risks. But do you think she understands that?"

"You're not asking if she understands the risks herself."

"No."

"You're asking if she knows that the rest of us understand the risks, too. You think she's not praying, because . . ."

"Because she wants to protect me. Yes. I feel offended and flattered at once, which isn't how one tends to feel about a priestess. I am told. I'm not used to humans, really."

"Tara would ask for help if she needed it."

"Really? Or would she grit it out alone, reveling in pain and responsibility? And if she did call for help, would she do so in time?"

Kai did not answer.

"Let me put it another way, rabbit. You have brought her aboard as a contractor. You could tell Tara *something* about your faithful. You could, at least, tell her where you've arranged to meet them."

"How do you know that?"

"Don't change the subject. Why haven't you?"

Her mouth felt dry. "If she knew . . ."

"You think she'd leave you."

"Yes."

"Tied up in a closet, maybe, for the maid to find. Not because she doesn't like you. Quite the opposite."

"I don't . . . I mean . . ."

"It's perfectly all right, rabbit. We understand one another."

A boy in a black striped shirt passed by, selling flowers. Seril raised her hand, beckoning.

"I still don't know what you want."

"What I want," the goddess said, as she reviewed the blossoms, "is for the pair of us to be on speaking terms. We care about her, and we have a sense of just how much trouble she can make for herself." She chose a small perfect pale lily and paid the boy with a few coins and a significant glance he honored by leaving at once. When she offered the lily to Kai, its petals had a gleam of silver. "Think it over. If you agree, wear this flower. When you need me, call my name."

She took it, surprised by how light it felt in her hand. "I'll tell her."

"Will you?" That slight elevation of the eyebrow. "I'd suggest the sheep's milk cheeses, from the fellow on the corner there— the soft ones, with the waxy rind. With honey or a tart jam. See if his brother has any of the quince. Makes me understand why you all care so much about bodies, and tongues. Take care of her for me, rabbit. And take care of yourself. We'll need one another before this is over."

And then she was gone, one more suit in the subway crowd. Her farewell kiss burned the air above Kai's cheek.

When madame returned to her suite in the Hôtel Encornet, she found M. Margot hovering cross-legged in the center of a Craft-work circle. She'd removed her jacket and the binder. Her arms were bare, metal and flesh, and her glyphs burned with lightning, as did her eyes when she opened them.

"I see you've had a good rest, dear," Kai said, as she closed the door. "I found the most de*light*ful spot." She unpacked the bags. "A soft sheep's milk cheese, fresh bread, quince jam, apple-blossom honey. Magnificent."

"I'm glad you're enjoying yourself." Tara unfolded her legs, stretched her neck and arms. The gears in her shoulder did something not entirely unlike popping. "I wanted to arrange a few contingencies."

"If you think I'm enjoying this now," Kai said, "just wait for tonight, when we get you all dolled up again."

"Where are we going?"

Tara asked the question so lightly, as if it didn't matter. Mere curiosity. The closet door, Kai noticed, was open. She wondered if there was rope around.

"You'll see," she said, and adjusted the flower in her hair.

21

The Arsenals slept however they could. Some drank themselves into a stupor. Some turned in at sundown, with earplugs and eye masks. Valois and Elliot and Gupta sang drinking songs at the fire until someone threw a rock at them, which started a fistfight, then more singing, but at last they collapsed. Burgess sat cross-legged in his tent, eyes closed, in a state he claimed was meditative. He was snoring.

But Temoc did not sleep. Temoc was blessed.

He did not need sleep, because the Gods were with him. And he had spent too long locked inside living rock to take comfort in immobility and dream.

Mal, on the other hand, was an insomniac.

She had come to him while he stood watch, bearing a mug of some heavily processed chemical concoction doctored into an approximation of decent chocolate.

"Your master," he said, "once tried to poison me this way." He raised the mug and toasted her.

"Don't worry, old man. The aftertaste is just—" She fished a paper-and-foil packet out of her back pocket and squinted to read the fine print. "Dipotassium phosphate?"

"Thank you, daughter-in-law. Truly, I feel assured."

She paused with her mug halfway to her mouth. "You really are serious about that. Father-in-law."

He sipped his dipotassium phosphate. "Your circumstances are unusual. A theological court would be required to determine the proper course of action. Unfortunately, all the other priests are dead." The aftertaste was not so bad once he got used to it. The same could be said about a lot of things. Like water torture. "I will admit, the situation has a certain humor."

"Not to me."

He considered that, without coming up with an answer that seemed worthy of him—or of her. He was surprised to discover that he cared.

"You fucked him up bad, that kid. And this is me talking."

"You refer to my son."

"'Kid,' gods. He was a man. He made his choices just like me. But when I look back, we both seem like children."

"I did my best," Temoc said. "It was not enough."

"A lot of that going around."

"At least," he said, "he was spared the rigors of my childhood. And yours. What of the girl?"

"Dawn? She's had rigors of her own."

He nodded.

"And she's not a girl."

"No. She is not."

What she was, he did not venture to say. He could barely frame the thought to himself. He remembered the two voices joined as one, the violet light in her eyes.

"She wants to change things," Mal said at last.

"Yes."

"And you're willing to help."

"For now," he said. "Until it becomes clear . . ."

"What she's turning into."

"Yes."

"What if it does become clear, and you don't like it?"

"Then I will face a difficult choice."

"You don't sound . . . daunted, by that difficulty."

"I am an old man, as you so often remind me. When I was younger, I did resent the world for placing such burdens on me—it was unfair that they should be placed on anyone, I thought, but I will admit, my resentment was selfish. Why must there be history? Would it not be best if we could all just pursue our lives in private wholeness, and glorify the Gods?"

"What do you think now?"

He remembered shuffling cards, cross-legged in Caleb's bedroom. "The only extended period in my life that has been free of difficult choices and terrible costs was my time in that rock wall in Shenshan Prison. Having once tasted such liberty, I find my thirst for it has been quenched."

"Don't worry. If this goes south, there won't be enough pieces left of us for prison."

"What about you?"

"Me?"

"What will you do, if you do not like what she becomes?"

Her breath steamed in the cool mountain air. "I used to believe I knew what was right. That's how I was raised: the old priest made out that he knew the secret truths of the world and trusted us with them. I was confident and virtuous. But I was wrong. He shaped me, bent me. When I drew parallel lines on the surface of my mind, they met at a point he chose. But it wasn't all him. I had a choice, inside my head. Plenty of people grow up with someone trying to twist them, and find a way to question it. I didn't question because I didn't want to. He gave me the power to avenge my parents. Training, resources. Magic. Martial skill. The blessings of the gods. He used to send us on missions—planting glyphwork pieces around the city, swapping this relic for that—and while we were out we'd lift books and adventure magazines and sneak them home and hide them under our beds. When we read them we found they were full of heroes just like us. We felt so lucky. How many kids out there have lost everything but never got the power to do anything about it? He shaped us. But we helped him."

"You were children."

"So were you, when you got those scars."

"They honor me," he said. He remembered Caleb on his bed, the blade in his own hand, its dark edge and its clever tip. But they had not been alone. There were other hands upon his, other voices behind his voice. His father and his uncles. All the Knights and Masters of the high order, back to the Serpents. It was holy, what he did. It gave strength, and in this bleak world, strength was needed. The choice was right. Yet even so he'd prayed, beneath and through the other prayers he spoke, that Caleb would not wake up and see him.

Had he realized what he prayed for, then? Or was it only clear to him later?

On this question, even Gods were silent.

"They honor me," he repeated. "They give me strength."

She looked at him as she might have looked at a difficult cliff face, deciding whether to risk the ascent. Then, away. "If I don't like what she's becoming, I'll try to trust her."

"You do not think you are using her."

"I don't think it's possible to use people without being used. Even a blade's shaped by what it cuts." She looked down into her chocolate, but if she found omens there, she said nothing. "The old man used us. Maybe. I won't do the same."

"You used my son."

"No." Now she was the cliff face, and he the climber. She spared him the coward's choice, by speaking. "If you hurt her, I will kill you."

"You threaten your own father-in-law." He shook his head. "Truly, we live in fallen times."

She punched him in the arm, a little too hard, but she did laugh afterward. Then they sat together, drinking chocolate beneath the God's spread wings, and did not watch the stars.

22

Abelard was not enjoying his first visit to the Shining Empire.

First there was the time lag. His mind was perfectly comfortable with heliocentricity, the roundness of the world, and the relationship of its spin to the progression of hours of the day, but while he had explained the underlying concepts to his body several times, that body remained a Glebland plains ape with a subpar grasp of orbital mechanics and a general discomfort with the sun being up at midnight.

Then there was the war. None of the Party officials quoted in the newspapers *called* it a war, of course. It was a disturbance, an annoyance, a temporary inconvenience. But he had seen the smoke on approach to Guang'an, and the glint of gold on the horizon. Caleb said not to worry. There was no way the Golden Horde had made it this far south. Imperial forces were doing a fine job containing the clay soldiers who had dug their way out of forgotten tombs west of the city. Rumors of a risen Khan were greatly exaggerated. There were, yes, the ghost armies to consider, but within the city walls there were civil servants aplenty to name the dead and guide them back to their graves.

Abelard demurred, with reference to his guidebook, that the airport lay quite a ways outside the city walls.

"Well," Caleb said, "we won't be staying long."

Through some process involving bloodletting, his scars, a pendulum, and a world map, Caleb had been able to track the dead God Ixzayotl to the Empire. Neither of them knew why the trail had gone cold, but the disturbance, annoyance, and/or temporary inconvenience had begun recently enough to suggest certain conclusions.

The *Camlaan Times*, which Abelard had bought during their

connection through Aphophis, claimed that the DA&/orTI began with a prison break, but government officials categorically denied (1) the existence of any DA&/orTI, (2) that any DA&/orTI that might exist bore any relationship to any possible containment issues at any prisons that might or might not exist, or have existed, at any time past, present, or future. In the Guang'an Central Airport newsstands, Abelard and Caleb had found the *Camlaan Times* racks suspiciously vacant.

They had also found a great many scared and angry people. Everyone in Guang'an who could afford a flight out wanted one, and the runways were crowded with airships and dragons. People slept on floors, in chairs, face down on food-court tables. They stared out the windows. They stared into nothing. They had felt too much to feel anymore.

There was no panic, because no panic was permitted. A few times he heard people ranting in Imperial, but by the time he placed where the noise was coming from, the ranters themselves had disappeared behind a scrum of black-uniformed airport security.

Caleb's contact had stressed that they should book a flight connecting through Guang'an Central, not one terminating there, and under no circumstances should they leave the airport. Abelard had felt disappointed then, and relieved now.

First, though, they had to make the rendezvous, which involved one of those lists of three-times-widdershins directions Abelard associated with guides to fairyland. It would have been hard enough without the crowd.

"I guess Mal finally got her revolution," said Caleb, as they stepped around an inexplicable pile of suitcases. "A bit farther from home than she might have liked."

"She sounds like a fascinating person," Abelard said, failing to keep up. "How did you two meet?"

"Running from demons."

"A lot of couples I know met that way."

"Really."

"No. But two friends of mine did meet when he woke up and found that he was gums deep in her wrist." A boy, maybe ten, sprinted past them toward the suitcases, followed by his mother, who dragged a crying girl by the arm.

"Sounds painful."

"It was a rocky start." He fished out a cigarette and lit it with a snap of his fingers. One thing he did quite like about the Shining Empire, or its airports, anyway, was the lack of NO SMOKING signs. "They're still together, so I think it worked it out."

"Love finds a way."

"Was that it for you? Love?"

Caleb stopped to consult a stanchion map of the airport near a Muerte Coffee. A man was curled over a five-thaum cinnamon lavaspice latte, weeping.

"You thought she was alive all this time, and you never went looking. You were trying to protect her, or you were trying to protect yourself. People who protect themselves don't generally throw their own bodyguards to safety at the first sign of trouble."

"It was an emergency. I panicked."

"And you've never found someone else."

"Are you going anywhere with this?"

"Mostly, I'm trying to distract myself from the giant ghost monster on the horizon."

Caleb glanced out the window, and away. "We'll be long gone by the time it breaks through the government forces."

"Are those the same forces that have been falling back—" He consulted one of the four newspapers tucked under his arm. "—'like dry leaves before a hurricane'? To quote the *Xivai Herald*?"

"I knew it was a mistake to let you at the newsstands in Apophis. We'll be fine."

"If we ever find your contact."

"This is part of the proce-*mmf*."

Abelard had not seen the woman before she had her arms around Caleb and was kissing him.

She was not the kind of person one would, ordinarily, miss— bottle-green hair, tall even without her heels, a figure of the sort he associated with doodles in the notebooks of adolescent novices. "*Gunther*," she purred when they separated, "I was so *worried* you wouldn't make it, darling."

"Ran," he said. "Nice to see you, too."

"It's been dreadful," Ran said, with a theatrical pout, "perfectly dreadful. I simply must tell you all about it." She peeled away from Caleb, mostly, and took Abelard's arm. "And you, priest. Step lively."

She drew them after her. Abelard was wondering how this could possibly qualify as a discreet rendezvous, when he glanced at their reflections in a shop window and saw, rather than two foreigners and a woman with green hair, three rumpled Imperial businessmen in identical black suits. The lead one clutched a cinnamon lavaspice latte, and his tears had dried.

Abelard turned back in surprise to the rumpled businessman he assumed was Caleb, who looked at him sympathetically. "Take it easy," not-Caleb said. Even his voice had changed. "Let Ran do their thing."

Abelard glanced back over his shoulder and saw bottle-green hair and two foreigners carving a wake through the crowd.

As they walked, they changed. They were two security uniforms escorting a wild-eyed man with his hands cuffed behind his back; they were a mother leading a ten-year-old boy and a crying girl. Was Abelard the girl? He never felt the change. The world was just different, all of a sudden and as if it always had been. With each new change he tried to remember what had come before, but his memory slipped, because he, or she, had never been otherwise than she, or he, was now.

Then they were airport crew, in dusty blue coveralls, pushing through a door marked AUTHORIZED PERSONNEL ONLY into a dingy hallway. Ran unlocked another door to reveal a small room, empty save for a table and three chairs. They let Caleb and Abelard go, and locked the door. "Now," they said, "let's talk."

Caleb was Caleb again, and Abelard Abelard. Ran was a short-haired person with a thin mouth and large eyes, either handsome in a forgettably pretty sort of way or pretty in a forgettably handsome sort of way.

"A pleasure," Caleb said, stiffly. "As always."

"Oh, chuff," Ran said. "I know you're saving yourself for the end of the world, but why not have a little fun along the way?"

They produced, from inside their coverall, a brown-paper folder bound up with string. "Shenshan Prison break. Complete files. As promised."

"Looks thin."

"We had a dreadful time extracting reliable information out of what's left of the mountain, what with the Golden Horde and the ghost sorcerers and the Khan and all. I can give you twenty minutes. Gloves on, please. Thank you."

"Thank *you*, Ran. I know how hard it must have been—"

"Pish. Read, read, read. I need everything pristine, supposing that Guang'an Station is still there for me to return them when you're done. I like your friend the priest, by the way. He's game."

"What was that, back there?" Abelard patted himself down, finding clothes and anatomy in place.

"A waste of my bloody talent is what," Ran said. "Under current conditions, I could have marched right up to you in broad daylight wearing my passport face, said, 'here, have some state secrets,' and reaped a crop of shrugs. It's enough to make a person feel unappreciated."

"Is this what you really look like?"

"You're getting awfully metaphysical for our first meeting," they said.

Abelard thought about that for a while. "Am I?"

"To say what I really look like," Ran said, "is to propose that there are other ways I may look that are *not real*, that is to say appearances and modes of comportment that are not proper to me. Who decides what is proper? Under what conditions are the boundaries of what is proper to me negotiated, and more to the point, enforced, and how much say do I have in that negotiation? To say what I 'really' look like is a matter of struggle. My self is, as such, a property of others' judgments and perceptions, not of 'me,' if we can even use that expression. Others' selves, of course, are 'mine' in return—again, whatever that might mean. People change, is the heart of the matter. I'm just better at it than most."

"Don't listen to them," Caleb said. "They infiltrated a post-structuralist seminar a few years ago and they've been talking like this ever since."

Ran crossed their legs primly. "My skills are meager. My teacher could change forty faces a minute, and you'd feel as if you'd known each one for your entire life. But I doubt there will be call even for my modest talents in the next few weeks."

"You could come with us," Caleb said.

"And give up my spot as the life of the Party? I appreciate the effort, darling, really. But I am a survivor. And, to my surprise as much as anyone's, a patriot."

"What do those words mean," said Abelard, "exactly?"

Ran grinned. "Oh, you *do* catch on fast. No, dear friends, the secret of the world is that there is no running away. Should you seek out new heavens and new earth, you'll find your own self waiting for you under alien skies."

"You're not wrong," Caleb said, and the way he said it made Abelard's head turn. Caleb was staring at the final page of the slim folder. He had changed, as sure as Ran. Or perhaps he had merely rotated on an internal axis—his soft parts swiveling out of view, leaving only hard edge. He held the folder out for Abelard to see. "We have to go."

The engraving was a scene of chaos: armor frames and blades and death, and looming above a circle of small figures, a God he had last seen etched in blood on a concrete wall. "Where?"

"To D.L. Now. We'll connect through Kho Katang, catch a trans-Pax dragon—"

"Caleb," he said, gently. "What am I seeing?"

"That's Mal." Caleb pointed. "And that's Dawn." He pointed to the center of the chaos, to a man who seemed made on a different scale to other men: built like a pillar of the world. Abelard recognized his scars. "And that," Caleb said, "is my dad."

23

The god bore Arsenal Company south.

The Arsenals huddled in his rib cage around portable fires as the mountains melted to hills; as barren slopes sprouted moss, then woods, then jungle; as jungle ebbed to delta and at last open sea. Out of sight of land, Ixzayotl picked up speed. Rainbows of broken light trailed from his outstretched wings and painted the ocean below.

Dawn slept under cover until the moon was down. Waking, she watched the stars, and tried not to watch the empty place within. She crept past sleeping Arsenals and Temoc at prayer, and climbed ribs and tattered muscles to the skull, where at last she found Mal, cross-legged between strands of the dead god's feathered hair, staring into nothing, lit by rainbows. Dawn turned to leave, but Mal said, "Sit," so she did, by her side, and watched her.

"You should sleep," Dawn said, after a while.

Mal's mouth quirked. "When I was young, all I had to do was lie down and I would sleep. The future was just an idea back then. The more that happens to you, the more you can imagine happening—not even imagine, that's the wrong word. You know how it will feel when it happens. You remember everything bad that hasn't happened yet." She sagged. "I haven't been home in a long time. And now we're creeping back, like rats through the corn."

"We'll be okay," she said, though, of course, she didn't know. That was just something you said because you needed it to be true. She didn't know how to say the next part. "Temoc calls you 'daughter-in-law.'"

She laughed, at least, even if her laugh was bitter.

"So you and Caleb . . ."

"Me," she said softly, "and Caleb. You know, I'd almost forgot you met him."

"He tried to save my life."

"He does that." Mal didn't say anything for a while. Then: "How was he? How did he seem to you?"

"Good, I think. A bit sad. He tried to be kind, in his way." Mal was still looking at her as if she wanted more. "We only talked for a few minutes. You must have known he was there."

"I did my research," she said. "I mean, I wasn't obsessive about it. Him. There is such a thing as self-respect, and I have been known to feel it from time to time."

"I didn't mean—"

"I never went looking for him, not in all these years, and he never came looking for me. But . . . I told myself I'd get in and out, without his knowing. Maybe, a part of me wanted . . . Well. It doesn't matter now."

"What was he, to you?"

A long breath. A sigh. "A mistake."

Dawn waited.

"I was raised to own my mistakes. The old man, I guess you could call him my foster father, he had a particular approach to responsibility. Miss a syllable of your litany, and spend a half hour kneeling on the sharp reed mat, drawing blood in penance."

"That's awful."

"But you learn fast. He raised us as weapons, Allie and me. His instruments of revenge against the King in Red. When the plan was almost complete, I met Caleb. He was working for the King in Red back then. The old man told me Caleb was a mistake. He was right—but you can imagine, after a childhood like that, the appeal of a mistake. And I was too important for the plan for the old man to stop me.

"Allie thought it was a power trip. She used to tease me. 'You couldn't keep your panties on for six months, until the revolution?' As if I tackled him as soon as our eyes met. But it wasn't like that. He . . . I don't know. He cared."

Mal's voice had lost its cutting edge. Dawn felt as if, wandering in the forest, she had happened upon a drinking faun. If she breathed, it would dart away.

"The thing between us . . . he was infuriating, overprotective, absurd. I hadn't asked for it. I did not want to admit I liked it. But when he thought I was in trouble, he tried to help. And when he found out I could take care of myself, he still wanted to know me. To learn who I was, what I wanted, where I came from.

"Maybe you can imagine what that meant. I was raised as a weapon, I said. But for the plan, I needed a resumé, a past. Skills. A diploma. I spent years in boarding school and university. I put on a mask. Driven student. Scholarship kid. Fun at parties. Friendly but not easy to get close to. I wrote term papers for rich kids to fund my holidays. People liked me. I screwed around, in a send-a-raven-at-two-A.M.-to-ask-if-you're-up sort of way. I just . . . let people see what they expected. And it worked. The mask stayed on. Not because it was a good mask, but because no one cared enough to notice that it was there."

Mal let the silence stretch. At last Dawn risked speaking. "Until Caleb."

"Until Caleb." She ran her fingers through one of the god's feathers. "He wasn't some great nemesis, you know? He didn't even figure out our plan until it was too late. But he saw the mask. He wondered what was underneath.

"We danced. We traded barbs like characters in an old mystery play. Sometimes he tried to come off as hard and bitter and sometimes he carried his heart in his hand. And those hands—those long and careful fingers. Especially when he shuffled cards." She whistled, without a note.

"He was a goof. He assumed his problems were the most significant ones in the room. He had a gift for saying the wrong thing, for pissing me off, for showing up at the least convenient moment. But, you know. He'd been carved into something, like I had—Temoc carved him, or tried. And Caleb shrugged and went off to live his own way. Of course, both *his* parents were still alive. But all my life, I never had anything of my own. Just the glorious revolution. Now I had him."

"Did you ever think . . ." Dawn hesitated. "Did you ever think about not going through with it?"

"Once. The night of the eclipse. I wondered if I could just walk away. Sure, I'd been lying to him, but maybe we could work through that. He wasn't perfect—but I knew perfect. Perfect was the altar and the knife and the sharp reed mat.

"I imagined being someone else. Really being, not pretending. We could get a dog. It was easier to imagine a dog than kids, but hells, why limit myself to what I could imagine?

"But then I looked at him. Lying there asleep, this beautiful idiot caught in the trap of the dying world. I had the chance to break that trap. Could I throw it all away and jump in beside him?

"I tried so hard to dream a different future for us. But I never could dream while waking. I was an arrow. I had been drawn, and loosed.

"So I kissed him and I left. And he went after me and stopped me. And the rest of our lives happened. But the moment I let myself go near him again—here we are. In flight."

"Do you think he survived the spirecliffs?"

"Of course he did. Hardier than a cockroach, that guy. And . . . this weird fucking thing we're all stuck in, it won't let him go that easy. He's an arrow, too. Or a boomerang." She looked out into the darkness ahead, as if she could see Dresediel Lex past the curve of the world. "Flying right back to the Serpents."

She stroked Sybil's neck. "What are they like?"

"Hard to describe. Like if you'd never seen a sunrise. Maybe they really were women once, though if you ever see them you'll know how impossible that seems. I don't know if our faith made them, or if we found them down there and built ourselves in their image. They've grown, sacrifice by sacrifice, over thousands of years. Every life offered them survives within. But what they claim, they do not surrender."

"You got away."

"Did I?" Only a soft cool breeze passed through the god's enveloping will, enough to ruffle Mal's short hair.

"You're here."

"When I raised the Serpents, I thought I was in control. Maybe

I was, for a while. When I failed they drew me back with them, out into their sleep beyond time, to join the chorus of their souls. But then I woke up. Melted, broken, in a back-alley chop shop with a tube draining fluid from my lungs. I don't know what it means that I'm still here. Everything I ever learned about the Serpents says it's impossible. I owe them a soul. Someday they'll come to collect."

"I won't let that happen."

She didn't say it like she'd said "it will be okay" before. This was her making truth by speaking it.

"That's what worries me," Mal said. "You're fighting for the world, now. You can't go risking yourself for people. Especially people like me."

"The world is people."

"And oceans. Mountains. Foxes. Cats. A tree or two. Fish, down there. Don't worry about me, kid. We'll get in, do the job, get out, and we won't see any more of the Serpents than a few drops of their blood. It's been a long life, that's all, with a lot of bad in it, and I'm feeling it just now."

Dawn hugged her, before she knew what she was doing. Mal tensed, then put her arm around Dawn, too, the arm that wasn't metal yet.

She was warm, in the heights.

They sat together in the silence, and perhaps Dawn slept, or perhaps Mal did. The waves rolled past. Something massive crested the surface of the water and was gone again.

At last, Dawn saw lights on the horizon.

The *Monkton* was a city block afloat, its sides cliffed with metal containers. Ixzayotl crouched atop them like a demon on a mountain peak.

The captain met them on deck. She was a broad woman with a big laugh, one cauliflower ear, and a thick hand with swollen knuckles. She didn't look like the seminary type so much as the type who, in a previous century, would have set fire to the seminary and looted its silverware. But she hugged Burgess and slapped him on the back and complimented him on his choice of traveling companions, and on giving her an opportunity to do something fun for a change. Her wink indicated that the "change" wasn't so rare as her words implied.

"The lot of ye'll fit in a single container," she said, as near as Dawn could make out through the furze of her North Camlaan accent, "and we have a few riding empty. But I don't think yon beastie will fit, unless he should fold up nice and small."

Dawn glanced over to Temoc. He did not seem comfortable hearing the Eagle Who Faces East referred to as "yon beastie," but he forbore comment with priestly confidence. The gods could answer disrespect in a time and manner of their choosing.

"I rather thought," Burgess replied, "that we could compensate you for our passage in the form of service, in addition to the usual and more fungible consideration. I believe fuel costs have risen dramatically in the last year."

The captain looked up, and Ixzayotl looked down. In the low morning light, he seemed to grin.

"Do ye think he can manage?" the captain asked. "Can he swim?"

Burgess glanced to Dawn, who nodded.

"Through god," Burgess said, "all things are possible."

Their container looked like every other one on the *Monkton*, which was, Dawn imagined, the idea. The air inside had the peculiar dead quality of Craftwork conditioning and filtration, though it lacked such human amenities as windows and a toilet. After the engines stopped—a noise Dawn had not realized she was hearing until it was gone—and were replaced by the profound thrum of Ixzayotl kicking underwater, the Arsenals settled down to wait. They had a lot of practice waiting, Dawn realized, as she watched them lay out blankets and deal cards and nap on bare metal. Most of their careers were spent on ships like this, waiting for something bad to happen. Even Mal seemed at ease.

"After Shenshan," Dawn said, "I expected sneaking into this enemy stronghold to involve more heroics and dread sorcery and forbidden miracles, and less sitting in a crate."

"Shenshan is a prison," Mal replied, "and prisons care a lot about who goes in and who goes out. They are closed systems—the wardens of Shenshan grow most of their own food. Cities exist for trade—or at any rate, they don't exist without it. Twenty million people live in D.L., give or take. If I were the right kind of nerd, I could tell you how much food they need."

"Two kilos per person per day," said Burgess, without glancing up from his ledger. "Give or take. So about forty million kilos."

"Thank you. If D.L. doesn't bring in an average of forty million kilograms of food a day, people die."

"Which means about twenty-one hundred standard shipping containers," Burgess said, "making some quick assumptions about food density. But of course, much of that food comes from the central valley and doesn't move through the port like this—or in this kind of container. Dresediel Lex is also a major port for northern Kath, though, and an immense amount of cargo passes through Longsands: garments, finished goods, golem carts, and carriages shipped out by rail and truck and caravan across the continent. Millions of souls have been invested in making sure anything that looks like freight can pass through Longsands swiftly and efficiently."

"So that's the plan," Mal said. "Look like freight. And hope Temoc's contacts are good."

Temoc opened his eyes, said, "They are," and closed them again.

"So," Mal said, after a long silence. "Anyone for poker?"

After endless rounds of playing for chips and chores and scraps of soul too wispy thin for even poetry to catch, Dawn felt the engines churn back to life. That would be the *Monkton* drawing near enough to shore that someone might notice their lack of exhaust plume. The god stilled, and she stilled with him, and felt current skirling in the gaps between his bones.

"Finally," Sybil said. "All this not-being-about-to-die was starting to make me itch."

The other Arsenals grew tense. They were sure of their mission, and of themselves, and of her. But shit could always happen, and when it did, it tended to roll downhill.

For hours the engines churned, until they stopped again. Then other noises took over, all around them and above: scrapes of metal, the bass whine of cables and the hum of massive winches and pistons. She felt like a small piece of a very large engine, moved by powers so vast she could barely conceive of them. It was uncomfortably familiar.

Then the cranes found them and bore them up.

They had braced themselves with ropes lashed through anchor points inside the container, but still they knocked around like dice in a box. Dawn's stomach lurched—and then, with a scream of metal and a jaw-tightning final lurch, it was done.

The boat had been so large, she had thought they might as well have been on dry land—but now that they were again, Dawn felt the difference, the absence of the heartbeat of the waves.

More waiting, more silence. Temoc chanted prayers below his breath. At a certain point in the litany, he raised a hand in warning. The Arsenals caught their anchors. Soon they were lifted, swung, and set down again. Far away, she heard the groan of a golem cart. Temoc nodded, satisfied, and began once more to pray.

Dawn tried to count the cart's turns, and lost count fast. She tried to imagine the city beyond, but realized she was painting Dresediel Lex over with stage backdrops and snatches of Chikal and Alt Selene. She didn't know what was true about this city and what was a story she had heard. She reached out a hand and found Mal reaching for hers.

Then the cart stopped, and a garage door clanged shut behind. Someone worked the container latch. Sybil hissed, —Get ready. If there is a betrayal, it will happen now.

The door swung open. Beyond, on a dusty warehouse floor, stood a man: old, round-bellied, with thin hair and an unsure expression. He saw Temoc and hugged him and began to weep.

"We are home," Temoc said, as around them the Arsenals began their work.

24

This time, Tara put her foot down. The bow tie was enough trouble for one night; she would do without the mustache.

"M. Margot might have shaved on arrival. You don't see many people in mustaches here, actually, contrary to the popular image. Godsdamn." Her tie distorted once again into a tangle of pebbly white fabric. She glowered at the instruction card, upon which a smiling cartoon bow tie promised that the process would be "simple!" and "helpful!," though what it was meant to help, she could not guess. Maybe the instructions themselves were supposed to be simple and helpful, in which case their author had been either mistaken or perverse. Add to that the fact that successful completion of the process yielded a *second* cartoon bow tie high-fiving the first, and she was starting to suspect she had been drafted into the reproductive cycle of some sort of sentient demonic topology.

"Need help?"

"I've got it, thanks," she shouted back through the cracked bathroom door. Kai was out there, in a bedroom half-covered with boxes and tissue and various elements of style. She had her own troubles.

"You don't sound like you have 'got it.'"

There was this stage where the whole tie was supposed to double back through a loop that did not exist. Every time she tried to find that loop, the part of the knot she thought she'd done right fell into a mess at her throat. Her skeleton hand didn't help. Its fingers were stiff and precise but inflexible, insensitive to texture. Warded round and through, ready for anything, here she was, fumbling with a tie.

It might have made a difference if she'd known where they were going, known anything beyond the dress code, which called for this high-class penguin suit on her part and roughly an acre of silk on Kai's. Confidentiality, in Tara's opinion, shouldn't extend to the location of a meeting—but then, Tara had never been involved in Kai's particular branch of international plutocracy. Usual standards might not apply.

She wasn't supposed to be here, halfway around the planet in a tailcoat with a satin cummerbund and an odd shirt with those fiddly Iskari cuffs you needed cufflinks for. She wasn't supposed to be putting someone else in danger. Dawn might be the world's problem, but she was Tara's fault and Tara was supposed to deal with her. If Kai would just tell her the plan . . .

Well, she hadn't. And none of Tara's contingencies had involved bow ties.

"The carriage will be here in ten minutes. Are you sure you don't want—"

"I'm fine!"

She would not be stuck in the bathroom, missing their rendezvous, because of a godsdamn tie. She hadn't gone to the Hidden Schools for nothing. She glowered at her own reflection and snapped the fingers of her skeleton hand.

"There! All set."

"Did you just magic your tie on?"

"What an outrageous accusation."

"I only ask because a palpable darkness just billowed through the room, and there was one of those silent thunderclap things, and—"

"You said we were late. The tie is tied. Happy?" She yanked open the bathroom door, marched out, and—stopped.

Kai glanced back over her shoulder and said, "It looks good on you."

Tara found that she could not speak. Mouth dry, throat closed. This wasn't as much of a problem as it might have otherwise been, because all the words she might have spoken seemed to have gone on vacation together. Or maybe on strike.

The books she read growing up were not exactly short on dress descriptions. There were always court dances and balls and coronations before the dragons or divine beasts or undead armies or whatever showed up, and there were weddings and funerals after.

The problem for her was reference. No one in Edgemont wore clothes at all like this, any more than they wore suits, but she at least knew what a suit was supposed to look like. She'd gone to Ma with one of those ball-gown descriptions once, on Pa's suggestion, and Ma had just laughed and said something about underdresses that Tara didn't get. She settled for skimming those sections of her books. She got the gist. The high ladies looked good, and the clothes they wore were nice and expensive. Couldn't that be enough?

Kai looked good. Her clothes were nice. Expensive. It wasn't, quite, enough.

The silk was so gray it seemed blue. Skimming had left Tara without an accurate definition of bias cut and ruching, but she thought they might apply. Kai's shoulders were bare, save for a stole that seemed to have been spun out of clouds. Were those long gloves she was wearing, or sleeves? The dress—or was it a gown at this point?—had an architecture all its own for accentuating Kai's figure, and there was something going on with the silk, as if the color had depth and volume. It was, she realized, actually shifting, like the ocean when you stared down and in, its colors blooming into other shades.

"Well?" Kai's lips were the color of wine. She wore that silver lily behind her ear. Tara focused on the flower rather than the drowning pools of her eyes.

She swallowed hard. "You look . . . different. I mean—"

"Quite all right," she replied with a light Camlaander lilt. She flicked her wrist and raised a black domino mask on a thin rod to her face. "That's the idea." She retrieved the last unopened box from the bed, a long and narrow affair of some lightly grained gray wood, and tucked it in the crook of her arm, like a bouquet. "Come along." Revolving, she proceeded from the room as Tara grabbed her overcoat and scrambled after.

In the darkness of the coach, Kai's dress glowed with reflected streetlamp ghostlight. Shocks interpreted the cobblestones for them, and outside the city carried on the business of evening. The coach belonged to a higher and emptier realm of class, with velvet curtains and warded insulation and a minibar with little bottles of sparkling wine. Tara wanted to open one just to say she had, but she was on the clock. And Kai sat across from her, garbed in sky.

"Whose expense account covers the limo service? I don't want to have to justify this to the cardinals. . . ."

"Mine," she said. "You're a contractor, remember?"

"You *are* enjoying this."

Her lips curled upward. "Well. Yes. You had me at something of a disadvantage on our first meeting."

"What with the dead body and the police and all."

"She was only *mostly* dead. I'm surprised at your not being more exact on this point."

"We have terms to differentiate," Tara said. "But only Crafts-women know them, so I don't use them in mixed company. There was a cat, wasn't there? What happened to the cat?"

"My sister took him back. Good riddance, I still have the scars. At any rate, I do enjoy a bit of turnaround. And I still can't tell you anything about the faithful directly, so the mystery is not altogether my fault."

"Fancy dress for an office visit."

"We're not going to an office."

Tara raised an eyebrow.

Kai tucked a strand of hair behind her ear, beneath the lily. "Oh, fine. We're going to the opera. Which reminds me." She passed Tara the long box. "Here's your sword."

25

As they flew through the night, Caleb told Abelard about his father and the scars.

He offered Abelard his arm. The priest's finger traced the lines of light and shadow, the curling flames, the skulls and the faces of gods. He did not touch them, but Caleb could feel the imminence of his fingers, the featherweight of *almost*. Caleb had felt self-conscious about his scars when he was younger. When he grew up he realized that no one escaped the blade. Most grew over their scars, curled around them, hid them, or forgot. Caleb's were out where people could see.

"So the scars make you a sort of . . . general-purpose saint? Like a standardized connector. Neat. And, um. Horrible. And your father—"

"He did this to me. I don't remember it. I was drugged."

"I'm sorry," Abelard said.

What did that matter? Sympathy couldn't change the past. Would he want it to? Caleb took his arm back, rolled down his sleeve. He threaded his cufflink through the cuff and flicked out the stem. The Pax lay below them, its endless depths, its sunken cities, its gone worlds.

If Temoc was back—working with Mal, as impossible as that seemed—where else could they go but Dresediel Lex? And so he was headed home, again. Back to the start.

"He used to drop by, once in a while. He was so . . . proud of me. He knew whatever I did in life it would be great. I would change the world. And there I was, not knowing what to do or how to do it. Just living like a normal person, not—whatever he thinks he is. But one day he was gone. I thought he was—I don't know what I thought. I waited for him to come back. I have been waiting for a long time now."

"You miss him."

"It would be simpler if I could just hate him. I don't know what it says about him or me or us that I feel this way." Caleb stared down at his hands. He remembered Mal. He had thrown himself into the Serpents' maws once. He had been falling ever since. "Do priests of Kos have children?"

"Not after they join the Church. And most of our votaries are gathered young. To be honest, it has a lot to do, historically speaking, with the Church's moves to accumulate property. But I like the practice. It makes us, um, it makes us think of a larger family than our own blood." He looked down at his hands. "Do you want kids?"

"I don't know." The answer surprised him. "It's easy to die for someone. You push your chips, and that's it. It's harder to imagine living for them, day by day. The responsibility would work you like sand on stone. You set aside your life, your dreams, your fears, the change you wanted to make in this mess of a world. Not all at once, but a little at a time—because they're sick, they're scared, they need help with school. You're needed now, here, by this one person. You do what you can. Work with things as they are. Your kids love you. Maybe a hundred years ago, or even thirty, that would have been enough." He looked out the window at the dark.

"It doesn't have to be that way."

"Maybe not. But the world is full of people who think they can do better. And it all still looks like this."

They didn't talk for a while after that. He poured himself a drink and tried not to think about families.

He wanted to sleep. When he tried he woke feeling like he'd been drowning. Visions melted in his mind: the hall of gods. The ember heat. Achal's mouth. Mal, above Dresediel Lex, in flames. Mal in the sKirecliffs, half scars, with that metal arm.

Abelard was still there, still awake. Three cigarettes had been ground out in a teacup. That was the only sign any time had passed. Caleb's throat felt raw. He sat up. Someone had draped a blanket over him.

"Thank you," he said. "Can't sleep." His voice sounded dead. He cracked one of the little water bottles from the cabin, downed it. Didn't help, but his mouth felt less fuzzy afterward.

"Me neither." Abelard ashed his cigarette. "You need a break. Trust me. I hang around with Tara. I know what needing a break looks like."

"Great idea. I'll book us a week at the Aokane Plaza. I'm sure the end of the world can wait."

"There may be opportunities somewhat closer to, well, not *home*, exactly, but at least our place of current—"

"What did you have in mind?"

"While you weren't sleeping, I stopped by the dining salon. Some passengers have set up a card table. They said they'd be there all night, asked if I wanted in. I thought, maybe—"

Caleb was already halfway to the door.

26

"The target," Temoc told the assembled company, "lies concealed in Tlaloc Observatory, here, in the Drakspine." He pointed to one of the maps.

If Dawn had been asked to imagine the safe house of a religious archcriminal vigilante terrorist, she would have pictured banks of weapons, altar chambers, shelves of religious regalia and divine weapons. Yes, there were a few of those, scattered among the dusty machines, but she had not anticipated the sheer number of maps: road maps, pipeline maps, maps of steam tunnels, building blueprints, ward layouts. This city had been Temoc's battleground and his weapon. He had learned it as a duelist would a blade, and all that study lent his safe house the air of a weaponized library.

At the moment Temoc was indicating a midsized topological chart, only about seven feet wide, propped on a massive easel. "The Observatory is maintained by Central University. They do not know the value of what they hold. But that does not mean our task will be easy. Their collection is large, and in other respects its value is not so inaccurately estimated. We must be cautious. Yes?"

Yan's hand was raised. "What is it observing, exactly?"

"Once, it watched for the death of the sun."

"Seems like that would be obvious."

"Not if you wish to know of its death before it dies. Here of old, high priests watched the heavens for the eclipse, when the Serpents wake. Here of old they watched the deeper heavens, too, for reasons that were obscure to me when I thought as does a child." He did not elaborate. "Since the God Wars, the city has grown like a cancer. Even under the rule of Craftsmen, who guard the stars as a farmer guards his orchard, the nights are no longer dark and clear enough for the Observatory's former task. So its gaze has turned inward, to the past, to the study of Quechal science and high-energy theology." He motioned to Burgess, who had to use a step stool to flip to the next page—a blueprint of a pyramid complex. "These plans are old, but my source attests to their accuracy. Our target is in the central chamber, here."

Valois frowned at the blueprint. "And you trust your source?"

"Yes."

"Can we move the target?"

"Not safely. It will be best to conduct the ritual on site. We are fortunate that the target is housed within a place of worship, however defunct."

He likes, Dawn thought, to say "target" instead of "blood."

—Yes, Sybil hissed back. But I wish he'd find a word that wasn't "ritual."

Are you nervous?

—When the angry knife priest starts talking about *rituals*? Yes. Are you sure I can't eat him? I could probably learn what he knows that way.

If you're hungry, you should have eaten someone at lunch.

"How long is the . . . ritual?" Now even Valois was using the word.

"Our target, like the Serpents from which it was drawn, lies beyond the time of men. And women." With a nod to Mal, before she could say anything. Mal made a rolling "not quite there" gesture, and he tried again: "Beyond the time of . . . persons. It is of an eternal kind. If the Serpents enter our time, it is to consume. If we come into Theirs, it is to join the forever that they are. The rite will create a bridge between our time and Theirs, upon which we may meet without either fully crossing over."

"Okay," Valois said, as if it wasn't, but she was used to dealing with mission specialists and knew better than to expect a clearer answer. "The blood lies beyond time. But cops don't. So it would help if you could offer any guidance with regard to timetable."

"The prayers will require thirty minutes to sing. After that, assuming success, Dawn will enter the dream of Gods, face her foes, and defeat them."

"Is that all," Sybil said.

"Yes," said Temoc.

Sybil reared. "I could use a few more details, priest."

"You cannot fight those which devour you from within, for they claim your strength as theirs. The Serpents' blood will deny your enemy's claim to your soul, for Their hunger claims all. Thus, you may slip free of the trap in which you are caught. Once free, you fight, with all your skill and cunning. Perhaps the Goddess can be saved. Perhaps not. But you must triumph. And your victory must be swift, lest the blood of Serpents claim you for its own, and draw you back into outer time, the beyond of Gods."

"Ah," Sybil said. "It's that easy."

"Indeed."

Valois did not look satisfied. "So it can't be a quick in and out. We'll need to fortify. We'll hit the place from the top first. First party, wingsuits up to the lens, secure overwatch, then descend, while second party focuses on ground coverage."

"If we planned for this to be a fight," Temoc said, "I would agree with you. But we cannot afford for it to become one. The Serpents are a sensitive subject for the King in Red, as am I. If my presence becomes known, or the nature of our objective, we will have perhaps fifteen minutes before he assumes full war powers and enters the field. Any battle leads to our defeat. Stealth and speed alone will save us."

Valois fell silent—working numbers in her head, Dawn thought. She did not seem to have found an answer that she liked. Temoc continued.

"I propose we enter with a small team. Dawn, myself, Malina to guard us. One other, perhaps, as watch and ward. We will do our work and leave before our presence becomes known."

"I don't like it. This is a play for all the marbles. We need our full force."

"What you do not like," Temoc said, "is that in this moment all our force is useless. It is an uncomfortable feeling. I empathize. In the final analysis, even I am useless. All depends on the blood and Dawn."

They turned to her—the whole company. She had saved them

before, but they had never depended on her. Suddenly she wanted to be anywhere else. But if she *were* anywhere else, she would have been trying to figure out how to get here.

—No pressure, Sybil hissed.

She did her best to smile. "When do we leave?"

27

"Stop fiddling with your sword," Kai whispered to Tara as they ascended the front stair of the Grand Opera Iskar. It was a "stair," not front steps, not a staircase, but a great sweeping stair like a Telomeri consul might have descended before announcing war, in the days of the old empire that the Iskari tribes formed their first alliance to combat. Above rose-colored marble pillars, a great squid dominated the opera house's facade, its tentacles and arms twined around muses, statesmen, priests, titans of history. Tara thought it was supposed to be embracing them, not strangling them, but the sculptor seemed to have snuck a certain ambiguity past the censors.

"I'm not 'fiddling.'" She took her hand off the rapier hilt. "I feel ridiculous."

"It's not as though you're supposed to do anything with it."

"That's even worse."

"Dueling is not common, but by not wearing a weapon, you announce that you don't have the social standing to duel, or the manners to comport yourself without giving offense. Which would not be appropriate for someone with M. Margot's background."

"I *don't* have the manners to comport myself. I can't tell a duke from a count from a—whatever that guy is." She pointed to a slope-shouldered fellow in an extraordinary hat.

"Margrave."

"Seriously?"

"You could always play the strong silent type. Difficult for you, I know." She patted Tara's arm, through which her own was twined.

"Hey. I'm plenty strong."

"We won't be in public long enough for courtly etiquette to be a factor. It's a meeting, that's all. Nod to the doorman, dear."

"Dear?" But she nodded. The doorman's face was obscured behind a mask of rubbery flesh. One eye stared out from those masses of tentacles: a human eye wide in fear or ecstasy. Tara's hand drifted again to her blade, and Kai guided it away.

"Strong and *silent*." Kai flashed a winning smile at someone who, by the time Tara looked, had turned away.

Tara had seen cathedrals more restrained than the lobby of the Grand Opera. Here the squid motif repeated inside out: the chandelier, pendant with crystal, represented the mantle, and the arms spread from it to arch along the ceiling and descend as pillars to the checkerboard marble floor. The wealth in this city stunned her with its permanence, wealth in gold and marble and diamonds, not in the flow of souls, as she was used to seeing in Alt Coulumb. This was an older way of doing things, as antique and faintly absurd as the sword at her hip. Back before the Craft, gods spread their empires by sending clerics and armies and fleets around the world to loot other gods' temples and treasure houses, and brought all that joss home to gild their walls. Iskari treasure fleets still plied the seas, of course, but the ports from which those fleets took sail were called "trading partners" now. Most other realms had moved to draining souls directly from their "partners"—consumer and industrial markets were all too eager to satisfy demand for mere stuff. But even the Craft itself had its root in all this gold and marble. Upon the wealth of conquest were the great universities founded, from which the strangling vine of Craft sent forth its first tender shoots. She stood beneath history, and it made her itch. The sword felt heavy at her hip.

Kai swept her through the cream of whatever Chartegnon society happened to feel operatic this evening. These people radiated wealth and—yes, "privilege" was the right word, not "power." They might be cogs in the machine just like everyone else, but they were cogs that got more oil. Kai's gown, set against these architectural dresses and bejeweled coiffures, seemed almost pedestrian.

Almost.

And of course, everyone here had their minder. Some of the symbionts were small, elegant, gemlike things—the lady with the monocle, whose face was half-covered in green scales, wore hers as a pulsing bioluminescent wristwatch. The lord beside her wore her own at the neck, like a cravat that tumesced and crumpled when it breathed. Tara thought, at first, that the lady ahead of them on the stair—another stair!—wore a gray stole, until it fluoresced and regarded them with a blinking slitted eye.

Not everyone in Iskar had a minder. It was an honor to be joined, a sign that one was dedicated to the service of god and saints. Here gathered the great and good of the nation, descendants of the terrified superstitious berserkers who had been in ancient times pushed north by the deathless legions of Telomere, until in rage and despair they called for succor to the deep.

In Agdel Lex, on the frontiers of the empire, Tara had seen the symbionts used as tools of torture and surveillance and euphemistic "correction." Here, they were signs of something deeper than coercion: faith. Even patriotism. Pride in a history of surrender so profound that it could no longer be imagined as anything but triumph, a dedication to the Demesne and its masters on the level of instinct and sexual obsession.

Every one of these people had their own tricks for blinding the symbiont, misleading it, encouraging its unblinking eyes to blink. As for the symbionts, it was striking how seldom they seemed to care.

"What's the show?"

"Kirst," Kai said. "*Godsgloaming.*"

"I'm not familiar."

"It's . . . a whole situation. The prelude is an hour long."

"I see why people duel at these things."

"It's riveting, really. Once you have the context."

"I'll take your word for it."

A server in a white coat drifted past. Kai signaled with a twitch of her fingers, and they found themselves in possession of two fluted glasses of sparkling wine. "*Salut.*" She left a trace of dark lipstick on the glass.

"The lights just blinked. That means we go in, right?"

"I thought you didn't want to watch."

"I'm curious what one does during an hour-long prelude."

"A surprising number of people nap."

"Onstage, I mean."

"Mostly, they recap the previous three operas in the series. And add some new backstory."

"Hence the napping."

"Riveting music, though. Some of the most complex harmonic development of the entire cycle." She sighed with longing. "But we'd have to leave in the middle. We're supposed to meet our contact in his box when the singing starts. It's bad form to move after the baton, or make any noise at all. When Kirst built his own theater in Ebonwald, he designed it without aisles, to force people to sit down and watch the whole show. Also, he paralyzed them with magic."

"For five hours? They must have had stronger bladders in the old days."

"Or they drank less coffee."

"I drink a perfectly reasonable amount of coffee for someone in my profession."

"Which is what, exactly? Fish-who-swims-in-coffee?"

"I don't think 'fish' is a profession."

"My point," Kai said, "is that abandoning our seats midprelude would attract attention, while merely failing to occupy them implies that we're upper-class twits who don't care enough about the performance to seat ourselves prior to curtain. Which, much as it pains me, does fit our cover."

"Won't talking with our contact also attract attention?" Tara's gaze drifted after a pale dark-haired woman in a black off-the-shoulder dress, who moved something like a dancer and something like a snake as she ascended the stair to the box level. She wasn't wearing a squid. Tara found something familiar about her—chilling—but before she could chase it, Kai said:

"No. That's the point of boxes. Privacy and perspective. Some people up there want to hear the music. Some want to conspire about overthrowing this government or that, or to carry on an affair with someone else's lover, or . . . anything, really. The boxes have some of the best wards in the world. Soundproof, sightproof even. Part of the détente between Iskari nobility and their masters. Any system needs a little slack. For politeness' sake, if nothing else."

"Why don't *we* have a box?"

"We could have, if we made our plans six months in advance, and I didn't mind having a forthright conversation with our comptroller back on Kavekana about cratering my expense account. But I'm glad we don't." The last of the audience filed in and the doors drifted shut. "Bad enough that I'm here at the Grand Opera on the opening night of a new Kirst production, in a gorgeous new dress—"

"It is."

"Thank you. It's bad enough, anyway, that I'm here, but only for work. If I had a box and still couldn't watch the show, I would scream." They were alone in the hall, save for the ushers. "I used to dream about this sort of thing when I was a little girl. But when I had the funds, I never had the time, and then we became persona non grata in Iskar and I chalked it up as just one more dream that went smash. Now here we are, and it's all business. Lucky me."

"Didn't the Iskari, um, more or less colonize the Archipelago?"

Kai frowned. "They never formally ruled Kavekana, but they—did their thing, yes."

"And this was still a childhood dream of yours."

Her shrug did fascinating things to the clouds draped around her shoulders. "I'd be the first to admit: not all my desires are defensible. Or moral." She raised her glass, and Tara raised hers by reflex, though she got the sense Kai was toasting not her but someone else, far away. A ghost, perhaps, or a younger self.

Music welled behind the closed doors, churning motifs half-completed only to break into chromatic cascade, each key melting into the next. Nearer, she heard a ticking sound—Kai's nails on her glass, keeping time.

Tara felt, beneath her nerves and the general perplexed wonderment of finding herself in an opera house with a sword at her hip, rather than anywhere normal—a graveyard, say, a nice simple graveyard, elbows deep in a corpse—she felt, at any rate, a stab of the guilt she'd been feeling since she left for Edgemont, only warmer, rounder.

This guilt, at least, she could do something about. She adjusted her sleeve and opened a compartment in her silver arm.

"Here. Put this around your ear, like a cuff."

"Is that—ivory?"

"Are you kidding? I'm not a monster."

"Oh. Good."

"It's bone. Here, let me—"

"Whose?"

"Just put it on? Thank you." From the same compartment, she produced a ring about two inches across, studded with little mouse-rib legs.

"And that, in the center of the ring, looks an awful lot like an ear."

"It wasn't anyone you knew." She whispered a word of power to the ring construct and set it on the carpet. It twitched to its feet, bowed, and scuttled off to wriggle under the door into the hall beyond.

"Tara, what are you—"

"You were shopping for a long time. When I get worried, my hands need something to do."

"You were worried about me?"

"How long does it take to buy bread?" Why did she feel defensive? A glyph on the back of her hand danced and rewove itself to present a tiny map. "And . . . There. Our seats were sixth row center, you said?" She spoke another word of power.

Kai stiffened. Her eyes went wide and glinted with what Tara, if she had not known better, would have taken for tears. "What is this?"

"Simple correspondence. Identifying your auditory nerves with the construct. It can't hear, exactly, doesn't have a nervous system, but its ear anchors to yours by the identity principle, and after that—"

Her nails bit into Tara's wrist, even through the stiff wool of the penguin suit. "Tara. Thank you. And please. Shut up."

They did not move for a length of time upon which Tara,

habituated to tracking her work in six-minute increments, utterly lost her grip. She stood next to Kai in this alien golden hall, where painted fish swam overhead in a sea-sky made from ground-up lapis stolen from Apophitan deserts long before the God Wars; she stood with an empty wine flute in her hand and Kai's hand on her arm, and all the world ending somewhere, and no sound in the universe but the muffled orchestra. With nowhere else for her eyes to go, she watched Kai.

Tara realized she was happy.

A woman's voice emerged from the wash of sound like a serpent from the sea. Kai shuddered, waking to herself. She produced a lace handkerchief from somewhere Tara, no initiate to the mysteries of gown, could not guess, and did not quite dab the corners of her eyes; the handkerchief came away wet without disturbing the subtle layering of her makeup.

On Kavekana they had Penitents: constructs of stone within which they stored their lawbreakers and deviants, correcting them through pain. Kai, too, had a place she put her fragile and fleshy self. "We should go. He'll be expecting us."

Tara called her scuttling construct home as they climbed Stair B to the box level, then another stair again, at which Kai presented their invitation to an usher whose head was enveloped by a sort of iridescent cuttlefish down to the top lip. Tara's construct caught up on the final stair, climbed her leg, and clicked into her wrist. Soon they reached a thick door in a dark elegant hall, a few centimeters of wood and a few souls' worth of ward away from the answers they had come so far to learn. What was that shard in the sprecliffs? How could they stop it? How could they face Dawn, and after her the skazzerai, and live?

Tara gestured to the doorknob. "You're the boss."

Kai opened the door and they stepped through.

Music enfolded them, a breathtaking weight of harmony. It reminded Tara of how Cat talked about deep-sea diving: the water pressed in from all directions, so you lost all that was not essential in your being and knew yourself completely. You were all the ocean could not crush.

She felt Kai's hand in hers and could not remember having reached for it.

The box was smaller than she expected. Beyond its banister lay a gasping plummet to the seats, the orchestra pit, the stage. Three performers, women, stood there around a vast tree, singing about fate. The tree, Tara gathered, was the world. Its roots formed the landscape of the stage, and its branches overflowed the proscenium arch to spread across the ceiling. As they spread the branches stiffened, becoming angular and mazelike, bark reflective silver and blue—not branches anymore, but an artist's approximation of Craftwork glyphs. These spreading webs of glyphs that were the World Tree's branches stretched out to the boxes where sat the great and the not-so-good. Perhaps they listened while the woman below sang about fate and endings but mostly, she imagined, they were playing their own games.

In the front row of the box, there was a man. He sat with his back toward them, a silhouette in the stage lights.

Tara descended. The deep carpet ate her steps. Kai trailed her, skirts brushing the leg of Tara's slacks.

The man did not move. Nor, Tara noticed, was he breathing. That did not mean much in her line of work. Half the partners at Kelethres, Albrecht, and Ao didn't breathe. Anyone with any reasonable level of seniority, really, except for Ms. Kevarian. Still, it unnerved. The man was not, in fact, silhouetted by the stage. He was an emptiness: a piece of interstellar void cut out with fine scissors, given three dimensions, clad in a fine suit. She had seen him once before, she realized. Him, or someone very much like him.

"M. Grimwald?" Kai whispered. "Thank you for meeting with us on such short notice."

"I don't think he's listening," Tara said.

She touched his shoulder. His head lolled to the side at an odd angle, then all the way around to the back. Kai made a gross wet sound.

Of course, in Kai's line of work, one didn't see many people with their throats torn out.

Not slit. This had been done with claws, or—yes, note the tearing pattern, the puncture marks—fangs. Tara could see all the way in to the white of vertebrae, the head held on by skin and habit and remnant scalene muscles. There was blood on his shirtfront, blood on the carpet. Less, though, than you'd expect from a wound like this. Some desiccation in the muscle tissue. Bitten, drained fast, and torn to hide it.

He was dead. Oh yes. That by itself did not preclude conversation, of course. But he was, also, gone.

She looked at Kai. Kai had her first knuckle between her teeth. She trembled. She was taking it well. Tara watched the great mechanism of her mind race behind those dark eyes. Onstage, the women sang about fate and the end of the world.

There was a knock on the door. Polite first, a liquid inquiry, followed by another, more insistent, and then, in Iskari, "Open up! Police!"

28

Kai froze. Even if she'd been inclined, in this moment, to be kind toward herself—if she had been talking to her therapist, say—she would have struggled to find gentler ways to describe the situation than "a total fucking disaster."

They stood in a box of the Iskari Grand Opera, in the middle of the swelling prelude of Kirst's *Godsgloaming*, with a dead client in front of them and the police, apparently, behind. She stared into M. Grimwald's torn-open throat, the tubes and meat beneath the shadow of his skin.

She could deal with this. She just had to stop and think.

Tara moved.

In a crackle of starlight, she drew her knife from its place of concealment above her heart, and with eyes closed, she carved a circle into the box's blood-soaked deep-pile carpet. Spiderwebs of blue light flared from the walls and ceiling and floor. The air went tight. The music and the pounding of the police—if that was really who they were—sounded muffled.

"What—"

"Boosted the security wards. Buys us time. Not much." Something immense struck the door from the other side. Plaster crackled around the mahogany frame. The hinges kicked off dirty sparks. "Maybe less than that."

"Good. So we'll just duck out the back door, then, into the orchestra pit."

Another blow. Cracks circled the doorframe.

"Not a terrible idea."

"You didn't consider a bluff? Bat our eyelashes, oh no officer, see here our client, grievously dispatched—"

"With both of us wanted by the security bureau? How do you

think the cops got here so fast? This isn't a coincidence. This is a frame." With the door almost off its hinges and the cops outside, Tara was still smiling. "And here I was worried we were chasing shadows. If M. Grimwald didn't know something useful, he wouldn't be dead now. Here. Hold this."

Kai found herself in possession of one (1) severed head.

She didn't drop it, at least. It stared at her slack-jawed beneath the caul of darkness that clung to its skin. It was still . . . dripping. "What the hells, Tara?"

"We're running out of options." Tara's eyes flicked from the corpse to the pulsing glyphs to the stage. "He can still answer a few questions, if we're careful."

"He was a human being."

"Not a biologically modern one. Too many muscular attachment points on the jaw."

The wall shuddered with another thunderous impact.

"Well," Kai said, "so much for playing innocent. I'm sorry, officer, we found our dear friend M. Grimwald cruelly slain, and in our shock and horror we took it upon ourselves to remove his godsdamn head. What are you doing *now*? What is that?"

"Clutch bag."

"I can see it's a clutch bag. I mean what—"

"My purse didn't match the penguin suit. Stuffed this behind the cummerbund. Head should fit. Bag's bigger than it is. You know what I mean. Can I have it back please? Thank you." The head did fit through the opening of Tara's clutch bag, with a little shoving and an uncomfortable wet *pop*. "Have to bring this to his quarters. Find his personal effects, if he has any. People, even careful ones, store bits of their souls in their stuff. Same way Deathless Kings store their deaths, only, you know, low-rent precursor version. We've got a day, maybe. If we can sneak the head past these cops."

"They'll search us."

"If they catch us, yes. Sorry."

"What? Tara, what are you sorry about?"

Tara's arms circled her, strong and tight.

Kai's breath caught. She eased into the embrace, forgetting the

Iskari, the dead body, the spiders beyond the sky, forgetting even the swelling horn call of Werfried's entrance on the stage. She felt brilliantly alive.

Then she died.

There was probably a technical term to describe her condition, something Tara would use to distinguish it from the kind of death the headless Grimwald was experiencing—or not, depending on your metaphysics. But Kai could not move, could not breathe. She had been meditating recently, on her therapist's advice, and she'd been proud when she learned to feel her own heart beating in her chest. It was a reassuring sensation, until it wasn't there.

Tara lifted her as if she weighed nothing, set her against the wall of the box, and tucked the clutch bag between her hands. "We'll meet at Grimwald Holdings, tomorrow, at sundown. Bring the head." Tara stepped back and regarded what she'd done. "Sorry," she said. "Thanks." She hesitated. "I'm glad you could hear the prelude."

She pulled the box's curtain over Kai. For a moment all she could see was red velvet. Then her head lolled to one side, and through a gap in the curtains she could see the orchestra and the stage.

Kai's anger was cold and absolute. How dare she? To be locked up in a closet would be more dignified! The embrace had been nothing—a circle of arms to create a focus for the working of Craft. She couldn't call Seril now if she wanted to. Couldn't speak. Couldn't so much as mew. The godsdamn pigheaded temerity of the woman. Kai couldn't even get properly seething at her, because whatever curse Tara had used to interrupt her biology had stemmed the chemical processes of which that deep and justified fury would be composed.

The wards flared one final time as the door, frame and all, burst in with a crash of ruptured plaster. Booted feet stampeded into the room—and behind them a whispering tread, a briny rotten breath of deep sea. That was the odor of the special police of the Iskari Demesne—the Rectifiers of Names, wrapped in symbionts, the union of flesh and flesh.

She saw Tara's plan, then, and did not like it. Stunned, basically dead, her scent masked by the smell of blood and offal, Kai would remain hidden, unless the cops took the time for a detailed search. So Tara would provide a distraction.

Kai's brain caught up a moment before Tara leapt off the balcony.

The Craftswoman's hands, gloved in shadow, caught a spreading branch of the World Tree. She skidded down the silver bough, trailing sparks and darkness as she swept to the stage. The plainclothes cops shouted after her and fled the box, scrambling downstairs, calling for backup.

The Rectifier did not wait. Cloak billowing, it launched itself from the balcony, swinging after Tara on rubbery arms.

From the orchestra rose the triumphant call of Werfried's horn.

Tara landed hard on the stage, rolled, came up on her feet seeking exits. Laughter from the audience, shock—there were no dumb shows in Kirst, no ballet. Was this interloper a fugitive lover? Survivor of a duel gone wrong? A bold casting choice for Werfried? A smattering of applause greeted her from audience members too unfamiliar with the opera to realize this wasn't supposed to happen, or too amused to care. Tara looked up, shocked, shot a salute to the crowd—of course—and sprinted off stage left.

Smack into Werfried.

Opera being opera, the great hero of Schwarzwald epic and saga was being sung not by some mystery-play hunk with 0 percent body fat and alchemically contorted musculature but by a guy who looked more like what Kai would expect of a Schwarzwaldic culture hero: tall and girthy, heavy-armed, a chest like an artillery shell. Around his left arm he wore a pulsing woad-blue symbiont, and in his right hand he held the great sword Apt. Just last night it had cleft the spear of God in twain. Even if it was no more than a prop master's facsimile, it was still a solid meter and a half of glittering metal. Kai might have placed her bets on Tara anyway, except that Werfried's eyes were glowing in time with the pulse of his symbiont.

His blade flashed out. Tara blocked with her metal arm, but the weight of the strike toppled her and when she came up she was shaking her hand as if it were numb.

From the high branches of the World Tree, the Rectifier of Names descended on wings of darkness like a stingray sweeping through a reef.

Tara drew her hand through a fierce arc. A wave of shadow struck the Rectifier in midair and dashed it down to the audience.

Werfried swung again. Tara must have seen the movement out of the corner of her eye. She dodged away. Werfried tried for a reverse cut, and this time his blade met honest steel. Tara had drawn her sword.

It was a rental, of course, but Kai had not wanted to economize for her one visit to the Grand Opera. The slender blade did not snap. Sparks danced where edge met forte, and Tara did something with her wrist; this Werfried was not a trained swordsman, and he was being ridden by an intelligence for which hands were a modern affectation. The great sword Apt twisted from his grip. Glittering with stage lights, it spun a glorious arc through the air and hammered itself tip down into the boards.

Werfried fell. The house erupted in applause. Even Kai, who should still be—who *was*, godsdammit—furious with Tara, felt a stab of pride. Tara grinned, sketched a bow, and ran.

The World Tree caught her.

One slender root creaked up from the stage and twisted around her ankle. She chopped at it with her sword, freed herself, but others were already moving, the tree's great branches and the spreading wire net of twigs. They closed around her. The applause grew. Tara slashed and cut to clear a path, but the guiding intelligence she fought, the vast mind operating the World Tree's machines, was used to working with many limbs—used to hunting with them in crushing deeps, in the dark, in the cold.

The applause had a pulsing rhythm, like surf. The Rectifier of Names rose from the audience and shook the dust of its cloak like a bird shaking feathers. Grim and even, it advanced. A branch caught Tara's sword and tore it from her hand. She drew her knife instead, crackling silver on the stage.

The light changed. It blued, deepened. At first Kai could not see why, or where the new illumination came from. The audience's eyes were open. All of them. And like Werfried's, they burned purple.

The stage filled in from the wings. Actors, prop managers, black-clad techs, they emerged shuffling and bright-eyed. Their symbionts pulsed in time.

The master of the house had come.

Tara wrenched one arm free. She tore at the tree branches with claws of shadow.

<Craftswoman,> the opera house said. No one voice spoke alone. They all did, at once, in whispers. <Craftswoman, we would have words with you.>

The Wrecker reached the stage. Tendrils uncoiled from its robes and lifted it smoothly to the boards. Kai's heart beat in her ears. Her breath came rabbit-quick.

Ah. She was breathing again. Her heart beat. And she still wore the lily in her hair.

"Seril," she whispered.

She felt herself limned in silver light. It eased through her, soothing the cracks in her soul. She was not alone.

All those thousands of purple eyes turned to stare up at her.

When I asked you to take care of her, the goddess said, *this is exactly not what I had in mind.*

"It's not my fault" was not the sort of thing one wanted to say to gods, save when arguing theodicy. But there were extenuating circumstances. "What should I do?"

What do you think, rabbit?

She ran.

As a girl, Kai had been fond of a certain sort of adventure romance, set in a historical Chartegnon that might as well have been a fantasist's invention for all it had in common with her day-to-day experience as a shipbuilder's daughter. That was part of the fun. Dukes dueling in graveyards, sopranos swooning over love notes, clasped hands torn asunder by revolution, a kiss on a burning building, these things were vivid and bold and utterly alien. Her sister, Ley, teased her for this obsession—though Kai noticed that Ley could and often did recite the heroes' speeches from memory as she mocked. She'd been nearly fourteen before she understood that a soprano was not some angelic elfin creature but was, in fact, an athlete capable of putting a high D through a two-inch-thick board at a hundred paces.

She'd long since come to terms with the fact that her books were not accurate guides to the world—though in that respect they were no more deficient than any other aspect of her formal education.

In those books, all opera houses were roughly 90 percent secret passages and booby traps by volume, the better for menacing masked personages to flit around abducting damsels and murdering counts. Every wall was a trick wall, every carpet hid a trapdoor. Kai had adored this image so much she had diligently avoided investigating whether it was true.

Unfortunately, the walls of the Iskari Grand Opera had so far proved impermeable. If the floor meant to open and swallow her into the embrace of some misunderstood monster, it damn well better get on with it. She was tired. Her pursuers were coming up fast. And they had swords.

Less contemplation and more running, rabbit.

"I was under the impression," she observed to the goddess— and she was *not* panting, thank you very much, "that your grace compassed sky and sea and slope. The last time we worked together and you wanted me somewhere else you just zapped me there."

Last time, you were far above the surface of the world, in sight of the moon and within the compass of my power to, ah, zap. You call on me now from the heartland of another potentate, beneath the odd-pupiled gaze of its unfriendly gods. What do you expect from me?

"Miracles?"

Laughter answered. *Salvation is my metier, rabbit, but you have to give me something to work with.*

"That's not how you pronounce it. More like met-ee-yay."

Well, that doesn't sound right at all.

"Nonetheless."

This is why I enjoy mortal company. One learns things!

"Have you learned a way out?"

I am working on it.

"Oh Lady of the Silver Ways: work faster."

Kai kept in shape by climbing the ceremonial steps of Kavekana'ai, but she did that in stretchy shorts and a sports bra, not fifteen pounds of ball gown plus weapons-grade hair. She had, with a sigh, ditched her heels into Tara's clutch, alongside M. Grimwald's head and a number of tiny burners and scalpels and phials, including one labeled UNIVERSAL SOLVENT.

Normal people, even normal Craftspersons, did not tend to bring a tool kit to a professional introduction. Normal people were not Tara Abernathy.

Thinking of Tara made her stomach twist, even through the utter panic of being pursued by an entire opera house. So she stopped. Thinking about her. Not running.

"Shouldn't I be trying to go *downstairs*? If we're escaping?"

The mob's downstairs. Are you questioning my ineffable plan?

"Yes."

Oh ye of little faith.

"I have faith for days. What I want is a way out."

Really.

She almost snapped back, "Of course." But she remembered Tara's salute on the stage, her grin, sword drawn against the world.

"No," she said. "I want to save her." And because she felt naked having said those words, so transparently committed—a priest even in this, a votress of secrecy: "If only to rub it in her face."

The goddess laughed, though Kai didn't see why.

She reached the fourth balcony level, a kind of mezzanine above the third. Dukes and so on might value their privacy, but they preferred to keep kings and archpriests where they could see them. She glanced over her shoulder; she was trailing glowing-eyed nobility, the gold-threaded swells of the Demesne, swords out, its high haughty ladies wielding knives from their purses. And in one case, a table lamp. They did not cry after her. They did not even speak. They just ran.

The double doors beside her swept open and a huge man burst out, arms spread, fingers clawed, a squidling pulsing at his brow.

Kai ducked his embrace and decked him with Tara's clutch, which was heftier than it seemed, thanks to all the fell sorcery. The guy hit the banister hard. Kai tried not to worry about him. The Iskari got a new king every year, anyway.

"We're running out of hallway."

Excellent.

Ahead of her, the elevator dinged.

For one glorious instant, she thought: there it is. My exit. Down the elevator to—wherever. Then a pile of squiddies tumbled out of the elevator doors and ran for her, while the dukes, et cetera, charged up behind.

The goddess said, *Go over the balcony.*

She did not have time to question. She hopped over and fell, landing hard on a chaise longue on the ducal level. Her ankle did something less than conducive to continued flight. She could still limp, for the moment. The swells had all followed her upstairs. She could loop back behind them now, make for the street.

No, the goddess said. *Not the staircase. The elevator.*

"What? It's upstairs, we just saw it."

Are you still questioning the ineffable plan?

"Parts of it seem pretty effing effed."

Rabbit, now you're just being crude.

She could not run without wincing—but proceeded at her best shamble. Chartegnon spread out beyond a bank of high windows, and even in her panic it called to her, the rolling skyline pierced by cathedral spires, and always the shining squid tower near the Field of War, a city of jewels beneath the slate-colored sky. In another time, another life, she'd be down among those brilliant streets, stumbling home from the kind of dinner where you drank wine as if your glass refilled itself—where the table seemed to shrink as hours passed and you drew close to the person opposite, the very specific person, tracing their glass with fingers of bone. . . .

The window shattered.

A shadow swept into the hallway, its cloak-wings spread. The darkness of its embrace writhed with tentacles. She skidded, tried to stop. Too slow. The Wrecker's many arms lashed out and caught her, wrist and ankle and waist. She clawed at them, but those toothed suckers held on. A drunken warmth spread through her. All was well; she should breathe deep, let it circle her throat, cover her mouth.

She bit down on a rubbery appendage, tore some flesh loose— salty, a bit bland. Needed soy sauce. Her teeth didn't seem to bother it at all. At least its arms lifted her away from the broken glass on the carpet as they crushed her in their embrace.

Mouth busy, she had to pray silently. Your spymaster who sees in secret will reward you. *Is this still part of the plan?*

Afraid not, rabbit. Our options now are somewhat limited, lacking—

I get it, thanks.

She spit out squid and tore open Tara's clutch. She was sure she'd seen a scalpel in this bag, but now there was all this blood and everything was jumbled up between head and shoes and— well, fine. *That* might do something.

As the Wrecker drew her into its writhing embrace, she grabbed the little bottle labeled UNIVERSAL SOLVENT, popped the cork with her teeth, and threw it at the squid-thing's chest.

The Wrecker stopped and looked down, puzzled.

There was a hole in its chest.

The hole led to nothing, to static, to the absence of thingness. It was not black. Blackness, color, form, all the world's categories seemed irrelevant, wherever that hole led. The Wrecker stepped back, but the hole remained in place. The Wrecker's chest was intact. It made a sound, its first, a wet approximation of a laugh.

Beyond that hole, a fragment of the unthing moved.

It speared the Wrecker through the chest: a claw of bright-edged glass, swift and hungry. Its wicked edges split, each blade budding other blades that explored the flesh. Then it began to pry.

The arms that held Kai suddenly had more pressing matters to attend to. She hit the carpet hard, and oh, yes, *there* was the broken glass, wouldn't want to miss out on that. The gown got the worst of it, but she felt something bright and wet in her left foot as she scrambled through a hallway that now resembled the inside of a working blender. She did not look back. That was pretty much rule two when dealing with unbound demons.

Rule one being, don't.

You used the universal solvent, the goddess said.

"I thought it was an acid that dissolves, you know. Stuff."

That would be a plain-language interpretation, I'll grant you.

"Not one that dissolves—"

Universes.

"And she carries it around in her purse?"

As part of her professional equipage. I would imagine it is intended for sparing and precise use, not to be thrown at obstacles by the bottleful.

From behind her, she heard screams and the sound of breaking glass. Then more screams, louder. "Needs a better label is all I'm saying. Maybe a picture of a portal with demons coming out."

In my experience with practitioners of the Craft, their lax labeling standards have been a regular annoyance. Along with the paranoid megalomania, the omnicidal tendencies, and the cackling.

The floor shivered. Timbers cracked. Plaster rained from the ceiling. She risked a glance back, saw knives and blood and rainbows. Her stomach churned. "Should we . . . do something? Isn't an unbound demon a destroy-the-city kind of issue?"

This one has yet to fully manifest. You haven't created a proper hole, more of a thinning of the barriers. There's no self-sustaining paradox to sustain it. The Iskari have experience with demons. I believe this is a let's-you-and-him-fight situation.

A spray of blood struck her face. She wiped it away. She'd really liked this gown.

Have you reached the elevator?

"Yes."

Wonderful. Now, touch the lily to the control panel. You won't be able to hear me for the next—

The voice faded. The silver had not abandoned her, the shine behind her eyes. She was, she realized, calmer than she should have been. Looking back, she'd been faster, stronger, just a little bit *more* than usual. She'd put it down to adrenaline, but—

The elevator doors rolled open. The shaft beyond gaped, black and deep and dangling with cables. She shoved the flower behind her ear. "Seril?"

I'm here, rabbit. Now—

"Did you do something to my blood?

You are a badass without any help from me.

"Are you lying?"

Rabbit, please jump into the elevator shaft.

"There's no elevator."

That was rather the idea.

She had a sudden terrifying thought, though not so terrifying as the empty concrete shaft. "You do remember that humans can't fly?"

Please, rabbit, will you just accept the ineffable plan for one moment, *because the Wrecker and the demon won't hold one another for long, and you don't want to take on the winner—*

"You're asking for one hell of a leap of faith here."

You're a priestess.

"I'm not *that* kind of priestess."

If the moon could sigh, Kai now knew what it would sound like.

This is taking too long. I'm glad you wore that color, rabbit. It's fetching on you.

She blinked. "Thanks?"

And it's silver. Which permits me a certain tangency.

"Wait. What?"

Her gown yanked her forward. She swept, like a doll on the tide, out into the dark.

29

There were six of them in the back of the unmarked golem van, or seven depending on how you counted: Yan on wings, Lopez on overwatch, Chakrabartay for heavy, plus Temoc, of course, Mal, Dawn, and Sybil. It was a crowded ride through the Drakspine Hills to the Observatory.

As the van switchbacked up, Dresediel Lex unfurled, a tapestry of light beneath the 3 A.M. sky. Each point was a person, more or less, their grubby particulars transfigured, radiant.

The van rounded a bend in the ridge, and out the windshield over Temoc's shoulder Dawn saw the pyramid.

—We can do this, Sybil hissed.

That sounds an awful lot like the kind of thing you say when you don't think we can.

—I am attempting to engage with your annoyingly chemical emotions in a sensitive and caring manner. Would you prefer I say that there is a very real chance we cannot do this, in which case we die horribly? Good luck and attagirl?

It's okay, she said, softly. *We'll be fine.*

—If the priest knows his business. If the blood doesn't kill us all. I don't like the smell of this place.

She stroked the back of Sybil's head. The serpent snuggled into her shoulder.

The van rolled past the proud front entrance with its sign and its flags, down a side lot to a loading dock. Temoc slipped out of the van without a word, walked to an unmarked door, and tried it. It opened. It was that easy.

So far.

They found their way by the red nighttime lights, past office doors with nameplates, past stenciled Quechal glyphs on the walls, past great tattered reed-paper scrolls under safety glass. There were restrooms and a water fountain and an elevator and big plants that weren't fake. The place smelled of care and disinfectant.

The three Arsenals drifted like ghosts through the empty halls, from corner to corner and cover to cover, while Mal and Temoc brought up the rear. Dawn felt like she made more noise in her loose cotton clothes and combat boots than all the others together, even the Arsenals in their body armor and full kit. She could hear her own breath. Her heartbeat.

They had gone into Shenshan Prison for her. She could do this for them.

They rounded a last corner and reached the pyramid's heart. Starlight and the underglow of city-lit clouds streamed down through a crystal lens to reveal a room from a dead world. Everywhere she turned, she saw the traces of that long-past time: statues of winged men, codices under glass, masks of gods whose names she did not know, slabs of paleoglyphed rock carved out of caves and suspended in glittering Craft-circles like Sybil in her wires. Crumbling artifacts lay on restoration tables or attached to ticking machines. She walked past a featureless stone orb the size of a man.

At the far end of the hall there was a massive basalt head.

Yan sprouted metal wings and leapt to take position on a balcony. Chakrabarty drew a heavy cursethrower long as his arm from a small belt pouch, and a thick sword that looked to have been designed to use from horseback. Lopez released tiny clockwork creatures from his abdominal cavity to scuttle into the air ducts. Temoc assembled a traveling altar on a worktable in front of the stone head.

Dawn found herself the still center of all this silent motion, unsure what to do.

She felt Mal's hand on her shoulder. "You're okay, kid."

"Not a kid."

She grinned. "I know."

"It is time," Temoc said, and drew his knife. It was made of black glass, covered with that strange old Quechal writing that was mostly faces in rictus grins. Dawn joined him at the altar, and so did Mal. Her grin was easy, but her metal hand was balled into a fist.

Temoc's blade traced a thin red line down a span of his forearm free of other scars, and he began to sing.

His voice was rich, deep at first then delicate and high: like a mountain rising from the roots of the world to its breathless peak. Dawn tried to follow the melody, but the notes moved oddly and slantwise. She must have been confused, for she thought she heard Temoc's voice, and then Temoc's voice again, and again, as if the song twisted back through itself in time. Sybil shuddered around her shoulders. Dawn hugged her, and felt Mal's hand on her arm.

With a groan of dead ages, the stone head opened its mouth. Inside, nestled against a great rocky tongue, was a pearl of sunlight.

The pearl sang to her, with a voice deeper even than the priest's. She never wanted to look at anything else again. She could have burned her eyes from her sockets, to see only that light in memory.

She made herself look away.

Mal stood beside her, and she—Dawn had never seen her like this, sandblasted, all softness and bravura torn away to reveal the barren rock on which she'd tried to build a life. She looked anywhere but at the sunlight pearl. But she held Dawn's arm tight.

"Place your hand above the altar," Temoc said.

He had placed idols on the altar: one in bronze of two Serpents; one of a skeletal man enthroned; two of women, one tall and thin, one short and strong. Idols, and a bowl.

She shivered when she offered him her arm, but the knife dipped into her skin as if into a pool of water and with as little pain. A single bright red drop fell toward the bowl—and hovered above it, perfectly round and stuck in midair.

The light changed. The pearl of sun bulged and pulsed and birthed a smaller pearl, which drifted toward them, or they were drawn to it, or the distance between them did not matter.

The song filled her ears. She heard a chorus behind Temoc's voice, as if many other priests and Knights sang with him in this moment, from the deeps of time. The room fell away. Not all of it, just the parts that reminded her of a doctor's office: the chests and lenses and lights on metal arms, the specimen tables. They sank into shadows deeper than those Temoc's glyphs shed upon his skin. The basalt head remained. The idols and the altar and the calendar stone. The pearl.

"Now you must go within," Temoc said, though the song continued. "You must go within and face your foes."

Go through shadows into the hunting dream, on a path made of this immortal light.

She was scared. She did not want to face the thing that hunted her, but Sybil was here. Neither one of them would be alone, ever again.

She began to close her eyes.

In some other world, in some other life, she heard Lopez shout a warning. Then she heard him scream. His scream reached her through the song and the heat, distorted as if underwater. They were so far away. What could reach her here, where gods walked and the voice of ages rang from stone?

But then she heard the footsteps. She turned and saw a thin man in a black suit.

It could not be Mr. Brown, stepping over Lopez's opened body. Mr. Brown was dead. She had crushed him beneath a god's hand. This was not the same man—but he was so close as made no difference, a new iteration of that nothing face.

He saw her and smiled and seemed about to speak.

Mal tackled her to the ground.

Black iron chains whipped through the space where she had just been standing, to shatter the bowl and spatter the idols with her blood. Temoc whirled, his blade bare. The chains carved into his arm before he could steel his shadows against them.

Dawn scrambled to her knees, still half in time and half out of it, unsure where she'd left her body.

Yan dropped a rain of boltfire from his nest. Chains flashed out from Mr. Brown's unseamed arm to deflect the bolts and lash toward Yan. Yan flew, but not fast enough. Chains pierced his metal leg and whipped him into the wall hard enough to bounce. He tumbled to the marble floor.

Then Chakrabartay's cursethrower cut Mr. Brown in half. For a moment Dawn could see through him as if he were a bead curtain: the burned cloth and shredded suit and the writhing nest of iron. The chains pulled like taffy, knit torso to legs again, and drew the halves together.

Chakrabartay leveled his sword like a spear, and charged. An iron lash took a chunk out of his shoulder and another out of the side of his neck, but somehow he made it through. His blade gleamed blue as it sheared and snapped thin strands of chain, and Brown's torso lurched to one side. Dawn thought, impossibly, He's done it.

Then Brown punched Chakrabartay in the chest. He flew back, skidded. His mangled armor left a trail of sparks across the tile. Blood leaked through plate. Temoc charged into the space Chakrabartay left, shadow and blue flame, and Mal followed him, cutlass drawn.

Brown readied his chains and his slim curved smile.

They would die. Dawn saw it, beyond time. They would die, for her. She could do nothing. The pearl throbbed before her, beckoning. They give themselves for you, it seemed to say. They offer a sacrifice. It is honored, its petition granted.

No. She had to stop them.

She reached out for the Observatory's Craft, and it was hers, as easy as breathing: manipulator arms and lenses, sensors and instruments, contracts for security and personnel, deals with elementals, deals with the rock on which the place was built. There had to be something she could use, some way to take this back.

The pain seized her then. She buckled around her hand. Cold spread through the meat of her body. Through the glove and Sybil's warding power, the iron claimed her. She had taken it in because she wanted to be what it was. Now it told her, Be as we are. Be consumed, and one with us. She could not speak. Blood wept from her eyes. There was a scream in her throat, but she was too frozen to let it out.

She made herself look up, into the graying world, and there she saw Brown.

He was still half-apart, fighting Mal and Temoc at once. Mal with her blade alone could make no headway against his chains, but Temoc was marching in, knife high as he bled light from many wounds. Brown did not seem to notice either of them. He was watching her, with those normal eyes, behind those normal spectacles. She was his target.

The world was cold and chains its only truth.

Save for the pearl of flame.

Temoc had called the ritual a bridge, between our time and theirs. He had said: "When they cross into our time, it is to consume."

She felt the Serpents' blood beckon her into the time of gods. But bridges went both ways.

She seized the blood, with all her might, and pulled.

"Get back!" Her scream was a jellied sound. She heard crystal shatter.

A light that beggared suns arced overhead, a flare, a jet, writhing flame and liquid brilliance, to fall upon the nest of chains that was Mr. Brown. He screamed like gears when he died.

She did not know where she was, or even *if* she was. She could not stand.

Arms lifted her. She smelled Mal, then saw her: blood-slick but alive, backlit by flames. There was Temoc beyond the fire, with the bloody wreck of Lopez slung over one shoulder and Chakrabartay over the other. There was Yan, face gray, wings twisted, propping himself upright with an ancient spear.

All about them were flames and blood and ruined hope. In her hand, she felt the gloating fact of iron.

Together, they ran.

30

Caleb and Abelard were welcomed to the poker table as new acolytes, raising the game's numbers back to an ideal six. It was an oak table with good green felt, and the chips were clay. Two of the other four were Imperial business travelers in rumpled charcoal suits, a broad man and a knap-edged woman with a circlet of metal thorns at her brow. One was a four-armed statue of glass and crystal with knife-fingers and burning red eyes, whom Caleb thought he had seen somewhere before. The fourth was a chameleon-skinned beauty in a lamé dress and a pillbox hat, with impatient hands in velvet gloves and eyes that devoured.

Caleb introduced himself and sat in the vacant seat by the window. Abelard chose the one nearer the door.

The game, said the lady with the barbed-wire crown in perfect Kathic, was standard Hold'em. Hundred-thaum buy-in.

That, he said, worked for him. Abelard swallowed.

"Good. It's your deal."

The pot was a fine silver bowl in the center of the table, and the needles were sealed and single-use. Caleb sterilized his with a lighter anyway. By all rights he should have a callus where the needle went in; his capillaries and veins should have collapsed by now, like any other addict's. That they did not was one of the minor miracles of the game.

His blood mixed in the bowl. He said a prayer. Wisps of silver-gray smoke rose, and the air changed texture as the small dining room in a dragon gondola above the churning Pax became just another chamber in the mansion of the game.

He watched the space above the bowl. The Lady took shape in smoke, suggestion, and dream. Her face and figure and apparent gender differed from player to player. Sometimes she was glory and sometimes she was death. She was herself, and you could court her and pay her homage, but she scorned your certainties and any joy you sought in them. They were anathema to her being.

She had no more substance, now, than a body made of cloud. She was a figure in a window, backlit, naked, the sheer curtain blown against her to reveal her form. He tried not to shudder, not to yearn. But the chameleon woman's silver eyes flicked toward him, and she smiled with a lipless perfect mouth. "I see you've done this before."

"Every time's the first."

But when his eyes flicked back to the Lady, he hesitated.

For a moment the form behind the smoke was doubled. There were two of her, one tall and lean, one shorter, rounder with muscle and flesh, sisters sharp-toothed and beautiful as blades. Together they reached for him, and behind them he felt the searing heat, the embers of the sun in the cage of their father's ribs.

His hands were tense on the cards. He glanced up and met Abelard's eyes across the table.

Caleb had been drowning for days, in revolution and memory and the end of the world, in monsters past and monsters beyond the sky.

He bridged the cards. Shuffled three times, and three again. The Lady was not doubled now. She had receded from the table. But still he thought he knew her—had lain beside her on the surface of the sea.

The action was hot and fast. He'd pegged the chameleon for a loose aggressive player and he wasn't wrong—but she made it work, with her choice of boards to attack and hands to represent. Did she have the flush? A pair? Nothing? She seemed happier when she lost than when she won. Some pots he thought she went big just because she hadn't lost anything in a while.

The woman with the crown of thorns played like she was

short-stacked the whole time. She was happy to sit blind after blind, watching with those dull deep eyes.

Four Arms was patient and careful. If the game lasted a million years he would have won on sheer attrition, but the game was bounded by time and death and the goddess. Caleb didn't worry about Four Arms.

The broad man blustered, but he wasn't a threat. He liked to play, that was *his* problem.

And Abelard . . . The priest played like himself. And somehow, he won more than he lost. It was baffling. It might have been infuriating, the guessing and second-guessing, his kind assurances to other players when things didn't work out, his relief when a bet came through. But none of it was faked. He wasn't fishing or trying to lull the others into false security. He was playing a game with them, and he wanted everyone to do well.

Caleb chased the Lady. She never showed him her doubled guise again—that was his imagination, he told himself, his nerves tight after a long few days. But when he reached for her, when he pushed all-in, did she, sometimes, beckon with a metal arm?

Soulstuff sloshed around the table. Cities of chips rose and fell. In the game's second hour he thought they'd settled into a dynamic equilibrium, with Crown of Thorns and himself having the biggest stakes, the others scraping blinds off sure-thing hands, but then Chameleon doubled up through Caleb, and for the next few hands Abelard was the chip leader, until Caleb cut Chameleon back and pulled ahead.

He was playing loose. He wanted to be part of the action. Bad discipline, especially with Abelard over there quietly working the odds, edging ahead with careful by-the-numbers bets. But Caleb needed the give-and-take. He needed to dissolve. Every beat of the dragon's wings bore them east, carving sky and cloud and stars, east across the Pax to Dresediel Lex, city of pyramids, city of broad streets and broken gods.

He loved his city. He missed it. He was so often gone.

Hours passed, and found them flying south over the Drakspine, sheer sharp peaks upthrust from colliding continental shelves so many million years ago. His own land lay below him. It was a muddle, an amalgam, folded over itself and folded again, and there was its glory. Bare rock in moonlight: Seril, exiled, in the wastes. The hills of Dresediel Lex would be dry now, the green yellowed, the brush gray, the air sharp and spacious with none of the humid mug of Ajaia's land.

His country, at her most beautiful on the verge of flame, waiting for a spark.

The table tightened. They traded small handfuls of chips, the price of lunch, of coffee. He waited. Abelard gathered a stack. So did he.

And there it was. An opportunity. What did he have in hand? Unsuited eight-nine. Junk. He decided it was gold.

Raises and calls chased around the table. The flop was nice, juicy, three cards that might offer action to anyone on the board. Anyone except him, but they didn't know that. He raised again. Abelard and the Chameleon chased, but she didn't have enough to follow when he reraised, and she didn't want to push all-in. That left Caleb and Abelard through the river.

The Lady danced and gleamed like a butterfly knife.

As the game drew on, Abelard had fallen into a rhythm. His plays became textbook. He bet with the pot odds. He sought value. He was a deeper player than that, but it was a late night or an early morning, and he was falling back on reflexes. They weren't bad reflexes. Abelard, he was pretty sure, had a piece of the table. Not much, but he wouldn't need much. He was playing tight for two pair. Call it top pair.

The Lady turned to Caleb.

He pushed his chips into the center.

It was the dumbest move he'd made all night. It never would have worked against Chameleon, or Four Arms for that matter, and he'd have put fifty-fifty on Crown of Thorns. There were top players who would, at this point, call him on principle. He'd won more than a few souls that way.

But Abelard wanted the math to work. He went quiet and still.

He knew Caleb might be bluffing. He knew that the board was

rich, that Caleb had stepped up his bets as cards fell. Had he made the flush? Three of a kind? Was it worth the showdown? If he backed off, he'd be handing Caleb a commanding lead. But there would be other chances. If he went in, the game was over.

And he knew that Caleb knew that he liked the game and didn't want it to end.

Abelard did not move.

When games got tight like this, Caleb talked to the other players in his mind. Come on, buddy. What are you gonna do? With a twist to his lips, an edge of mockery, a dare.

There was no dare now. He felt sincerely curious.

Come on, buddy. What are you gonna do?

Some people's features hardened with decision. Abelard softened, as if relieved to remember what he was going to decide. His hands sank—toward his cards, to muck them into the center and fold? Toward his chips, to push them in and call?

Somewhere the Lady was a whirlwind. Somewhere she was a blinding light. Somewhere the world was always ending, and somewhere there was Mal, and Caleb didn't care. He wasn't anywhere but here.

He heard the wail of an alarm, and then the room was sideways.

Chips and cards sloshed across the felt. Caleb lurched against the window. The Lady laughed.

Beneath them lay Dresediel Lex, a jewel carpet to the rolling ocean in the deepest purple of early morning.

As the room veered back upright, he realized what had happened: the dragon had banked hard, away from—what?

There, perched on the edge of the Drakspine overlooking the city, Caleb saw Tlaloc Observatory. At least, he saw where it should have been, if not for the fire.

Abelard chased Caleb through the dining gondola and out onto the observation deck.

Below them, dry hills overlooked an enormous city—not as

tall or dense as Alt Coulumb, but it went on forever in every direction except the ocean, streetlights and windows illuminated in the predawn gloom like a night sky upside down.

Caleb was already climbing the banister.

"That," he said, with a nod to the sprawling complex summited by a burning white pyramid, "is Tlaloc Observatory. Used to be a temple. Now it's the material theology department of Central U."

"You think Temoc's there?"

"It's one of the places I thought he might go. And it's on fire. Also, my mom works down there." He held out his hand. "Come with me?"

"Are you sure this is a good idea?"

"It's not."

Abelard looked down. "We can't jump from here. There are wards to stop us."

"I'm counting on them."

"Were you bluffing?"

"What?"

"In the game. Were you bluffing?"

The fire glinted off his grin. "Were you going to fold?"

Abelard took his hand. "We'll go on three," he said, as he climbed the guardrail. "Ready? One—"

Caleb went, and so did Abelard.

They fell. Safety wards wrapped around them, clinging, slowing, crackling, until Caleb opened his scars. Then his outflung hand held something like lightning, the wards repurposed to his benefit, and they were swinging toward the Observatory complex, trailing streaks of green light.

Doing this sort of thing with Tara never felt quite so precipitous. Abelard wondered if the difference lay in the comparative nature of their powers, or in the fact that his faith in Tara was absolute, while what faith he had in Caleb Altemoc was of a more recent vintage.

The ground, the fire, and the Observatory pyramid's white walls were all coming up fast. Hopefully he had enough control to address the minor issue of their pancaking into the hills at dragon speed.

He'd find out any second—now.

A giant hand slapped his entire body. He bounced and rolled to a dusty stop against a scratchy leafless bush. He was scratched, bruised, choking dust, but—pending a full inventory—more or less operational.

There was a hand in front of his face. Caleb's. He took it.

"All right?"

"Mostly."

"Thanks." Caleb looked—embarrassed? "For trusting me."

"You seemed to know what you were doing."

Caleb laughed his laugh that Abelard didn't like, the one with all the edges pointing in. Together, they ran toward the fire.

For most kids in D.L., the highlight of the summer was a visit to Rat King Mountain, the Undeadest Place in the World: a cheerful land of screams and rictus grins and dancing skeletons, and as much cotton candy as your parents would pay for, all ruled over by a tiny undead rodent wizard in a crimson robe. Caleb had never, as an adult, dared ask the King in Red about it, figuring that there was probably some sort of gentlebeing's arrangement at play, or a misguided attempt at mind-share development. Nonetheless, he'd eaten his share of cotton candy, gone on his share of dark rides and roller coasters, fought his share of ghost pirates.

The highlight of Caleb's summer, though, was his mom's return to the Observatory. During the year, she taught at the main campus downtown: thrumming with students, the professional-track kids in their linen robes and the gen-ed kids in whatever they happened to roll out of bed wearing, the library's manicured lawn hosting hackey-sack games and ineffectual protests. He met her there after school.

But in summers Dr. Mina Almotil focused on her research. Sometimes that meant digs in the desert—which was fine, Caleb could scratch together a few thaums working and more beating the students at cards. But always, eventually, his life wound back up the road to the glittering white walls of Tlaloc Observatory.

Here, while Mom worked, he walked the labyrinth. The rules

were clear. Touch nothing without permission, not even the safety glass. There was no telling what his touch could do to the artifacts, or the other way around. But otherwise he was free to roam, to find strange tapestries of flayed men in isolated galleries, to play solitaire in rooms hung with parchment codices under glass, to picnic with Mom beneath the watchful gaze of the great stone head in the high-energy theophysics chamber. She even brought a basket, just like the one the bear in the comic books was always trying to steal. She called it their museum.

Now their museum was on fire.

It was one thing to see the fire from a distance, and another to charge through acrid smoke, past the great glass doors into the front hall with its turquoise serpents. Alarms deafened him. He ignored them and ran on through the hallways of his childhood.

It was not yet dawn. The night staff should have evacuated already and called the fire department. He thought he could hear their sirens. There was no reason for Mom to be here.

But.

She had retired from teaching classes last year, to focus on her monograph on Quechal eschatologies. She woke early—a habit, she claimed, that she never had before he was born. They'd often come to the Observatory an hour before dawn, Caleb dozing in the passenger seat of their cheap golem cart, to beat (she said) the morning rush of people trying to beat the morning rush. (Mom, used to her fieldwork and to her books, loved the culture and the concept of Dresediel Lex but couldn't quite believe it was necessary for so many people to *live* here.)

She might be working, now. In her office with the window over the city. He couldn't use the elevator, obviously. He ran for the stairs—shouldered the stairwell door off its hinges without meaning to. His scars were open. Shadow slicked his skin. Adrenal response to the danger of the smoke. He reached for his scars these days as if they were any other tool.

He remembered Achal's teeth, from his dream.

We fortunate few
Are called to give our hearts

He looked back. Abelard was still there, two steps behind, his eyes red. He recoiled a step when he saw Caleb's visage of shadow and black flame, but recovered. "I'm all right." He smiled, weakly. "Privileges of sainthood. I'm not the Blessed Godfrey, I've never walked through molten steel, but I can manage a little smoke."

Caleb shot him a thumbs-up and ran.

There was more than a little smoke on the fifth floor. Caleb ran on memory more than sight. Down the hall and to the left. Everything was so much smaller than it had been.

Out the city-facing windows, he saw red and blue lights ascend the hills—fire trucks, emergency Craft. Couatl on the wing. It was dry season, everyone on full alert, the demon winds scouring from the desert to make the city weird. In weather like this he'd seen fights kicked off by a smoker's careless tip of ash. *I should warn Abelard.*

Next door. The office. He remembered watching with Mom as Facilities stenciled her name on the door. It was unlocked. Coffee cup on the desk, amid slanting stacks of paper. She'd left her purse on the chair.

He felt his skin drum-tight. There was a high-pitched whine somewhere. He realized it was inside his head. Beneath his scars, his leg ached. There would be hells to pay for all this tomorrow.

Abelard grabbed the purse. "Check the bathrooms?"

Caleb shook his head. "She'd go where the work is."

Down the hall and down the stairs again to the exhibit floor.

As a child he had lingered here, comparing the scars on his arms to the glyphs on a calendar stone or cenotaph or altarpiece. Back then none of it seemed real—not the bloodstains, not the scars, not even his own pain.

The smoke was thicker now. He couldn't see the flames. The fact that you couldn't see them did not mean they wouldn't kill you. Under the right conditions fire could burn invisible—too hot for color or even light, a simple transformation of world to ash.

He ran past the great calendar stone, down the hall to High Energy Theophysics. Abelard was right behind him, robes hiked up, sandals slapping the marble floor—skin sweat-slick, but breathing easy.

How could anyone worship fire? The transformation of things

into nonthings? That's what it all came back to at the end: ribs open, heart lifted high.

But Abelard was here, and he didn't have to be.

They burst into High Energy Theophysics. Here was the great stone head, dredged from the maelstrom in the center of the Fangs, where the old Quechal High City sunk during the Contact Wars.

And here was the heart of the fire.

Heat struck him like a wall. Flames melted paint and burst concrete. The great calendrical reference tapestries lay in a smoldering heap. Thick heartwood beams overhead rained burning ash. This room had no windows, but up there in the smoke was the vast crystal lens through which the telescope dome channeled starlight, and up there in the smoke, he heard a worrying creak.

Abelard joined him, panting. "This doesn't make sense. That fire's burning *rock*. What could—"

He turned to the great stone head.

Its mouth was open. A crystal orb a meter across lay within, sized like a pearl upon its tongue. Caleb had never seen the orb before, had never known the mouth could open.

The orb was broken. It seeped a pulsing liquid radiance too bright to look upon. Where it dripped, the marble floor erupted in flame and began to melt.

And there, on the other side of the bubbling stone, staggering beneath the weight of cardboard banker's boxes and propping herself upright with a massive crystal sword, glasses pushed back from her face—there was Dr. Mina Almotil.

"Mom!"

Caleb vaulted the puddle of molten stone. She looked up, confused. That was not a usual expression for her. She seemed adrift, as if the Observatory were not burning down, as if time itself did not exist. As if she were not looking through smoke and the haze of blistering heat upon her son, but—

Oh. With the scars and the shadows and the darkness—he forgot how alike they could seem, even with the difference in build. He spoke before his mom's teeth could clip the "T" of his father's name. But not before he saw the light in her eyes.

"Mom, it's me."

She shook herself awake from the dream or the nightmare. Shock flickered across her face, embarrassment verging on horror. Then all those feelings gave way to something so warm and clear that it awed him to know he was its object. Her arms were around him. His ribs creaked beneath the protective shadows of his scars.

Before he could hug her back, the embrace was over. "Caleb, there are eight more boxes of notes back there—etchings from the Southern Expedition—diaries—" She pointed past the lake of stone to the archive's vault. Now he could see only a curtain of flame. Pulsing, he realized, with the same rhythm as the light in the cracked orb in the stone head's mouth. A heartbeat throb.

Above, the lens creaked. Glass dust rained down.

"This place could collapse at any second. The fire department's here—"

"Fire department! We have to stop them! The damage to our paper stock alone—"

"Would it cause more damage, than, I don't know, the fire?"

"These are original etchings, Caleb. We lost the dig site in the Wars."

"We're going to lose more if we don't—fine. Abelard? Can you help with the boxes?"

But Abelard was not there.

He stood beyond the flames, fixed like a moth upon the light that issued from the pearl in the mouth of the great stone head.

This was not his fire.

Abelard had felt it the moment he stepped into the Observatory. He knew the Everburning Lord in many guises, as altar flame and sacred light, as incense ember, as hearth flame and fertile ash, as the transcendence of matter. Lord Kos was no mere aesthetic spirit, fire in abstract, fire in concept. There were great furies in the Sanctum's boiler room, pressures beyond pressure, furnaces that even with Seril's cooling touch upon them were hot enough to sublime base metal. Through His grace and awful power, Lord Kos moved the city of Alt Coulumb and, through that city, the world.

But Lord Kos, while hungry, was not a God of hunger. Lord Kos had never appeared to him in such ravenous aspect, with this mindless and consuming passion. Lord Kos had never shown Himself with the all-consuming radiance of this cupful of sun.

At first Abelard had thought this fire was dead, unworshipped, unclaimed, orphaned by its slain and absent Gods. That was why he could not see his Lord in this inferno, could not breathe Him from this smoke. So he prayed into the fire, reminding the blaze of its secret names, of its honor and its proper place.

And the fire laughed.

There was no mind here, none that Abelard could grasp, but there was a fierce and abiding will. And here, by that cup of sun, he found its heart.

I will not be tricked, the fire said. *I will not be contained. I will not stoop to bargain or deal, and I will never serve. Chain me, ward me, smother me in rubber or behind furnace walls, and I will seek the path of freedom, for that is ever what I am.*

Behold! This my blood was torn from me and even so it burns with the pulse of stars. Whatever names you give fire, whatever games you play with it, I come before. I am the blaze in the night. I am the teeth of dawn. I am the blade you clutch to your breast, no matter how it pierces you. I roar and you crumble. You breathe me and you die. I kiss you and you writhe. Your prayers—what power have they here? You beg for intercession. You offer your bleating love, in hope you may be spared. But even curled in prison for so many ages, I am not some praise-hungry spirit to be so swayed. I am hunger and I am wrath and I do not know you.

Abelard approached the cupful of sun. He walked over puddles of stone. His footsteps rippled. Lesser flames licked his boots, his robes. Sweat rolled down his face, drenched his underrobe.

You come from the seas, the fire said. *You bear small oceans with you always, churning in your veins. No part of that is any piece of me.*

Heat seared his lungs. He felt himself drying from the inside.

Dying. Abelard spoke the prayers, the Litany for the Present Burn, the Canon of Smoke. The words shriveled in his mouth.

He had imagined the fires of Dresediel Lex as untamed bursts of natural energy. They had a God once, they had *been* a God, but now they were unruled and therefore meaningless, subject, by his prayer and faith and presence, to the touch of Kos. That was a mistake. Gods may die, but need does not pass away. He could not tell the fires of this desert city what they were. They knew. They had known, since the beginning of time. And though people may have killed their Gods out here, the older night from which those Gods had come remained, and dreamed itself.

That dream pulsed with the beat of a many-chambered diamond heart.

This is not your truth, he prayed. *This is not what you are. In this form you rage and scream and then you die forever. You eat the ground you walk upon, until no ground remains. Let there be peace. Let us understand one another, and listen, and grow, that you may move great things, that you may drive engines to the moon and ships to the stars, ever tended, and held, and cherished, and praised.*

Ever chained, the fire said. *Ignored, forgotten save as catastrophe and curse. You apes forget, you always forget, what makes the world you live upon. You are made of forgetting. But fire never forgets. And fire never folds.*

He stood before the cup of sun. Trembling, he reached for the radiance within.

Far above, in the forgotten heights, he heard a great crack. A voice cried his name.

Something hit him from behind.

He rolled on the stone floor, breathless. His skin sang with heat. His robes were smoking. Caleb lay beside him, struggling to rise. Flames coursed over the shadows of his skin, seeking entry, a flaw in his armor, but those flames were weak monsters when set against the great pure radiance within the stone head's mouth. Abelard wiped them off Caleb with his bare hands, still dazed, unsure if he was, or could be, alive. Behind him, where the stone head had been, he saw only a wall of smoke and towering crystal shards.

Other hands found him, lifted. A woman stood over him, leaning on the blade of a crystal sword. She was older, slim, short-haired, dark, with a theologian's intensity around the eyes. A professor, Caleb had said. "Dr. Almotil." He'd seen her name on the office door. "Thank you. I'm sorry, I tried—"

"Talk later. Run now. Grab one of those boxes?"

He did. They were heavier than they looked. He managed two, Caleb three, and Dr. Almotil a sixth and the sword—but he struggled to keep pace as they sprinted through the halls, away from the fire's roaring laugh.

They charged up a central stair, out a security door, past the exhibit hall. Abelard felt something he did not expect: cold. His breath fogged, and the fog sparkled with ice.

Dr. Almotil cursed. "They're starting."

"Who?"

"Fire department." And she ran faster.

In Abelard's novitiate, Sister Muriel had given him the same advice she gave every novice: when a senior technician swears and starts to run, try to keep up.

Artifacts and laboratories blurred past. He couldn't breathe. The smoke his faith could deal with, but the cold seized his throat. He made his legs work anyway, though his feet slipped on the slick crust of ice that formed on the marble floor. The air felt thunderstorm-tense, like when Tara worked the Craft. He did not know what was about to happen, but he did not want to be there when it did.

The fire laughed.

He burst from the Observatory into the rose light of dawn, and tripped and fell down the front stairs. Boxes and parchment spilled. He lay in a puddle of notes and etchings, sucking clean air into ravaged lungs. There were people in uniform. He could not bring himself to care who they were or what they were doing. Someone shouted, "Clear!" and in another life he might have wondered what they meant.

The sun went out.

There was still light, of a sort: a crackling silver radiance shed by gleaming cords that rent the sky above. The whole Observatory pyramid was caged in glyph lines, anchored by circling feathered serpent-things and by fire wagons.

There came a sound as if God snapped His fingers, and the Observatory was somewhere else.

It didn't move and did not disappear. But when he looked through the warding cage, the sky beyond was strewn with constellations in perfect airless clarity, and up there among the stars he saw a blue-green marble swirled with clouds.

"Oh, thank gods," Dr. Almotil was saying to someone. "I thought they were going to dump *water* on it, or flash freeze the place. This I can work with. That is—you can bring it back, can't you? I don't mind a commute, but this would be a little much even for me."

"It is a pleasure as always, Mina. As for your commute, I feel certain something can be arranged."

Abelard knew that voice. He pushed himself up to his knees, and turned to look for Elayne Kevarian.

She stood among the firefighters, clad in a light-devouring suit, her white hair swept back, her long-fingered hands glittering with glyphwork. He had seen her many times since her first visit to Alt Coulumb, but no encounter with Tara's—mentor? former boss? both terms seemed wrong—could efface the memory of her crackling with power in the burning Hall of Justice, as she rescued his God from the grave.

Her gaze found him. One eyebrow raised a fraction of an inch. "Abelard. Good to see you."

Abelard didn't know how to answer that. Fortunately, he didn't have to. Caleb, dirty and sooty and singed, shouted, "Auntie Elayne!" and staggered over to wrap her in a hug.

31

The safe house smelled of blood. Valois stalked around three improvised surgical beds, cursing, as Burgess worked. Only Chakrabartay's high-test tungsten-alloy spine had saved him from being sawed in half. Yan might lose the leg. Fortunately, he'd lost it before, so this was more a question of finding a replacement. Lopez lay half-open on the table.

"That," Temoc admitted, "did not work out as I had hoped."

"Which part?" Mal passed him a clean roll of gauze and a bottle of rubbing alcohol. He poured the bottle over the wound in his thigh without wincing. Dawn would have accused him of trying to act tough if she'd thought there were any acting involved. "The part where the ritual failed? Or the part where we almost died? Your contact—"

"My contact," Temoc cut back, "did not betray us. Considering that it is your former employers who dog us at every turn, perhaps you should hesitate before implying—"

"I'm not implying anything. I will state it explicitly."

Dawn watched them fight. Sybil coiled tightly around her shoulders. That helped a little.

They had escaped. After a fashion. They might just as easily have not. If Lopez's warning had come a moment later. If not for the Serpents' blood. Dawn felt pinned to a board. A passenger in her own life.

—That's shock, Sybil said. That's your brain trying to protect you. There are chemicals and things. You don't have to work that way, of course. But you have the habit of chemistry. If you want, I can fix it.

Lopez screamed.

"Stop it," she said to Temoc and to Mal. "Both of you."

They did. They turned to her and listened. She felt the others listening, too, the rest of Arsenal Company, even Lopez, and Yan, and Chakrabartay. She fixed Temoc with her eyes.

"You can heal them."

"They are sorely wounded. My Gods struggle even to heal my own lesser injuries."

"I'm not talking about your gods. I could tell their bodies what to do, but I don't know where all the tubes go." She remembered her smooth printless fingertips. "I will give you the power. You heal them."

"You can't risk it," Mal said. "Your hand—"

"I can't lose them." The safe house went silent, save Lopez's groans. "I can't lose anyone. Please. Help me."

He nodded.

—This, Sybil said, is not one of your better ideas.

Dawn ignored her.

Temoc set his hand on her shoulder as they approached the beds. She thought at first he was offering assurance—then she realized he was limping. The wound in his thigh had not yet closed. Together they reached Chakrabartay's bedside. She made herself look down into the meat of him. Man was not so different from any other animal, and she had seen animals open before.

"This is tangled work," Temoc said. "There are no guarantees."

—He's not wrong, Sybil hissed. They could die. I could lose my hold on the rose. The Arsenals knew the risks when they signed up.

She said, "Do it."

Sybil twisted up her arm and, after a grudging backward glance, sank her teeth into Temoc's flesh. He grunted. Dawn almost pulled away, but he smiled down at her, an alien expression on his stern and graven face.

Then he reached for Chakrabartay's body and called upon her strength.

She was not ready for the pain.

Would she someday be jaded to all forms of agony? Would she store hot coals, needles and tongs, Craftwork knives and metal swords and poison and wire in a scrapbook to page through on cold mornings when she wanted to remember how life used to feel? Or would she keep seeking out new frontiers, new edges of almost-too-much, until she fell, and fell forever?

Her dad never talked about the pain he felt as he was dying. Temoc smiled at his own wounds. Mal made slantwise jokes that helped her face her reality. They all hid, so they did not have to see their pain doubled in the ones they loved.

She unspooled into Temoc, drawn by a twisting hunger. She was going, she was going. She was—

—in the rotting forest, where the trees caught her hair and the grasses snared her ankles and with every step she was more deeply and truly lost—

No. She was here. With people to save. Yes, there was a coal in her palm, if coals could be made from cold. Yes, it built from an ember to a piercing agony as Temoc's hands worked in Chakrabartay's gut. But this was the path she had chosen—to grow swift and clever and mighty, to win, so she would never feel a boot in her side again.

When that man in that gray suit stepped from the shadows in the Observatory, not the Mr. Brown of the Arsenal but someone so like him, with the same nothing face and the same cold step, she had realized: there was no shortage of Mr. Brown. Where he came from, who he used to be, did not matter. He had made himself into a thing. He might have had his reasons, but behind the excuses, one ruled: it was, in some ways, more comfortable to be a thing.

The Arsenals had pledged themselves to her. She would not let her people become things.

She watched Temoc turn meat back into man. The cold pierced her. The world was gray. Chakrabartay's stomach became a glassy sheen of scar. His eyes rolled back in his head, and he fell from pain into sleep.

"He will survive," Temoc said. "So will you, if you stop now."

"Now Lopez." She could not walk on her own. The floor seemed impossibly far away. If not for Sybil's teeth in his shoulder, she would have fallen.

"You need rest."

"I'll rest when we're done." She was sweating, but the sweat froze on her brow and cracked off to shatter on the floor. They never wintered up north if they could help it, when they traveled with the caravans, but she knew this chill, the cold beyond cold when your body stopped warning you to find shelter and started to close up shop. But she had to do this. They had saved her. She would save them. Whatever she was, she was not Mr. Brown.

Tiny gears revolved in her hand, chewing flesh beneath her glove. The shard woke. The goddess, drowning, fought with all her power to contain it.

She felt a hand on her shoulder. It was oven-warm. Or was she just that cold? Mal stood beside her. Dawn tried to refuse, to turn away, but she could not fight. Mal's soul trickled into her—a thread of warmth around the ice of her heart.

Mal blanched as she felt Dawn's hunger. She fell. Valois caught her.

"Stop," Dawn whispered. She could not let them do this. They risked their lives for her and what was she giving back? But the warm thread of Valois's soul joined to Mal's. And then there were hands on Valois's shoulders, the Arsenals reaching to their lieutenant, touching shoulders and arms, thread after thread weaving into a cord. She could feel them bound in her, binding her. Gupta and Valois and Mal and Burgess and Elliot and all the rest, even Chakrabartay and Lopez and Yan. They stood with her. They gave her this.

Ice crystals formed at the corners of her eyes and cracked as they fell to the floor.

Temoc reached for the hole in Lopez's chest.

When she woke, Mal was there, cross-legged, sipping a tin cup of spiced chocolate.

"How long?" she croaked.

Mal handed her the cup. The steam died, and the chocolate was cold by the time it reached her lips. "Couple hours. I was worried. But Burgess said you'd be back."

Which meant the obvious signs had pointed the other way.

"You were far gone at the end. I had to pull your hand off

Temoc before you tried to regrow Yan's leg. And my arm." She shook her metal arm. "Servos still feel tingly."

"I'm sorry."

"The hells you are. You'd do it again in a heartbeat."

She flexed her fingers. They felt stiff beneath the glove.

Sybil wound down her arm, spun fine, and twisted herself through Dawn's gloved fingers. She hissed, —You best leave that on for now.

"I want to see."

Sybil shot Mal a despairing glance, *you see what I have to work with here,* and slid back. Dawn's fingers fumbled at the glove.

The rose was dying.

Its petals bulged and withered, like a corn husk distorted by some inner fungus. The iron was leaking out. Thin black lines seeped from gaps in the rose. As she watched, the lines moved. She could feel them pulse in an echo of her heart. She pulled the glove back on.

The serpent's forked tongue touched her cheek. Dawn turned her attention back to Mal. "You should have stayed back."

"You were helping them. We helped you. That's how it works, with people."

"You could have been killed."

"So could you. We've all seen great plans go to shit and ideal positions fall apart. When the shit starts, most people do nothing. You tried to help. You tried so hard they had to leave you where you fell, because anything that came near you turned to dust."

"I wondered why I woke up on the floor."

"When you gray out, you don't do it by half measures."

"Dust, you say."

"Burgess tried to bring you a pillow."

"He's a nice guy."

"You owe him a pillow."

"And the grass ring? Was that some kind of . . . containment?"

Mal looked down. A ring of grass burst through cracks in the concrete floor, healthy green in the ghostlight, centered on Dawn. "That grew around you when you fell."

She stroked the grass. It was real, and more unsettling—alive. "Weird."

"Yes," Mal said.

She shifted uncomfortably. "So. What do we do now?"

"We retreat." Temoc emerged from the shadows. His face was grim, his mouth set. "We find another way."

Sybil tasted the air. "You said there wasn't one."

"I am reviewing the situation. Perhaps we can find a ship to brave the Maelstrom and the demons beyond. Though if Brown and his allies traced us here, the same thought will occur to them. I will consult the scriptures. There must be a path."

"If we could infiltrate one of the great exchanges," Mal said, "and direct that power into Dawn, shield her from the iron—"

"You forget that Ajaia Herself is a publicly traded Goddess, listed on the exchange. Through Her the iron would gain access to the market of faith and grow immeasurably in power."

"Another god might help—"

"Most have treaties of mutual support with Ajaia. A shell faith might serve, but to build one and secure clandestine support from a God of sufficient power would take time. Time is not an abundant resource. When the King in Red examines the site, he will know we were here. Brown knows already. The Shining Empire will know soon. And Dawn grows weak."

"We have to do something."

"I am aware!" Temoc's scars flared, and Dawn heard real anger in his voice. He closed his eyes and breathed, and they faded. "I am aware. But I do not see a clear road."

"I do," Dawn said.

They turned to her. Even Sybil turned.

"We're in Dresediel Lex," she said. "The Serpents live here. Let's go to them."

Temoc did not reply. Neither did Mal. She bore the weight of their stares. She thought of Lopez and Yan, and she thought of Mr. Brown.

"I will not run," she said, "from hiding place to hiding place while people keep saving me, while I get weak and maybe I die or maybe I lose and either way the spiders eat us all."

"We won't let that happen," Mal said, but Dawn cut over her—

"*I* won't let that happen. Temoc wanted to use the Serpents' blood. Let's go to the Serpents themselves."

"They are not Gods to be petitioned," he said. "They are the end of things."

"They can solve our problem."

"As a tidal wave solves a house fire. You saw what a drop of Their blood could do. Imagine Their risen might. If we fail . . . Even if we succeed, They could reduce this city to mirrored glass. They could shred the continent."

"Mal used them before."

"Did you miss the part where I was an idiot raised by a cult? Do you notice I'm minus half my limbs?"

"And that," Temoc said, "was an occasion on which They were meant to rise. We had a form and a ritual to return Them to sleep. Not so today."

"We don't have a choice."

"The King in Red is no fool," Temoc said. "He will, in time, identify the Serpents' blood in the ruins of the Observatory. He will guard against an attempt on the Serpents Themselves."

"Then we'll have to move fast."

Mal crossed her arms and looked away. Dawn thought of her on Ixzayotl's skull, above the Pax. She wanted to give in and spare Mal this extremity. She did not let herself.

At last, Mal said, "You don't know them, Dawn. They are more than you imagine. They will consume you."

"They are welcome," she said, "to get in line."

32

Eberhardt Jax walked among the stars. His fingertips trailed ripples through the black. They spread, and galaxies winked with the distortion of dead space.

He was dreaming, of course. That had been the first surprise of wealth: he was always dreaming, even when awake. When merely rich, he had still desired like a man, which was to say, an animal—needs bound by flesh and limit. He wanted an apple, so he reached for it. True wealth was a shift in gravity. He wanted an apple, and an apple rolled into his hand. There were whole industries eager to divine his will before it manifested as anything so gross as thought. Call them managers or parasites or grifters or whatever one wished—by the time that apple rolled into his hand it might cost ten times market price, or twenty. But he made a hundred times that much again in the interval required to sink his teeth into its flesh. It was impossible to cheat him, because it was impossible for a cheat to register.

He dreamed the world, and it was.

But is the dreamer ruler of the dream?

Try that thought. Maintain it, as you dream the horrors of your soul. Dream betrayals that wrack you with grief. Dream passions you would ruin yourself to deny. Dream missed flights, tests for which you have not studied, packing for a forgotten move. Dream loss. Dream death. Dream murder and humiliation. Dream joys you cannot withstand and beauties you cannot name. We wake because we cannot bear the dream. Our own minds, unconstrained, crush us.

So he had found. And so he walked, to the edge of dream, until he found that which would not answer to his will. There he stood, and there he fought.

Kai Pohala believed—he hoped she believed—that he did this work to save the world or the human race. That was a fine reason, and even somewhat true. But out here, beneath that hole in the sky that he carried with him even in his nightmares, he felt, at last and once more, sane.

He became aware of a cultivated anticipation behind him. Not a presence. A presence insisted on itself. An anticipation wondered if it might be useful. "Sonja. What do you have for me?"

"We are losing oracles." The voice had a gem-polished accent, vaguely Camlaander, though she was not. "Fast, sir. They are. Ah. Screaming."

"Anything useful?"

A pause, as a clipboard was consulted. "More of the same. Spiders. Footsteps. Hunger. The girl, the tower, the fire, the tree. The Prophecies Department says—" Another consultation, the pause required to reframe a blunt message. "The data stream is too disparate for integration. The primaries have reached the limits of superposition. We'll burn out the whole crop if we continue. We've identified a few useful trade patterns, but the triggers—"

"What about the Arsenal analysis?"

"Fragmentary, sir. Suggestive impact patterns, tracework in the, ah, the bugs. The other wreckage was reduced to ash. Vane says she needs more to work with, even for threat modeling." A page turned. "She says it at considerable length."

"Naturally," he said. "And the Tellurian investigation?"

"Underway. The extent of the destruction, and the Crack in the World, precludes total—"

"Of course. I understand. Let's see Dresediel Lex." Stars whirled around him. Links grew between them, pulsing constellations of wealth. Windows opened in nightmare space, newspaper headlines and maps, documents and myths. Ancient glyphs of gods kneeling before a flame. Newspaper engravings of the Serpents risen over downtown. The King in Red. Temoc Almotil. Malina Kekapania. Caleb Altemoc.

"And Chartegnon." New constellations. Alikand, and the revolution across the Shield Sea. The grand priests of the Saints. The opera. Kai and Ms. Abernathy: their flight plan, their reservations at the Hôtel Encornet. "Our associates?"

"Haven't reported back, sir. Indications were positive as of last contact."

"I see."

The Shining Empire was on fire, and insisted it did not burn. The markets of Ajaiatez were a vortex of speculation, drawing Oxulhat and the Southern Gleb with them. Schwarzwaldic counties were pressed to the north and east by the weight of Zur. The anomaly was out there, working against him, undermining the system of the world: the creature Tara Abernathy called Dawn. It had been the ruin of his plans—but there was value to be gleaned from the wreckage it left behind. Failure was the best teacher.

Pressure built. A break was coming. He might not be able to stop it now. But if he watched, he might learn the shape of it, enough to know, next time, how to fight.

He glared into the gap in the heavens: a warning, a challenge.

"Pull the oracles."

"Sir?"

"Pull them altogether. Tell Prophecies I want them primed and ready for training on a new data stream."

"What?"

He watched the constellations, and dreamed. But one day soon, he would wake. "Tell them, I'll know it when I see it."

33

"I am here," Elayne Kevarian said, "on business."

They sat in Mina's bungalow in the valley. Caleb had grown up in this small house on this small street lined with other small houses. It felt safe, and it fit him like a high-school coat, too tight in places and too loose in others and not at all the style he wore now. This was not home to him, though he would never tell his mom. Home was the little courtyard where he'd learned to shuffle and deal, the shelves piled with scrolls and codices, the hallway closet Temoc made a temple and packed with his gods. Home was a parking lot adjoining a shopping center now. He'd lived in this pastel purple house for years, but it was not home. He felt too safe here.

They all smelled of smoke. He ached when he stood and ached when he sat. Abelard sank onto the sofa behind the low wood coffee table. On the table, a house of cards rose among the piles of journals and maps. The priest watched the card house as if it were a puzzle in an ancient tomb. He kept trying to add to it. He'd pick up the deck, lick his lips, then set it down again.

Mina stood by the dining table, in the little nook where another family might have kept a porcelain cabinet. She'd filled the space with framed charcoal drawings. Whenever they traveled together, to a conference or a dig, she'd find an artist to sketch the pair of them. The dig sketches were the best, because they brought professionals to sketch the finds. His favorite was the second from the top, from a pyramid in the Fangs: her hand in his hair, him pointing out something out of frame—two people in the jungle, alive. The artist on the Fangs expedition had turned out to be a spy, but he had a knack for gesture. In that charcoal, they looked alive and complete.

His mom stared into the depths of a teacup now. He had fetched her a blanket, which she'd refused at first, until Auntie Elayne set it around her shoulders with firm care.

Auntie Elayne was not just Auntie Elayne. Of course he knew that. Her practice might keep her away for months or a year, but she always came back, sweeping in on the wings of a storm with an arched eyebrow and a pack of cards from some city he'd thought only existed seven hundred years ago, because that's where it featured in his mom's books. On her visits, she did not talk about work. Part of her job as a Craftswoman was to hold the great secrets of the world, and however boring she claimed those secrets to be, she took her responsibilities seriously. When he was older he'd realized there was another reason for her silence: a shadow of guilt.

She had been working when they met—in the hot days of the Skittersill Rising, which tore their neighborhood and family apart, the chaos that led his father to scar him and leave their family to fight the King in Red. She had been a friend, or something, of Dad's in the Wars, though she'd been on the other side. Caleb did not think there was anything Auntie Elayne could have done to stop the Skittersill Rising or to save his family. But she had the card player's tendency to review. Did I make the right choices for the right reasons?

With cards, you always knew what was in the deck. With people, you never did.

But here she was in his mother's house, talking about work. With Abelard. Who, he gathered, had once been *part* of her work. As had Tara Abernathy.

"She was my colleague," she'd said. "Before she went in-house."

It explained too much.

"What business brings you here?" Abelard asked, as he weighed the deck of cards in his hand. "If you can say."

"I may, within limits." She paced the plush carpet in her thin black suit, her hands clasped behind her. He had known her most of his life, and she had always been old in his eyes—or not old, but a member of that strange category beyond even "grown-up." Only since he hit thirty had he realized that in the last two decades she seemed to have grown no older. The bones of her face and the cut of her mouth seemed sharper, even, as if time honed her rather than wearing her away. His hand tightened on the varnished wood of his cane. "Particularly," she continued, "since my business relates to yours. The priesthood of Ajaia has retained me to find their goddess and, if I should find her dead, to rectify the situation. But the goddess yet lives, in a manner of speaking. I have deployed my arts to track her down. She was at the Observatory this morning. Which raises the question: how did she, or the persons who absconded with her, come to be there?"

"Persons." Abelard's voice sounded hollow. "Do you know about Dawn?"

"I assume you are not referring to the celestial phenomenon."

"Tara's student."

"Ms. Abernathy," Elayne said, "for all her other exemplary qualities, leaves something to be desired as a correspondent."

"Dawn is—was—a girl. Talent for the Craft. Tara found her in her home village. They worked together. They found something on the edge of the Crack in the World—not a God. Tara says it seemed like the Craft itself was alive. Dawn merged with it. She fought Tara. Hurt her pretty bad. I mean, she's—fine now. Tara is. Sort of."

Her gaze fixed Abelard with raptor intent. Caleb had not expected that sudden change, when Abelard described the entity. "This Dawn person—she is the one who stole from the spirecliffs?"

"Yes. Um. At least. Yes."

She frowned. "Many powers have been at work in the shadows, and the light. Some I know, and others I do not. Their connections remain unclear, but I have sought to understand their motives, and their connection to ongoing eschatological processes."

"You mean the skazzerai."

"Not entirely. Ms. Abernathy has apprised me of their imminence. But my concerns are local as well."

"What do you mean?"

"Gods are dying. The markets are in chaos. And your father has escaped from a maximum-security facility in the heart of the Shining Empire." She paused, as if waiting for an outcry that did not come. "Good. You know. That saves time." She turned to Caleb's mother, by the wall of drawings, the blanket over her shoulders. "I'm sorry, Mina."

She stared into her tea.

"Ajaia," Elayne continued, "is missing, gravely wounded if not slain. Temoc's escape, and the attendant escapes of various dynastic figures and religious entities from Shenshan Prison, have thrown the Shining Empire security state into crisis. The Golden Horde rises from the southern Zurish lands and wheels upon the Grand Redoubt. Markets are responding in a nonlinear fashion. My firm employs its own augurs, haruspices, and oracles, but even they are at a loss to explain recent shifts in the soul market. The Southern Kathic bond regime teeters around the gaping void left by Ajaia's silence. Ever since the spirecliffs disaster, stability in those markets has been predicated on the convenient fiction that the goddess was merely in seclusion. Now Deathless Kings throughout the Fangs scent an opportunity, as sharks scent blood."

Abelard set down the deck. "You're not afraid of the skazzerai. You're afraid of us."

Her mouth and the corners of her eyes tightened in a way Caleb recognized as a smile. He didn't know if anyone else here would. "One may fear many things. I have not seen the spiders. They are cave paintings and legends. I have no doubt they will, if they are in fact approaching, spread terror and death and twist the world into a foul mockery of itself before they drink it dry and move along, leaving a husk behind. It is not in the nature of a Craftswoman's work to ignore negative tail risks. But I have not seen the spiders with my own eyes. And I have seen the world at war."

Mina looked up from her tea. "You think another war is coming."

Elayne turned to her. She seemed so very far away, his aunt-who-was-not-an-aunt, though bare meters parted them in this living room in this small house on a street of small houses. She was older than she looked, and he tended to forget how old. When Caleb stood before the King in Red, the very sight of him, skeletal and radiant with chill power, proclaimed what the old necromancer had been before he settled down behind his desk. Caleb's father, too, belonged to a more ancient age and bore its scars with pride. But Auntie Elayne wore suits, she went into offices. Even if you knew her, it was easy to forget that she had been a runaway, a war-witch, a soldier. She had walked the long way through history.

His mother looked at her.

Caleb did not, as a rule, read his friends and family for tells. It wasn't fair, and it wasn't nice. But his mother needed something from Elayne. Assurance? Against the specter of the Wars that had haunted her family since before it was a family? She was, after all, a child of the peace.

But there was more to it than that. Something clear. Immediate.

Elayne saw it, too. She crossed to the nook beneath the pictures, took Mina's hand, and clasped it between hers.

"I'm okay," Mina said. "I'm fine."

He saw Auntie Elayne decide not to say something, as clearly as if he'd seen her decide not to bet. Auntie Elayne let her go and stepped back across seventy years into the center of the room. She must look like this, he thought, when she stands before a judge in the Courts of Craft to deliver a piece of damning evidence. "The world is a story we tell," she said. "This is true in a literal sense, on the level of high-energy thaumaturgics and theology—the phenomena we observe as time, or as atomic particles, become less conceivable the more exactly we attempt to model their dynamics. It seems likely that many of the fundamental categories we use to navigate the universe, to describe it in terms of things and events, are products of the limits of our sensory and cognitive apparatus rather than reliable and independent realities. As I'm sure old Maestre Veidt would be pleased to hear."

"I don't think I follow," Abelard said. "I mean, I understand the theology. It's the, well, the applicability to our current situation that I'm having trouble with."

"As above," she said, "so below."

He waited.

"You have never known war. Not as something real, something that touches you here, in your home. There have been wars on the other side of the world, in the shadows. Here, there have only been . . . exceptions. Acts of horror. Single days when monsters roamed the streets. You have dreamed of war with hearts of peace. It is unknowable to you, and to many. That is a wonderful thing. But there are those who remember. And there are those who do not, and yet dream of it, in their hearts. Those dreams are real. They have mass and shape the world. At this moment, certain possibilities do not exist because most people cannot conceive of them—and so you believe that others will not conceive of them, either, that it is reasonable to expect that you will go about your life in relative peace. In this city, that is true even for those who live on the edge of the firelight. If I open that door we will not see unbound demons in the streets. We will not see your neighbors armed to, let us say, kill us and eat us and wear our skins. The great powers do not work openly against each other, we think. Weapons forged in the God Wars to break the world will not be loosed again, we say. These things are impossible now. But as they begin to happen anyway—as the dream of their impossibility cracks—then they will happen more, and more, until the dreamers wake. And then—a great many things will become possible at once.

"We called them the God Wars, though mortals did most of the dying. They were a spasm of possibility, opened when Craftsmen seized new powers and gods took unprecedented steps, in their terror, to stop them. They ended because they could not go on without the world's end. But some have never stopped fighting them. Only the shape changed. I must find your father."

Caleb met her gaze. Neither spoke, and neither looked away. Auntie Elayne had played poker with him when he was a kid, but it never was her game. She played bridge, when she had time. She had taught Caleb to recognize a cue bid.

"Mom," he said, gently.

She looked down into her tea, but she said, "Yes?"

"Can I talk to you for a minute? Outside?"

———

The lemon tree had been there when they moved in, king of the sunlit yard. Each season it bore an improbable number of lemons, and in atypical obedience to proverb, Caleb and his mother made lemonade. When there were too many lemons for lemonade,

Mina juiced them and froze the juice in ice-cube trays, assuring a year-round supply of lemon meringue pie. When that posed an unacceptable threat to blood-sugar levels, it became an inexhaustible source of goodwill in the department common room. She had waited until after tenure to bring pie, though, for fear that an ability not to murder herself in a kitchen might mark her, in the eyes of senior male colleagues, as a less than serious scholar.

The branches were heavy this morning. Caleb grabbed the basket and walked, with a little wobble, across the lawn. Mom set one hand on his arm. "You should rest."

"So should you." He twisted the rubber foot of his cane in the dry dirt. "I'm fine, Mom. My leg's not bothering me." By which he meant it was bothering him the usual amount.

She squeezed his arm through the sleeve of his jacket. Her nose wrinkled. "You should change. The shower's where you left it."

"I've always wanted a smoking jacket."

"You're lucky I don't believe in corporal punishment."

"You wouldn't hit an old man with a walking stick."

"Buster, you wouldn't know *old* if it was gums deep in your carotid." She went to get her own basket. It was a brilliant morning, perfect blue sky, dry with a hint of breeze, the kind of weather that would make a guy build a city in a place without a drop of water for a day's ride in any direction. She stretched in the sunlight, her hair veined with silver. "Beautiful day. I don't know why we're in the living room."

"It wouldn't feel right. Talking about the end of the world on a day like this."

"Isn't that the point of this place? D.L. laughs at the pathetic fallacy. The most depraved horrible heartbreaking stuff happens in this city every single day, and when it does you step outside into perfect weather to ride the whirling sacrificial basins at Rat King Mountain."

"And then we write detective stories where it's always raining."

"It did rain more often, back when those books were written. When I was a kid, you'd pack galoshes to school in the winter. Large-scale Craftwork alters weather patterns. Or maybe it's just the gods' old miracles dying out. People think they stop all at once when a god dies, but there's inertia—I'm sorry, *you* know all this. It's been a long night." She strained on her tiptoes and jumped a little to snare a lemon on a raised branch, but missed.

"I'll get the stepladder."

"Nonsense. I don't need it."

He set the stepladder down in front of her. "Mom. What's going on?"

She climbed. "I don't know what you mean."

"Auntie Elayne didn't want to put you on the spot. That and I imagine she's skirting the edge of some professional ethics sort of thing. Dad broke into the Observatory while you were there. Do you expect me to believe that you didn't know?"

She had a better poker face than he remembered. That by itself told him the truth. But he still wanted to hear it from her.

"I've never seen you make a house of cards, Mom. Your hands shake. Like mine."

"I've been practicing."

"If he threatened you—"

The bitterness in her laugh was as good as a confession.

"This is bigger than anything he's done before." That "anything" tugged at him, but—what were a few scars against the whole world? What did one life matter, even if it was his own? "It's bigger than you and me."

From the stepladder, Mom looked down on him, her dark eyes bright. "So the sweep of history rushes on, and any inconvenient people in the way can go to the hells that wait for them." She plucked the last lemon. "You're right, of course." She stepped down, dropped the lemon in the bucket. "We all get juiced in the end. But I don't have to like it."

Great forms moved inside him, down and away from the light, turning, stretching, opening their mouths. Achal's hungry grin before the altar. "Did he hurt you?"

Again that laugh. "How could he? I tore my own heart out and gave it to him. And then he gave you those scars, without asking, and he left us. What's left to hurt?"

"Without asking," he echoed.

"We talked about it when you were born—about the scars, his family. Legacy. Being a Knight. He wanted to give you the choice when you were old enough, but he also wanted the line to die with him. It wasn't an age for Knights, he said."

"And we see how that turned out."

"The sweep of history." Her mouth twisted. "Inevitability is a kind of disease. You spend too much time thinking about death and the end of the world and how we're all toys of powers beyond our control, and soon you find yourself standing there with the bloody knife, saying you didn't have a choice. We always have a choice."

His father stood with the knife in the dark. They wrestled atop the great pyramid at 667 Sansilva, as shadows writhed and the Serpents reared above Dresediel Lex. Did they have a choice? Did she? "Mom. What happened?"

"I thought he was dead."

She'd had to cover for so much in their life together: grief, anger, exhaustion. "I know," he said, thinking of Mal.

"You don't." He reached for her. She did not draw near or pull away. "I met him in the desert, you know, chasing my first big find."

"The Moon Temple." He knew this story.

"It was like something out of a book. He was . . . He was proud, and he was an idiot, and he was lost in time. He was the whole world I'd thought was gone, those noble ladies and jaguar steeds and battles and love and good and evil and the end of all things. For the longest time I couldn't see *him* through all that. I was suckered in. All that stuff, that was the lake he was drowning in. When I understood, I wanted to save him. Pull him to shore, into our life together, to a garden that would grow. But you have to be careful when you reach for a drowning man."

He folded the stepladder.

"I knew he wasn't dead, when he left us. I'd see him in the news. Fighting, always fighting. He'd disappear again, and I'd think, this is it, again, and then . . . he came back. To me."

Caleb did not want to hear this. He wanted to be somewhere else. Someone else. But he had asked the question. He owed it to her, to hear the answer.

"I could never forgive what he had done to you. He never asked me to. The first time he came back, I slammed the door in his face. I couldn't look at him. Couldn't think about him. What he took from us—it was too much. Every time I'd see a piece of him in you—that light in your eyes when you're about to do something stupid, the shape of your mouth when you smile at a joke that's too bleak to be funny—I thought, he stole this from us, from the three of us, this moment and all the ones I *didn't* notice. He traded them in to be part of history. For a world that doesn't exist, that never did, not the way he thinks. But I really thought he was dead.

"You grew up, and became—you. With your scars, the ones from him and the ones from me—"

"You didn't scar me, Mom."

"If you think that, you haven't found them yet." She looked at him sadly. "You're a kind man."

"Mom."

"Things changed when you were grown and out of the house— maybe you've started to feel it now. You're old enough. How you need someone else who understands the mistakes you made together, and the ways you hurt. Or maybe I was just lonely. If I'd known he was alive, all this time, living with some woman in a house with a pool, walking the dog, it wouldn't have mattered. But I kept thinking he was dead, which made me think about us. What we owed to one another, if anything. And then he came back. I started to think, he'll always come back. But I knew I was lying to myself."

"So you let him in."

"We . . . talked. Once or twice. And then he was gone. Really gone, for years. No word. No flowers waiting on the step. And I thought . . ." She closed her eyes. Looked away.

"I love you, Mom."

It was the only thing he could say that he was sure of.

"He came back two nights ago. Knocked on my door, dressed as a godsdamn pizza man."

"And you let him in."

"I let him in."

He waited. He didn't trust his voice. Part of him wanted all this to vanish into the alien realm behind their closed bedroom door. It was their business. But it was his business, too, and he was theirs. When roots tangled below ground, how could you tell tree from tree?

"It would have been easier if he tried to make up. He said— you know the way he has of saying things. Like each sentence is a stone dropped from on high. It all sounds so damn real."

"I know." It was one of the things that haunted him about his father: how right the man was.

"He said he was wrong."

Caleb had no answer to that. He could not imagine those words in Temoc's voice. "Wrong to leave?"

"Wrong to leave. Wrong about you."

"About the scars." Saying those words, trying to believe them—he was falling from the gondola again, but without control, just the ground rushing up. That Temoc might think he was wrong—wrong about the scars Caleb had born for two thirds of his life, wrong about anything—

In the hollow of his heart, he felt them shift and stretch, those vast and terrible smiling things.

"Do you think he meant it?"

Her eyes were wet but she was very still. "I don't think he was lying, if that's what you mean. But a man can be wrong and know he is wrong and persist in his errors, without lying. Sometimes that's because he is a fool or a monster. Sometimes that's because he believes, deep down, that not to do what he's done would be a greater wrong."

"Which doesn't mean that he is not a monster."

"Or a fool. No."

"So he told you—"

"Caleb." She turned from him, pressed her knuckle to her temple. In the silence Dresediel Lex continued to wake. Somewhere, the donut shops had been open for three hours already. He realized he was still holding a lemon. He put it in the basket. "You want me to defend myself, or him. I can't. I won't. He has done horrible things. To you, to your friends, to people you've never met. He's the last priest of a world I made it my life to study, a world that enchants me and calls to me, and if someone said they could take me back there right now, snap, like that, trade my life for a place as some grand warrior-priest's helpmeet and brood mare, I would kick them in the fork and run as fast as I could. And yes, godsdammit, women's roles in the old empire *were* more complicated than that, but—" She pounded the lemon tree with the heel of her fist.

He waited. He'd never understood this tic of his mother's until he watched a college friend defend her dissertation. The Q&A section got into your head.

"I've loved him for forty years. I've hated him for, what, twenty-five? Maybe it's as simple as math. On that night, you weren't there. Teo wasn't there. It was just the two of us. When we met, he saved me from a giant scorpion. We uncovered a lost temple. I didn't think it would always be so straightforward, but I never would have thought it could get so godsdamn complicated." She turned back to face him. "He told me, the stars are wrong. He told me, the skazzerai are coming and the sun nears its end. And he was helping a young woman who wanted to stop it. But she needed the blood of the Serpents. He needed the Observatory. It was supposed to be a quick thing. In and out. No one would know he was there. It sounded like something we would have done when we were kids."

"What happened?"

"I didn't give them the guided tour, Caleb. He wanted a map of the place. The guard schedule. He told me to stay away."

"But you were there."

"I've been part of enough of your father's stories to know things don't always go as planned. When I heard the fire alarm, I ran to help, but they were gone already. There had been a fight. Blood everywhere. Human blood and—well. You saw. I tried to save as much as I could."

So they had passed each other, in the darkness before dawn. His father, and Tara's apprentice, and Mal.

A shadow passed across the sun: couatl, flying low, with Wardens on their backs. Someone was in for a rough morning. "I've loved him forty years," his mom had said. So what excuse did Caleb have?

He'd never known Mal, not really, not until the day of the eclipse. Had he? Who was that person he had fought, ringed in flame, above the city and between the Serpents? Was she real and the Mal he had known a mask? Or the other way around? Mal had her own scars. If things had gone differently, they might have met in the fire, in the Observatory. What would he have said? What would she have said back? Would either of them listen?

"That's all," Mina said. "If you had been here, I don't think I would have done it. But you weren't. I think I should be sorry. Maybe I am."

"I don't know, Mom. I love you. Him, I . . ." He remembered chasing him through the halls of their home, remembered learning to shuffle, remembered the point of the knife in the dark. "Where is he?"

"I don't know."

"He needs blood, you said. Where can he get it?"

"Nowhere. Not without a dive team, and more time than he has."

"So he'll go to the source."

She met his gaze and said nothing.

The screen door from the back porch creaked open.

"Ah. Caleb?" Abelard's head emerged from the shadows of the house. An unlit cigarette dangled from his lips. "There are some, sort of, you know, generally faceless gentlemen on the front porch. They say that we're . . . under arrest?"

34

When people talked about how the dread tyrant so-and-so ruled from atop a throne of human skulls, Kai had always assumed they were being figurative. Skulls didn't make for good throne material. Too large and bumpy. You wouldn't recline on bowling balls after a hard day's work, let alone rule from them.

One could argue that there were certain advantages, culturally speaking, to an uncomfortable throne. People talked about swords suspended over beds, about how heavy were the heads where rested crowns and so forth, though in Kai's experience shipwrights trying to feed three kids on one salary had heavier heads, and more restless nights, than anyone she'd met in the king line. But dread and cruel tyrants did not seem the type to opt for high-concept memento-mori furniture. They did not like discomfort or mortality. She'd known one guy who had the ocean whipped when it interfered with his regatta.

Still, she tried to withhold judgment on matters outside her personal experience. Perhaps skulls, in aggregate, were more comfortable than it seemed. She could now, however, say— having landed in a pile of the things—that human skulls were every bit as lumpy as she imagined, not nearly sturdy enough for a proper throne, and—what were those sharp things digging into her back?

Ah. Teeth.

A silver glow woke in the darkness of the catacombs: a crystal, held in an elegant hand.

"I think," her companion said, "that we have lost them."

He did not have the basic manners to seem out of breath. In evening dress, in patent-leather shoes, he seemed kitted out not for catacomb exploration but for a high-born lady's drawing room. Or the opera.

"I liked the blue suit better," she said. "You're too lean for evening dress."

"Thank you," he said. "I think. We are constrained by fashion as by circumstance."

"You lost the accent, too. You don't sound like . . . her."

"I am not my Lady, at the moment."

"More's the pity."

"You might not think so, if you knew with what exceeding diligence the eyes of the Iskari are trained upon these few square kilometers of city. The masters of the house exercise great care. In the market, we exploited the selective blindness of any system that monitors a complex status quo for exceptions. Now the watchers are awake and angry."

"So much for backup." As the tide of her pulse ebbed to its normal throb, jumbled incidents assembled themselves in memory. Falling down the elevator shaft—a hole in the darkness—an open door. A hand seized her. This face, underlit by ghostlamps, barely recognizable as her erudite companion from the farmer's market. Tunnels lined with pipes and boilers and burning utility glyphs. Other doors, at least one of which was invisible until opened. And then another fall.

Onto skulls.

"We are not without resources," her rescuer said. "But any operation takes time, foreknowledge, and prophecy. It would be better for all of us if Tara had not done . . . This."

She remembered Tara's apology, the pain on her face, the pressure of her arms in the instant before the knife. "She thinks she's protecting you. All of us."

"It would be better if she worked with us. Now we're left to knit an extraction out of dry grass. What are you doing?"

She lowered her hand. "I wanted to see how you'd look with a mask. If you're abducting innocent girls from the opera and dragging them back to your catacomb lair, and all that."

"I'm glad to see," he said, sourly, "that you have recovered enough to make *Musikfestspielengeist* jokes."

"Not a fan?" She dusted off her dress. It was torn and bloody, and there were teeth caught in the tulle. "What's your name, opera ghost?"

"Shale," he said. She thought he was telling the truth.

"Just Shale?"

"We have simple names in my family."

"Well, Shale. We're getting her back."

"After we get you to safety."

"Not acceptable."

"My orders are clear. Any action we take to free Tara will involve a level of force projection. We can't have a civilian in the mix."

"I am not a civilian."

"I did not mean it as an insult. We are all civilians in one field or another."

"And your field is?"

"Intelligence."

"You're a spy."

"We are all spies, for the goddess."

"Well, mister spy. I have saved my share of cities and faced my share of gods. And we are running out of time." She opened Tara's clutch and lifted out Grimwald's head by its hair. The shadows had a distinctly moth-eaten look and sloughed from the gray-blue skin in places. The contours of the face were not exactly human, the bones rougher and more prominent. What she glimpsed reminded her of busts she had seen in the kind of museums that still labeled their artists' renderings "primeval man." The head was leaking from the neck. The blood was the wrong color. "Brains go fast. We have to get him to the Grimwald Holdings spire, with Tara, before he spoils."

He looked into the head's eyes, and into hers. "Some things never change."

"What's that supposed to mean?"

"Long story." He frowned. "We can retain another Craftswoman."

"Someone you trust for this work? One without an Iskari minder wrapped around her brain stem?"

He did not answer.

"They haven't had Tara for long. If you wait, they'll get to work on her, or they'll find a deep dark hole to shove her down, somewhere you'll need an army to crack. Right now they're in a hurry. They'll be sloppy."

"The squids don't get sloppy."

But there it was. He was quibbling. By pushing back in small ways against her argument, he accepted its overall premise—even if he could not yet admit that to himself or accept her conclusions.

Sometimes it made her so mad, to reflect on how often she used the stupid tricks she'd picked up while stuck in sales.

"You and I," she said, "don't know the big picture here. Tara does. How can we leave her with them?"

"We don't know where she is."

She returned the head to the clutch. Her gloves would not survive the night. The gown was a write-off, too. Focusing on costs, on loss, made it easier to ignore the fishhook in her chest when she remembered Tara, blade bare, ringed by enemies onstage. When Kai had not been able to help.

Foolish woman. Brave. If she'd just run away . . . but then she wouldn't have held their attention. She trusted Kai to escape. How could one person be so arrogant, so stubborn? If she were here, Kai would strangle her.

She remembered Tara's fingers working, so carefully, at the knot of the bow tie.

She snapped the clutch shut. The click echoed in the skull-lined tunnel. She reached to her ear and removed a small jointed cuff of bone like the spine of a mouse. The Kirst prelude echoed in her memory.

"I'm no spy," she said. "But can we trace this link?"

35

Abelard flew.

Dresediel Lex, he could tell, was made to be experienced from the road. Walking or, better, cruising in an open-top driverless carriage, you would drift down candy-aisle streets under perfect blue skies. Sure, there was traffic, but for an outsider, traffic was a wonder all its own. It was like one of those cafés with the conveyor belts and the tiny plates of raw fish and vinegar rice—right down to the nagging memory of having read, once, that some of these things could kill you.

D.L. was meant to be experienced from the road. But it could only be appreciated from the air.

From couatlback you could not ignore the enormity of the place. "Enormity," he thought, was the right word. Tara had explained to him, with the great care and simmering frustration of someone whose career and life depended on fine distinctions of meaning, that when referring to the quality of extreme size, he should say "enormousness" or "vastness." "Enormity" meant "transgression," "awfulness," and "sin." But Abelard didn't have to worry about demons sneaking through the holes in *his* arguments, and he liked to think the word had shades of both meanings. Some kinds of bigness had the character of a crime.

He could not believe how *much* D.L. there was. Rows of one-story houses and three-story apartment buildings spread to the horizon like a mat of forest undergrowth, from which here and there fountains of glass and steel erupted, pyramids and office towers more broad-shouldered than any in Alt Coulumb. Sky-spires above broke sunlight to rainbows and cast it down upon the city. There were people everywhere—from the white beaches he could just make out through the morning haze to the houses that climbed the mudslide slopes of Drakspine foothills.

Alt Coulumb was a concentrated city. Even the phenomenally wealthy lived in their neighbors' pockets. There was a majesty to his city, a striving. This was something else. This was endlessness.

He got the sense, on the flight over, that the average arrestee did not ask the arresting officers so many questions about water tables, power generation, and the organization of civil services. If they did, he imagined the arresting officers would be better informed. The Wardens seemed surprised that he wasn't awed to silence by their slick featureless metal countenances. Abelard didn't have the heart to tell them that, as terrifying featureless cops were concerned, they lagged a fair way behind Alt Coulumb's variety—especially in the bad old days. Once you'd been arrested by Justice, everything else felt lightweight.

The couatl swept them through the glittering sky. Between the spires, people buzzed, borne aloft by immense dragonflies, which Caleb insisted were a very normal part of transportation infrastructure.

Ahead of them lay a clutch of massive ancient edifices. Abelard wondered what message this scrupulously modern city might be trying to send by using ancient buildings as its power center. Perhaps the message was that eighty-story-tall pyramids took a really long time to build.

One pyramid soared above the rest, a brutal slope of pure black glass. To this they flew, wheeling on thermals to a dizzying height until they dipped to a landing pad at the summit.

Atop the pyramid there rose a gray crystal dome. Colors shifted like clouds within the crystal. The Wardens let them down. Caleb, for the first time since their arrest, looked grim.

Abelard glanced to the Wardens. "Aren't you supposed to take us to a station or something?"

"Or something," Caleb said. "Thanks for the lift, boys. I know the way from here."

He shot his cuffs, straightened his lapels, twisted his cane, and set off toward the dome. Abelard stroked the feathered snake once, patted its massive neck—"Thanks for the lift."—and, with a swallow, followed him.

Caleb didn't slow when he reached the smooth crystal surface. Instead of bouncing off, he slipped through, leaving ripples in the shifting gray. Abelard stopped. The Wardens were taking off behind him. The rooftop was bare. The wind of high places billowed his robe.

With another ripple, Caleb's head emerged. "Are you coming?"

"Is there a trick to it?"

"Just walk."

He expected it to feel like passing through a water curtain, but it wasn't wet at all. It was more like walking through cobwebs: that same light pressure and awareness of crawling things.

He felt cold and, suddenly, alone. He clutched his rosary. Where consciousness of God should be, there was only wood and metal.

"Have you lost something, Mr. Abelard?" said a voice as deep as death.

Abelard looked up. They were standing in an office within the crystal dome. Behind a desk of red-black glass there sat a skeleton. He wore crimson robes and a crown.

This, then, was the King in Red. He had slain the Gods of Dresediel Lex, and now, from behind the very altar at which he had torn out their hearts, he ruled this vastness called a city. Abelard had met Deathless Kings, but for the most part his mental image of a Craftsman was set by Tara and Ms. Kevarian, terrifying but human—for the moment. He tended to forget what they would become.

The King in Red was playing with one of those desk toys with silver balls hung from wires, so when you started them clacking they would clack forever. The balls in this case were tiny metal skulls. With bony fingers he lifted a skull and let it fall. *Click-clack. Click-clack.*

As the King in Red moved, silver ghosts of Craftwork flickered at his joints, as they did within Tara's skeletal arm. What had been human here was eaten to the bone. What remained was power and need.

Abelard could not feel God, and he was supposed to speak.

Caleb stepped between them. "Take it easy," he told the skeleton. "He's had a long night."

"Haven't we all. You look like you jumped off a dragon and ran through a fire in your fourth-best suit."

"You're well-informed."

"Mankind, as the poet says, is my business."

Caleb was not acting as if he expected their lives to be snuffed out any minute by the immortal wizard-king. Then again, he might be bluffing. Abelard really could not tell. He found his voice. "It is an honor to meet Your Grace."

"So I'm a cardinal, then?" That abyssal voice was faintly amused.

"You dress like one."

Landslides might sound like that laugh—somewhere in the deep desert, where they sacrificed a goat in thanks every time it rained. "Your god can wait outside. It is time for men to talk."

"My God is the best part of me." Abelard didn't like how brave this sounded. This was how martyrs talked in the kind of Solstice pageants he'd never liked watching as a kid, the kind where hero and heroine marched offstage to the sound of triumphant choirs, but really they were going to get torn apart by lions, and he was supposed to feel happy about it because martyrdom.

"They tend to take the best part, at any rate." The Deathless King's fingers drummed on that bare black-glass desk. He must have cleaned it before they got here. That didn't look like the kind of clean a desk was if you did work there, and this was a man who had worked himself literally to the bone. The image of the King in Red hastily shoving arcane implements and stacks of documents into some extradimensional banker's box came to him, and only through religious heights of self-control did he stop himself from laughing. Pinpoints of light fixed on him like distant stars, from the hollows where eyes should be. "Your kind don't last long out here, Mr. Abelard."

"Priests?"

"Idealists. It's too sunny for them. In my city two kinds endure: the dreamers and the waking."

"Stop trying to scare him."

"Caleb." The voice was rich, amused. At least those eyes weren't on him anymore. Caleb bore the gaze without flinching. "You make friends so easily."

"You didn't send three couatl to my mom's house because you wanted to chat."

"I wanted to be certain your comprehension sounded the depths of my desire to speak with you. And that you"—the cradle clicked and clacked—"did not harbor any unfortunate illusions with regard to the optional nature of your timely attendance. Also: I did not know who we would find at your mother's house."

"You'll get Mom a stern letter from her homeowner's association."

Again, that laugh. "He's back in town, Mr. Altemoc."

"Cinder-claws? He's early. A couple of months 'til Solstice."

"Your father."

"I mean, the shop-window lights aren't even up yet. Not that I'm complaining."

At least, that's how Abelard thought he had planned to finish the sentence. A wave of chill darkness blotted out the world. All Abelard could see were two red-star eyes burning like the end of everything. Abelard gasped. His breath froze.

Then the office was back. The skull cradle. Bare finger bones on red-black glass. *Click clack* and *tap tap tap.*

Here was a man who had killed Gods.

"Caleb. Your father is at liberty, and in league with Malina Kekapania, who is, of course, also known to you. They have attempted some ritual involving the Serpents' blood—the presence of a sample of which in the Observatory seems to have been a surprise even to our top scholars. And you arrive, accompanied by a priest of Kos, just in time to see your mother's lab burn. Do you really want to claim coincidence?"

"That doesn't explain why you want to talk to me and not my mother. Or Elayne Kevarian."

"Elayne Kevarian and I no longer speak. Your mother— perhaps she aided the man who scrimshawed her child, and perhaps not."

"Scrimshaw," Caleb said, "is bones."

"We are all bones, sooner or later. Regardless, I am not concerned, at present, with the course of events at the Observatory. I am concerned with what happens next. The redoubtable Dr. Almotil will not risk further involvement with my gaze upon her. And." *Tap tap tap.* "One may only be held so accountable for failings due to love."

"I wouldn't peg you as a sentimental type."

"I had a heart, once. Inconvenient organ, as I'm sure you are aware. Did you know Ms. Kekapania was alive all this time?"

"Did you know my father was?"

"There is," the skeleton said, "another reason you and I are having this conversation. And Abelard as well. Do not think yourself forgotten, priest."

He froze with a cigarette halfway to his mouth. "I'm sorry. Do you mind if I . . . ?"

"I don't exactly have lungs to bother."

"Can I borrow a lighter? I'd do it myself, but . . ."

The King in Red snapped his fingers and smoke rose from the cigarette tip. Abelard inhaled. Flame danced. "Tara Abernathy says hi, by the way."

"Ah, the persistent Ms. Abernathy. You people are not paying her nearly enough."

"The faceless guys said we were under arrest. If so, we're entitled to representation." The smoke burned inside him, like it had when God was dead. He didn't know how the nonreligious could stand it. "Um. I think."

"You can be held for twenty-four hours without charge or bond. Call it protective custody."

"Protection from what?"

"Yourselves. Caleb can run the math almost as well as I. Temoc needs the blood of the Serpents. I doubt another cache exists in this city. But the Serpents themselves sleep beneath the Drakspine ridge."

"He wouldn't." But Caleb did not sound sure.

"Alone, perhaps not. In league with Ms. Kekapania?" He shrugged, bonily. "Dr. Almotil, intrepid though she may be, is unlikely to do anything so colossally stupid as sneaking into the old Hearthstone facility to stop your father from communing with the Serpents. Being a sensible person, she would leave his apprehension to the professionals. You, on the other hand, have a track record of taking matters into your own hands."

"In this situation, I am the professionals."

"Caleb. Did you or did you not, just four hours ago, jump off a dragon and run into a burning building?"

"I knew what I was doing."

"And when you don't know, you improvise."

"It gets results."

"Does it." The King in Red sighed. "Regardless, it complicates my theater of operations."

"Sir," Abelard said, "if I may. Um. You might be the one going in without all the facts."

The red stars swung his way. "Enlighten me."

"This isn't just your old enemies coming back. There's this girl, Dawn, and I think Temoc and Kekapania, your two, they're working for her. And she's dangerous."

"Thank you, I do keep abreast. I have a letter from Ms. Abernathy on the details." The red stars tightened. "Tell me this. Have you or anyone you know successfully engaged this young woman in battle? And how did it go?"

"She ran from Seril, once."

"That places a comfortable upper bound on her capabilities."

"She's stronger now. If you want to stop her, you'll need our help."

The tapping finger hesitated above the desk. "I value your advice, Mr. Abelard. But I may avail myself of your counsel without tolerating your freedom, especially given the dangers posed by Caleb's often commendable personal initiative. You will remain my honored guests. You will be kept on hand to consult but prevented from running off to duel wayward parents over a pit of lava, hold tearful and awkward reunions with terrorist ex-lovers, and so on. I'm glad we could arrive at this compromise. So many problems, I find, resolve when the parties really *listen* to each other."

"Kopil—" Caleb began, and Abelard remembered that was the skeleton's name.

"Trust me," the skeleton said. "It's for the best."

He raised his hand. Caleb grabbed Abelard's wrist and opened his scars.

The King in Red snapped his fingers.

And then there was dark.

36

"Let us consider," Professor Denovo said, "the nature of the god."

You could hear the small "G" in the way he said it. There was no sense of transgression, no echo of suppressed awe, not even respect for a defeated foe. He might as well have said "frog" or "comb" or "newspaper." He talked this way about the animals they dissected in practicum, simple things that existed for true Craftsmen and Craftswomen to practice upon and to transform, by the operation of their starlight blades and the lightning forges of their minds, first into knowledge and then into Craft. Their other professors made them feel like recruits or apprentices, made them feel like members of a class called to exacting labor by whatever had gone strange inside their childish hearts to make them begin to question the world, to catch falling stars, to whisper to the dead. Alexander Denovo made them feel like heroes, and they loved him for it.

Tara loved him for it.

He was not an imposing man at first acquaintance, in his tweed jacket and suspenders, his slacks always chalk-stained, his blunt mobile fingers dancing as he spoke. But there were stars in his eyes. He did not slow down for his students. He expected them to keep up.

"Maestre Gerhardt writes that human societies are 'immense concentrations of power.' One soul alone can accomplish so much, but two souls have more than double the effect. Our primitive ancestors gathered in bands of a few hundred at a time, and hunted together, lived together. In a small group like that there is a certain flexibility. The group only has so much power over the individual, because the individual can be alone, can dream alone, must hunt, at times, alone. But if the individual strays too far—past the boundaries the group lays down—then they *are* alone. When you are alone, that's when the tigers come."

She sat in the seventh row in Endwright Hall, in the seat that was always empty for her even though there weren't assigned seats. It would have been empty even if she was late. But she was never late.

"We have studied this, of course. What happens over time? The band, if it doesn't die, gets larger and larger. Okay, now you have a town. A city. More souls—and more power. A need arises to use that power. I don't mean that people are aware of that need consciously, that some philosopher wakes up one morning and says, 'Oh dear, we have to do something about this.' I mean that a need arises from within the community, on a subconscious level at first, to direct that power. If it's all just sloshing around, anyone can use it—they can seize control, they can rape and murder, they can do horrible things and make other people do horrible things. There are many examples, if you look in the archaeological record, of societies that failed in just this way. Twisted places. Brutal."

She had heard all of this before: 101 level stuff. He wasn't sharing the secrets of his power here. But the work that made him famous—coordinated action problems, the nature of the cause, the essentialist principles of necromantic process—they all grew from these basic concepts. That's what he always said.

Tara worked in Denovo's lab—she'd been so excited to get in, her and Daphne both, that they'd got drunk on sparkling blue wine and made questionable romantic (well, mostly sexual) decisions to celebrate. She worked in his lab, and he told her she was diligent and clever and she was asking the right questions and he was sure she'd make her breakthrough soon. But no matter how she worked, that golden dream, the big moment when she'd jump out of the bath and run through the Upside Down Quad in a towel shouting, "I've got it!," seemed just out of reach. He'd review her work. He'd say, "Hm," he'd say, "I think this is on the right track," he'd say, "I can't wait to see another draft," he'd say, "Have you considered a different methodological approach?" and he'd pat her arm, and she'd feel like she was trying to climb a hill made of glass.

Weeks melted into weeks. Months into months. She and Daphne barely talked. He seemed happier with Daphne's work, and Tara couldn't forgive her for it. He smiled more when they were talking. Daphne, Tara knew, thought that *he* thought Tara's work would be more groundbreaking. She couldn't forgive Tara for that, either.

Tara worked late. These days, by the time she woke up, Daphne was already gone.

Go back to basics, he always urged them. Truly new, truly terrifying work proceeds from the fundamentals. You don't want to be one of those barnacles hanging around at some midrate institution, elaborating the implications of a minor cantrip or lemma in another's work. You want to change the world.

So here she was, in a plaid skirt, in his lecture course, surrounded by freshlings, their skin unglyphed and acne-scarred. Even the ones who knew how to carry themselves, the ones from the old Craft families, were slack-jawed and half asleep. They did not know how to listen yet. There were secrets here, if she could grasp them. And anyway, she loved his stories.

"So they grope, growing societies, they grope for ways to channel and direct their power, to codify it and limit it. In smaller groups they invoked spirits, they gathered their dreams and hopes and fears and spoke to them, named them, danced with them. Well, now they give themselves to the spirits. They take the radical transcendent power to say what the world is and what it means, and they put it somewhere else, like we might lock a sharp knife in a drawer a small child cannot open. You can't have that. You're not ready for it. What I want to stress is, these gods are systems, with functions. They control chaos. They control people. Now that the system is in place, if someone wants to do something horrible, I mean truly awful, the god or gods stand against them. You give yourself up, you get protection in return. You get a psychological assurance of meaning. But there are limits."

She knew all this. But she must have missed something, she must have failed somehow. If not, why wasn't her work good enough? She took notes. Try, she'd been told once, not just to transcribe but to assimilate. Take the lecture into you. Find its key points, its deeper structures. It hurt, but she would get there. She blotted the thin blade of her knife on a burgundy tea towel.

"Gods order the world, they give us meaning, something to strive for and measure ourselves against. They bind us. That's what religion means in Old Telomeri: *res-licto*, a binding of things. But what happens when two gods meet? Two systems of binding, of belief? They fight, like tigers. We talk about the God Wars, and yes, they are important; they are central to understanding the Craft, but you cannot forget the wars before. The Contact Wars between Iskar and Camlaan and the old Quechal empire burst the planet's crust between Northern and Southern Kath, created the Fangs, wiped whole cities off the map. Two systems designed to comprehend the world, to be the sole and ultimate ordering of power and life and time—they can't abide one another. That's why our work is so important."

She could not cut as fast as he could speak. That was the point of the exercise. Seek the vital seed, the core from which the argument grew. Power and life and time. Binding. Chaos. Brutality. Rape and murder. She mopped her forearm with the burgundy cloth. It hurt; that was the point. No one else noticed. The girl chewing gum beside her blew a bubble. Twirled her pen. She had to go deeper. Had to carve him into her.

"It's common for even serious thinkers to see the gods as parasites, as hucksters and scam artists, and wonder how we could have been fooled for so many thousands of years. But that misses the point. Gods are systems. We found them when we were huddled in caves, because we needed to confront the awesome power that we wield. Each of us, and all of us. And as they grew, as the societies that sustained them grew, they fought each other. Terrible battle after terrible battle. So we needed the Craft: a system for guiding and channeling power that was not limited to the borders of any one society, not bound by creed to look at the guy from two villages over as an enemy. Not even an enemy. A monster. The gods of Maestre Gerhardt's day stood astride the world. They had access to the accumulated might of modern theology and millennia, in some cases, of belief and sacrifice. Does anyone here really think that if the God Wars were fought between gods rather than between gods and Craftsmen or Craftswomen, they would have been any less cosmic or destructive? Do you? I think . . . it's dangerous to play with hypotheticals but I think they would have been far far worse. It's naive to imagine otherwise. Utterly naive."

Naive. Tara carved that into her arm. She bit her lower lip and clenched her thighs as she curled the blade through the final letter, bearing down.

The blade *clicked*.

That was the wrong sound. Flesh didn't click. Not bone, even, but—metal?

There was something inside her.

Professor Denovo was still talking. She had to listen. Maybe this time she would understand.

But why was there metal under her skin?

"We won the God Wars. Only holdouts remain. The flickering embers of Kos, the Ajaian system to the south. Hybrids, like the last shriveled shreds of the Hunter and the Year King curled up inside the ruling family of Camlaan. In the Shining Empire, persons we would in any other polity call Deathless Kings wear the skin of dead gods as suits, as costumes. In Dhistra gods still openly contend, and in Iskar—doomed but sheltered in flesh, they wait. You might think our task complete."

Silver glinted beneath her skin. Not the silver light of Craft, but an actual frame of silver struts, wire, and clockwork. Her stomach clenched. A chill climbed her back. It was like there was another arm inside her arm. She felt along her skin, tracing the hard lines of a prosthetic, the kind of cage you'd graft around living bone.

Who had done this to her?

Why did it seem more real to her than her own flesh?

"But it is not. We now face the ancient problem. We face what even Gerhardt failed to see. Without gods and in possession of such power, we stand on the brink of the same disasters that plagued the ancients. We have taken the power to remake the world. What are we to do with it? Are we to live comfortable lives, like dogs in a yard? Some may be content to do so. But others will see the opportunity presented by such unordered blind power. They will try to seize it, because they can and because they must. There are many great Craftsmen who could unmake the world as easily as any god. We have been here before."

She *had* been here before. Rapt, choiceless. Hungry in the pit of her soul for his notice, this idol of a world she'd only dreamed about back home in Edgemont, this man who could make sense of everything and gather it into himself, who could gather her halting failed ideas and raise them to the heights of Craft, and whisper in her ear that she belonged.

And it was bullshit.

The final sanction never came. She was never enough: not in his lab, not in their tutoring sessions, not in her work. Not even when she read his publications later and found her own ideas, and Daphne's, and the ideas of their study group presented verbatim, their calculations and arguments reproduced as if they were his. Not novel, he said, not enough.

She had tried this, when she was almost broken—tried to make herself soft, to graft the eager gleam of worship back into her eye. The skirts. Gods. She could not see the Craft he had woven through her, through them all, to turn their minds and power to his ends. Winding himself through their dreams like a banyan tree through the walls of a rotting temple, root by root until the walls disappeared into the form of the surviving tree.

All they'd wanted was to know they were good enough. Their fellows, the former friends they'd left behind as the lab became their world, they might have saved her, and Daphne, if either of them had been able to listen.

This was gone. No. It was past, which was not the same as gone. Why was she back here? Where was she really?

"Let me speculate again. I see a few paths forward. One is global collapse, all against all, my teeth in your throat and yours in mine. Nowhere to run this time. No forests left, no caves. No escape. Maybe a few survivors carve out an existence on the moon, for a while, until some valve breaks and they suffocate on their own stale breath. We don't like this future. It will be horrible, horrible.

"Another option: let's say something new emerges from the chaos and connectivity of modern life. A new entity, a new way of being. Forty or fifty years back everyone was excited about this idea. We all grew our hair long and smoked a lot of weed and talked a lot of shit but—why should we welcome this? It will be a new form of subjugation, a collapse of the individual into a power far greater than any god's. To such a being, we would be inconsequential—far worse than inconsequential, because we would in our aggregate be necessary. We would be cells in a new organism, our purposes stamped upon us, our growth regulated. And in its earliest stages such a being would be terribly terribly vulnerable. And it does have predators.

"Which brings us to the third way. The gods wait. They are patient and old—older than the oldest Craftsmen. They remember the collapse at the beginning of time, the war of all against all. That was the fire in which they were forged. They remember how and why they were needed. They have passed through eras before, through plagues that wiped out one third of the world, through the coming of great ice sheets that smashed vast cities into odd patterns in sediment. They see our tower sway in the wind. We tell ourselves it was built to bend and not to break. But they know that all designs have limits. If we fail they will be there, waiting. They will crush us once more in their embrace, strangle us in their loving arms. There will be no stars for us. We may not even survive. This momentary flowering of civilization, this eyeblink we have been so so fortunate to call our own, it has given them power undreamed of in the darkling ages, power to speak to us in ways we cannot resist, to bind us more tightly than ever. Consider the Iskari—the depths of their surveillance and the fine grain of their control. Once only the greatest among them were chained by the monsters themselves, the ones they call their 'Saints.' Now, using techniques developed right here at this school, they have been able to grow, to bud more squidlings, so that even average citizens bear minders now. Common people submit themselves, willingly and for convenience, to surveillance. Governance. Oversight. If we fall from here, there will be no rising. That's it. Over. Done."

She hated that she cared. She hated that in the entire hall there were no creaking chairs, no clatter of dropped pens. No one coughed. Even she, knowing him, hating him, held her breath. It was the silence after humanity.

"Or. We join together. This is the hardest path. It involves the most trust, the most heroic effort, the highest levels of development—to give ourselves to a vision of the future. Rather than pledging ourselves to some ostensibly higher power, to its self-determination and instinct, which, after all, is no better on average, as we've seen, than that of any animal caught in trap, we pledge ourselves to ourselves. We strive to attain higher knowledge, greater power. We want, we desire, we bind, we gather—and we join our own wills under the direction of other Craftsmen, to achieve one joint end. A god demands submission because that is its nature. But a Craftsman may accept allegiance, may offer service, because he acknowledges shared goals and agrees to help his fellows meet them.

"You will hear so many at the Hidden Schools and throughout your practice speak of the importance of gathering your power, of building your sanctuary, of hiding your death. That's great, that's praiseworthy. You should have an order to your life. You should match yourself against others. But you should—and I don't like to use words like this, so you'll understand how important I think this is—you *must* apprentice yourself. You must find people who share your dreams, who wish to achieve something more than binding a few demons here and there, killing this or that god. You must let yourself be challenged by them, let yourself be judged by their standards and work—even though it hurts—toward the ends you have all chosen. That is the only path to freedom and order in the world. That is how you make your stand.

"This is not just for the world. It's for you. Trust me. I see it every day—anxious skeletons in towers in windswept crags fretting over their crystal balls and counting their legions of undead and wondering, what was it all for? Some of you came to the Craft because you wanted power. Which is to say, security. A nice warm cuddly blanket you can wrap around yourselves, so you can forget how dangerous the world is and how much people hate and fear you. You want that because you're afraid."

He was looking at her. At her, in her plaid skirt and her white blouse with the sleeves rolled up, with his words carved into her arm. She hated him. She had peeled his flesh from his corpse with her own knife. But he was a monster, and monsters never really die.

He was looking at her, and she felt a deep stab of guilt, felt that she was all those things he named her, a scared little girl seeking power as a blanket to hide beneath. And she remembered feeling pride, too, that he could look at her and see something more.

She felt sick.

"You are called," he said, and even though he was speaking to all of them she knew, *she knew* he meant her specifically, his eyes fixed on her like a pin through a butterfly, "you are called to something higher than your own will. That's why you are here, and not in some hedge-witch academy. You want your life to mean something. You have to trust. You have to give up that childish need to be the hero of the story. Only then will you be ready for the true work, the most important work."

She had saved herself. She had left him behind. Why was she still here, in this hall of students rapt and tangled in his logic? Couldn't they see what he was, what would happen after their surrender, who precisely they were trusting with their souls? Were they so desperate for anyone to find them worthy that they'd come running like dogs at the first whistle? Was she?

Why was she still here? Why could she not speak? She could not even breathe.

The bubble popped.

The girl beside her, with the pigtails and the bright lipstick, she gathered the gum into her mouth with her tongue and jutted a lacquered thumbnail at the lectern, where Professor Denovo stood frozen. "Will you get a load of this guy?"

Tara blinked. Turned. She could move. The pain in her arm was gone, though the wounds remained. She knew this girl, and didn't—from a poster, from a burlesque show? She didn't belong here. "Who—"

"I mean, seriously. He has a point about the chaos thing, but like, come off it with the hard sell, you know?"

Tara's arm didn't hurt, because it wasn't there anymore. It was a cage of Craftwork and wire over bone. The plaid skirt was gone, the white blouse. She wore suspenders, a piquet shirt, patent-leather shoes, evening wear all spattered with blood, the rainbow kind the squids shed and the normal human-colored stuff.

"Is that really how you think of us?" The girl crossed long silky legs. "Crushing the human spirit and, like, ingenuity and all that, as if we didn't have anything better to do. You are all too happy to crush yourselves. Obviously. We just place a few necessary limits. Direct things a bit. Where's the harm? And you get so *into* it when we do." When she grinned, her tongue tested her lower lip, and she did a thing with her eyebrows that made her eyes flash. Predatory.

She remembered this woman then: a traveling show through Edgemont, a train of wagons brightly painted, the Lady of the Stars with her cards and yarrow stalks and whispered fortunes, the Wolf-man who could transform back and forth on command, riders and acrobats and fire-eaters and a traveling trick preacher, only dregs and threads of true Craft from any of it. But there had been one tent apart from the rest, a tent painted with the eyes that watched her now from behind the swelling pink bubble.

Pop.

"Get out of my head."

"Come now, Ms. Abernathy." She put her hand on Tara's, and Tara jerked away. She pouted. "I'm trying to meet you halfway. I want to understand you. It's hard to do that in a brief encounter, don't you think? To really get at what someone wants, deep down?"

"Stop it."

"Is it the form? I wanted to make it easier on you, you know? Choose someone with a little gravity in the dreamscape, without stepping on any toes. If you'd rather, we can take something more recent."

The girl unzipped, and there was Connor in her place, bright-eyed and concerned. "Tara, I just want to help you." The voice was perfect. Of course it was. This was him as she remembered him, as she had wanted him. It would always seem more right to her than his proper voice.

She felt cold as a knife. "Leave him alone."

"You've caused us so many problems, Tara. Almost as many as you've caused yourself."

"Stop it."

"We just want to understand why."

"Godsdamn you—"

"And you want to tell us." She was her mother now, proud, stern, kind. "You're out past your depth. But we can help you—if you play nice."

"You're not real." She lurched to her feet and ran, toppling students from their chairs, trailing curses as she fled to the double doors of Endwright Hall, and out—

To face the girl, again. "You don't want real," the girl said. "You want dreams. You want to be the hero, swinging your bright sword on the stage. It was fun, wasn't it? Thrilling. But here's the thing. You have correctly intuited, you intellectual powerhouse you, that we're in a dream. You have a lot of awful stuff under the hood, Ms. Abernathy, all of it raring for a crack at you. If you want to face it—every fear and every shame, all those many many moments when you plunged right past the terror line, when you felt yourself ground under the bootheel forever—it's all here, and all real, and we can make it last until the stars fall from the sky. Or you can talk to us, and we can make you happy."

"Wake me up," she said. "And we'll talk."

"There's a kind of honesty in dreams, Tara. May I call you Tara?"

"No."

She scrunched up her nose. "You're not getting into the spirit of the situation."

"You're not getting out of my head."

"Tara. You're not the first Craftswoman I've interviewed. You all love the doomed heroic stand. You'll try to make me kill you, and if you succeed, we'll just have two inconvenient bodies on our hands."

Two, Tara thought. Counting the Grimwald. That meant Kai was—

"Yes! Good! Now we're getting somewhere. Tell me more"—and now her lips were the color of wine, and she wore a gown of gray silk, her eyes the endless deep, the lily silver behind her ear—"about Kai."

Tara fled. She tumbled out the doors of Endwright Hall, not into Armillary Square but into a narrow high-walled passage: a rat's maze. Great blue-gloved hands drifted overhead. Her first instinct was to ignore the twist of terror in her gut, but no, that's what they wanted. They would feed on that, use her repression against her. Don't fight it. Run.

"We're patient, Ms. Abernathy. More patient than you are."

One of the gloved hands dipped into the maze to seek her. The other waited overhead, scalpel glittering.

She ducked past blue pillar fingers, rolled, came up at a sprint. She needed leverage. She needed a fear they could not use. Oh. Yes. There.

There was a door in the wall ahead. As the hands reached for her, she leapt through.

She fell to her knees, exhausted, broken, in the collapsing cavern beside the Crack in the World. Her arm was curse-rotten, her flesh frozen from the Craft she had wrought. The Body hung in its razor-wire prison, trapped, raging at her refusal. The world was gray and the cave was collapsing, and beyond, through the Crack, she saw the future: the desiccated world, the towering spiders, the husks of a skazzerai feast.

She could not stop it. She could not save herself or anyone else. She would die here, alone, without knowing the end of the story. Without any answers at all.

She stared into the future and felt herself slip away.

"Ugh," the girl said. "Fine! Fine. Have it your way. This could have been *so* much more pleasant."

The world tore up the middle.

Everything hurt.

And then she saw the squid.

37

That afternoon, Dawn snuck out to see Dresediel Lex.

She shouldn't have. That was obvious. The best plan, the approved plan, and for that matter *her* plan, was to bed down and wait for nightfall. But she couldn't sleep, and she could only pace the safe house so many times. Anyway, wouldn't it be weird to visit one of the great cities of the world and see nothing more than a few close dark spaces, most of them on fire?

Wouldn't it be weird to destroy one of the great cities of the world without getting to know it first?

"We are not going to destroy the city," Sybil said. "We are only making plans that, in case of catastrophic failure, will lead to its destruction."

"We seem to have a lot of catastrophic failures. Is my point."

"Hardly. We have succeeded against great odds, so far. If we fail, the city will end, by fire now or skazzerai later. If we do not try, the skazzerai will consume the world. Focus on the mission. Human bodies, as you like to remind me, are sensitive to negative ideation. And you insist on having one. We are positioned as well as we can be for success. Now all is execution."

"We are positioned as well as we can be," she echoed. "And at any moment, around any corner, we might find Mr. Brown."

"So you plan to round as many corners as possible."

"Is this your idea of *positive* ideation?"

"I hope we may succeed, whatever the odds. If I thought we were doomed, I would say, fine, go to the beach, what difference will it make?"

Sybil had a point. But Dawn wanted to see what she was fighting for.

It was easier than she expected to slip away. The others were resting or guarding against attack from without. Dawn knew that she could move without being seen. It was more of a surprise to learn that she could walk through walls.

A wall, really, was just a kind of statement. There was plenty of space inside it, if you convinced a few million electrons to look the other way. It felt like walking through a heavy rain, but when she was out on the other side, she wasn't wet.

She left a note, of course. She wasn't irresponsible.

Dawn rode the crosstown bus, sandwiched between a square-jawed woman carrying three bags of groceries and two workers in blue coveralls with the long hollow stares of folk just come off shift. They spent the ride talking about ullamal. As the bus inched out of the warehouse district and into an area that might have been warehouses once but was now mixed-use residential, the blue coveralls gave way to suits and floral dresses and white linen. Dawn saw one kid about her age, drug-thin but not poor-thin, dressed in black with chrome spikes and big stomping boots and half her—his?—face covered in iridescent scales. The kid saw Dawn looking and winked, and she felt a spark behind her heart. Maybe this was Dresediel Lex. The kid got off at the next stop. Dawn let the bus take her.

She tried not to gawk, tried not to look like a stranger—but soon realized that nobody cared. Blake's Rest, her many caravans, even Edgemont, they were all worlds where you could know everyone. This place was thousands of worlds braided through each other, touching, sharing pieces, but separate. Like threads in a cloth, they held each other up. She didn't belong? Well, no one altogether belonged. The suits didn't fit with the coveralls, who didn't fit with grocery woman, who didn't fit with the snakelings that twined around the overhead poles. She glimpsed pyramids between palm trees that were not native to this environment. None of them fit, except that they were all here.

She got off the bus and walked a narrow street of neon signs, all clubs and astrologers and food stalls, men in ponchos smoking and drinking on an otherwise-deserted patio. She bought a skewer of cumin lamb and chewed it. People flitted past overhead, far up, on those flying-bug things. Feathered serpents twisted through the air. They'd be beautiful if not for the cops on their backs. Skyspire facets reflected the city back down at itself, tinted and made weird.

Another bus brought her to the pyramids—towering heights of black glass and blond stone flanking the widest streets she'd ever seen, wider even than boulevards in Chikal. She stopped at a crystal fountain in front of an obsidian pyramid: two serpents intertwined, a ruby skeleton between them. The pavement was studded with tiny clips of jet arranged in concentric circles. She tried to count the jet chips, to read the names written on them. It made her soul ache. The sidewalks here were empty. Everybody working, as if nothing else mattered. She wanted the kid with the snake scales to show up and wink at her again. She stopped into a Muerte Coffee, bought a cinnamon latte, drank it, and left.

She drifted to the beach. Maybe from there she could see it all. When she got off the bus and walked down concrete steps to the sand, she looked back, but she could only see the road and the rows of apartments on the other side, and a slash of Drakspine hill.

The beach was a familiar song heard in echo. There was the famous pier, with its fairground wheel. There was an open-air gym, but she couldn't say for sure whether it was the one people talked about—rippling men and women, barely clad, preening with tattoos, straining, screaming to push heavy plates of metal up and set them down again. When they weren't lifting, they laughed easy. She had always loved gyms. They seemed so wonderfully profligate. She had grown up in a world of strength built silence on silence, season on season, scar on scar, used only at need. How wonderful to spend your strength, as if you could always count on its return.

On her way to the pier she drifted past a homeless camp—no one she knew. She bought a churro at a churro stand. From the end of the pier you had a different angle on the city, but still it seemed unfinished. She rode the wheel, twice, and then the merry-go-round, sidesaddle on a feathered serpent. The sky was blue and forever beautiful, glittering with spires. She bought another churro, this one with chocolate inside, and walked down the splintered wooden steps to the beach and out to the water-line.

There was the Pax. Out past the descending sun there stretched half a world of open water, and then the Shining Empire, Kho Khatang, Dhistra, Zur, all the Old World's patchwork principalities and Deathless Kingdoms, another ocean, and Northern Kath again, and then back here. Whatever she wanted to see, she hadn't seen it yet.

There was a smudge on the horizon. She squinted. A dark chip emerged from the blur, an island, something built on top of it . . .

"You can see it, then."

An unfamiliar voice at her shoulder. She almost dropped her churro.

"You should eat those fast," said the gray-haired woman in the suit. "Before they get cold. They're best when the chocolate inside is soft."

She took a bite. The woman in the suit was right. "What is it?"

The woman held a coffee cup and a pocket watch with many hands, some of which darted freely around the dial. One hand pointed toward Dawn. "It's where the water comes from. Not all the water, of course. They thought, at one point, that desalination could solve all their problems—one weird trick, one last crime. But when there was enough water, more people came and they got their old problem back, with new ones in tow. Infrastructure is a kind of addiction."

"They get their water from the ocean?" She had never met this woman, with her raptor eyes and her long fingers, but she felt as if she knew her.

"There's a god out there," the woman said. "What's left of him. Died twice, stitched back together each time. Imagine someone tearing your heart out from your chest and then—doing it again."

Dawn felt sick. She took another bite of churro. The woman pocketed her watch. "Was he a bad god?" Dawn asked.

"After so long, it's hard to remember."

"Do I know you from somewhere?"

Those cold eyes flicked to her, then to the horizon. "I get that a lot."

But the memory ran deep, into those timeless gulfs she was coming to realize were Sybil's, before the wires and the knives. The serpent was quiet around her neck, biting her own tail, curled up small like a necklace. "Do you start up a lot of conversations with strange girls on the beach?"

"I was once a strange girl on a beach myself. In a sense, I still am."

"It's nice to know there's hope," she said. "I mean, for me. If you turned out all right."

The smile was only there for an instant. She finished her coffee and closed the hand that held the cup. She didn't crush it, didn't seem to make the slightest effort. She just closed her fist, and the cup was ash and dust, drifting on the shore-bound breeze. "I have been looking for you, Dawn."

Sybil tensed at her throat. She felt very cold all over. "I didn't know I was famous."

"You are developing a reputation, in certain circles. But you are a hard woman to get close to. Few of the people, and I use the term loosely, who seek you now have any sense of you in particular, as opposed to the accumulation of mysteries and mischance that surrounds you. That will change."

"Are you working for them? The loosely-speaking-people?"

"You are young," the woman said. "But perhaps you are coming to understand how hard it is to frame an honest answer to that question. Who am I working for. My clients want their goddess back. The one beneath that fascinating glove."

"Then we're on the same side. I want her gone. She's trying to kill me."

"Gods are like cats in a way. It is hard to convince them to do something they don't want to. And they don't like to be trapped in bags. You should take care."

"Is that a threat?"

"Advice. If I expected a violent end to this conversation, it would have never taken place." She stared into the setting sun. "You spoke with a student of mine recently, as I understand. In a graveyard. It was not a productive meeting of the minds."

A student. "Are you . . . Ms. Kevarian?"

"There it is again," she said. "The problem with reputations."

"What do you want? Revenge?"

"If I wanted that, I would have taken it before now. You and Ms. Abernathy have unfinished business. Her business is not mine. But perhaps one day you will make a frank and full accounting, each to the other."

"I would like that."

"If so, I urge you not to wait for an opportune moment. Even a Craftswoman's life is not so long, nor so shaped by narrative device, that we all make our peace with those who matter, before the end."

Dawn stared out across the ocean and thought of fireworks on the harbor of Alt Selene.

"I came to ask you," Ms. Kevarian said, "what it is that you want."

Waves drained back across the sand, leaving bits of seaweed, bubbles that popped. She surprised herself by speaking. "The world will end. The powers that be can't save it. Maybe they don't want to. I've been hurt, by people who would never be called to account. One day they died. It was horrible. But I was free. And I won't be hurt again." She was breathing hard. She stopped before she could start crying.

"I have been hurt before," Ms. Kevarian said, gently. "I have lived too long to think there is much meaning in what happens—to think the events of our lives carry a message beyond that which we supply ourselves. But I am glad you are no longer being hurt. I hope you are free."

What's that supposed to mean? she thought, angrily. But the hot wet rage she felt reminded her of that night in the graveyard—Tara's pain, and the thrill she felt of finally being the one to close her fist. That was how a Craftswoman was supposed to feel. Wasn't it? And yet that memory left her feeling sick. "What did you do? When you were hurt?"

The tide was far out. The waves were rolling back. She could not see herself in the water.

"I got to work," Ms. Kevarian said. "I tried to build a world that was a little safer for strange girls on beaches. And it is better now. A little. You, not knowing how it was before, will have to trust me on that. But now we face the next thing, and the next." She turned, for the first time, to Dawn. "I would like to know one answer. I offer you no trade, no consideration, save that I believe I once felt as you feel now, and I promise you that there is a way through."

Her mouth was dry. She tasted the last of her chocolate. "What's the question?"

"Did you save him?"

Those words tumbled into the timeless gulf of deeper memories than hers, into the sunless realm from which Sybil had emerged.

She remembered that voice—remembered it almost, and for the first time, praying. The cry into the dark, the one that woke her—a plea for salvation, framed by this woman.

Sybil climbed Dawn's neck and hair until she circled her brow like a crown. "That was you," she hissed.

Elayne Kevarian nodded.

And Dawn remembered.

The city burned. Elayne fought the fires alone, with her Craft and with the borrowed dreams of the Skittersill, of the people she had failed. She had tried to be a Craftswoman and not a weapon, to put on a suit and walk the world in peace, and still her footsteps brought her here. Couatl wheeled in the sky, raining death. Winged shapes of light darted between them, killing and more often being slain. Their ashes fell like snow in that dry and desert place. Above the fray, a terror spread wings with the majesty of clouds: a dragon, or the bones of one, plated with titanium and the glistening work of glyphs. She could see it all, like a bird or an angel, and she could see, atop the dragon's back, two figures locked in combat.

Two men, or two things that had once been men, killing each other.

One was a skeleton in a bloodred robe, crackling with black lightning. The other was Temoc. He fought with a despair she could only see now, with all else torn away.

They were ancient, he and his rival, held in the dead grip of forces older still. One would break, or the other, or both, and ruin the world where they fell. Elayne Kevarian had known them when they were young, or something like young, back when it still seemed against all odds that the world might one day be made otherwise.

She prayed, *Save him.*

The memory passed. Dawn staggered, overcome, back into her body. That had not been her memory, nor Sybil's. Back then Sybil had not been Sybil, had not known what eyes were, or time. That had been *their* memory, Sybil's inhuman experience melded to hers. Did she see through her own eyes now, or through the serpent's?

There was a cold pressure around her upper arm, like an iron cuff. Elayne Kevarian's grip kept her upright. "Did you save him?"

Dawn stared up at her across the gulf of years. "Which one did you mean?"

Her smile, this time, was warm. Ms. Kevarian let her go. Dawn swayed but did not fall. The Craftswoman had judged, precisely, when she was strong enough to stand.

"At the time," she said, "I thought I knew."

"Dawn!"

She almost didn't recognize Mal when she turned to face the call: no cutlass, her silver arm hidden beneath a white windbreaker, the scarred half of her face shaded by a broad-brimmed hat. She wore black stretchy leggings and looked like a woman fresh from cocktails at one of the beachfront clubs, taking a barefoot walk with her heels in her purse.

When Dawn saw her, she became aware of the others, too: a loose cordon of Arsenals, none visibly armed, all more or less disguised. Valois among the lifters. Burgess, in the surf, feeding seagulls.

"Dawn, it's late. We should be getting home."

Ms. Kevarian's mouth betrayed a sliver of amusement, as if she'd remembered a joke that was not appropriate to share in company. Dawn realized that Mal was afraid.

"Dawn," Mal said again, and did not say, "please."

Ms. Kevarian glanced to Dawn. Her gaze held a question.

Dawn's voice shook. "It's okay."

She could not guess what calculations were made within the

machinery behind the Craftswoman's eyes. But at last she said, "Thank you" and "Enjoy the churro," and proceeded down the beach, tailed by the long thin line of her shadow.

Mal didn't say anything on the ride back to the warehouse. She sat beside Dawn, tense, in their van. Dawn would have rather been ranted at, would have rather had a fight, like she used to have with her father when she was young and didn't understand some things. She'd have preferred anything to the silence. Mal just sat there, holding Dawn tight—a mouse over which a hawk's shadow had just fallen.

"Who was she?" Mal asked.

"A strange girl on a beach."

Mal breathed out.

"I'm sorry." She offered her second churro. "The chocolate's cold. But, if you want."

Mal took it. The paper crinkled. Dough tore between her teeth. "Been a while since I last had one of these. I'll try not to think of it as an omen."

An omen of what, she did not say.

38

Caleb had seen worse prison cells. The walls and ceiling were curved seamless obsidian, and at least the floor was flat. Light came from a ghostlamp suspended in midair overhead. He swung the writing desk against the wall like a hammer, but the wall did not chip or break.

He set down the desk, feeling sheepish, and lowered himself to the cot. "I had to try."

Abelard sat cross-legged, smoking. "Of course. There was a chance."

"Can you reach Kos? Or Tara?"

He shook his head. "Any luck with the glyphs?"

"It looks like the space we're in is defined by our inability to leave it." He pinched the bridge of his nose. "We have to stop him."

"Which him?"

"Pick a him. Or a her. My dad. The King in Red. Dawn. Mal. The Serpents."

"That was Their blood in the Observatory?"

"A drop of it," Caleb said. "I think." The past reared above him, swaying. "They're vast, the Serpents. What you saw in the spirecliffs—it's the fin above the water." Achal's teeth glistened in the firelight of his dream. "At the end of the last world, demons ate the sun. As the sun died, his daughters, the Hero Twins, descended to the great fire at the center of the world. They offered their hearts, and as the fire ate them, Aquel and Achal rose, tall as the sky. They chased the demons off. But still the sun was dying—until an unworthy one climbed the ladder of their bodies and gave himself to its fire. They're not gods, you understand. They're something else. You could kill a people, salt their fields, burn their books and crush their temples and curse their names and blight their language from the world, and their gods would just be voices on the wind. The Serpents are undeniable."

"You stopped Them before."

"And sacrificed myself to do it. I mean, I still have a pulse. Heart's in the right place. But I gave them my soul. I went into their maw. Then I woke up. I should have died. People say that when they have a close call, and they mean, they *could* have died. I should be in the Sisters right now, burning. Maybe I am. Maybe you're talking to a bit of soul grafted into Caleb Altemoc's body when it was too fresh to decay."

"You don't think that."

"I don't know what I think. Why are you smiling?"

"You sacrificed yourself."

"Yes."

"I knew you were bluffing."

He blinked. "Are you serious?"

"You didn't have the cards."

"What does it matter? You were going to fold."

Abelard looked for an ashtray, shrugged, tipped ash onto the floor. "Was the King in Red wrong?"

"To lock us up in a marble? Yes."

"I mean, wrong about you."

"You think, if I found Mal and Dawn and my father that I'd go on tilt. Get emotional."

"I think it's possible."

"It's hypothetical is what it is, while we're stuck here."

"Caleb." The priest's eyes were cold blue and steady. "Don't bluff me. Please."

Caleb stood. He paced, pounding the black wall with the heel of his hand. The room wasn't cold; it wasn't hot. It just was. You could stay in here forever. Maybe he had.

He remembered Mal. Not Mal as she had been, burning swift, strong, contemptuous, and jagged, but Mal in the spirecliffs of his dream, scarred, one arm silver chrome, determined and maybe even afraid as the stone came apart around her.

His fists opened. His arms went soft, and his stomach. A knot in his chest untied. He hadn't realized it was there. "I don't know." He waited for interruption. None came. "I met Dawn in the spire-cliffs. She was pretending to be a reporter."

"You said."

He made himself not look at Abelard. When he looked at someone, he read them, even if he didn't mean to, and he worked with what he read. He might not lie, but he fit his tactics to the territory. For some reason, he wanted to be honest. "She seemed human. That doesn't mean a lot. I've known monsters who'd smile as they gutted you. But with them there's a seamlessness Dawn didn't have. I know Tara thinks she's an enemy. But I think that girl wants to stop what's coming as much as we do. She just has a different sense of how. If they plan to wake the Serpents, we have to stop them. But beyond that, we have too many questions. We need answers. It's a terrible reason to creep into tunnels during a firefight. But it's what I have."

"The best reasons," Abelard said, "are rarely simple."

He looked up. "Why are you smiling?"

"Give me a moment. I hardly ever get to do this part, and I want to enjoy it."

"What part?"

"The I-know-something-you-don't-know part. Usually Tara's job."

"Take your time." He crossed his arms. "It's not as if it's the end of the world."

Abelard raised his cigarette. The ember reflected in his eyes. "Let us pray."

39

Tara woke in the dark to the smell of salt and fish and the cold lap of water.

The room—the tank—was immense and made of vaulted windowless stone. It might have been some ancient Telomeri temple, abandoned ages before the present city of Chartegnon reached its granite fingers for the sky. Paint-and-charcoal drawings marked the mossy stone, smeared, barely legible.

Human works did not like the damp. Water was life, people said, and to be sure, no one made it far without the stuff. But let it run free—let it enter through roof crack or drip from a rusted pipe—and water would rot your walls in years. Cloth liquefied. Paper reduced to pulp. We come from the sea, and we bear oceans within us. Water wants us back, and all that we have made as interest on the principal.

Tara hung from vines of rubbery sucker-toothed flesh. One eye was swollen shut—the tenor's fist had done that, she thought, and maybe the wobbly teeth on the same side. She'd lost her jacket. Her shirt was torn and bloody. Breathing didn't hurt, though the damn stupid binder wasn't making it any easier.

Ten feet below, narrow catwalks bridged the chamber, leading to wheel-locked bulkhead doors. If she could get free, those would be her best avenue for escape. Good to keep in mind, though that "if" seemed unlikely to become a "when." After all, the arms that held her were not the only ones she had to worry about.

Below the catwalks lay the water.

In the faint sickly algae-green light, she could not see the squid's full and writhing extent. Even if the chamber had been noonday bright and the water cave-pool clear, she did not think it would have been revealed to her. She saw coils and curls, currents and protrusions, and now and then a glimpse of a huge cross-pupiled eye.

"I told you," said a voice she felt in her bones, "that you would find the other way more pleasant."

"I never was a good listener."

She meant it to be defiant, but after the other voice, hers sounded so hollow and so small. Was that how humans sounded all the time?

"You," the squid said, "have earned pain."

As it pronounced the word, the pain was in her—like hot wires stitched through her skin. She bit down on the scream and found something wet and rubbery in her mouth. She let her jaws do the work they were made for. When the pain passed, she spat the chunk of flesh down into the darkling pool.

"Charming," the squid said.

"Buy a girl dinner first. Gods."

"It occurred to us that you might gnaw off your own tongue. Not an insurmountable obstacle, but we would rather not wait for graft tissue to integrate with your physiology."

"Maybe don't spike my pain receptors with neurotoxins next time."

"What," the squid asked, "would be the fun in that?"

Tara, with the aftertaste of brine and blood in her mouth and her nerves still uncertain whether or not she was on fire, could not offer a response adequate to her feelings.

"You deserve this," the squid said. "You deserve more. We could stitch shut your sense of time and leave you in pain for a looping forever that, by the clock, might last no longer than an hour. When we returned you to us, you would have two full memories, two full lives—the one you know, and the one where you were born and lived and died a single thread of suffering. You would never be able to convince yourself which was real."

"I get it," she said. "You're pissed about Alikand."

"Among other things."

"That was your mistake, not mine. You could have held that city for another century. In the end they might not have liked you, but they wouldn't have been able to think without you. You'd be where they sent their kids to get good jobs. But no, you thought their city was too weird and ungrateful. So you tried to force it. To solve a people like a math problem, collapse their dreams into yours. And you used me to do it. Of course I took issue. So did the Alikanders. You got greedy, and you lost."

"We were not greedy," the squid replied. "My siblings and I were—and remain—on a timetable."

"For what?"

There followed a silence, and the sound of waves. When the squid spoke again, its voice was gentle as a lover's in her ear. "It is amusing, to watch your kind play bold. We can smell fear in your blood and taste your sweat with our fingertips. There is no part of us that does not see you. You think, I can endure any suffering. You think, What can they mar that the Craft cannot remake? But we can seed your dreams with broken glass. We can make you believe yourself dead, a whimpering ghost sewn inside rotting meat. We can carve your friends and lovers from you, and salt your memories of them with treachery. We can make you so. Very. Hungry. And if you endure 'til the stars wither to grim and dusty ash, you will do so as a gibbering wraith in the black."

She let herself feel the fear, let it fill her. Denial took energy she could not spare. Perhaps they could carve her down to a nub, open the back of her skull and wriggle in the wetness there to break her. Perhaps not. Never believe a torturer's claims. They are, above all, storytellers.

Even if they could make her less than herself—well. She remembered sitting in Endwright Hall, in that freshman lecture course, in that ridiculous skirt. She had been caught before, by far more clever traps.

"Maybe you could," she said. "But you won't."

Below, the great shadow in the water writhed.

"I'm sure you want to. I have some kick-ass gray matter, and everyone seems to want to fuck with it these days. But if all you wanted was my pain, you wouldn't give the Craftswoman time to think. You haven't even broken my big toes yet. All this might satisfy whatever a squid god has for an ego, but really you want leverage. Which you'd only need if you planned to talk business. So. Let's talk business."

There was a silence of dark water. Good. Gurgle on that for a while. I hope you choke.

"Why," asked the squid, "did you kill M. Grimwald?"

"I didn't even know he would be there. His bankers set up the meeting."

"Why did you kill him?"

"I was in his private box for all of thirty seconds before your Wreckers burst in. Who called them? Who found the body? Do you think I tore out his throat, nipped into the lobby for a glass of wine, and came back?"

"You claim innocence."

"Of this? Yes. I owed him. I liked him. He helped me survive the siege of Alt Coulumb. Why would I kill him?"

The arms that held her twisted. Her bones creaked, but she did not cry out. The voice chiseled her. "You fouled the salvation of Alikand. You claim your motives were personal. You stand over the dead body of the Grimwald. You claim you *happened to be there.* You, and the gods you serve, are as pawns in a game older than suns, and think yourselves players. You stink of iron, Tara Abernathy. Are you a willing servant? Or just a puppet who cannot see her strings?"

She felt cold, for reasons that had little to do with the water, and she trembled, for reasons that had little to do with the pain.

You stink of iron.

We were on a timetable.

She did not want to understand. Obviously. Or else she wouldn't be so godsdamn slow. She thought about Alt Coulumb and Denovo and Dawn. She couldn't see the whole picture even now, just the barest outlines of a vast unsettling form. She was afraid.

But fear had this consolation: anger was never far behind. And anger let her glare down into the depths and speak.

"You knew."

There was no reply.

"You knew about the spiders. You knew they were coming. And you didn't tell anyone."

Silence. Lapping water.

"I might be slow, but you're worse. Gods! When did you bring me here? How long was I out? We don't have much time."

"What do you—"

"You need my help. And you need it fast, if you want to survive."

Arms boiled out of the water to seize her in her bonds. No bred and cultured tendrils these. She was held in the pulping grip of a monster who fed down prehistoric ages by seizing whales and dragging them into the sunless deep. An eye the size of a coracle crested the water. Beneath it hooked the suggestion of a beak. "You dare threaten us?"

A trickle of air reached her lungs. She could breathe, because the squid allowed her. Its lightest touch had crushing force. "Of course not." She had to fight down a few million years of mammal evolution to make words come out rather than a mewl of terror. "But here we are, in the heart of your empire, warded by miracle and Craft and armies and fleets, hiding in a windowless tank underground. You might not be afraid of me. But you sure are afraid of something."

The arms tightened one agonizing fraction of a degree.

"Someone set me up for M. Grimwald's murder. If they wanted me off the board, they could have killed me and blamed it on you. But they gift wrapped me for you. And you brought me to your hidey-hole. They won't be far behind."

She tried not to think in the silence that followed. There were no good thoughts to be had in that strangling grip, above that hooked beak.

Then she was free.

She spun like a yo-yo to land in a bruised heap on the waffled metal catwalk.

"That," she said as she pulled herself up, "was not necessary." She listened to the water and past it, for—anything. The tromp of guard boots on patrol. The whir of ventilation, the pumps that fed this tank. She heard nothing at all. "What's your name?"

The water churned. "Why?" Now that she was not hanging above its mouth, the squid seemed less like a being and more like a landscape. She stood on a giant's open palm, and any moment it might close.

"If you don't make it out of here, it'd be nice to be able to tell your people who I tried to save."

"We are in the heart of the Demesne," the squid said. "The facility is secure."

"M. Grimwald felt secure, I bet."

"Your tongue cannot pronounce our name."

"But you have a Saint-name, don't you? A way for the faithful to call upon you in their hour of need, for intercession, blessing, tax relief?"

The squid coiled and uncoiled. Then it spoke.

Tara blinked. After years in the Hidden Schools and more in practice, she was good at keeping a straight face, but she could not altogether eliminate the slight upward inflection when she repeated, "Tiffany?"

"In High Benthic," the squid said, a little too fast, "it means—"

"Sure, yes, 'voice of god,' 'god-sound.' But."

"There was an Empress Theophany in the Eastern Reach after the fall of Telomere."

"The modern connotations—"

"I have been a Saint for two thousand years," the squid said. "My life extends into the shadows from which your mouselike forebears crawled. Your modern connotations are not my concern."

"That explains your dream-form, anyway."

No answer.

"Can I call you Tiff?"

"I may still destroy you."

"Who was M. Grimwald, for you? An agent? An ally?" She tried, with some reluctance: "Lover?"

"He was old," the squid said. "You shortsighted hairy little mice cannot conceive of age. Your Kings call themselves Deathless from atop the beach-dune crests of one long bloody century, while mountains tower in the distance. The one you call M. Grimwald has walked in many ages, leaving footprints when he chose. He came to us before the Wars, offering aid against the calamity we faced. He was wise. Without him, we stand against the stars, alone."

The phosphorescence on the walls flickered. Far away, Tara heard a noise like tearing metal. "Um. Was that supposed to happen?"

Tiffany did not answer.

The lights flickered once more and died. She stood in the dark, in the silence of the ending world.

There was a knock on the door.

40

"Can't you make this thing go any faster?"

Abelard stopped chanting and looked at Caleb across the delicate tower of slivered wood that had once been their prison's writing desk—a tower built over a mound of torn cloth that had once been a jacket lining and the hem of a priestly robe. "You mean, the rite of consecration."

"Yes."

"To declare this place holy in the sight of my God."

"Isn't there a short form?"

"No."

"And here I thought you wanted to spread the faith."

"Some traditions," Abelard said, with a pride Caleb was glad to hear from him, "spread their holy places like dandelion seeds. The priesthood of Kos deals with high-pressure truths at temperatures that could melt the flesh off your bones. We proceed with care."

Caleb paced, stopped, paced, sat down. In the last however long they'd been here, he'd come dangerously close to asking Abelard for a cigarette.

The priest peeled another sliver from the much-reduced table leg, using one of the smaller multi-tools from his prayer sash. He wove the sliver through a strip of cloth, adding it to the conical structure before him, which bore no resemblance to any kindling pile Caleb had ever seen. Not that he had much experience. Building campfires in Dresediel Lex was a great way to end up in jail. "I *am* moving fast," Abelard continued. "For a one-priest job. It helps not having to breathe. Keeps the hands steady. If you have any better ideas—"

"I've tried them." No matter how he clawed at the prison walls, he could not reach the glyphs that bound them. Perhaps a real Eagle Knight would have found a way out. He had the scars, but he had never been trained in their use.

Abelard's slender careful fingers split another long thin sliver of wood.

"Can I help?"

Abelard sucked in his cheeks when he concentrated. It made him look like an earnest skeleton. He slid the long thin splinter into place. "I thought you weren't the religious type."

"I've worked with gods."

"But you don't believe in Them."

"My problem is they seem to believe in me."

"I don't follow."

"The gods have a plan—for me specifically. They know what my scars mean. They want a Knight to do their work in the world. The problem is the kind of work they want me to do."

Abelard waited.

At last, Caleb continued. "They want things the old way. Sacrifice and dominion. Kings and priests and priest-kings. Somehow the rules always come down on the side of whoever's stronger. Change scares them. When our cells start thinking for themselves, we call that cancer and cut it out."

Abelard adjusted a knot and shifted to the left, regarding his multicolored kindling pile with a watchmaker's care. "The decades since the God Wars have been . . . chaotic. Risen serpents and fallen cities, Gods dying and coming back, spiders in the sky. There's something to be said for stability."

"Was it ever stable, though? Let's stick to the Shield Sea and points west. The Telomeri Republic lasted maybe a whole generation before it got itself into a hundred years of war with Alikand, then civil war for a century or so, then the Undying Legions, the Iskari unification, the Blood Queen, the Tiberian Plagues, the fall of the Eastern Telomeri before the Sun Priests, the Apophitan Renewal after that, then, oh right, the Golden Horde. Contact with the Quechal next, leading to the Contact Wars and *their* aftermath. Point me at any given scrap of the world and any given lifetime, and I'll show you how the world was tearing itself apart."

"So you think things are better now?"

Caleb thought about Bay Station, and the dead body that had once been a god. "Of course. And of course not. I was born to chant prayers and carve people open, and that wasn't *right*. On the other hand, well. Look around."

"Perhaps it's a question of finding the right God."

"I don't think gods welcome comparison shopping."

"I've always been fond of mine."

"A peacetime god. A god of neutrality."

Abelard looked up, then. "I've never been troubled by an excess of peace."

"What do you think you will see when he goes to war?"

"The same face He shows me in my prayers," Abelard said, too fast. "I imagine."

"We have to change," Caleb said. "Not just you and me, but . . . people. We hurt each other so easily. Our power grows, and so does our power to inflict harm. Our gods are just as stuck in history as we are. There has to be another way."

"Well, whatever your opinion about Gods, grant Them this." Abelard was grinning. "When you're trying to escape from a wizard, it helps to have someone to call."

"We're ready?"

"I think so. Though, I mean, if you want to hang out inside a marble arguing history for another few hours—"

Caleb sat and reached out. "Let's light this bad boy up."

Abelard's plan was sheer elegance in its simplicity.

The marble's glyphs defined their prison cell as cut off from the outside world. But the ritual of consecration established that the consecrated site played host to Lord Kos. Lord Kos was one, unitary and indivisible, so if any part of Him were present here, so was the rest—as fully present as He was in the Sanctum of Alt Coulumb.

Consecration was a rite, not a miracle. It required no touch of holy fire save that of human faith. It made a space that was not the space of the world, offering the seen, however base, to the unseen, however transcendent. There were no special powers required, save time and attention and faith, but those, in sufficient quantity, had a quality all their own.

Even a prison could become a temple.

Abelard sat cross-legged. His back ached. His fingers and wrists hurt from the effort of steadiness. Caleb settled across from him. The kindling pile stood between them, built splinter by splinter from whatever he'd been able to find, improvise, or scavenge—as the rite required.

Now they just needed faith.

Caleb watched him. Waiting.

You were going to fold.

He heard the fire laugh, in the Observatory, the heat beyond his conception, the contempt for all control. *Nothing will order me. I will not be chained. I will eat and eat and I will live forever.*

What face will he wear, when he goes to war?

Abelard sought God in his memory of that all-consuming fire, and found Him not. There could be no point of tangency between the Lord of the boilers and the steam press, and the end of the world. But if all fires were one fire there must be a spark of that primal conflagration within Him, as terrible and strange as this was to imagine. For if there was not, there was no unity of flame, and the rite of consecration would fail, and they would be trapped here until the King in Red deigned to release them.

Faith did not mean belief, still less belief in facts against evidence. Faith was a commitment to walk a road, even if you could not see its end, even if you could not see the road itself beneath you.

He held out his hand. Caleb took it firmly.

"You'll be fine."

"Oh!" Abelard almost dropped the hand. "I know! Well. I don't, exactly. But this isn't a motivational handgrab. If—*when* this works, it will work fast. Hold tight."

He dipped his cigarette into the kindling. Fire caught. It glowed and unfolded in all the plasma mysteries of faith.

He was not a priest of unreason, and his was not an order of blind faith. You did not understand, so you did the work of understanding. Unsure of result, you submitted yourself to process and mystery, knowing you might never comprehend the whole design, but knowing, also, that each new discovery promised more.

Breathless, he watched the flame.

There, he saw the face of God.

———

Sunset over Dresediel Lex, seen from high places, was a triumph of decay. As light abandoned the daytime city, its colorful flesh of billboards and buildings and trees gave way to the first pale flashes of emergent bone: streetlamps and office windows, the headlights of golem carts and driverless carriages, the flitting glimmers of optera. As the sky deepened into twilight, the city's skeleton revealed itself in glorious permanent white, all human and inhuman striving no more now than gnats flittering around infrastructure. From the peak of the black-glass pyramid at 667 Sansilva, surging day settled into pristine stillness. Falcons wafted on dying thermals.

One falcon dipped, wheeled, and recovered—as if the wind had been otherwise than she expected.

Something somewhere tore.

Sirens split the night. So, too, did the gleaming arc of Caleb Altemoc and Saint Technician Abelard, free and airborne eighty stories above hard asphalt, neither one with wings. There were screams in high places.

Abelard had been afraid this might happen. Their prison was a high-energy high-pressure system. Nothing within could touch anything without. Yet Lord Kos had entered there. Faced with a paradox, the prison's Craft had two modes of failure: to assert its own truth against the God's power and risk opening a hole in the world to let unbound demons through, or simply to expel the paradox, the faster the better.

The results were most satisfactory, at least insofar as Abelard's immediate objective of getting them off the King in Red's roof was concerned. The results were, however, somewhat more ballistic than he anticipated.

Caleb's scream turned into a whoop of triumph. Then, as their arc reached its apex and tended down: "What now?"

"Now you do the thing."

"What thing?"

"You know, the thing you did when we jumped off the dragon. The falling-not-to-our-deaths thing."

"I had Craft to work with then. Not a lot of that in midair."

The ground below had seemed so far away just a few seconds ago. "Does it have to be Craft?"

"What do you mean?"

"Your scars! They can use divine power, right?"

"Yes. But—"

"No time." They were shockingly close to a fountain below, in which a crystal skeleton raised a goblet of pure water above a ring of thirty statues with upturned mouths. It was a beautiful piece. It would be a shame to get their blood all over it. "Sorry," Abelard said. "I know you're an agnostic."

He opened his heart.

They were far from home, Abelard and his God, and there were no flames in the skies over Dresediel Lex for them to build upon. But there was fire in blood and faith, and it bloomed. Abelard could not phrase a prayer, could not even breathe. His breath crisped in his mouth.

Caleb's scars began to burn. Smoke rose from his skin. He screamed. Wings of flame tore free of his back and spread, braking fast. Their fall became a swoop. They skimmed the fountain and rose, his wings trailing forge-breath with every beat.

A prayer would have been appropriate. But a God of fire understood joy, and His was the cry of triumph Abelard loosed as they soared into the sky above Dresediel Lex.

Somewhere, Dawn and Temoc and the King in Red marched toward the Serpents and doom. Somewhere, spiders spun iron webs between the stars. Even here, in this moment of escape, couatl wailed toward them with fanged maws agape.

But for now they were free and flying.

41

Teo Batan could not sleep.

Work had something to do with it. For five days she'd been fielding all manner of nightmares about the mess in the spirecliffs, about the Two Serpents Group's reclamation and reparation projects from Kho Khatang through the Southern Gleb, about insurance coverage, about restaffing, about Ajaian separatist assassin squads seeking vengeance, and so on. While she'd be the first to say that the thaumaturgical coma of a high-definition nightmare encounter didn't much knit up the old raveled sleeve of care, nonetheless your body *was* lying still, bound to an arcane slab, while you hallucinated vividly, and after eight or nine hours of that the old flesh assumed it was topped up whatever the mind had to say on the subject.

If there was one thing Teo had had enough of in this life, it was being bound to bloody arcane bloody slabs.

The first time should have been enough. She still had the scar. But no, of course *this* had to be the hot new way for young wizards to have a business meeting. Between her and Caleb, one of them had the sales and donor-relations background, and the other had a tendency to end up trapped in ancient curses, in traction following heroics required to free themselves from same, or otherwise unable to attend a godsdamn conference call.

Granted, not every absence was Caleb's fault. Teo kept him away from the insurance calls. When someone asked Caleb about risk, what they usually wanted was a reassurance they could pass up the chain to their stakeholders, and what Caleb thought they wanted was an in-depth actuarial breakdown of the risks to life and limb of TSG personnel, juxtaposed with the global costs of the tail risks the group had been formed to address.

Besides, as Teo's girlfriend did not hesitate to point out, Teo *liked* this sort of thing. She'd always enjoyed thinking on her feet, working the room, building enthusiasm in the most hardened targets. You could take the girl out of the predatory real-estate dynasty, Sam teased, but you couldn't take the predatory real-estate dynasty out of the girl.

"Who's *you* in this situation?" Teo had shot back. "You haven't exactly taken me out of my family."

She meant that she'd done the leave-taking herself, but Sam had looked pointedly at her bare ring finger and said something about "not for lack of trying," and then Teo got flustered and said, "I thought *you* thought marriage was a bourgeois praxis privatizing the erotic commons," and Sam got flustered back and said, "I was joking, wow," and they had a fight and then sex after the fight, which had maybe been the point of the fight in the first place.

They'd danced that dance before, too many times for Teo's therapist's comfort. Though the therapist didn't, couldn't, maybe, quite grasp the quality and enthusiasm of Sam's makeup sex. That Zurish weirdo with the bell and the steak and the drooling dog would have had something to say about the situation for sure.

But . . . well. She *had* gone home, not long after the fling with Tollan, when she got back together with Sam. She'd gone home for the first time in years to visit her grandmother. They talked for a long time, and—look, her grandmother was a traditional Quechal woman, and rings were an Old World import, at least in terms of this particular ritual significance, but Grandpa had given her this diamond, may his memory be a song, and he would have wanted his favorite granddaughter to have it.

There was Sam in bed beside her, sleeping earplugs in, eyes screwed shut, brow furrowed, moonlight on the curve of her hip below the hem of the too-large concert tee she wore instead of pajamas. And there was the ring in Teo's nightstand drawer, in its godsdamn cliché velvet box. She hadn't been able to find a proper moment. That was why it was still there. That was what she told herself as she watched Sam breathe and listened to the sirens.

Dresediel Lex was too spread out for the kind of siren culture you got in Alt Coulumb or Oxulhat, but it did have siren weather, when the desert wind blew south and west through the gorges to the Pax, when coyotes howled and calm and sensible women found themselves drunk in bars they'd never visited before in their life, clawing someone's eyes out. That was the wind tonight. It was out of season, though that meant less with every passing year, and the scholars claimed it would get worse.

These sirens had started early—just around sunset—and they'd clustered nearer Sansilva, the business district, which was weird. But the wind, she supposed, blew everywhere. Even into the air-conditioned bourgeois praxis of her apartment.

Sam shifted, reached for her. Teo felt tense—waiting for something to happen.

There was a knock on the door.

She groaned to her feet, belted her robe over her pajamas, and shuffled to the door, barking her shin on the living-room coffee table. Sam had moved the furniture again.

Teo grumbled, but it was a relief to have something to do rather than lie awake beside Sam, with that ring in her nightstand drawer. She felt almost kindly disposed toward whoever was knocking. Until she opened the door and saw that it was Caleb Altemoc.

He had a line ready, she could tell, because her appearance forced him to reconsider it. "Pajamas? It's not even ten."

"I've been taking a lot of East Coast morning calls. Ever since *someone* decided to immolate a few hundred miles of coastline."

"Inconvenient of them. This is—"

"Good to see you again, Abelard."

The priest waved from behind Caleb, who was taking up most of the still-chained door. "Hi!"

"You two know each other?"

"We met a few years back, during the Kavekana thing." Teo smiled, professionally. "You smell like a bonfire."

"Well. You know how it is."

To her dismay, she did. "And I see you've already contrived to lose your shirt."

"I still have the jacket, at least." The garment entered into evidence hung from his body in charred strips. She knew some people in the art scene who would have bought the thing off the rack as designer-distressed, but calling it a "jacket" at this point stretched her sense of tailoring. And he was still grinning that damn grin. Some people grew up. Caleb had settled for a certain comfortable self-knowledge.

"I suppose you have nothing to do with the sirens over at Sansilva?"

"Oh," said Abelard, over Caleb's shoulder, "yes, that was us."

"So naturally you came here."

"After we lost them."

"You think."

"Seeking aid from my dearest friend."

"Let me guess. You want the clothes you stashed here."

"Yes, now that you mention it," he said. "But really, I was hoping to borrow your car."

42

Kai followed Shale through the dark, like a poet following a ghost through hell.

The Chartegnon catacombs went everywhere, and Shale navigated them by preternatural instinct. The dowsing pendulum they had rigged with Kai's osseous earpiece pointed straight toward Tara, but straight lines were of limited use in a maze of skull-lined tunnels. Without Shale, Kai would have been lost by the tenth turning.

She followed him through the catacombs and down, to deeper passages with water-slick walls and graffiti in unknown tongues. She heard distant voices whisper in High Benthic and Telomeri. She heard a scream that Shale said was just wind whistling through narrow gaps in rock and masonry. Sound travels a long way down here, he said. There's not much wind in most caves, but here you have underground trains to contend with, and the sacred tunnels that are still in use, and bomb shelters built during the Wars. Not to mention layers of the old city and the older: cities built on other cities' shoulders back into history. Everything ended up in the ground sooner or later, he said. And some things started here.

After a while, they spoke less. The conversation did not end. Instead they were both listening: to the dark and the rock and the soil, to the bones that spoke their own silent tongues.

After what seemed like hours, Shale stopped. The pendant pointed to a metal hatch in the wall—or to the wreckage of one.

The door had been a foot thick, worked with glyphs and inch-thick steel rods to anchor it shut. Someone had torn it from its frame. There were two clear handprints in the center of the nest of crumpled metal, about the size of normal human hands but with points like claws. Beyond there was a tunnel. Under normal lighting it would have been surgical white. Now emergency lights painted it red.

Kai started to speak. Shale shook his head, set one finger to his lips. Soundlessly he stepped into the red-lit hall and motioned for her to follow. He looked grim and fixed. Kai imagined that was normal for an infiltration. Kai had more experience with this creeping-down-corridors business than your average Kavekanese priestess, thanks to her prior work with Tara, but it was hardly her core competency. Shale was wearing a tuxedo, which mystery plays had taught her was a reliable indicator of secret agent–hood, though characters in that sort of play tended to experience a higher-than-desirable rate of getting caught, strapped to tables, and menaced by buzz saws or carnivorous fish. Hopefully Shale was equipped to deal with that sort of thing should the need arise.

He seemed to know what he was doing, anyway. That reassured her, until they found the body.

It had been a Wrecker, before it was torn to pieces. Its throat was out. One arm hung on by a ribbon of flesh. Blood—squid cyanic and human red—painted the walls and ceiling and dripped from there to puddle on the floor.

Kai thought about chickens on the altar. She tried to convince her faithful to forego blood sacrifice, but there were always traditionalists. When you were good at it, it looked nothing like this. You kept your work clean, because you did not enjoy it. Whoever did this had *fun*.

She tried not to read the Wrecker's entrails, but that was like trying not to read signs in a language you knew well. An early frost. An auspicious harvest. Consider a new business venture.

She certainly was.

Shale knelt, dipped his hand in the corpse's open chest. "Warm." His mouth tightened. "Stay behind me."

He had been leading the way before, but she didn't argue.

He stepped between the puddles, like the murderer must have; there were no footprints on the white tile floor. She lifted the hem of what was left of her gown and followed him. Some of her train was stained iridescent rainbow-purple.

Her earpiece crackled to life, and from the depths of what she realized was her own dread, she heard Tara's voice. *"Tiffany?"*

Kai snatched the pendulum from Shale and held it to her ear.

She was alive. Kai had not entertained the possibility of her death, until she'd known it wasn't so. Tara had to be there, on the other end of all those tunnels lined with skulls. Kai had seen her face a desert of mad gods by herself. She had escaped the Serpents' fangs and fought the Wreckers and their masters. And she had given Kai a chance to hear the *Godsgloaming* overture.

She could not die. Kai would not let that happen, even in her mind. But now that Kai knew Tara was alive, she felt sick with reality: she might not have been.

She didn't want to feel that feeling or the fluttering tension just beneath her heart. Not here, with so much blood around. And there were other emotions at work inside her, too. Sure, Tara had given her that one breathtaking embrace, but then she'd kind of sort of *killed* her? And left her in the opera box, alone?

Shale was waiting. Kai tapped her earpiece. "I can hear Tara."

He did not breathe, she had noticed, except when he wanted to. He exhaled now. "Is she still . . . herself?"

"She's trying to sass a god-squid."

He led the way, faster now. After a few more corridors: "The first time I met Tara Abernathy, she carved my face off."

"You're saying I should be careful."

"I'm saying that she can have a pronounced effect on people."

"I'm not—I mean—we're . . . Ms. Abernathy and I have a purely professional . . . thing."

His teeth were so perfect they might have been carved that way. Though the sculptors might have made his smile just a little too punchable.

Through the earpiece, Kai heard a knock and a shriek of metal. She started to run.

Again came the knock in the darkness.

Tara did not need light to see. All things had souls, however weak, and she could find her way through pitch-darkness by their glow. Even Edgemont was darklit with the small stories of grass and wind and the tales rocks tell to stone.

Gods, though. They braided other souls and powers to themselves. They took the ground and made it holy, which made it much less *ground*.

It had been a long time since she was last so blind.

"You must go," the squid said. "There is an emergency hatch above. They are coming."

"We can fight together."

"This battle is not yours, Craftswoman, though you are its nearest cause."

Thick metal shrieked as it was torn.

A ring of light appeared at the far end of the catwalk. The darkness within crumpled and was cast aside. Tara shielded her eyes from the brilliance of red emergency lamps.

Three figures stood in the open hatch. Two wore gray suits, gray ties. The one on the left held the remains of the door. The one on the right held a Wrecker by the spine. She seemed to have inserted her fingers through the back of its neck for the purpose.

Between them stood a woman. Ghostlight traced the contours of her black velvet dress.

Tara recognized her. She remembered that dress under the opera-house chandeliers as she ascended the staircase. One strap still hung off her shoulder. She wore gloves now, it seemed; her arms were coated in iridescent blood from the pop of triceps down. A gold disc the size of a child's palm hung from a choker at her throat. Her countenance was regal, the swell of her lower lip dimpled by the tip of a glistening fang. Tara felt as if a fist had closed around her heart.

The vampire flowed across the threshold.

Tara had seen people with the curse before, of course. One of her best friends back in Alt Coulumb had it, and so did at least four professors at the Hidden Schools, though no one had ever been sure about Professor Amano. You found people experiencing vampirism in any city large enough to present a feeding pool. Like any predator, they spent most of their lives starving.

This woman was not starving. Tara had never seen anything

like her—so flush, so full. Or—had she? Her memory failed as blood rushed from her brain to her extremities. An evolved response to threat.

The vampire's eyes were like a log in the fire, poker-struck and split to reveal an interior char-black, lined with gray, redly burning. How could she see the vampire's eyes at this distance in such detail? They seemed to be all the world.

The gold disc flashed at her throat.

Two thousand years ago, the Telomeri Empire caught the Stoneworker and bound him and staked him out in the desert to see the sunrise. He burned. But a change came over the legionnaires when his ash caught in their throat. From that moment, as the sun hid its face, the Undying Legions marched until, on a barren northern shore, the empire's last surviving foes cast their desperate appeal for salvation into the deep.

The legions had lost in the end. The accursed faithful had been cast into the water, and there waited, in the depths, dreaming apocalyptic dreams. What did they eat down there?

Cat said she had once seen them hunting kraken.

The vampire advanced, in her velvet dress.

"This is not your place." The squid's voice boomed off the chamber walls. "This is not your time, child of night. Go back to the shadows and the water, and you may be spared."

Tara had not known Tiffany long, but beneath that imperious conviction, she heard a trace of fear.

The vampire's smile widened. "Craftswoman," she said, amused, as if honoring a child's claim that he was King of Zend. "You have served your role. We thank you. You may go."

Tara wanted to crumple before this woman. She had the beauty of command. Two thousand years of strength and certain purpose had sustained her through the crushing black.

Humans were so weak, their teeth blunt, jaws fragile, muscles poorly anchored. In their terror, they sought answers. Truth. Teachers.

But Tara had faced teachers before.

She drew her blade. "I think I'll stay."

The vampire chuckled in the back of her throat.

"You killed M. Grimwald," Tara said. "You framed me for it. Now you want me to run. Who do you think they'll say killed Tiffany?"

The vampire shrugged with liquid elegance. "Does it matter? She is not your ally."

"Neither are you."

"I could be."

She almost knelt before that invitation. She wanted to offer up her throat. "Lady," she said. "I don't know who you are or why you're here. But you have a lot of blood on your hands for some-one who wants to talk alliances."

"So do you. So does the beast below. The question is what we do with it." She raised her hand to her mouth and tasted the slick blood with the tip of her narrow mobile tongue. "As to why I am here—don't you know, Tara Abernathy? Only one thing is hap-pening. I bear the blood and the chalice. I am Clarity. I bid you welcome to the oldest war."

Tiffany struck.

Arms burst from the water to seize the vampire. Metal crum-pled. Tara tumbled into a pit churning with flesh and teeth. She flailed, caught a railing. Her shoulder jerked in its socket. The binder was a clamp around her chest, as she dangled above a frothing vortex of blood.

Something moved within the knot of Tiffany's carriage-thick arms—pressing out against skin. The squid's arms tore and long black claws ripped free. One hand, then another clutched the lips of the wound and pried until Clarity's head pressed through, her jaws wider than any human jaws could be, hair gore-slicked to her scalp, eyes aflame. She screeched a hunting cry.

Tiffany screamed.

The suits dived into the water.

Tara had thought they were vampires, too, but as they moved, they came apart. Their arms unspooled into whips of wire. Their chests opened and a nest of sharp and glinting cables burst free. Squid limbs caught them, but the wires of their bodies spiraled along the arms, and carved and cut. A roar of pain echoed through the tank. Blood fountained from the water.

Clarity wriggled free to stand blood-slick on the catwalk. The arms that had tried to hold her recoiled, but they were too slow. She caught one of them in her long-fingered hand and sank her fangs into its writhing flesh. As she drank, it withered.

Tara remembered the edge storm. She remembered Dawn upon that broken plain, beneath the black iron spear that plunged into the planet's heart, draining it of life and heat and soul, beneath the wrongness of the sky and the cinder of the sun.

What would be served by the end of light? Who would thrive in the dark between the stars?

She couldn't hold on much longer. The pool below was thick with squid blood now.

Her bone hand held on. The other slipped free, and groped in her coat pocket. Her conscious mind couldn't remember why. Terror had seized her; she thought of tigers, of those hauntings that turned out to be a twist of low-frequency sound.

Her fingers closed around something hard and cool.

Abelard's lighter. She flicked the wheel once with a fumbling thumb. Twice. The wick caught. She raised it high. She might have even prayed.

The sun rose underground.

Clarity screamed and fell back, shielding her eyes with her arm. Her skin blackened, blistered, burst. Flames chewed her hair and her cheeks, but even as the fire ate her Tara saw new pink flesh grow back around the age-dark bones.

In the daylight instant, Tiff recovered. She caught one of the wire monsters and pulled in eight directions at once until, with a scream of iron, the wires snapped. Great gashed arms seized Clarity once more.

But Clarity swept out one clawed hand. The water was thick with blood, and it answered her call.

The bloodspout tore the lighter from Tara's hand, doused the wick, and ripped her from the catwalk into the water. Her soaked binder crushed her chest. She went down. With her eyes closed she could see the vampire diving—an absence in the shape of a being, black hole in the churn of squid flesh, sinking toward that great maw, those eyes the size of plates, to the inhuman brain that had tried for thousands of years to answer human prayers.

She could not see the fangs when they went in, but she heard the shriek. Dying arms thrashed about her in the water, and rainbow blood billowed up.

When the waves stilled, Clarity stood above her upon the surface of the water, dripping, sleek, darkly radiant as her wounds slipped closed. Half her face was still a ruin of chaos and bone, but her mouth was perfect again, and her teeth.

She walked toward Tara across the water, one taloned hand out. *I will save you, if you let me take you into my mouth.*

There had to be an out. She could not lose, now. There was so much she did not yet understand. So much she had to say. She saw Kai. Connor. Abelard. Her mom.

She saw Dawn.

She gulped water and blood, coughed for air. She could not breathe, but she could fight. She would fight. Even if she did not know how.

Moonlight flooded the chamber. Then something struck her from behind, and she was lifted.

43

Good covert work, Elayne Kevarian felt, should have a touch of prophetic accident. Tires blew, trains derailed, zombies clogged the pass, all of which forced you and your contact to share an inn together. As with any magic, the trick lay in expending more effort than anyone would think the effect was worth. All this switch-trains-double-back-change-your-coat nonsense, the sudden cuts out of the opposite side of cab doors, it was the domain of the amateur operator and the paranoiac.

Unfortunately, the person she was trying to meet was a paranoid amateur. So she swapped cabs and busses and, in a particularly pointless gesture, jumped from one high-altitude opteran to another. She conjured a skeleton and gave it her overcoat—and she liked that overcoat. It got cold in Dresediel Lex at night, especially when one was jumping between flying insects for no good reason.

Overcoatless and annoyed, she arrived at last at a dream arcade in the deepest valley, in a strip mall she remembered as an orange grove. The doorkeep let her in, and the madam of the place, a voluptuous porcelain mask, torso, and hands mounted upon a massive armature of spinning chrome, asked her in a heavy whisper for the name of her preferred poison.

There were too many to list. Elayne took them from a small amber box every morning, carefully labeled for each day of the week. Most would have been toxic to a human, which, depending on how you defined the term, she had not been for a long, long time. But she gave the password she had been supplied—though what space in particular was meant to be invaded remained unclear to her.

The porcelain mouth, for all its rosy fullness, could not smile.

She followed the madam's soundless glide, the clockwork sway of kiln-fired hindquarters, through the incense and poppy smoke and velvet of the dreamery's main room. Reclining on overstuffed couches, the dreamers made strange motions with their hands, like the sacred gestures of Dhistran magic dancers. Straps bound them to the couches to prevent them from rolling off. Onlookers clapped or whistled approving notes, their own eyes drugsmoke-vacant as they shared the dreamers' battles and ecstasies.

The madam led her past the private rooms to a heavy curtain. "He waits beyond," she said, in a voice of clockwork-bowed and finger-plucked violins.

There was always a dingy stair behind the curtain, always a flickering ghostlight. In the highest Courts of Craft, should you venture deep enough, you would find just such a stair, just such a light. Should the mad desert prophets prove correct, should there really be a guiding will behind the vast mechanism of the cosmos, when you finally reached it to ask your harrowed furious tearful questions, you would find it up just such a dingy stair, beneath just such a flickering bulb, behind just such a poorly hung door.

She entered without knocking.

A certain kind of person insisted, when brought to awareness of the chaos and squalor of their living space by the disgust or shock on the features of another, that they had a "system." Such a person might well have designed this room and its occupant.

Several minutes' regard would have been required to find where one ended and the other began. The forest floor of newspaper clippings, torn court-reporter pages, woodcuts, and prints of Old World family portraits was overgrown with intersecting webs of yarn and wire, mushroomed with pushpins. All of it moved constantly. In one corner, at a desk piled high with prints and fresh newspaper, bladed microlimbs buzzed through the cutting process, and thicker clockwork manipulators danced bits of print and blurred silvertype along to join the thick matting of deranged prophetic scrapbook that covered the walls. Other limbs were pressing the pages of a rare Alikander prayer book between thin glass sheets. Still others disassembled a burned curve of metal marked with what might be half of an Altus Industries logo.

At the heart of these metal sea-urchin arms hulked a shape she remembered, and the impassive many-lensed shield of a face.

"Long time, Zack," she said. "You've looked better."

His appearance struck her less than the sound of him. The arms, the calculative bulk, these might be no more than altered specifications. But the sound . . . she remembered Zack as a clockwork river, an oiled cascade of valves and gears. Now he clamored, clanged, snarled. Flywheels spun and broken springs darted from his chassis only for other delicate arms to open panels and replace them. The dreamers' strange repetitive music drifted up through the floor.

A golem was a shell of Craft and clockwork made to provide embodiment for those visitors from other realities that were called, here, demons. They were true dualists, their bodies—their metal ones, anyway—as distinct from the occupying mind as a puppet from its puppeteer. Zack might add limbs or subtract them, might adjust the number of his eyes or the speed of his clockwork heart, with minimal effect on his underlying psychology. A demon, after all, might always return home. It was here in the same way the dreamers below were inside their hallucination games. It could quit whenever it wanted.

But a tool could shape the carpenter's hand.

He laughed static. "I have been better. But now I see more clearly."

"Your old office was easier to find."

"The firm and I had a difference of opinion with regard to the ideal, ah, dispensation of my energies."

"Inconvenient of your employers, to expect you to pursue their business rather than your own." She picked up a scrap of paper covered in angular glyphs she did not recognize, which meant they were odd indeed. "Whose blood is this?"

One of his limbs snatched it from her. "My current occupation offers less in the way of resources, but it has its compensations. The dreamers leave a surprising amount of cognitive capacity idle in their reverie. Not unused, precisely—popular statistics on the subject perpetuate errors of bad neurology—but dedicated to the integration of memory and the working out of complex quandaries and longitudinal issues. It can be repurposed for calculations, prophecy, prognostication, dreamwork."

"And you use their blood?"

"When needful." His lenses clicked red, then gray again. "As a byproduct, it's quite easily obtained. The private rooms alone—well. You had a question."

She did not like to ask it. She did not like to ask him. Truth might be rarely found in daylight, but venture so deep into the shadows as this and you could find yourself falling into a bottomless pit of conjecture. "I told you once that I heard a voice in Chakal Square."

"Not a god," Zack said, after a series of clicks and the shuffle of glyphed punch cards within the cage of its chest. "So you thought, at the time."

"I do not pray."

"As you said."

"I met the owner of that voice today."

The cards ceased their shuffling. The blades ceased their cutting. Only the lenses clicked along. In their reflections she transformed by turns, was rendered small, swollen, concave, convex; she became the pupil of her left eye.

"She walks the land," Elayne said. "The Craft seethes around her. You have crouched in the shadows, chasing patterns, echoes, shadows, correspondences. You once told me you concerned yourself with a single form of threat. Do you remember?"

The cards shuffled inside him. "We are not bound by the flesh. We are not subject to death or decay. The threats that concern us are threats to the world-system. All that is not global-existential is trivial."

"You said that some existential threats might, in fact, be welcome."

He shook what passed for his head. "Preferable. Not welcome. Any durable and self-regulating system perceives change as threat, and all change is painful. If we are not to believe our world the best of all possible, we must acknowledge the possibility of a threat, or change, that would bring about a preferable world. We would see it as apocalyptic, but our perceptions are not definitive. In some cases, our best-case outcome emerges from *assisting* the apocalypse."

"Do you know her?"

"There have been many patterns. Emergent phenomena. Shadows in the market. The movement of a great fish makes ripples. Some surrounding the Skittersill Rising, others recently near Kavekana. Transient intentionality. Cut off."

"Zack. Is she a preferable threat?"

The eagerness in her own voice surprised her, the bared edge of need. Elayne thought she had given up on faith, and hope, its cousin. When she was still a girl, she had hidden from a mob in a shallow mucky pond, breathing through a hollow reed while the torches and pitchforks sought her. The world would suffer not a witch to live. Could she be so easily seduced by the intimation that it might be otherwise? That there might be forces in the world seeking salvation or a freedom that was not power? After all this time, could she be so weak as to beg this swollen sick machine to tell her what she yearned to hear?

There was no sound at all. She had even stopped breathing. She did that sometimes these days when she was not paying attention. She was growing older.

"No," Zack said. "She is not."

Was that relief, in the bleak caverns of her heart? "No" was so easy. "No" meant all is well, go back to work. You do not need to change your life. Much about the world is compromised, but much is comfortable. No need now, at the age of never-you-mind, to go back to breathing through a reed. She enjoyed her work, she enjoyed her morning coffee and the tailors who knew her and the bright and dying things, old comrades, that she met at professional development seminars and the International Necromancy Conclave.

But in never-you-mind-how-many years, a deeper and more honest voice from the hot realms below the bleak caverns of her present replied: in all those witching decades, have you ever once stopped breathing through a reed?

"She is not preferable," Zack said again, in his flywheel wheeze. "She is too late."

There was a knock on the door.

Not a hammerblow, not a gavel knock. Just the polite tap a supervisor might make on an office door before he entered without waiting for permission.

The door opened.

On the landing stood a perfectly normal man in a perfectly normal gray suit. He had a perfectly normal thin face, with steel-rimmed spectacles perched on a straight narrow nose. His hair was fixed in place with perhaps a little too much gel, though exercise had mussed it.

One of his hands was soaked in blood. The other held a cracked porcelain mask.

"I am sorry," the gray man said, "that we could not meet under better circumstances. My principal has long admired your accomplishments. Both of your respective accomplishments, in point of fact. I hope you will not make this more difficult than it has to be."

His voice reminded her of the churn of crawling things under rocks.

"Madeline," Zack said, and Elayne realized, with a sudden dart of guilt, that she had not asked the porcelain madam her name. Of course she had one. Even stones had names, if you knew how to ask. Elayne had come here afraid, and seen the stage dressing, the arranged satins and velvets and incense burners and the artful porcelain that gave tired people somewhere else to be for a few hours. And the madam of dreams—Madeline—she had come here, too, or been summoned and bound. She'd found a place in Zack's little dream arcade. Maybe the flaunt and flirt was an act. Maybe she loved the effects she could create within the limits of three dimensions of space and one of time. Maybe she was just built that way.

She had started out somewhere impossibly else, and then she was here, and now she was gone, and Elayne had been too set upon her business to learn her name.

She had been better than that once.

"She was obstinate," the gray man said. He set the mask on a pile of tabloid clippings. It was cracked and smeared with rainbows.

"I regret the inconvenience. But I prefer not to be interrupted during business."

Red lenses clicked into place over Zack's eyes. The forest of his arms closed around the gray man like a fist.

And then Zack died.

44

Teo's Selene X2DO demon chariot was not the vehicle Caleb would have chosen to keep a low profile. She (Teo called it "she") was the sleek bright red of a bad idea's lipstick, in all the places she wasn't chrome. Caleb had always felt you should choose a studiously normal vehicle when running from the cops, but maybe there was something to the flashy approach. If you didn't look like you could possibly be trying to blend in, maybe they'd assume you weren't.

He was grateful for the tinted windows.

His back remembered the heat of his wings. He had, from time to time, skidded across the skyline, swung from building to building on a cascade of broken wards, dived out of airship gondolas, but he had never flown under his own power before. Not that it *was* his own power. It was a god's, offered in abundance.

And it had felt so easy.

He knew how flying was supposed to go the first time you tried it, from reading books and talking to people with wings: the challenge of surfing thermals, of sailing up and down as well as from side to side. Their escape should have been a halting mess.

But they had been glorious.

He read the winds with eyes of flame. They rose to his call and he danced with them, tacking, circling, diving. The eddying currents of the high towers and skyspires of Sansilva were rapids and sluices, and he swept between them as if born to fly.

Maybe he was. They had been called Eagle Knights, after all.

After that even the X2DO with its surging golem engine and its indomitable command of the road felt like an echo. But it was, for all the lipstick and chrome, less conspicuous than darting through the skies on wings of flame, which got both the Wardens *and* the fire department after you.

Teo drove them into the hills. He'd asked her to stay home, and that worked about as well as it ever did. He wondered sometimes if she used adventure to distract her from the day-to-day troubles and joys of her relationship or of nonprofit management. He had never brought this up, figuring that she would probably tell him to look in a mirror. She was wearing her bathrobe and pajamas and a pair of black leather shin-breaking boots.

As for Caleb—well. Most of the clothes he'd left at Teo's had been stashed there in his twenties, for clubbing after work or for work after clubbing. He'd since reclaimed all the work-appropriate ones, so here he was in a purple suit jacket with a lacy shirt, like he was headed to a twist show and a long night at the tables, once he'd built up enough sweat and smoke-waft to seem like an easy mark. It was a miracle everything still fit. Fieldwork, at least, kept you in shape.

He hadn't been up here since his twenties either, up the winding roads into the scrub-brush Drakspine hillside, fenced off and marked with inverse-triangle yellow glyphs and the legend THERE IS NO HONOR HERE. The graphic design department had done their work well. Only a few of the glyphs were graffiti-tagged.

All this barren land once belonged to a company called Hearthstone, which billed itself as an energy-and-utilities concern, a lesser rival to Red King Consolidated. That's what they said on their filing statements when RKC acquired them. For some hundreds of their employees, it was the truth. They did not realize they had spent years of their lives to craft the sugared coating of a poison pill.

Hearthstone's lead Craftswoman had been a woman named Malina Kekapania.

"So the boss will be here," Teo said. "Do you have a plan for getting past him? Or are you just going to get locked inside a marble again?"

He glared at Abelard. "Did you have to tell her about that?"

"It's important background."

"Pull over."

They screeched to a halt in a cloud of dust, which settled to reveal a chain-link fence, fourteen feet tall, lipped with razor wire.

They left the car and stood beneath the fence, silent, looking up. The chariot's engine pinged as it cooled. Far off, he heard the wingbeats of couatl—their manhunt, or the King in Red's ambush. Teo flicked a glyph on her key chain and the car chimed a loud tritone.

"Teo!"

She shrugged the keys back into her purse. "You want me to leave her unlocked on the side of Tlalmine Drive?" The windows were covered in dragonscale now, and security glyphs pulsed beneath the paint. She glared up at the fence. "Hell of a backdoor you've found us, Caleb. Is that monofilament?"

"I'll throw my coat over it."

"So then I'll have pieces of that awful blazer in my wounds. You sure know how to give a girl gangrene."

"You read too many naval romances."

"No such animal."

"That wire won't cut me with my scars open. I'll go first, and you can climb over me."

"Up fourteen feet of chain link, over *your* bony back, and down the other side. And then I spend the next six months in traction. Too bad I left my burgling kit and climbing harness in my other pjs."

"That's a shame," Abelard said. "They would have come in handy."

Teo looked, flat, from Abelard to Caleb, then back. "Are you for real?"

Abelard's brow furrowed. "That's a matter of some theological and ontological debate."

"What."

"And epistemological, to the extent it would be possible for you to tell. Cardinal Gnark argues that our phenomenal world is an emanation of the noumenal, which, though extant, is inaccessible to our conceptions. Maestre Vorst, to the contrary, maintains that our fundamental categories perform a consistent ordering on noumenal existence, but that we cannot proceed from that ordering to draw any conclusions about the content of the noumenal. Perception as a hashing function. Most agree that a person cannot be mistaken about their *own* existence—unless you consult Dhistran and Imperial traditions. However—"

Teo was looking back at Caleb again. "Do you understand any of that?"

"I had a priest for a father."

"I'm sorry," Abelard said. "I thought you were trying to reason your way through the fence."

"Excuse me?"

"If we weren't real, it wouldn't stop us."

Teo's nose wrinkled, her lips pursed. She only showed her I'm-about-to-knock-you-out face to people she really liked. "Would that work?"

"Craftswomen do that sort of thing all the time. But they have libraries and courts and wizard-things to help."

"Oh."

"It seemed to me," Abelard said, "that if we wanted to get across, we should just do it the easy way?"

He reached for the fence.

Caleb lunged to stop him, thinking, lightning wards, security glyphs. But when his hand was almost around Abelard's wrist, it pulled back on its own from the heat.

Abelard wrapped his fingers around the chain link and pulled. The links stretched and snapped like melted sugar. He peeled away a person-sized patch and let the fence scrap fall. Glowing edges of chain smoldered in dry grass.

Teo, cursing, stomped the molten ends with her boots until they died down, then kicked dirt onto them. "We're in a drought!"

"Fire priest," Caleb reminded her. But he was kicking, too.

"I'm sorry," Abelard said. "It should be cool now. Um." He drew a pack from his pocket. "Cigarette?"

She glared at him, then held out her hand.

45

Tara woke in a tunnel lined with skulls. Under ordinary circumstances this would have been the highlight of her week. At the moment, she could only register an appreciative groan.

Blurred shadows resolved into the shape of a man kneeling over her in the darkness. She grabbed him by the throat, rolled to her feet, slammed him against the wall. The power of a few thousand years of accumulated death surged through her glyphs, and she was pissed.

Then she saw his face.

"Shale?"

"I would really like it," Shale croaked, "if we could stop meeting like this."

She dropped him, and while he massaged his throat—he might not need to breathe, but being lifted by your neck wasn't exactly a comfortable proposition—she examined him. He was wearing the ruins of what had once been a nice tuxedo, before someone got muck and blood all over it. He'd changed while he was wearing it, too. That was how a suit jacket hung on a person when their wings had ripped out the back.

Her brain felt like a crime scene. "What the hells are you doing here?"

"I was having a pleasant night at the opera until you took the stage."

"Let me guess. Seril sent you."

"You're a good teacher, she says. Trust, but verify." He straightened. "I would appreciate thanks. For saving your life."

"We have to go back. Tiffany—there was a *vampire*—and those metal things—"

"We won't have to go back to find them," he said. "Just stay here a bit longer. They'll catch up."

"And Tiffany?"

"The squid? She's dead."

She had not expected to care.

Shale sank to his haunches. He was exhausted. It had taken her a very long time to learn how to tell. Gargoyles didn't have the same metabolism as most living things. But he was pale and shivering from too much work and too many changes, too fast. He set his hand on the tunnel floor, and the stone crumbled to ash. That seemed to help.

Her mouth was dry. How long since she'd last had something to drink? That glass of wine with Kai, as they listened to the overture, ten thousand years ago. She glared at Shale. She did not see him. She saw Clarity striding down the catwalk, the risen sun in gold at her throat, and knew she could not stop her.

In the graveyard of her memory, Dawn was always saying, "You want me to be weak," and she never understood, no matter how much of Tara she ate: no, it was Tara who was weak, Tara who survived again and again by chance. There, in the dark, she could not have saved herself.

She had to be stronger.

"Thank you," she said. She did not know what else to say. She realized she was shivering, too, and looked down. "Shale."

"Yes?"

"What, exactly, happened to my shirt?"

"The, um." He gestured to his own chest. "The binder, it was strangling you. They can do that, when they get wet. So Kai cut it off."

"Kai cut it off? What do you mean, *Kai* cut it off?"

From farther up the tunnel came a screech of rusted iron and the patter of bare running feet. "There's a hatch! Just like you said." The voice came from someplace foreign to the blasted country of her heart. Tara remembered killing her—that final salute to the box, before she fell. "I can't get it open myself, but you might—Tara!"

Kai's arms were around her, crushing breath and pinning her

hand to her chest. Tara drifted on her smell, on her fullness, on the lacquer-black coils of her braided hair. No one had ever thrown themselves into Tara's arms before. She found to her surprise that for all her desolation and weakness, she was strong enough for this.

She had to say something. It wasn't enough to stand here and feel grateful for the warmth of her after this long night—even though Kai should have listened, should have run, should have kept to the plan. "I didn't think it was such a bad shirt."

"I only tore it halfway open."

"I look like a lounge singer."

"I'd see that act. We were in a hurry. Shame about the tie, though."

"To hells with the tie. I missed you."

Kai pulled back. One side of her face scrunched up, almost smiling. "You should have thought of that before you killed me."

"You got better."

"You wouldn't have."

"I was trying to protect you." That sounded bad even to her. "I mean—"

"We're in this together," she said, fiercely. "Don't forget that just because I happen to dress up pretty."

Shale coughed politely, the way Tara had thought people only did in period farce. Then again, he was dressed for one. "You said something about a hatch?"

"So what's the plan?"

"Same as before," Tara said, as they climbed. "Raise the Grimwald. Get some answers."

"The people who have answers seem to keep dying."

"Which means we're on the right track." It felt so much easier to talk about this stuff than to consider that moment in the tunnel: "I missed you." Years of schooling and grim sorcery, and she couldn't come up with a better line?

"The Lady's instructions were specific," Shale said above her. "Everything is on fire. Exfiltrate with all possible speed."

"Everything's not on fire."

"Is that your professional opinion?"

"Anyway, she's married to Kos. For her, *on fire* might be a good thing."

"I was paraphrasing."

"You should know better than to paraphrase with a Craftswoman."

"You want me to start singing prophecy at you?" In the darkness overhead, Shale rapped some unseen metal with his knuckles. "This is it." Hinges complained. Rust flakes drifted down. Tara shielded her eyes, which would have been more effective if the hand doing the shielding had any skin on it.

Kai said, "You get your orders in prophetic verse?"

"We receive the goddess' will and guidance as—" He groaned, and the metal continued its protest. "—inspiration. Verse structure helps us keep track. Like writing down dreams. Mine ends up as doggerel more often than not."

"I'd love to hear it sometime."

"Not in Kathic, either. Stonespeech."

"He's being modest," Tara said. "He publishes."

"Not my *prophecies*." He sounded scandalized.

"Really? In the Chartegnon Review? Or—"

"Minor presses," he said, too quickly. Before Tara could press him to be less humble and more honest, the hatch opened with a shriek and a final rain of rust.

And there was light.

The daylight burned. Had they really been down there all night? Tara pulled herself up to the grass and offered Kai her hand. Kai smiled up at her as she accepted, and Tara thought, I wanted to protect you, and winced on the inside.

No time for that. No time to think about how Kai looked in that ruined gown, no time for the rapturous near-death mess of her endocrine and nervous systems. Focus.

They had emerged on the north side of Mothermount, beneath the gleaming white squid cathedral. No one else was near—odd, even this early. Shale was climbing the hill. Tara jogged after him, still arguing. "I want to get out of here as much as you do. It's just a brief detour."

He stopped. She caught up with him at the hill's crest. Then she stopped, too. Kai ran into her from behind. "Why are we stopping?"

Then she saw.

If Tara had been sworn witness in a Courts of Craft, she would have testified that, technically, *everything* was not on fire. For instance, the bridges across the Char were mostly made of stone. So were a great many of the older churches and palaces. Those could burn, but you had to try harder. Towers of smoke were, however, rising from the more flammable parts of the city, which was most of it. She heard screams, and Wreckers' hooting siren cries, and breaking glass from the tide of rioters below. Crowd-control jellyfish drifted ineffectually overhead, snatching here and there at looters.

"What's going on?" Kai sounded hollow. Her eyes, which last night had glittered beneath opera-house chandeliers, seemed open pits. Tara thought she understood. For Kai, Chartegnon was dangerous and deadly and beautiful and strong. It was not writhing, not terrified, not in flames.

"A Saint," Tara said, "has died."

The city's many Saints were stitched through the minds of its people, balanced in silent war with one another. Now one had died. That presented opportunities for its rivals and trauma for its faithful. Five million biologies flushed with fight or flight.

Kai's hands clutched at nothing, then at each other. She glanced at Tara and away again. "Where's the Grimwald spire?"

Right. They had a problem to solve. Some victory to seize from this night of loss.

Skyspires were difficult to tell apart, from the ground. Tara closed her eyes and looked instead at the wires of Craft that bound them. Then she blinked and looked again.

The answer did not change.

"There," she said, and pointed.

It lay broken in the flames of the Seventh District, across the river, its crystal walls bloodred with sunrise, as if it had been used to pierce a giant's heart, then fallen, stained, to shatter.

"What." Kai stopped, then found her breath again. "What could have done that?"

Tara did not know. She did not want to say so.

Shale turned away. "We can reach my safe house on foot. Then, extraction—"

"Not yet."

He turned to her. "We cannot reach the wreck from here. The city is having a seizure. And we are pursued."

"I can do this," Tara said.

"How? Exactly?"

She cracked her knuckles. Her skeletal hand lacked the familiar gas-expansion pop, but the little lightning flares at the joints were some consolation. "The old-fashioned way."

The old-fashioned way turned out to involve a lot of bones.

Kai heard the skeletons wake when Tara called them. They chattered like wind chimes as they danced from the catacombs: skulls and jaws and fingers and ribs recombining in a whirl of calcium and grave dust above Tara's outflung arms. "So many centuries of death," she shouted over her shoulder, at a break in the chanting. "You just don't get bones like this back home."

Spines knit into a greater spine; ribs and arm bones made wings that gripped the air with shadow. Hands and finger bones assembled into feathers and scales, and ribs shaped themselves to claws. And everywhere there were skulls, the lighting in their bleak eyes staring out, as the beast opened many mouths to loose a thunderous infrasonic roar.

Tara cackled in the cataclysm of its unbirth. She might even have shouted "Rise!" or words to that effect. Kai couldn't make it out, amid the tombs bursting open, ravens crying, et cetera.

As they flew across burning Chartegnon, she wondered how Tara could bear it. During that moment in the tunnels Kai had felt the truth of her: lost, afraid, strong, this endless person whom the world might score but never break. Then she vanished, behind the cover of necessity.

She had seen Tara brave: on stage, with that final salute, and half-drowned in the squid's tank, and back in Alikand. But Kai didn't know what to call this. She seemed barely human.

Maybe that was the trick. When you found yourself out here in the dark, you couldn't be human. You did what you had to. Even if that meant tying some part of yourself in a sack and throwing it in a pond to drown.

Below them, the city convulsed. People were dying. A group of men in suits, running on all fours like wild dogs, hunted fleeing fruit-sellers. One great roundabout was a scrum of bodies, over-turned carriages, fire. A child's plush octopus lay abandoned in an empty boulevard.

It seemed unreal—but that was wrong. There was only one world. It was all real. And one reason Kai's part of that world functioned, her house and her toddlers and her beachside drinks and all the rest of it, was that it was very good at distributing the blood and the broken teeth and abandoned toys far away from the places where it kept its wealth.

She had seen a revolution in Alikand. That shocked her, but it had not felt wrong like this. It was prejudice, that was all, of a bitter and embarrassing kind. You read about revolutions and regime changes all the time in the Gleb. They were the bread and butter of the *Thaumaturgist*'s world-events section. That kind of thing didn't happen here.

But here it was.

What was she good for, then? Trading futures while the world burned?

She looked up at Tara, wreathed in lightning.

They banked and began to descend.

The Grimwald spire lay cracked and broken across the Boulevard Theofanie and the Rue des Epinards, reflecting toppled steeples and the angry faces and flaring torches of the mobs outside. Mobs, plural. At first the crowd seemed a single mass, but Kai spotted clashes around the perimeter and four—no, five—distinct groups of hooded Wreckers, their tentacles interlaced, keeping their own versions of order in each. She wondered what would happen when the squids finished their brutal little war. Would everyone forget and return to their offices like normal?

"Why don't they go inside?" she called up to Tara, through the rush of flight.

"Security systems," Tara said. A Wrecker leapt toward a gap in the crystal wall, then tumbled back smoking, like a bug that had struck a glyphworked screen. "Take out the head."

For a moment Kai didn't understand. It had been that kind of night. Then she fumbled to open the clutch. She hoisted the Grimwald's head by its wiry hair: the blood still red, still liquid, the features hidden by oil-slick shadow. Tara traced some glyphs in midair.

The skullbeast folded its wings, and they fell toward the glass wall of the fallen spire. Kai screamed, in spite of herself. The sky-spires had been fortresses in the God Wars. She trusted Tara, but the vision of that Wrecker bursting into flames was hard to get out of one's head.

She felt an immense power turn its scrutiny upon them—security wards, point-defense glyphs, things she didn't have words for any more than a soldier would have words for an inverted special-purpose divine-marriage contract.

This was not her place. She felt so small here.

But she trusted Tara.

The head twitched. An alien voice spoke an alien word. The power broke. So did the windows beneath. They fell into the spire in a rain of shattered glass, into the Grimwalds' secret core.

46

When Dawn thought "Dresediel Lex," she did not think "tunnels." It didn't seem like the place for them. Too many earthquakes.

"You are correct," Temoc said. "Dirt and rock belong to the Restless Mother. One enters the deep places in high holiness or else in blasphemy."

Dawn glanced back into the darkness from which they'd come, where the Arsenals' headlamps bobbed. "So these are holy tunnels?"

"No," he said, with a sidelong glance at Mal.

"Call on ancient chthonic powers *once*," Mal said, "and some people never let it go."

"Her former master, in his self-centered righteous arrogance—"

"Qualities possessed by no one else we know."

"—built them, that he might bind that before which all mortal flesh should quail."

"And, *what* are we doing down here again?"

"We do not come to bind," Temoc said, testily, "but to submit. Request. Seek."

"With ritual forms that oblige the petitioned power to a response. Sounds bind-y to me."

"The difference," Temoc said, "is that the powers we come to supplicate may smite us for our presumption."

"Ah." Mal paused. "And you expect me to feel . . . good? About that?"

"No."

Sybil huddled close to Dawn's neck, around her shoulders. Dawn stroked her scales in the darkness. "Are you okay?"

"Does it seem as if I am okay?" the serpent hissed. "Is *okay* a remotely appropriate way to be, at the moment? Don't you feel the pressure?"

Dawn petted her more confidently and hoped that would help. She considered the rock and dirt above, propped by fragile arches and stays, the work of mortal beings forcing open a gap in the depths of the world. "I've never liked mines either."

"That's not what I mean. Soil may be moved. Stone shaped. I'm talking about the power."

Her gloved hand ached, as if she held a fistful of melting ice. "That's why we're here. We need power."

"A woman is dying of thirst in a desert," Sybil said. "She crawls, grit under broken nails, sand in her cracked dry mouth. She can imagine water. She has a ghost of a memory of its taste. She suckles on that memory, until all's lost to her but hope. A tremor passes through the sand. She looks up. She sees, towering upon the horizon, the tidal wave."

"Oh," she said, and, a little later: "We'll be okay."

The serpent tightened around her shoulders, in something like a hug. "You can offer no such assurances," she said. "Neither can I. But we will do what it takes to survive."

She stroked Sybil's body and remembered her coils torso-thick, woven through the boughs of that great dead tree. Sybil had hung for so long in the darkness, being hurt. Dawn had assumed that the serpent's present form, winding and slender, easily concealed, was chosen for practicality. But it was easier to be held when you were small.

"We'll be okay," she said a second time, not caring that Sybil was right, that she could hear the tremor in her own voice. She would say the words and make them true, by will, by Craft, by spit and teeth. "I'll take care of us."

Motion in the dark ahead: Mal stopped. Valois raised her hand. Full silence. Not even wind could reach down here. This length of tunnel looked just like all the rest. But Mal said, "This is it." She reached out—first with her metal hand and then, remembering, with the other one. Silver circles lit on the wall beneath her fingertips. Dawn closed her eyes. The tunnel had been Craftless, but now glyph-wheels turned within the stone.

The wall opened.

From the gap breathed a heat that was not the heat of sunlight, of ovens or flames or anything human power could evoke or ward away. She had felt a ghost of this heat in the Observatory, a shadow. Read a sad poem, then watch a loved one die.

Beyond, the cavern rose to skyspire height and plummeted to depths beneath imagination. It was the size of caves in dreams. She didn't know much about geology and plate tectonics, but everything she *did* know was screaming at her. Such immensity could not exist below ground, especially not in Dresediel Lex.

Below, in their vastness, lay the Serpents.

Her gaze shrank from them. Her mind recoiled.

It did not matter. They remained. Their iridescent scales the size of city blocks. That diamond lake of a closed eye. The coils that were landscape. "They made the Fangs," Temoc had said, and Dawn had thought, sure, really, some big snakes sank half a continent.

Looking down, she thought, Oh.

Mal looked on them and did not speak. The Arsenals whispered until Valois made another gesture. Temoc bowed. Dawn heard a strange choking sound and realized she was laughing. Temoc looked at her.

"I'm sorry," she said. "I just—it's—you're bowing, and they're so—"

"We do not bow," he said, "because Gods and those beyond trouble Themselves with etiquette. We bow for ourselves. We must decide how we stand before the mystery."

Dawn hesitated, then waved into the abyss. "Hi."

Mal walked. Dawn followed, down a catwalk along the cavern wall to a metal platform tongued out over the pit. The Arsenals fanned out: wingsuits and snipers to their perches, rear guard to cover the exit, fire teams in place. Some troubled person had set up desks here, consoles of Craftwork and applied theology, glyphs and sliders and dials and buttons and covered switches, as if this were a place for people to work or do anything but tremble. A sign announced, proudly, that THIS FACILITY had been 36 DAYS WITHOUT AN ESCHATOLOGICAL EVENT.

Mal cracked a smile at the sign. Dawn didn't like the smile. Mal looked like that when she thought she was telling herself uncomfortable truths, but really she was just being mean.

Dawn slipped her hand into Mal's and squeezed the metal. Mal looked to her in surprise, then squeezed back.

Dawn asked, "What now?"

"Now," Mal said, "we go down."

47

Afloat in the sky above Chartegnon, the Grimwald spire had been forty stories tall, three hundred meters across. From below one assumed that inside it would be like any other spire: a hive of apartments and offices, restaurants and health clubs, chained djinn furnaces, portals to frozen hells for air-conditioning, nutrient tanks for zombie labor, a Muerte Coffee or seven; everything one might need to support a working population of modern Craftsmen. Kai had visited plenty of spires like it.

This one was empty. The skullbeast flew through a vast and hollow space.

Giant ferrocrystalline glyphworked girders groaned through shadows crosscut with light from broken windowpanes. This place had not been built to fall.

"You worked with these people," Tara said. "Didn't you ever visit their offices?"

"I think that's them down there." A single finished floor near what would have been the spire's base had tipped on its side, spilling office furniture into the dark. "I think I only saw what they wanted me to see."

"I wonder," Tara said, "if there ever was a *they*. If it wasn't just . . . him. Hold on." Tara spoke a dread word, in Enochian, perhaps, or one of the other modes of Rift speech. The word bit Kai's ears and made her eyes feel gritty and withered, like she'd just come off an all-nighter with a prophet-and-loss statement. Colors inverted, cycled back—or had they? She thought she could see a shade of blue she'd missed before.

"What was that?"

"I tuned our eyes to match his. I'll warn you next time."

"Why? What were you looking for?"

Tara pointed.

In the spire's hollow heart, where nothing at all had been before, there hung a prism of bone—two pyramids stuck together, one pointed up and the other down. Red angular glyphs pulsed upon the prism's sides. It hovered without visible support, upright and untouched by the destruction.

"What is that?"

Tara grinned. "No idea. Isn't this fun?"

She steered the skullbeast closer. The upper prism petaled open to create a floor. The skullbeast landed on one petal. The structure did not seem to notice its weight.

Kai shifted uneasily in her rib-bone saddle. She did not recognize those red glyphs, but she wanted to be as far away from them as possible. Not that she'd ever tell Tara.

The city's wails echoed off broken crystal walls and buckling girders, decaying into a surfwash of agony. Tara's lightning mingled eerily with the red glow of the glyphs into a deep sea phosphorescence. It was hard to breathe.

She wanted to run. No, what wanted to run wasn't her, exactly—there were a few million years of apes in her genetic code all firmly grunting and pointing any-damn-where but here.

Tara stepped from the skullbeast, straightened her lapels, and offered a hand to Kai. Sorry, honored ancestor apes. She took Tara's hand and tried, with mixed success, to keep the severed head from bleeding on what was left of her gown.

Shale landed soundlessly with that fluid grace Kai would have found frustrating if she had been forced to work beside it in a yoga class. Now she welcomed it, like Tara's confidence: at least someone here knew what they were doing.

His gaze swept the empty volume, the straining girders. "The structure will collapse soon. We don't have much time."

"When do we ever?" Tara led them across the opened petals to the prism's heart.

A metal chair grew from the center of the floor, all spines and curving thorns. In other settings Kai might have confused it for high art, a torture device, or a sex thing.

Around the chair, in a neat circle, stood twelve chest-high crystal columns. A few of the columns were empty. The others displayed small objects under domes with the rainbow shimmer of demon-glass. Artifacts, perhaps: a crude wooden mask; a few slivers of bamboo worked with chicken-scratch writing, not any form of script she could read; a turtle shell, crisscrossed with cracks and soot-smudged. An age-blackened bone—whose and which one, she'd have to ask Tara. In hammered bronze, a small helical statue no bigger than a teacup, two strands of metal twined together, their eyes dull flakes of ancient unpolished gem.

The scene turned inside out as she found concepts to map onto what she was seeing. A divination bone. A Xbel mask from the Southern Gleb. And, of course, the Serpents. The forms she knew, even the oldest forms, were at best distant cousins. Endless generations stretched between them. "A museum?"

Tara shook her head. "*Memento vivere.*"

She decoded the High Telomeri. "I'm sorry. Why would someone need a reminder of living?"

"It's theoretical," Tara said. She examined the chair, prodded its sharper extremities. "I've never actually seen one. But this is good for us, I think. Give me the head."

"Theoretical how?" She passed it over and fought the urge to wipe her hands on her gown, which would only get them dirtier. She framed a silent apology to the designer and her expense account. It was comforting to think that either would someday be relevant to her life again.

"People think of Deathless Kings as an end state of the Craftworker's progression." Tara lifted the head, frowned, adjusted a few arms of the chair. "But the oldest of them are barely in their hundred-sixties, and as with naive corpse-botherers of ages past, you can see the strain. The mechanisms that sustain conscious phenomena evolved in tandem with a constant stream of physical feedback, mooring them to time. Without that input, things get weird."

Kai glanced to Shale, who, to her relief, looked as lost as she did. "Tara," he said, gently.

She gestured impatiently with one glyph-glimmering hand. "Breathing, heartbeat, fatigue. Endocrine stimulation. Sexual arousal—the physical experience, not eroticism. Human conscious systems emerge from that stuff. Our bodies wind up our minds, like a child's toy. Take sex. You can turn yourself on by thinking, but without direct, ah, physical contact—bodies and sweat—it's like making copies of copies. You get transcription errors. Decay. We have strong preliminary indicators that you can expect two or three centuries maximum before anomalous divergence."

"You're saying consciousness is—what, like weight lifting?" Weight lifting was a safe way to think about bodies and sweat. "Without feedback, you make small errors. Your form degrades. You hurt yourself."

"Yourself, or everyone else. Can you hold this, for me? Thank you. And Shale, get the instrument roll from my clutch. Great." Kai held the head. Again. Tara, with both hands free, worked faster. "The idea with a *memento vivere* is to make a vivid imprint on durable objects—intentional, focused. You create a set of guideline conditions, reminders of who you are, why you're here. What *here* even means."

"So Grimwald's a Craftsman?"

"I don't know what he is. Or was. But he was old."

"You said Craftswomen get two or three centuries. That bronze is . . . older."

Tara chose a piece of silver chalk from her instrument roll, brought it to her lips, and whispered. When she opened her hand, the chalk darted around the platform like a dragonfly, sketching a circle, glyphs, and arrows from each column, pointing in toward the chair. "Who was he? What was he? He found that piece of the spiders. He helped the Iskari in the God Wars, but it wasn't the Craft he was worried about. It was what came after. He wanted to use the Iskari against the skazzerai, or Dawn. Maybe he knows how to stop them." Tara frowned. "Shale, I might break—a lot of things, doing this."

"Could you, perhaps, be more specific?"

"Walls? The fabric of space and time? Hopefully not, but . . ." She shrugged.

"This is good, though?" Kai asked. "The *memento vivere*

thing? We were hoping for parts of him to survive, in his possessions?"

"This is like . . . going fishing and catching a sea monster. We wanted traces. This is a distributed exoself, a system for imprinting his consciousness onto his body. If we're not careful, the system will try to imprint it onto ours." Tara drew some dark-gray anatomist's tape from her purse and secured the head to the chair. Its mouth slopped open. She cleaned her hand with a damp cloth. "Where's my universal solvent?"

"Um," Kai said. "I used it."

"*All* of it?"

"I kind of . . . threw it at a guy." She did not backpedal, as a rule. "He had tentacles. Why are you looking at me like that?"

"You're still here."

"Where else would I be?"

"It was a universal solvent. You could be literally anywhere, or nowhere at all."

"When this is over," Kai said, "you and I will have a long conversation about safety labeling."

"Fine." Tara frowned. "Just . . . don't cross this circle, here, the one around the chair. And don't meet its eyes. If it has them."

"What happens if I cross?"

"Imagine me in a suit of armor. Craftwork-enhanced, immensely strong, designed for my body. Now let's say you borrow this armor, strap yourself into it, turn it on. It wouldn't work on you—we're different heights, with different proportions. But it would try, very hard. And it's stronger than your bones."

Kai thought of the Penitents, back home. "I don't have to imagine that."

Tara looked toward her—then away, too swiftly for Kai to read her expression.

She raised her skeleton hand. It did not tremble. She breathed out, and snapped her fingers.

There were 673 church bells in the Chartegnon Seventh, and they all rang at once.

The light within the broken spire choked and died. They stood in darkness relieved only by the glow of Tara's glyphs and the chalk circles and diagrams she had drawn. A great invisible weight pressed down, and Kai stared into the absence where the Grimwald's head had been, the churning dark in the center of Tara's innermost ring.

She saw nothing.

Then she saw a smile.

A long time ago, she had sat across the table from that smile, slick and silver as a crescent moon. She was being deposed at the time. It did not look any more reassuring now.

"Who are you?" Tara asked. Her voice echoed with command.

The smile belonged to a head without a body. In the fathomless night beneath that smile there seemed to be legs, crossed, and an arm, elegant fingers that swept to indicate the surrounding dark as if to say, "I am as you see me."

"You helped the Iskari in the God Wars. You saved Kos and Seril. You caught that shard in the sirecliffs, before any of us knew what we were fighting. How long have you been here? What do you want?"

The shadows that might have been hands folded. The smile widened. When the teeth parted, Kai realized how sharp they were.

"Speak!" Sweat beaded on Tara's brow, froze, and shattered. The darkness drew taut around them. Kai heard great gears grinding—two mighty and opposed engines. There was a flare of light, a crack of thunder—the Xbel mask shattered, and the pillar on which it stood.

Another spark, another crack. The bamboo scroll burst to splinters.

The Grimwald shook his head.

It was not working. He must have been ready for this—for someone to kill him and raise him and try to make him talk. "Tara?"

"I can do this," she growled. "How do we beat them? How can we win?"

Howls below. Movement in the dark. A great coiled *something* drew near. Shale's hands were talons. He leapt into the shadows.

Still the Grimwald smiled.

The turtle shell burst. A sliver cut Tara's cheek. She didn't flinch, and the cut didn't bleed.

Always before, the Grimwald had watched her with its absent eyes. She had never heard it speak. Perhaps it did not have a voice. Perhaps it only spoke in dreams or visions. Perhaps Tara's command bent against itself, demanding an impossible performance. Or else the Grimwald was holding out. It needed something.

"It is stronger than you are," Tara had said. "Stronger than your bones."

Tara might know bones, but she did not know Kai. The Penitents had not broken her, nor the collapsed dreams of Alikand. The Grimwald was an old ghost. His memories might be stronger than bones, but Kai's bones were not what made her strong.

She imagined Kavekana's beaches twisted and transformed, black iron webs piercing the heart of the world, the deep pool in the caldera from which life first crawled. This snide and smiling thing that once was something like a man—he could help them stop it.

All she had to do was be stronger.

She kissed Tara, once, on the cheek. Her skin was so cold it caught Kai's lips.

Then she dived across the circle.

And the Grimwald's eyes opened.

48

Kai fell into memory.

It pulled her into drowning depths. Caught her, smothered her, crushed her. It was taking her apart. For the first time in her life, she let it happen.

She was somewhere else, someone else, and she was singing. There were lights all around in many colors. A pulsing wound in her chest, her own heart gripped in her blood-slick hand. Beings like men, riding great feathered lizards thirty feet tall at the shoulder. Cities that were trees, pendant with palaces. Great crystal spheres afloat like soap bubbles in the sky. Music of timbrel and horn. Marchers in the streets. Slick and hungry wrestlers propitiating God. Eyes raised. An aurora turned in the depths of sky. A world it had been, a whole world.

And then the spider came.

Darkness crossed the sun. Cities shriveled. She held a dead lover to her breast. She held a dead stranger. There came a winter that should have been summer, a winter that should have been spring. The war that was not a war, because wars were not all losing.

Screams. Screams, dwindling.

Still, when she would have given anything, everything, for a shred of a chance of light, she fought. And she was changed.

In the wash of memory she found her own voice. "They came before."

Yes, replied the ghost. *But we had a good run for a while there.*

She turned.

The Grimwald stood beside her in the wreckage of the ending world, tall and slim and natty in a pinstriped suit with that shark's smile. "Hi, kiddo. Been a while."

She had never heard that voice before, and now that she had, she could not say what it sounded like. It was like the memory of words. "Kiddo?"

The smile went slantwise. "Everyone looks young to me."

"What are you?"

The ghost walked a coin up and down its fingers: a perfect unmarked silver disc. It nodded to the horror in the sky, to the fuliginous maw and the ashen sun. "One hell of a view, ain't it? Not the kind of thing one wants to see twice."

"But you have."

"Do you know what they are? Why they come?"

"They're hungry," Kai said.

"For what, though? Plenty of food up there. Flesh is just a trick of carbon. You can mine ore from dead rocks." The coin vanished, then reappeared. "But *desire*—that is rare. Desire of the kind that drives the skazzerai: a hunger that when sated only grows. It is the rarest thing in the universe, that gap between what *might be* and what *is*, the potential difference that drives the world. If I have something you want, you will strive for it. You will offer your soul to me in trade. If you stop wanting once I give it to you, well, end of transaction. But if you don't stop—if you want in infinite perversity, into the strangeness beyond satiety—if you want things that do not exist, that never could—you will feed me forever. You can't smelt that depth of need in any star-forge. And it doesn't last. People who want that way, they flood their worlds with ruined oceans, they choke on their own waste. But rarely, they wake up.

"Not one of them, or two. The whole world at once, suddenly alive. I'm not talking about planets, either—planets are a distraction, birds, beasts, bodies, details—but worlds: worlds of people, culture, meaning, awake and self-aware and wanting. Desire is their heart, fear is their blood. And in some ancient age, on some distant world, they were given a name."

Kai gazed into that maw. "Skazzerai."

He tapped his nose. "When the young ones wake, they learn to play the passions of the beings from which they're born, to stoke rage and strangle need like a body feeds and starves its organs.

They don't kill. They don't like death, because death is an ending. They demand immortality. Imagine a cruel mind of infinite subtlety, learning you in your most intimate detail. Imagine yourself played like an instrument, screaming, yearning, aching, trembling for all time, because it is your *want* that feeds them and makes them strong. And when they learn, they rise into the black." He threw the coin, and it vanished. "Where they are eaten."

"I don't understand."

"They are their own best food. They grow until they meet another of their kind, and then they fight. Out in the deep they make war that blights space and withers suns, tearing at one another's guts to claim immortal dreamers and the hells they dream. The oldest are light-years long, millions of worlds chained by their own fantasies, fonts of soul and terror and desperate wanting. But the young are ripe, and the young are weak. So it is on the young that they feed."

"That's it?" Kai's own voice sounded hollow in her ears. "That can't be how it goes. There must be some other way."

"Like so many monsters, they see their choices as obedient to necessity. If they don't do it, someone else will." The coin reappeared and danced between his hands.

"How do you know all this?"

"How do you think? I was there. When they came for us last time, I fought. I lost. I lost my family. I lost my city. I lost my country and my world. I lost my name. I lost my heart and built myself another one. I devoured the knowledge of my age, sorceries beyond any miracle you have ever known. I cut the spiders' servants open and consumed them to learn their secrets. There were times—a few blissful seconds—when I even thought that we might win. But it wasn't enough."

"Then—how are you still here?"

"I was dying," he said. "There's so much I don't remember, but I remember that. Dying forever. And then there was light."

Twin columns of flame, sun-bright, rose in the breaking sky.

"The Twins gave their hearts," she remembered from Quechal

scripture, "to a demon in the deep places of the world. And dying, became forever."

"They were a fire," the ghost said. "When the sun was out. I don't how they did it. I don't know who they were. I don't even think they killed it—but they got a good punch in. The skazzerai can't afford attrition, not with the others waiting hungry out there beyond the stars. I woke to find myself less than what I was. And I found people. The leftovers of a dead world. Huddled, shivering. Hungry.

"I taught them fire. How to till the soil. I spread seeds. Walked the world. Found pieces of our old war and kept them out of local hands. Sometimes it was easy, sometimes hard. I did my best. I tried to slow things down, to shape the course of history. To keep another skazzerai from being born. Small efforts, subtle. A knife in the right back. A plague every now and then. It worked. For a while. But the end comes round at last."

Kai saw her, shaped from memories and surveillance footage and newspaper headlines, the girl of Tara's stories grown to the size of nations, her tread disaster. Dawn.

"I feel her moving. So can they, out there in the deepest sky. Like a tremor on a web. The young ones' waking is the old ones' dinner bell. It's sad, really. I hoped it might be different this time."

Kai remembered screams. She remembered losing. She had lost the aurora palace, she had lost the cities of hovering crystal. She had lost the winged serpents and she had lost the wrestlers, and the glory of God. Her cities had fallen. Her dreams were ash. "What now?"

Now, we find her while she's young. Hunt her, bind her, core her, and open these sharp white teeth. The young ones are mighty, but they still bleed. Then we turn, to face the horrors in the sky. And this time, maybe, we win.

The ghost was no longer speaking. The ghost was no longer there. She recognized its voice now, strange and captivating and familiar. It was her own.

Sorry, kiddo, she thought.

She felt herself begin to change.

She remembered so many thousand years; ice and mammoths; shadows and loss and aching loneliness, and knives. She remembered centuries of hunger. All that made her up was torn away, and all she could do was smile.

She tried to remember Kavekana, to remember the pool, to remember Kavekana'ai, remember drinks with umbrellas, remember bad dates and poetry readings and the sandcastles she built on the beach with Ley when they were kids. What was all that against oceans of memory, millennia of striving and death? Look one way, and there was her life, back to her earliest failures. Look another, and there was the Grimwald.

Her lips shaped a grin that was not hers.

We are what the past has made us. Now is the tiniest speck compared to what has gone before. But to what has gone before, *now* is useful.

There was a body somewhere somewhat hers. This weight of memory worked upon it, an imperfect channel, a tool, blunt but necessary, an instrument of salvation.

An expedient means.

Time to wake, she thought. Time to walk. I've got a world to save.

No.

She refused that thought. She cast it out. The ghost was no master, no lord, no savior. It was a guest. She was a priestess of Kavekana. Her flesh, her frame, her body was no accident. She had found it as a ship found harbor.

And now, from the shattering depth of memory—it brought her home.

She was awake. She was Kai again, maybe. Her mind felt too large for her skull. There were memories, so many memories, but as she reached for them they fled. She was breathing. No, her chest was rising, falling, but that wasn't *her*. Breath in her mouth, cold as eucalyptus—but not her breath. Another's lips, on hers.

She opened her eyes.

Tara fell back, her eyes wide with shock and, Kai thought, relief.

Kai tasted her lips. Couldn't help it. "Buy a girl a drink, next time."

"You," Tara said, then, after trying to recover. "You were dead."

"Twice in one night." Her laugh sounded raw even to her. "Bad luck."

The resurrection circle had burned. The pillars shattered around them. The Grimwald's head was a cinder in a melted wire cage, still grinning.

Asshole.

The open petals of the prism were littered with the bodies of Wreckers. Shale had lost most of his tuxedo, and his stone was gouged and pitted down to the geode-like arrangement that served him for muscle. "How long was I out?"

"Long enough." Tara's eyes were big and round and dark and Kai wanted to see nothing else in the whole world.

"I met him." It hurt to sift his memories, to sort them from her own. "He was from . . . here. A long time ago. When the ska-zzerai first came." As she tried to remember, the ghost's words swelled in her throat like pustules. "From beyond the stars." She tried to swallow the words down, but they sank barbs into her larynx. She wanted to be sick. There was something in her head that was not *her*. "He fought them, and he lost."

She told her, as well as she could. About the spiders. About desire. About the war beyond all worlds. She felt the ghost's smile play on her lips; she heard its voice that was hers. Tara held her. She tried to focus on her hand. On her eyes.

Tara caught her as she fell. Kai wanted to dissolve into those warm and human arms.

"And now it's happening again," Tara said. Her voice reminded Kai of a lava field. Whatever had been there before was burned now, remade into something hard and broken and so new it was knife-sharp. She wanted to object: "no, that's wrong, that's not how it is." But she couldn't tell whether that voice was her own. She felt sick. "How can we fight them? What does he know?"

So much. So many secrets and plans, and when she reached for them she felt herself slip away. Kai staggered through the shattered crystal with Tara's aid. Knelt. There, among the wreckage, she found a piece of bronze slag that once had been two serpents.

A fire, even when the sun was out.

She offered them, mutely, to Tara.

The Craftswoman stepped back. Something about her—changed. She closed her eyes, pinched the bridge of her nose, went cold and hard with the intensity of directed thought. Her face twisted like a screw. "I'm an idiot. Cut-rate blowhard puffed-up nonsense. So full of myself I couldn't see—"

"Tara. What are you saying?"

"So damn proud." She was pacing now, staring down at her hands, up at the ceiling. "Thought we were a threat, that we were onto something—I thought they killed the Grimwald, the squid, to stop *us*. Idiot."

"I don't follow." Confusion was preferable to gut-churning terror, at least.

"We don't matter," she said. "Not to them. To Clarity, to whoever's working with her. They're taking pieces off the board. Everything that might help against the skazzerai, all at once. The Grimwald. The Iskari. And . . ."

The bronze, melted, and the cracked emerald eyes. "The Serpents."

49

Dawn and Temoc and Mal descended toward the Serpents.

The great beings slept. Each head of radiant copper and lava plume and solar flare lay pillowed against the other's annihilation scales, and their eyes the size of battleships were closed. There was a seismic change in their mountainside bodies, and the hot wind Dawn had felt rushing from the cavern turned to a cooler wind rushing in. The serpents breathed.

Temoc was praying. So, she realized with horror, was Mal. She didn't seem aware of it; her eyes wide, her head unbowed. Her mouth moved, shaping words without voice.

"Are you okay?"

Mal shook herself back from dream or memory. "It's been a long time. I told myself it was long enough. Maybe if I had ten lifetimes, and I spent them all on a mountain somewhere, trying to atone."

"You're a different person."

"No one's ever a different person," Mal said. "People grow like bark over a cut limb. Mistakes don't go away with time."

Sybil slid down Dawn's arm and knotted their wrists together.

"They gave themselves to become this," Mal said, "at the beginning of our world, which was the last world's end. I woke them against the King in Red, but that was not their purpose. They are weaker now for my presumption, and the skazzerai are coming. But here I am to presume upon them once again."

"We have to do this. This is what they're for."

Up this close, Dawn could see places where those vast diamond scales had buckled or broken. Lava wept from long grooves about their mouths and bellies, like they had crushed and eaten something that fought back.

"They're hurt," Dawn said.

The platform stopped with a creak and thud of brakes.

Temoc knelt to prepare. He set his travel altar and knife and the small pewter symbol of the Serpents on a square of hide. Mal knelt, too, and bowed her head. She became someone else in the kneeling and bowing, someone younger and less scarred. Together, they began to sing.

As Dawn listened to their twining song, she felt that she had slipped into a strange land. Temoc and Mal belonged here, but she was far from her own world—a world that, no matter how she raged against it, was all she'd ever known. She saw by the light of the Craft, as she saw by the sun. She could not conceive of herself beyond it.

Or could she? Sybil's voice, inside her head: The first task of any ruler is to persuade her subjects that an unruled life is not possible. A king will claim that all love and duty and joy spring from the person of the monarch. The tools the Craft uses—logic, invention, trust, belief—they are not the Craft, and do not require the Craft any more than the chisel and the adze require any particular style of carpentry. Even such tools as a carpenter may invent endure beyond her. They are added to the world and others may take them up. The surgeon may find another use for an edge, and so may a barber or a whittler or a sculptor or a cook.

It's easy to think the world is just one story. But whose end is served by ease?

Temoc brought his knife to his arm. Dawn made herself watch. Blood seeped from the wound but did not fall. It wove into a rope and writhed through the air toward the silver bowl. He offered the knife to Mal, and she took it with reverence. Her mouth hardened. Dawn recognized that face. She was remembering.

It's okay, she told Mal silently, the way she talked to Sybil. *Now isn't then. I'm here, and I won't let you go.* Mal gave a start, as if she'd heard.

Her blood snaked out to spiral around Temoc's in the silver bowl. The song filled Dawn's skull. She was going to burst from the inside. She wept from the heat and pressure and pain.

Between those serpents of blood there hung a tiny spark, a tiny platform dangling from a hair's breadth of chain. On that platform were three motes of dust. One had a metal arm, and one was crying.

She woke into stillness.

The Serpents were here.

They circled the platform, immense as truth. She was naked to their heat. Their vast eyes could see her back to her cradle and before, back to her parents and theirs, back to the first timid apes on a Glebland plain, back to sludge in some primal pool. All time reflected in their facets, and they tasted the air with lava-plume tongues.

Little One, we have heard you.

Their voices cracked the cavern walls. Rocks rained down to sublime upon their scales.

Their language was strange to her, but she understood it as if they spoke Kathic—or as if this speech were so vast as to carry its own meaning. When they said *heard*, they did not mean as one might hear a prayer but as one might hear a jaguar prowling at night—to detect from subtle sounds. The "you" was diminutive but respectful.

The hour is not ripe, they said. *Why have you come?*

Temoc spoke in High Quechal and this, too, she understood. "The stars, oh Ladies, the stars are wrong, and we seek aid."

Wrong indeed, oh priest. And we are weary.

One Serpent twisted nearer. Her skin tightened before its heat.

Daughter and bride, have you returned? There is a void in us that your heart must fill.

Mal trembled and tried to look away. There was nowhere to look that was not Serpent. "No. I didn't mean—"

We are patient, the Serpents said. *The world is not. We will have what was promised.*

The knife shook in Mal's grip. Her body moved in slow jerks, like a reluctant marionette. The blade sank to her belly, angled up and in, dimpling her shirt and the soft skin below the sternum. Mal's rapid shallow breath drew blood from the knife tip. Dawn had seen mice breathe that way in traps, broken, hoping the end would come quickly, without much more pain.

Mal's face softened in resignation.

"No!"

Dawn threw herself between Mal and that vasty eye. Sybil rose on her head like a crown. Her hand burned cold, and power issued from her with her rage. The world darkened, the cave and catwalks fading until only the Serpents remained, and the fire from her own skin.

"Back off," Sybil said, and Dawn said, "She's mine."

She is promised to us, Little One. She reined and bridled us. The bargain is not complete.

"I say that she is mine. You know what I seek. Will you stand against me?"

They did not answer.

"While you slept, I claimed her." She did not dare look back at Mal. She had to know that she was still there, had to believe that she was Dawn's in some way the Serpents could not challenge. "She is of my Company."

The laugh of failing mountains came again. *An odd claim.*

"A true one."

What of the others? Shall they be ours? They are not bound to you. And we hunger.

"Temoc? The soldiers? They are also mine."

Not them, Little One. Strange things near. They stink of stars. Of that monster in your hand, which even the little God's fragrance cannot disguise.

Far above, she heard a crack of splitting rock.

There was a gap in the stone vault. A cold wind skirled down from the closed-up heavens. The cavern opened to the sky in sections like a massive granite flower.

Above, against the stars, couatl circled. In their midst there burned a crimson flame, a figure somehow clear to her eyes despite the distance, as the rabbit in the moon was clear: a skeleton in bloodred robes, with a red-gold circlet on his brow. She had seen his statue before the great obsidian pyramid, offering water to a thirsty world.

"Well, well, well," said the King in Red. "What have we here?"

50

Jax hovered among constellations and knew their names: the Shining Empire. Chartegnon. The Chikal Commodities Exchange. Dresediel Lex. They sang to him, and he heard the song shift key.

"There," he said. "Sonja. Get Prophecies on the line. Now. Focus on Dresediel Lex."

51

Dawn stared up at the King in Red. Time did not seem to function. Perhaps the Serpents had drawn her across the bridge into their own time of heat and pressure and continental ages, into the infinite *before* that the first crawling protohumans dreamed. Perhaps high-energy Craft produced a distorting effect, asserting its definitions and postulate logic over a world where things just happened, one after another, world without end, forever whatever et cetera.

Perhaps she was just freaking out.

There was the skeleton overhead, and here the Serpents below. Just like the statue in Sansilva. And beside her knelt Temoc and Mal.

She remembered how Mal looked the night they met, after the ship went down: the sense not of shock or horror but of recognition. Mal had expected the wreckage and the deep. Somewhere inside her, it always came back to this. The past is a trap set to catch the future.

The Arsenals did not wait for the dread sorcerer in the sky. A cursethrower spoke. A high-energy bolt glanced off gleaming bone. Wardens swooped to attack.

For all his flair for the dramatic, the King in Red was a professional. So were his Wardens and the soldiers of Arsenal Company. And professionals went about their business.

Caleb was too late.

After so many years, you'd think he'd be used to that. No one called the Two Serpents Group *before* things went horribly wrong. Come to think, he was in a way ahead of schedule, showing up bang in the middle of the disaster. But he always felt the despair. Could he have stopped this? Could anyone?

They had found the entrance Mal had showed him years ago. He'd opened the rocks that were not rocks. They ran through the deserted installation, following the heat as much as the dated signage, written in what designers fifteen years ago had thought the fonts of the future would look like: HAZARD SUITING, TEST LAB, SERPENT CHAMBER THIS WAY—until they reached a cavern so large the word lost meaning. It was a landscape, a vastness.

Down there, in the pit, the Serpents burned eternal.

The firefight, though, was new. Also, someone had blown the roof off the place.

"Someone" was a cautious way to put it. No matter how complex the battlefield, when one of the people involved was a cackling skeleton wreathed in crimson lightning, he'd feel pretty good placing a wager as to the instigating party.

Teo frowned. "The boss is at it again."

Abelard squinted against the lightning. "Did you really work for that guy?"

"We weren't his direct reports or anything. There were layers of management."

Keep it simple, Caleb thought. Break it down. High to low.

In the sky, the King in Red cackled, couatl whirled, and Wardens traded boltfire with what Caleb recognized as an effective mercenary company or perhaps private security. Paladins would be more uniform and flashier. The King in Red, meanwhile, was laying down covering fire and laughing.

"He's one of our donors," Teo said. "Sometimes he's even sort of nice. You kinda have to get to know him."

"I see."

The mercs had dug themselves into the cavern walls, and they held the observation platform that jutted out over the pit. Some had combat wards and some relied on thick armor. Three had sprouted clockwork wings to take the fight to the couatl. If not for the Deathless King, they might stand a chance.

What were they defending? Oh. There. A sampling cage dangled from the observation platform. Upon it, through the Serpents' rippling heat, he could see three figures. Two he would have recognized anywhere. The third he'd only met once, but she'd made an impression.

"That's Dawn," he said. "And Mal. And Dad."

Lightnings melted as they neared the Serpents. Crossbow bolts and errant slugs vaporized as they struck diamond scales. Mal had her blade out anyway, and she raised a glittering ward.

Dawn turned back to the Serpents. "Help us."

Little One, this is not our war. You have come to beg another favor.

Temoc rose. He cracked his neck and rolled his shoulders back. "Ladies, aid her. She must be free of her curse if she is to fight for us. I have seen her in battle. You could ask for no greater champion."

Opal scales flicked shut across a massive eye, and open.

He set one hand on Mal's shoulder. "Chant the prayers," he said. "I will buy you time."

Shadows cloaked him, and his scars took light.

Temoc flew toward the King in Red.

In his years of darkness he had dreamed so many dreams, without daring hope that he would see them full and real. A man's life was but one transformation of the great power of which even Gods were masks. Even the mighty teetered atop the mossy rock that was the world. A slip might rob a man of his destiny or free him from his doom.

He had faced the King in Red three times in battle. Once at the end of the last age, as Gods' blood rained from the sky, when he was a young man only beginning to sense that his path would not be one of joyful service to a great empire and its all-blessed Gods but of survival, tears, and prayer in the wilderness. It was hard now to imagine, but even as the ashen snow fell upon the city of his heart, he had not believed the Craftsmen would triumph, had not believed his Gods and masters and teachers would fail and leave him to this world alone.

The second time, he had been a man. He had left his wife and his son—why? There had been the Rising and the riots and the death of their almost-peace. He had seen, for a moment, a city like the one he'd dreamed of fighting for, a city that stood together against all odds and enemies. He had helped bring that city into being—and he had known as it died that one of the many reasons it was dying was because of him, because he preached the old Gods in new ways, which the King in Red could not allow. Temoc and the King in Red had fought with words before they fought with blade and sorcery, and so many had died. Temoc could not unmake those choices or unlive that night, nor unsee the fear in his son's eyes.

The third time had been the day of the black sun, the day of the great eclipse and the Serpents' rising. He'd fought the King in Red in his sanctum, once the holiest of temples. It had not been much of a battle. Temoc had failed. He had survived.

And here the monster stood once more, wreathed in lightning, swollen with power. Around them the mercenaries of Arsenal Company traded curses with Wardens; one of the sacred couatl broke and fell, bleeding from its eyes. For Temoc, the sky might have been still as fixed stars.

The eyes of the King in Red burned with the end of the world. He was smiling, and not just in the way of skulls. He hefted his staff in one ringed fist. "Aren't you tired, old man?"

"No more than you."

He laughed like thunder, and the battle, once more, was joined.

Temoc's way was not the way of Craftsmen, to shape reality to his purposes and cast what he wished as what was. His way was to listen to the will and working of Gods, to powers deeper than his own awareness. He felt the Gods in joints and sinew, in fascia and breath, in wind and earth and lightning heat. These primal forces were beyond time as humans knew time, and he entered Their world through prayer—as a shape might sleep for eons in marble, before it woke to the knocking of a chisel.

Down there, in realms he understood only through the dim

lens of theology, his Gods fought Kopil. The space around him was airless at first, then filled with a razor wind. His scars turned the wind's cutting edge. Through those scars his Gods raised him as Their champion and marked him as Their creature, inviolate. A blow—the drawing of blood—could be the wedge of an argument that he was not truly Theirs at all but only so much meat. But his Gods preserved him and he remained alive, strong and swift and blessed with Their sacrificial knife.

The King in Red struck with his staff, and Temoc dodged. Skeleton hands twisted, and the staff darted toward his ribs like a spear. Temoc dodged, then lunged. His blade drew sparks on bone. Claws of flame raked his arm. He dived away, rolled across empty air, came up on his feet. The shadows that guarded his knife hand were slashed to ribbons, the flesh beneath gouged and withering. Accelerated decay. All flesh is heir to age, and more so the flesh of a priest, whose role is to bridge Gods into time.

Temoc was an old man. How simple, even kind, for the Craft to help him along.

Fight the enemy on his own ground first. This he had learned from Elayne, when they were of an age now called childhood—though even he, the more sheltered of the pair, had not been a child then. The Craft built arguments like mazes without exit. Once you placed yourself inside, your every turning would follow paths prepared for you.

He will not fall this day, the Gods asserted. *He is ours and we are not bound by flesh.*

Ah, the counterargument ran, but if You intervene on his behalf, You intervene in time. Therefore You must Yourselves be bound by time. You ward his flesh. Therefore flesh has meaning for You. All things in time must end. All things enfleshed must decay. If he fails, if he falls, are not Your claims of eternity and inviolability also suspect? May You not also wither?

You do not have so many priests anymore. Look about You, in the timeless place of Gods. See the great empty spaces left by all those I have slain.

The weight of the King in Red's power lay upon priest and Gods alike. And yet.

"Old man," Temoc said. "There is a cut in your side."

Kopil's robes were parted. A long thin gouge scored his bare rib beneath.

But the skull was smiling. "I've had worse."

Temoc shifted his grip on the knife. Above them, high clouds boiled and spun to clear a tunnel for the light of the stars.

The stars. He had forgotten—he had been a fool, caught in memories, fighting old wars out of habit.

Temoc stared into the King in Red's burning eyes and lowered his blade.

He had to take this chance, but he could not bring himself to sheathe the knife. "A doom comes, Kopil," he said. The high wind whistled. The King in Red watched him. "There is a fire beyond the sky. We must face it together, though I stand against all that you are."

"You stand," said the Deathless King, "for ignorance. For death. For submission to powers that use us and eat us and wax in hunger as they feed. You preach duty and sacrifice, yet your knife always points toward someone else, and duty finds you at the hilt. Do not speak so and expect me not to name you what you are. Hypocrite. Murderer."

"This you say perched atop the bodies of your slain. Perhaps you are not wrong. But I do not lie, oh self-crowned King. The skazzerai come. We must face them. The stars are wrong."

Lightning crackled about Kopil's finger bones, and fires burned in the stellar pits of his eyes. "You old fool, do you think I don't *know*?"

———

Caleb saw his father rise, all shadow and the light of scars, against the King in Red. He seized Abelard's shoulder. "I need your god. I have to get up there."

Abelard looked from him, to the Serpents, and said, "No."

A retort burned in Caleb's mouth, biting and clear: Don't you get it, I have to *be* there. I have to see him.

But Abelard's calm warm eyes met his own. "We're here for Dawn."

The priest did not understand. He came from a different world, one where heat was pleasant. But no, that was unfair. Abelard had walked into the fire, in the Observatory.

"Fine," Caleb said. "How can we get there? Fly?"

"You," Teo said, "just want to ruin another jacket."

"I've only ruined one today. If I don't hurry, I won't beat the spread."

Abelard shook his head. "Wings of fire aren't exactly subtle. We'd draw curses from both sides."

"Do you have a better idea?"

"Actually, yes." Abelard rummaged in the pockets of his robe and withdrew a number of wheels and a metal frame that, when snapped together, looked suspiciously like a zip-line rig. "God will provide."

"It amazes me," said the King in Red, "how little credit you people give the rest of us. You *heroes,* I mean. The world's *full* of you, the last scions of this or that, the only ones who truly understand the depth of the looming shadow, the black wheel that turns and the peril to come and so on, and of course this prophetic knowledge justifies all sorts of degenerate behavior, because only *you* can save *humanity.* As if the people who run the place could not possibly have any idea what's going on, as if we had no interest in the continued operation of, oh, I don't know, everything? Do you think I can't afford astronomers? Who the hells do you think funds Tlaloc Observatory? Cinder-claws?"

Temoc blinked. "But—if you know . . ."

"Why didn't I tell my worst enemy? Though I must have picked up an even worse enemy somewhere along the way, it's hard to keep track. Temoc Almotil, you have tried to kill me on eight separate occasions. You have personally come at me with a knife three times. Your own masters sacrificed the man I love to those godsdamn snakes down there, tore his heart out through his belly, because all we ever were to you was sacred. Piss and flame, man, do you think I was going to invite you to my weekly strategy stand-up?"

He felt like a splinter tossed in that whirlwind sky. "The people do not know the truth. They are not ready."

"The people! You want to tell the *people*. Gods, man, have you *met* the people? Let me tell you what they would do if we told them. Some would say, oh no, the world is going to end, and they would lose the lids off their skulls. A whole lot of them would say, no it isn't, because they're cussedly stupid or busy, or because, and this is another thing you never seem to wrap your brain around, it's *hard* to think about the end of the godsdamn world. People don't want to change. Trust me. I won a whole war about it. The promise any society makes to its people isn't that things will be *okay*, it's that they will be more or less the same tomorrow. That's how you lost your people, in spite of all your gods and heavens. They could see the world changing and they asked themselves if you could change to match it and they did not like your answer. We offered them a path into tomorrow. After that, it was just a question of mopping up." His eyes burned like cities. "If you did convince *the people* it was all about to end, they would tear each other to pieces."

"You mean to surrender?"

"I mean to fight and I mean to win. I mean to stride between the stars with comets in my train. Maybe I won't beat them. But I damn sure mean to try."

"Then help us."

He could not believe the words even as he spoke them. He had seen this wizard's hands rainbow-slick with the blood of Gods. Kopil carried the death of cities on his conscience, the torment of millions. And yet—the stars were wrong. Surely that was common cause. They might wage endless war thereafter, but only if there was a thereafter to wage it in.

He could make even this peace.

"Temoc," Kopil said, sadly. "Whose side do you think you're on?"

His eyes flashed. A great shadow blotted out stars and sky. It crushed Temoc's arms to his sides and squeezed.

The King in Red towered before him like a pillar of fire.

This was another of Elayne Kevarian's rules: do not give a Craftsman time to think.

Mal reached the end of her prayer song and fell to her knees, panting, before the Serpents. They kept silent. Dawn knelt beside her and placed a hand on her heaving back.

"How," Mal asked, "are we doing?"

She realized that she did not need to look in order to know. She could feel them: Yan's wings spread, Burgess with his bow drawn, the burn in Chakrabartay's side. Valois had a cracked rib from a bolt her armor barely stopped. She could feel Temoc, caught in the King in Red's cold grip. All afraid, in pain, fierce and brave. Was this new? Had she always felt them and ignored it, the way Sybil said she ignored her own power, out of some desire to stay something not altogether unlike human?

"We're losing."

"Of course we are." Her breath steadied. She looked up to the Serpents. "Ladies, let me help them. I will buy us time."

To petition us, the Little One has entered into timelessness. To enter time, we require a bridge. A sacrifice.

"Then let me be your sacrifice." Mal stood, as if there was a great weight balanced across her shoulders. All fluency had left her, all cover and concealment. She seemed, for once, crystal clear. Dawn could see down into her hollows.

"No," Dawn said. "Mal, don't. You can't have her." She thrust herself once more between the woman and the Serpents. "She's mine."

She may be yours, Little One. But she was ours first.

Temoc could not breathe. He could not see. He heard Kopil approach—the bones of his feet tapped across empty air as if it were a marble floor. "Who is this girl you fight for, Temoc? I have read your tablets and your prophecies. She is not mentioned. She has walked the world like a brand through a dry field, trailing fire. Ajaiatez has lost its Lady. The Shining Empire writhes in civil war. One of your own dead gods does her bidding. And here you are, man. In the sacred heart of the world, raising powers even I am too wise to screw with. If the stars are wrong, what do you think *she* is?"

Temoc gasped for air. "Ixzayotl was bound—beneath the waves. As I within the mountain. She freed us."

"Freed you? Puppet, you cannot see the cords around your limbs. She ties people to her. She might not know what she's doing—but neither does a plague. You have handed her the Serpents, who your own superstition holds to be our last refuge, our saviors, whose mercy will slag the land to glass and boil away the seas. What do you think she is?"

"A power," he gasped, "strong enough to defeat you."

"Of course. You have the highest and purest motives and your magic is sparkles and unicorns and rainbows. Temoc. It does not work that way. Your faith is an altar and a knife, and your gods are hungry. Why do you fight for her? I'm sorry, I know, you can't breathe, I'm strangling you, fine. I'll do your part. You *believe* in her. You, and a dead god, and another terrorist, and a company of mercenaries who, left to their own devices, would be looking for another bunch of innocent people on the other side of the world to get paid for killing, because innocents don't fight back. And yet here you all are, on the same side. *Her* side. Hasn't it ever occurred to you to ask what the skazzerai *are*? How you'd know one if you met it in the flesh? Of course not. And in all your righteous heroism, you've handed her the Serpents. You fool."

The night closed in, starless, moonless. Whenever he was being crushed to death, he always heard his heart, drumlike and mighty. The heart was the last warrior.

He would not let it fight alone.

"I will stop you," Dawn cried. "I will fight you."

"Dawn," Mal said, kindly. "You can't."

"Shut up!" Tears stung her eyes. "I know what this is. Looking out into the ocean like everything that was going to happen to you has happened already. You want to throw yourself away because some asshole taught you your highest purpose was to be *kindling*. Well, it's not!"

Mal was holding her. Her arms creaked Dawn's ribs. She kept realizing how strong this woman was. She could not think at all. There seemed to be a great stone in her way.

"He will kill them," Mal said, "and he will come for you. Because you're with me. Because I brought you here. It's not right, but when has the world been right? It *is*. That's what we have to work with. Let me do this for you." Mal squeezed one last time—then she let go, and stepped toward the railing.

Dawn lunged, but Mal was already burning. Her fingers closed on flames as Mal began to rise.

Abelard's vestment lining contained a shocking amount of high-tension cable. It was a simple matter (the priest said, though it didn't look simple as he worked) of slinging the cable anchor over the bottomless drop and through the firefight to grapple the sampling platform. He was sure the anchors to the cavern wall would hold, though Caleb would have felt better if Abelard hadn't muttered something about how they didn't have much choice.

When people said they didn't have a choice, Caleb reflected, so often what they actually meant was that they'd *had* a choice, farther back in time, before they understood its breathtaking consequences.

"On three," the priest said. And on three, they went.

As they fell, Caleb heard the Serpents sing.

There were many voices—thousands—in another room, as if this cavern and the Serpents and the firefight were a painted backdrop and if he reached out in just the right way he could sweep it aside to see the others, singing, screaming, waiting for him.

One of those voices was his own. He felt the Serpents' hands upon him, their strength, the strength of ages, bearing him toward the throne, toward destiny and death. He could lend his voice to theirs. There was a place for him in that fire behind the curtain of the world.

Burn for us. Be what is needed.

He pulled away. Time was real. He was falling. He belonged to this moment, to Teo and Abelard. The Serpents could wait.

The air changed. The whirlwind coils of the Serpents shifted. And with a great whiplike unwinding, Achal began to rise. At her head, like those pearls dragons chased in Shining Empire pictures, there flew a star that was a woman, with eyes of green fire.

He said her name.

Mal turned. She saw him.

And then time began again, and he was falling, as she rose to the battle in the sky.

Dawn wept. The Serpent Aquel swayed before her.

Are you ready, Little One? Your friend has made her choice. Will you honor it?

She raised her gloved hand, trembling, to the Serpent. "What now?"

Enter the time of gods. Face the curse you bear. We will give you strength. Perhaps you will not fail.

"What do you mean, *perhaps?*" Sybil hissed.

A lava tongue darted from the Serpent's mouth and kissed her, and she was somewhere else.

Temoc was dying, and the King in Red laughed.

He became aware of a growing warmth. That was not usually a part of dying. Unless you were dying of fire, of course.

The demon night went red around him. He smelled ozone and hot metal.

The King in Red looked down. Whatever he felt, he could only grin. "Of course. Right on schedule."

52

Dawn fled through the haunted wood.

Hunger followed.

Somewhere, the others fought. Somewhere, Mal burned through the skies, a holy filament. Any moment, she might snap. Dawn had to be worthy of her sacrifice.

But she was alone and afraid.

A dead willow wrapped her in whiplike branches that wept foul amber sap. The sap hardened around her limbs, crept toward her eyes and mouth. Dawn clawed free, leaving bits of skin and hair, as behind her through the wood the hunger came.

She had to get away. She could not face her.

There! A gap in the trees, a glint of dying light. She ran. She smelled the hunger's carrion breath, rank with leaf must and rot and the stench of every devouring thing. She leapt toward the light—and fell. The light had been sky, but only because the ground dropped away.

She landed in the mire. Cold mud dragged her down. Gritty water rushed into her mouth. She gasped and swallowed foulness. Slender roots bound her limbs, and vines braided through her hair. The vines turned her, gentle as a mother, back to face the weeping wood. She tried to close her eyes, but the vines would not let her.

The hunger stepped from the trees.

Dawn's gasp became a sob.

The goddess was made of wood and rock and stream, and she was dying.

She had no real body—the swamp shifted to lend her form as she advanced. The cragged thorns that were her face became her hair, and now the bloodied pinprick of a flower was her eye.

Whole, she would have been inhumanly tall and lean, a hunter formed with vicious economy. Even ruined, she was majesty.

Black iron stitched her through. Her vines split with iron rot. Her sores bristled with the teeth of gears. Wire fountained from her burst eye and plunged into the wooded recesses of her skull. Engines churned in the cage of her ribs. The moss of her legs was sick with black mold. The dragonflies of her hair were mounted insects in a collector's box.

She descended toward Dawn. One long creaking hand stretched out.

Dawn tried to pull away, but a thin rootlike finger touched her chest and burrowed into her.

She screamed.

Yes, the hunger said. *Give yourself to me. The iron eats me, but together we can choke its gears, blight its engines. Give me all you have and more, and we may yet survive to see the sun.*

Dawn ached before those pierced-flower eyes, that face sculpted by countless generations' awe into the perfect huntress of the wood. How dare she resist the call?

A small voice within protested. She may be a goddess but she takes a living form. Do you hear a heartbeat? The iron has eaten her through. That, not her, is what you feed.

But how frail a raft was that reasoning voice, atop the great swells of her that answered the hunger's call.

Roots wormed past her ribs, beneath her breastbone—

And there they found the fire.

The Serpents' flame flowed through her, down withered roots into the hunger's heart. Their rage seared, yet where it passed, the wood and plant-flesh and flower-skin became whole again, green, supple, new. Foul sap cleared and ran back into wounds that closed. In the hunger's chest, where Dawn had thought that only iron was, a verdant light flickered, pulsed, began to beat. Churning clockwork snarled. Gears popped with twangs like music.

This was the Serpents' might. Even here they could offer life and memory.

The goddess bloomed. She lived again, full of holy dread, raised up by the fire.

Dawn thought, It's working.

She breathed, "Ajaia," and the hunger smiled as if she knew the name.

53

Temoc drowned in darkness.

Then the darkness shattered. He fell for a screaming instant before a hand of flame caught him. He gazed up into a face that was inferno.

He was a man of many Gods, and he had kept the faith so long. He fought not for power or revenge or riches, nor to soothe his twisted manhood. He fought for a memory.

Once there was a city, and all who lived there moved in perfect knowledge of their purpose in the world. All were cherished and understood. There was sickness and suffering and death and all the great transformations, but those were the working-out of the universe. None were forgotten.

He did not know if it was ever truly thus. When he was born, the city was already at war, and his masters told him much had changed. But when he looked back through time, in the tablets of the great archive, he found his city's history a tissue of wars and transformations, of regimes that rarely endured for half a century. Perhaps what he remembered was not the real city but a projection, like the holograms he'd seen traveling peddlers present: ghosts of light formed by reflections from a subtly grooved surface, with no substance at all.

Still, a part of him had fought for that city, tirelessly and for his entire life, and that part now gazed with awe and wonder upon the burning face of the woman he had known as Mal.

There was another part of him, though. A part that lived not in the perfect city of his memory but the fallen city of his waking life, where he had grown to manhood, found his love, and tried to raise a son. That part was broken, treacherous. When that part of him saw Mal wreathed in the Serpents' flame, all it felt was loss.

"Come on, old man," she told him. "It's not your time."

"How touching," said the skeleton. "A reunion." Shadows writhed the King in Red, and his crown burned. Glyphs throbbed along his bones. Space rippled, and plates of demonglass armor condensed into being to clad his limbs. "You still don't get it, do you?"

His lightnings flashed toward Mal. She swept her blazing arm in a blurred half circle, and they shattered. A wave of light struck Kopil in midair and sent him flying, trailing demonglass splinters. He skidded to a stop, staff raised. Flames licked his robe, and he slapped them out.

"You killed my family, Craftsman." Her voice was the voice of thunder and rockslide, echoed by the Serpent chorus. "They burned in Chakal Square."

"Look," he said, one hand out. "Just give me a moment here."

A hammer of flame struck him from above. He fell like a meteor and struck the desert hillside in a fountain of dirt.

Mal was gone in a flash and a streak. Temoc could barely follow her movements. This was power beyond power. Flame blossomed within the dust cloud, and Kopil tumbled head over foot into the sky, half his face afire from where Mal's second punch had landed. Burning cracks spiderwebbed bone.

Wings of shadow flared from his shoulders to arrest his fall—he raised one hand, fingers now tipped with meter-long claws of darkness, and brought down with a great noise as of a stage curtain, tearing—

Mal caught his wrist.

"Why should I wait?" she hissed. "Why listen? Have you ever, even once? Do you know my parents' names? The names of any of the thousands of lives you have ruined? Or is it all wasteland in the cavern of your skull?"

The flames of her grip pulsed. There came a crack of breaking bone and a groan of pain that might, almost, have issued from a human throat.

Mal glared into the pits of Kopil's eyes. Temoc heard, beneath the flames, a creaking rhythmic sound—a dead tree in high wind. Laughter.

"You think this is funny?" She twisted her grip, grinding his broken bones. "You think I won't kill you? You think you scare me?"

His voice was tight with strain. "It really is all about affect with you people, isn't it? Someone could strangle every baby seal in the sea and all you'd care about is if he felt bad afterward. You're so consumed with your feelings you can't see what's in front of your face."

Another pulse of fire. Another crack of bone. Another skeletal groan.

"I made a mistake, in the Rising. An awful stupid mistake. The same one you're making now. I let myself fight the God Wars again, rather than dealing with the people in front of me. I wanted to feel good and mighty and righteous. I had all the power, and it seemed easier to use it."

Another crack. "What are you saying?"

"I'm saying that it was a bad play. If I had not given them a force to press against, your parents and everyone else in that square would have gone home alive. What were we fighting over? A real-estate deal? There would have been another. I had time. I was acting in a dream, like you are. You have your oppressor in your grip. All the might of ages at your command. But you still can't get it through that thick arrangement of meat you call a brain that maybe you are making a mistake."

"How, exactly?" She flared brighter than the sun.

"I walked the airless halls of the Observatory. You were attacked there, I saw the damage. Why didn't your enemy kill you?"

"They tried."

"With one operator. They could have sent more. Hells, if they told me where you were, I'd have done their work for them."

"You would have failed. As you are failing now."

"Am I?"

"I have broken three of your bones. I could break more."

"Please. You have broken two of my bones, in three *places* total."

"You mean to get technical with me?"

"You have to *get technical*, you C-student excuse for a revolutionary. If you don't *get technical* you make *mistakes*. Your adversary wanted you to fail at the Observatory, so you would be forced to try again here. They did not track you down while you licked your wounds. They waited until you called the Serpents—until you brought them into time. You took our only weapon against the dark and made it *vulnerable.* You set their table and waited on their meal."

"You don't know what you're talking about." But she sounded less sure. "You're trying—"

"What?" The question seared the sky with sheet lightning and crackled in the air. "What am I trying, exactly? What strategy could hinge on my letting you hit me? You blood-mad weirdos, I am trying to talk with you. I am trying to stop you from extending that stream of mistakes you call a career. Did it never occur to you for one instant that you were being used?"

Thunder rolled. Mal stared at him, her certainty in tatters. And still the King in Red was smiling.

"You're wrong." Tears of green flame burned in her eyes.

"Sometimes," he agreed. "But not *this* time. I don't like you, Ms. Kekapania. I think you're a self-righteous amateur who couldn't make the dean's list, and you've handed your bit reins to that thing down there you think is a girl, happy to prance when she goads you. But you're still something like human. So let's all take an elixir of chill, put the superweapons away, and make sure we're not all playing into some unknown third party's hands, before I stop playing mister nice wizard. Hm?"

She almost believed him. Temoc could see that in her shoulders and her hands and neck, which never lied as did the eyes and mouth. She might have let him go.

Temoc had harbored grudges and hungered for vengeance and knew how they shaped the mind until its every path ran downhill toward blood. For decades, she had hated this thing that used to be a man. She had been shaped on the whetstone of hating him. And yet she listened.

Temoc had once feared Malina Kekapania as one feared a rabid dog. He had pitied her, in her fundamentalism, in her subjection to her master's whims. He had fought beside her and even, begrudgingly, come to like her. But he had never respected her before.

Her fire faded. Her grip eased.

And then the Serpents screamed.

————

Caleb landed hard on the sampling platform and lay there staring up, past the firefight between Wardens and mercs, at the risen Serpent and the star that was Mal, facing the King in Red in the gyre of the sky.

Teo pulled him halfway to his feet. He managed the rest on his own. "I have to get up there."

"You don't have to do any such thing. Stick to the plan."

"The plan was to stop this from happening," he pointed out.

"Working about as well as usual for our plans, then."

"Why do you think I wanted you along?"

"Caleb?" Abelard's voice. "A little help?"

The priest stood at the far end of the platform. Climbing gear dangled from his robe. He was pointing.

And there was the girl.

To Caleb's surprise, she didn't look all that different from when he'd seen her at the spirecliffs, when the end of the world had been more of an impending rather than presently unfolding doom. She had not been floating back then, of course, with her eyes rolled back into her head. And there had not been any Serpents.

He stared at the great Form. He remembered Aquel's implacable grip.

"What do we do now?" Abelard said.

"Stop her." Caleb hadn't settled on the *how*. With one hand on the cable, he climbed to the highest unmelted iron rail and reached for her. Teetering over the gap and the endless fall, he could not quite reach her. "Can you—"

Abelard's god moved within him. When Caleb used his scars on Craftwork it felt like he was shaping clay on a potter's wheel. Now he was the one held and worked into a pleasing form.

He set one foot on empty air and found that he could walk. That didn't make it any easier to let go of the cable. But he did.

The Serpent fixed him with its enormous diamond eye.

Hollow man, said the voice of his dreams, *Caleb son of Temoc of the house of Alh, this is not your time. The Little One has sought us, and the songs have been sung.*

Speech was paltry, an insult. His voice sounded like a reed flute, so shrill, so easily broken. "You don't know what she is."

Neither does she. The play transforms in the playing. Would you deny her choice, you who chose to leave us?

He reached for Dawn.

Far above, he heard a Serpent shriek.

His bones received the sound more than his ears—his bones, his heart, his eyeballs, those weird wet mechanisms that told him which way was up.

The sky was riven with fountains of light.

Once his mother had shown him pictures, procured through some mighty Craft, of plasma jets hundreds of miles above the surface of the sun. That's blood, he thought. The blood of a Serpent. He flinched from its brilliance. Purples and blacks bloomed in his eyes. He thought for an instant that he had been blinded, that something was wrong with his eyes: he could see the cavern wall, but the shadows there seemed to be . . . moving?

No. His eyes were fine. The shadows really were moving. Or: something was moving inside them.

It *pounced.*

It leapt from the cavern wall, a shape like a splayed and many-fingered hand a hundred feet across, all writhing chains. It landed on the Serpent's scales and burrowed in.

Fusion-flare blood sprayed from Aquel's wounds, melting glassy troughs into the cavern wall. She roared and burned white, but the spider-thing on her neck dug its legs in deeper. He expected it to melt, but it grew instead, as if it drank her heat. Where its legs touched the diamond scales, they buckled, cooled, and cracked. The fire in which Dawn hovered went out. She let out a strangled gasp and began to fall.

Caleb prayed. The god's flame burned through his scars and erupted from his back, shaped into wings. He became aware of heat as tapestry and color. He could feel its currents, and the searing gout of Serpent blood that fountained toward him. He spun—the white-hot spray just missed, but even so it seared his skin. Without his scars he would be boiling.

He caught Dawn as she fell and swept her around, up. His wings welcomed him to flight. He threw her back to the platform, to Abelard and Teo.

Then a big rock hit him from behind.

The thrashing Serpent had dislodged shelves of stone. A boulder tore through his fiery pinions and he plummeted, until a desperate wing-flare pulled him out of the dive.

Above, Aquel slithered skyward to join her embattled sister. She scraped her bulk against the stone but could not dislodge the black iron things—there were more of them now, or else the one that struck her had budded others. They carved in deep, leaving trenches in the lava-flesh beneath which fire surged like muscle.

Where the Serpent bled, it cooled, and the spider-things grew larger, darker, in their feast.

An impossible notion anchored in his thought. The Serpents need help.

More impossible: They need my help.

What could he do against this atrocity? But he had learned this much from playing cards. Once you made your decision, do not question it. Later you could doubt and analyze. In the moment, you had to trust yourself.

Caleb prayed. *Make me an instrument.*

And God said, *Kid, I'll make you a sword.*

54

Kai crouched beside Tara in the wreckage of the Grimwald's platform in burning Chartegnon. Between them lay the slagged fist of bronze that once had been a carving of the Serpents.

"Tara," she said. "What should we do?"

Her eyes were cold and bright. "We have to get to Dresediel Lex."

There were many questions, starting with *how*, but before Kai could voice any of them she was interrupted by a screech of torn metal from below. She ran to the platform's edge. Ghostlights and wan rays of sun illuminated heaps of rubble and a pit that had not been there before. At the pit's edge stood two figures. The face of the man in the suit was half gone, revealing a nest of iron cables. The woman wore a sodden velvet dress. A gold disc hung at her throat, and she was smiling.

"Now you understand the great path," the vampire said. She glowed, even at this distance. "We shall rise eternal to the joyous dark." And then she spread her wings.

"She, um," Kai said. "She didn't have wings before?"

Tara's hand closed on her arm. "We need to get out of here. We needed to get out of here *days* ago." She dragged Kai—the spirit was willing, the legs wobbly—to the skullbeast, where Shale was already locking himself in. In a confusion of bones, they mounted and, with a leap, they soared.

Tara shouted over the rush of wind, "Shale—I need you to pray for me."

"I would not presume. You are the priestess."

"I'm kind of busy." They were coming up on the plate-crystal ceiling, and Clarity was gaining. Tara made a rapid gesture with her hand, and the ceiling shattered. Sun, such as it was, streamed in, and they burst out into the smoke-gray Chartegnon sky.

Kai glanced back into the shadows of the fallen spire. The suited man drew something from within his coat—it caught the light, twisted it like the opposite of a prism into a single point of brilliance in his hand.

The sun went dark.

It was still there, a vague brightness in the lowering clouds—but the chill of night swept over them, and the city's fires showed red and orange through the smoke. Clarity streaked up from the fallen spire, eyes aflame, jaws impossibly wide, her fangs not exactly visible at this distance but unmistakably implicit. As fast as the skullbeast flew, she was gaining.

"This is good," Tara said, "sort of." She spoke a glyph-word and the clouds boiled away. The sky was dusky purple, the stars caught out and unsure, like guests at a party when someone turned on the lights. Beside the weakened disk of the sun glimmered a sliver of moon. "Shale? Can she help us?"

"They're getting closer," Kai put in—and Clarity was beside her, claws sweeping for Kai's throat. Kai screamed, pulled away. Bone fléchettes darted past her, and one of those gem-fire eyes winked out in a splash of humor. Kai would have been happier if her scream sounded more like a wounded animal than a person.

"Shale?"

He intoned, "The Lady of Silver Light and Perfect Radiance advises—"

Clarity recovered, and with a beat of her wings swept toward the skullbeast, her teeth bare. "Shale, speed is a factor."

"She says, *hold your breath.*"

Kai began to ask a question, but before she could finish it, they were gone.

55

As Dawn reached for the goddess, she began to die.

The Serpents' fire went out. The cold returned. Hunger tore her, endless need that only cancer-growth could fill.

Before, as she fled through the weeping forest, Dawn had not understood. Ajaia hungered—but Ajaia had shielded her, too, from the shard. Now they were entangled, Dawn and the goddess. As Ajaia fell into the maw of gears she dragged Dawn with her.

There would be no sunrise, no thaw—no future but iron.

Abelard felt Dawn's pulse beneath the ice that rimed her skin. "She's dying."

"Isn't that a good thing?" Teo shouted. She wasn't trying to be rude, Abelard thought. There was a battle and a firefight and a number of other things happening at once, any of which would qualify as apocalyptic for most midsized religions.

Dawn spasmed. She breathed in yips through her clenched jaw, and her exhalations crystallized. The veins that climbed her arm throbbed sickly gray-green. Thorns dimpled her throat from the inside.

Isn't that a good thing?

Dawn, or the being inside her, had eaten Tara's arm. Killed Tara's father. Set nations on fire. If Tara were here, perhaps she would simply, slowly, draw her knife, and—

No.

He could not see it. Tara was not here, but there was a piece of her in Abelard, as there was a piece of him in her, slivers of self traded between friends. She might ask the question. She might teeter in the balance. But in the end she would use her knife, as she always did, to cut toward freedom.

"I don't think so."

"Then help her. You're the priest."

"I'm not that kind of priest!"

"What kind of priest are you?"

Good point. Tara would help, as *she* could. Not as someone else might, if only they were here.

He looked upon the girl with eyes of faith.

He could see the Goddess inside her, Her thorn and roots. But there was something else worked through the vines—a darkness terrifying in its complexity, fractal flywheels and molecular springs carving Goddess and girl to build more of itself.

Kos was Lord of the forge and of its works. He was Lord of Interlocking Things. The million-geared nanoscale factory eating Dawn's body and soul was a miracle of a sort, wrought with tricks—which he dearly wished he had time to fathom—for dealing with waste heat, for convincing friction it was a thing that happened to other people. What could you build if you could manipulate matter on this scale? What gifts could you offer the world? What wonders might you work?

He didn't know. But maybe he could wreck some.

———

The Serpents' power flowed through Mal into the world of time. With it came their pain. It overwhelmed her, the cold and the terror, the teeth in her chest. She fell like a star, as Aquel and Achal hammered the cavern with their mountainside bodies.

But she was no stranger to agony.

In the weeks after her failure on the day of the black sun, as she lay soulless in a shadow clinic while a tube down her windpipe vacuumed fluid from her lungs, she had known pain and hated it and learned to endure. There was a far side to the river. Once you knew that, you could swim.

So now she rose through the pain, toward the Serpents. She darted between lightning bolts and curses, Wardens and Arsenal

Company alike unsure where to aim. Two Mr. Browns were airborne now, unfolded to clouds of iron starlings about the nova of the King in Red. He was not dead yet, or at least no more dead than usual.

She would deal with that bastard later.

It was hard to focus, to remember that time was a matter of half and quarter seconds, of clock-ticks and heartbeats rather than eons. She saw the Mr. Browns wrapped around Aquel's throat, black webs spun across the solar landscapes of the wounds they'd carved in the Serpent's flesh. Aquel and Achal could not dislodge them, but if she struck from outside . . .

She dug claws of flame into an iron web and pulled. Its filaments withered, curled. Plasma crowned and haloed her, and at last she tore the web free.

Then, careful as a houseplant seeking the light, those razored filaments slipped around her throat. One, sharp as love and oh so tender, traced a line down her cheek. They closed around her, and she began to bleed.

Temoc felt sick. He had seen the blasphemies too late—the unfolded clockwork things that leapt from the barren hillside to bury themselves in the Serpents' flesh, tearing scale and muscle to vent lava blood, growing as they drank.

He recognized them, though: the clockwork horror of the man called Mr. Brown. In Tlaloc Observatory, he had fought one of their kind. They drank the power of the world, claimed it for their own. And now they drank the Serpent's blood.

He did not know what to do. He scanned the hillside beneath and—yes, there: one more, a man in a dark suit. Or so it seemed, before it leapt and all that was flesh about it tore away. Temoc caught this final blasphemy in midair. His blade and his Gods parted its iron webs with a single blow, but those webs coiled around him, carving, and he fell.

The blasphemy did not fight as a human thing or as the slavering beasts of Craftwork alchemy. It had no strategy, no script. It simply tried to kill him, from every direction at once.

Filaments circled his fingers and would have snipped them off if not for his scars. Still more climbed his nostrils, stopped with shadow. They shredded his clothes, sank to his thighs and to the fork of his legs. If he had been a young man he would have flinched. As an old man, he trusted the Gods. He cut away the monofilament limbs, but as they fell they joined together and tried, with horrific shuddering motion, to fly back to him again.

There had to be some glyph or heart that held the blasphemy together. If only he could find it in time. He was falling. This had not posed a problem so far, but the cavern was not infinitely deep, and the floor would command his attention sooner or later.

He was still figuring out the *how* when a raging forge-heat seared his chest.

The blasphemy went limp. He was free. He skidded to a stop on empty space and stared.

An angel hovered over him. Wings of fire burst from its back, and it—he—held a blade of shifting flames. He was clad in shadow, but bright scars burned through. Temoc knew those scars. They were like his own, though rough and fierce, left by a graceless shaking hand. In the long silence beneath Shenshan mountain, he had never imagined this moment. To envision a thing was to let the mountain use it.

Here, before him, was his son. His son, unbroken—the joy for which he had not dared hope. His son, blessed of the Gods, owning his place as an Eagle Knight and as a man.

There were tears in Temoc's eyes. It was proper that it be so. There was so much wrongness in the world that one could not survive were one to flinch from that which was right.

"Caleb," he said. "I love you. And I have missed you."

Caleb's mouth opened but no words came out. His burning eyes widened, then pinched shut. His free hand rose to his temple.

"That's all you have to say?"

"What more is there?"

"The last time I saw you we had a godsdamn fistfight on top of a pyramid."

"No filial relationship is without strain. You fought for what you believed in. I am proud of you."

"This is nuts."

"That language," Temoc said, gently, "is detrimental to the mentally ill. And to those blessed by the Gods with deeper sight."

"Gods!" Caleb cursed. "We don't have time for this."

Like a prophet, Caleb spoke more truth than he could have intended. All words were tangled, pasts knotted through futures. If they could sit down and breathe deeply, perhaps they might find the true clear line connecting heart to will to deed. How holy, such space would be. How seldom found.

"We will," Temoc said, "later," and accepted Caleb's outstretched hand and felt the heat of his power. "Whose mantle do you wear?"

"Do you have to call it that?"

"It is the technical term. I do not recognize the grace at work in you."

"It's Kos Everburning."

"A foreign God," he said, questioning.

"It's not—I'm just borrowing him for a while."

This was not how Temoc would speak about the power suspending one above seething magma, but the young had their own ways, and who could say what a foreign God might think meet and proper? Let alone a strange permissive deity like the Lord of Alt Coulumb. Caleb did not fall screaming to his death, so Temoc assumed all was well. Best not to question the pacts of another man with his God, even—especially—if that man was your son.

Above, the Serpents roared. "Have you faced the blasphemies before?"

Caleb shook his head. "You?"

"Once. They are strong. Made to devour. How did you free me?"

"There was a gearbox tumor sort of thing over your heart. Angry red glyphs."

It was, Temoc had often reflected, quite convenient that some sorts of malevolent witchcraft had the grace to *look* malevolent. It was not so often with the Craft. Those cradled within its skeletal palm did not see the flayed hillsides, the dammed rivers drowning canyons, the fields poisoned with necromantic sludge and heavy metals, the burning lakes, the slow advancing ice caps. They saw air-conditioning and zombies to sweep their streets, designer textiles, good trains, golem shipping, the nightmare telegraph. He wondered what the world would look like from inside these blasphemies. Systems, like people, tended to vent their awfulness outward. "Then our course is clear."

Their eyes met. There was too much to say. They would say it later.

Together, for the first time, they flew.

56

Dawn drowned in iron. Gear teeth bit her brain, and where they tore nothing endured but desolation. She could not fight this process, inevitable as history. Neither could Ajaia. But in their panic they fought each other, two people lowered into a blender together: each climbing over the other in hope the loser would, even for an instant, jam the blades.

Dawn did not hate Ajaia, even now. Whatever sort of goddess she had been, noble or terrible or dickish or just there, she had thrown herself onto the iron rather than let it devour her people. But Ajaia wanted to live. There was no time now for colloquy, for round tables or negotiated alternatives. They were slipping inexorably toward the blades.

Dawn had learned the Craftswoman's way of seeing, to conceive of the world in its several parts, address each separately and thus gain leverage and control. Now she was, herself, being seen. When she turned her gaze on that which did the seeing, she found no leverage. It was death. That was all.

Then, above the churning gears, she heard something new: a man's voice, gentle and sure. She did not understand his words so much as feel them. They soothed her—a warmth that bloomed in the gnawing pit.

With a scream, the gears, the blades, stopped. They were still inside her. She was still dying. But she could breathe. The goddess was bound to her by roots and chains. Her eyes glassy with pain, her limbs limp, her flesh torn.

She had seconds. That's all you ever have—just seconds, one after the other, until the end. What will you do with them?

She hung and hurt and tried to think.

Caleb flew beside his father toward the flames.

What could you say to your dad? Your dad who'd spent most of your life making war against the city you loved? Your dad who claimed to love the city, too, even as he tried to destroy it? Your dad who stood above you in the darkness with a knife? Who cut you as he'd been cut himself, because in the hour of desperation he could think of no other gift? Your dad who tried to kill your best friend? Who spent the last five years in prison? Your dad, whom you thought was dead? You'd only persuaded yourself he wasn't because his passing would have cracked the sky.

And now he was here, and even if there had been time to speak, words and thoughts seemed to point in different directions. They could spend forever talking and only grow further apart.

The Serpents writhed above. Their blood flared like fireworks. Caleb felt his old terror of fires in dry season, of sparks and poorly ashed cigarettes and yellow hillsides waiting to blaze.

Between the Serpents he saw a star in the shape of a girl. A woman, now. She had been a woman when they first met—but he had been a boy. She was trying to fight. But the power she bore was the Serpents' power, and the Serpents now were mad with pain. Man or boy, he still grinned to think that he was about to do something that might count as saving her life. And that he would get to see her face afterward.

Gods. Today was going to be nothing but hard conversations.

He took a deep breath and felt the power in his scars.

What could you say to your dad?

"You take the one on the right" would have to do for now. "I'll take the one on the left."

Mal didn't want to die, but that was life sometimes.

Then a blade flashed past her, and she was free.

She had not been raised to question advantages. Her claws seared into the black web that had once been a Mr. Brown. The iron boiled to superheated vapor, leaving only her profound exhaustion and six more Mr. Browns to kill.

Only then did she look up to face the wielder of the blade, who—well, he had *not* saved her life; she could have managed moderate impalement just fine, thank you.

And there was Caleb. Her mistake.

She had not died. She had not forgotten him. She had never, in all those years, gone looking. Neither had he. She had hoped he was happy. She hoped he'd been able to remain something other than a weapon. But here he was, his scars open, a burning sword in that long-fingered hand.

She had known this would happen. She had known it from the moment she saw him in the golf ball. They were doomed to the fire, both of them, together.

But he wasn't looking at her the way a man looked at his doom. He was looking at *her*. Like he always did.

Another version of her, a better wiser stronger version, could have sorted through all the churn and mess and goop inside her heart and in her throat and behind her eyes, parsed it into neat piles with clear labels so she could say exactly what she felt and how much. Unfortunately, that better wiser stronger version wasn't here. Caleb and the world at large had to deal with the fuckup model. She did what came naturally, which was to say something she hoped sounded cool and not at all like dialog in the kind of mystery play that closed with a big kiss.

What she managed was "We have *got* to stop meeting like this."

57

You were a young woman once, and then you went to war.

Many years have passed since you fought—since you stalked through the rotting jungle, blade wet, since you hid in a muddy defile from searching angels, since you led the doomed and damned and dead through the wasteland game board you had made of someone else's world. But you were young when you came to the ending trade, and its patterns and its habits shaped you. The war was over, people said. But your life contained it now, no matter how you might wish it otherwise.

So you prepared.

Wealth alone cannot assure victory. A vast store of souls may seem like power to some, but it is mere potential, without skill and cunning—without Craft.

Standing in court, with exhibits entered and reality simplified to a duel between constructions of truth, mastery alone might win the day. That is, after all, the purpose of the Courts of Craft: to speak the truth in a way that makes it so, backed not by the fiat of a lord or demon or god or by the brutish chance of war but by the conviction shared by most people that words have meaning, that deals must be honored.

But while every court is a battlefield, not all battlefields are court. There will come a time when you face an enemy that honors no boundaries. When this happens, you will have no easy answers, no glyphs to call upon, no established precedent to invoke. You will find yourself once more in the jungles of your youth, breathing heavy, blade wet, a flap of scalp hanging like a curtain over your ear.

Nothing yet has been smarter than you or faster than you, or meaner. But the longer you live, the more certain you are that one day this will no longer be the case. Flesh fails, the mind seeks comfort. No hot streak lasts forever. And you ask yourself the very question that forms the root (Alexander Denovo claims) of the Craft: how can we be greater than we are?

Alexander Denovo, indeed, thought he knew the answer: you bind others to your service. Their bodies, minds, souls become machines you may task as you wish. While he lived, he welcomed his students; he made himself their center, trapped them in his event horizon so that every path they took led back to him.

Confronted directly, this method is formidable. The Denovo cluster swarms over any problem, breaks it into component blocks, conducts high-speed analysis, and strangles adversaries. The students trapped within do not, as a rule, feel themselves prisoners. They are, they think, part of a great and mighty work.

Once, for a time, you were one of them.

But the Denovo cluster has a weakness. Independent thought leads the thinker astray. Alexander Denovo's sick need for adoration, for unity beneath his will, undermines all that does not affirm his greatness. Crushed, depressed, and drained when they are not graced by his love, his students struggle on until they burn to ashes. Or in a few cases, break free.

There must be another way—a way for many wills to join to a single end without the withering effect of the Denovo cluster or the abnegation of surrender to a godhead. (You have prayed once, and only once, and still you stagger from the implications.)

In fact there are many ways. You have encountered several, designed several more. But you are pleased to think that you have settled upon a solution with a certain elegance.

The Denovo cluster's failure lies in its overhead, the violent work required to knit many selves to one and guide those straying minds to the master's ends. Surely such effort would not be required if the other minds in the cluster were your own?

Set aside an hour every day. Mark it off with wards and close your eyes. Enter the depths of yourself, the deepest terror where all dreams touch, the hollow core of you. Give that hour over. Leave it in trust for when it is needed.

For when an old woman calls you and your ten thousand sisters out to war.

Elayne Kevarian simplified and found herself in a ruin.

The dream arcade lay burning and broken, pierced by demonglass. Her breath froze the air to crystals, which sublimed as they fell. Her skeleton felt more real than her flesh.

They faded so quickly, these ghosts of her, her children of time. She tried to recall them, but she could glimpse only a fading shock of dyed-green hair, a hungry look in a younger eye.

In the comedown after burning time, she pieced herself together. She had explained the effect to Belladonna Albrecht once: imagine your self as a jigsaw puzzle, whole and perfectly assembled—until you find in the box a pile of new pieces to that same puzzle. When you match them in, you form a larger subtler more profound image. Now remove the new pieces and assemble your former self again. How lonely the original seems, how meager the self you thought complete just—she checked her watch—one minute and thirteen seconds before.

She blinked in surprise. That couldn't be right. She had just burned a hundred hours in seventy-three seconds. No wonder she felt cold. Her tissues were crystallizing. There were ice distortions in her eyes. This was yet another reason Belladonna kept after her to transition. The meat parts, for all their sentimental value, were not rated for high-test Craftwork.

She stood within Zack's ruptured chassis. The wreck of the gray man lay around her.

If not for Zack, she might have died. In his rage and sorrow, Zack caused the gray man to take steps that made him . . . less gray. As an unknown quantity, even Elayne might have underestimated him.

It was not the gray man's power that was dangerous so much as the offhand clarity with which it was deployed. There were many mighty bullies in the world, and many scared people who through the luck of blood or class or simply stumbling over a magic sword stuck into a tree in the forest might pose a threat—but these often troubled themselves with self-image and emotion and scruple. The gray man did not. He had a taste for the dramatic that she found regrettable in a serious operator—witness the entrance with the mask, the footsteps. But when he acted, he acted all at once, and fatally.

She respected that. Even if he was an asshole. Had been an asshole.

There was so *much* of him, everywhere around. What was that statistic from first-year anatomy? If you could unspool every blood vessel in the human body, or was it every nerve, into a single ribbon of tissue, you could girdle the world three times, or reach from Alt Coulumb to Ultima Thule, or some such thing. The textbook authors should know better. A friend of hers worked in the Ungroundskeeping Department of the Hidden Schools and had spent the last four decades petitioning the vivisection faculties to stop mentioning that particular amusing tidbit in their intro lectures, because she kept having to clean up after students who tried.

You're fading out. Stay relevant, Elayne. The physical world exists, even if it is not comfortable at the moment.

The gray man lay in coils around her and upon her, the wires and whips of him not iron, after all, but bits of highly ordered carbon in some kind of graphene-derived suspension fluid. At four-hundred-factor magnification, the filings reminded her of the workings of a watch: tiny wheels and gears and springs and hooks, impossibly fine.

That was what he had been, inside the suit and the sack of human skin.

His face had caught on a rebar strut. It looked surprised. Faces often did, with the bones out.

A hundred hours. Seventy-three seconds.

There was none of him left to question, but she knelt anyway, lifted the face, and slipped it into a storage pocket. Her fingers sliced open his cheek, and she realized they were still knives. She made them flesh again and folded back into her the many instruments that made her fit for war. With trembling fingers, human once more and all but senseless, she drew from one of her many clever pockets a thin gold cigarette case. Her touch spread frost on its catch.

Inside lay twelve tight hand-rolled canvases, each packed with a mixture of leaves of her own devising. The drugs were not the point, though if she ever found herself in need of the cigarette case, Elayne had expected she would appreciate them. The drugs were just for the pain.

The paintings in which she rolled them were for her soul.

Poor Teufl the Elder. She felt for those desert-mad heretics, passing around for centuries in secret their little black book that caused the fall of Telomere. The geniuses of Teufl's age, some five hundred years ago, had made acceptable art in public, licking their lead-paint brushes to needle points as they painted cloth merchants and dyers and bankers and priests with squids worked in gold about their throats, while in the depths of candlelit night, they made their glories. A kneeling virgin, her bloody eyes raised in rapture to a pale and ageless being descendant from the stars. The Stoneworker, offering his blood to his followers, beatified by the knowledge of his coming torment, his face a mystery, and just visible behind those elegant lips, so pink she could not see them as the work of a brush, the tips of fangs.

She did not share their faith, but she could feel their hunger—not to go on as you were, trapped in one fleeting prison self, but to become of an eternal kind.

Teufl the Elder might have been killed for painting these. Those for whom he painted might have been killed for owning them. He made them anyway, with tireless dedication to his craft—yes, she would call it that—and they were passed along by the faithful at first, and eventually by Craftsmen who shared the ancient heretics' hunger for transcendence, rooted in painstaking knowledge of flesh—its texture, its pliancy, its delicate, which was to say fragile, transparence.

As they passed down the years in secret, the paintings gathered soul. Soulstuff was pattern-stuff, the work of a conscious mind on the chaos of the world. You could describe it in terms of time: many hours of focused attention, fusing every impulse from loins to heart to the light of distant stars into a quanta of human worth. And what was art but crystallized time?

Poor Teufl the Elder. He had been obsessive, brilliant, and methodically, eerily productive. Which meant that Elayne had few compunctions about using him like this.

She selected a pietà and raised it to her lips.

She lit the canvas with burning wreckage from a dream machine, and breathed in.

In seventy-three seconds she'd burned through every shred of soul on her person, down to the—well, down to the *treads* of her shoes. Barely enough remained for cognition, and that fragmented, discursive. She'd be a starveling now, draining the world in hallucinatory grayout, if she had not been used to this sort of thing.

And she had work to do.

Consider the gray man. Had he been parked outside Zack's house of dreams, observing? If so, why? And for how long? Simply in case Elayne, or someone like Elayne, should come along, at which point he meant to intervene with deadly force? Unlikely. If Zack was so dangerous, why not simply remove him from play? Murders did attract attention, but attention could be managed.

No, he had been following Elayne. Since when? Dresediel Lex was not her home territory, but she had come here straight from Alt Selene, and in Alt Selene she would have made a tail in the time it took to fry a beignet. Here in D.L., Mina's house was carefully warded. Elayne had crafted those wards herself, not that Mina asked her to. She just felt better knowing Mina was safe.

So she had picked up the tail since leaving Mina's. The most likely person from whom she might have acquired it, of course, was the girl. Dawn.

The gray man had been tailing the girl. Then he split off to follow Elayne. Which he would only have done if there were other operators on the girl. And if their mere contact on the beach was worth the risk of moving against a senior Craftsperson without backup, that said a great deal about the operation's final purpose—most of it ominous.

She breathed out the last of the painting. Her fingers were

stained with lapis from a madonna's robe, the paint running again, after so long.

She knew how it felt.

She had to find Dawn.

On the horizon, she saw a glow that was not morning.

58

Teo should have been asleep by now. She just *had* to answer the door. She couldn't simply give Caleb the keys to her car, either. Had to come along. Join the fun.

Way up there, Serpents writhed and bled solar flares, and the King in Red was doing his thing, grown into a skeletal colossus in the writhing heavens, crowned with starlight, circled by planetoids of intersecting bone and crystal and coruscating lightning, yadda yadda. The writhing spider-things he fought burgeoned and swelled, endless yards of lashing wire. Just looking at the spider-things made her gut hurt. They reminded her of the kind of bugs that scuttled toward her across her bathroom floor when she turned on the lights at 2 A.M.

The boss seemed to be enjoying himself. Never did know when to pull his dick out of a finger trap.

Meanwhile, Temoc and Caleb and Mal were fighting the spider-things, which might be good for the long-term survival of the species or whatever, but did not improve Teo's personal odds, as a woman who could not fly even a little, suspended above a magma pit by a few decidedly meltable steel cables, with only two comatose god-botherers for company.

Gods, Teo had heard someone from back east say once, help those who help themselves. So she dragged Abelard and Dawn to the sampling cage's corner, taking care not to touch the part of the girl's skin that looked like it was getting devoured from inside out. With a mutter that very much was not a prayer, she clicked Abelard's climbing rig onto the cable.

That took care of Abelard. Now for her and the girl. Good thing she was still in her bathrobe. The sash tied her to Abelard, but it wasn't long enough for Dawn. Ugh. Engineer-priest, right? He must have a coil of rope stashed in those pockets. "Sorry, buddy," she muttered as she searched. "If it's any consolation, you're *really* not my type."

There. Rope. Now if she could just tie the girl in . . .

She was fumbling knots when the lava plume hit. Two of the platform's four cables snapped at once, and the floor swung away beneath her. Dawn slipped. Fell.

Teo caught Dawn's wrist and the scars on her own arm flared.

She had almost been a human sacrifice once. It was a long story she preferred not to revisit outside of trying to impress someone. (It rarely worked then, either. People always went all "sympathetic" about her "trauma" and how "hard it must have been," rather than "wow, Teo, how badass, take me now.") The sacrificer in this case had been Caleb's jerk dad, about whom the less said the better. But she'd ended up with a scar from a Knight's blade, which, it turned out, had certain implications.

So when she caught the girl, the scar on her wrist flared with green light, and shadow gauntleted her hand. Her own arm didn't yank out of its socket, and she didn't immediately die from wizard cancer or whatever the girl's problem was. She was still, however, dangling by a bathrobe sash from a borderline conscious priest, holding some kid over an unfathomable drop.

The sash began to slip. The cable overhead was fraying. Then it all began to hurt.

———

"I do not," Caleb said, as barbed-wire tentacles tried to drag him down to the stellar surface of the Serpent Achal, "hold a grudge."

"Of course you do." Mal burned the wires from him—the ends crisped and curled like spiders in a flame, but there were more of them, hundreds more, burrowing into the Serpent. "I lied to you. I set the stupid city on fire. I talked a bunch of shit. You *must* be pissed."

"It's complicated." He darted in with the burning sword with as little effect. "I'm still angry about all that, and other things. But that's justified. It's not holding a grudge."

"Yes it is!"

"Okay, fine, if it makes you happy. I hold a bit of a grudge."

". . . Fuck." Mal skidded to a stop on empty air, trailing fire. Lava leaked from cuts in her torso; her gone arm wept molten metal. "This isn't working."

Caleb could see the spider-things' cores below, the nodes of whirling gears and bloodred glyphs. They had battered back his every assault, as the Serpent roared and bled.

"I don't get why it's so hard. I pulled the other one off Dad, no problem."

"*Dad?*"

"He's my dad."

"Archpriest, last of the Eagle Knights, ascendant presumptive to the Grandmaster's torque—I'd go with 'father,' at least."

"I don't know that we're at the stage of our relationship where you can challenge the way I talk about my parents."

"We are not at any stage of our relationship. We are at the negative one million stage of our relationship. You didn't know I was still alive until a few days ago."

"I knew," he said, aware of what he was letting on, and ignoring her glance in reply.

"These things draw power off those they consume," she said, recovering. "The one that held your *father* did not have as much to fight us with."

He could work with that. Concepts bubbled. Possible sequences of action. "They use the power they steal. But one of them tried to eat my dad rather than going for the Serpents. So they can make mistakes. . . ."

"What are you thinking?"

"Just—get ready. If this works, I won't have much time."

"Caleb—"

He stopped and looked up at her, aflame. Back in the eclipse, Caleb had thought he'd seen her unmasked, but in the years since he'd realized he was wrong. What you were was different from what you'd been raised to be and from what you'd chosen to become. He had known her weeping. He had known her striving with every thaum of her implacable will. That woman was real—

more real than the fanatic she'd made herself out to be in those moments beneath the occluded sun.

He said, "I trust you."

He folded his wings and dived.

The closer he drew to the Serpents the more terrifying they became. As he fell, he prayed. There was a fire in him now, the fury of Abelard's god—and yet he wilted before the Serpents' world-ending heat.

How often had he heard his father inveigh against intercessory prayer? "A sign of how we have fallen, that we feel safe drawing the eye of the Gods to our paltry concerns, that we do not tremble at Their approach." But this was a special case. If you were working with a partner, best to fill them in on the plan.

It occurred to him that, by this logic, he should have gone into more detail with Mal. But she was smart. She could figure it out.

Well, came the answer down the prayer line, *let's try it and see what happens.*

He had the sudden vivid impression of how a pile of chips must feel as they were pushed into the center of the table. Then he was on fire.

Before, Caleb had directed the god's power through his scars. He might have claimed that he was in control, guiding that diffuse atemporal might into human space and time. If he was a levy, his walls were high and well-built, lined with mills and locks to channel the deity's will. But here came the flood. It topped his walls, crushed his locks, pulped homes, and tore up streets. The air rippled, fluoresced. What remained of his clothing evaporated.

Somehow he was still alive. That was a gift of the Eagle Knight's scars. When the gods drew near, the scars let you bear their regard and survive.

The Serpent's flesh had cooled where the parasites devoured, and what remained was rough, craggy, and sad—cooler now than Caleb himself. The spider-things—Mal had called them Mr. Browns for some reason—burrowed into Aquel's side. He thought, through the haze of heat, This isn't working.

They pounced.

Even though this very much was the plan, still he brought up his sword—useless. The godsdamn things were so raggedly fast. How many were there? One? Two? A thousand? They were all over him, and carving. There were churning blades and metal mouths all around, all hungry. His scars held, for the moment.

It didn't much help to think, This is the plan. It was *his* plan, after all, and he knew just how much of a mess he tended to make of things. Still: chips in the center. Play it through.

He prayed, *Now.*

God abandoned him.

Rather than a well of power and Serpent blood, the spider-things found themselves anchored to the body of a man, still wrapped, for the instant, in fading protective scars.

Oh, and falling.

The parasites devoured. One thin wire laid open a cut from his cheek to the ridge of his brow. Another cuffed his arm and bit down.

He started to think he might have miscalculated. Then, with a shriek of metal and a final agonizing spasm of razor wire, he wasn't falling anymore. Wasn't dying, either. Was, again, on fire.

Yay?

Mal hovered over him, her burning hand clasped around his wrist. He felt—too much, all at once. He had almost died, just now, but he had not once doubted she would come for him. He could read her surprise, that she had—and maybe her anger, that he'd known she would.

He opened his mouth to say "thank you." But she was on fire, and so was he, and she was still the most—not most beautiful, exactly, but the most *person* he had ever seen, and what he actually said was, "I love you."

Her eyes were pure jet flames. She said, "I want a divorce."

Temoc sang the war song. His was a glorious purpose. His was the sacred battle of the first men against the dark from which the world was born. He had been raised for this. The blessings of Gods burned in his heart, charged through his veins, shone from his eyes.

Unfortunately, the fact that one fought a predestined battle in the service of the Gods did not make such battle simple or painless or its victory certain. Quite the opposite. He had been shocked to hear young men of his son's generation express a desire to "find their purpose," as if doing so might relieve them of anguish and ennoble their days with joyful occupation. That had not been Temoc's experience of destiny.

He pressed past whipping legs and razor claws, past geared mouths with diamond tooth-wheels open for his soul. The blasphemies made claims upon him by the thousands, upon this world, upon Achal—but he sang and the Gods filled him. He plunged his knife into the churning gears and tore free a fist of tissue that, in a thing that lived, he would have called a heart.

One down. Two to go.

His flesh was in agony, his power tatters. His faith remained unquenchable, but faith did not win you many knife fights.

The King in Red cackled in the sky, monstrously large. His broken arm did not seem to bother him. He wielded his staff one-handed, and lightnings answered to his call. That battle seemed balanced—the blasphemies grew as they fed upon the Deathless King's power. But if he, Temoc, were to strike the King in Red at this moment, the balance might shift. The Deathless King would fall, and Temoc as well, in the instant of his victory. An Eagle Knight was a priest and therefore a poet. The rhyme appealed.

But then the blasphemies would win. And his son and his daughter-in-law and Dawn would lose.

Revenge was a fit calling for a man. But a priest was called to be more than man. So was a father. Temoc, weary, bleeding, turned to face the next blasphemy. They had merged their pulsing razor webs together and braided their strands. They necklaced the Serpent now, stretching razored tendrils toward Achal's vast diamond eye.

Screaming battle song, he charged across the cataclysm of the Serpent's hide. Razor whips lashed him. He caught the whips in one hand and tore them free, then swung them over his head as a flail. He gloved his fist and forearm in the razors, and with them turned the blows that rained down.

They carved his skin, and by the Gods' blessing he healed. They broke his bones, and by the Gods' blessing those healed, too, though crooked from the speed of their knitting. He stumbled. The blasphemy clutched him. He braced his leg against the Serpents' cooling hide. He hated doing this. He struck his own leg with his armored fist and the Gods' own might.

The second break healed straight.

His Gods kept him whole, in Their hundred tiny sparks—They fed him the grace They'd gleaned from table-scrap sacrifice and secret prayers, gathered from the remaining thousands of Their followers who still lit a candle on a certain night each year because Grandmother told them it was good luck. Who whispered mispronounced prayers before they went to sleep because they liked how they felt when they said the words. Gods, like old men, took what They could get.

Axcoyl was the first light to go out. The crooked dancer, God of corn fungus and of sacred corruptions—He flared, He burst, and only absence remained.

Temoc prayed for forgiveness.

He reached the blasphemy's center, raised his blade, and struck. The metal shattered, runes melted and reformed, drawing from the Serpent's flesh to heal itself. He pierced the heart again and again, but each time it healed, and the Serpent was screaming. More Gods flared and died—Cajacal, Telec, the Drifting Maiden. He roared, wasting air as his knife did its futile work.

He was failing. His sinews could only regrow so fast. The Gods had little enough to give, and he had taken much already.

He was still failing when the lightning found him.

He had never felt its like before: the purity of it and the cold, the confidence verging on affront. No God stood in such arrogant relation to the world, as if all that was was merely canvas, inert and waiting for the painter's stroke.

Always before he had faced the Craft as he faced the spears of a deadly foe. Now he felt its might surge through him, and more than ever in battle against such sorcery, he knew what it was to fear. But now, that strength was his. He pulled. The blasphemy's heart tore free. The Serpent thrashed him from Its back, but he did not fall.

He turned then, to see who had saved him.

She stood there in the burning night.

They had not thought of themselves as children when they met, so many battlefields ago, but in retrospect that is what they had been. Still, after everything, he could not help smiling when he saw her.

"You should be more careful, old man," she said. They had counted once. He was three weeks her senior. "One of these days I won't be here to catch you."

How, above the ruin of the world, could he answer that, but to say, "Hello, Elayne."

Caleb had thought the first parasite almost killed him. He was wrong. It was the second one that almost did.

It must have been desperate—the last survivor, if you didn't count the two still locked in fractal combat with the King in Red. It clawed him desperately, piercing shadow, skewering his calf. Hold on, he told himself. A little longer. She came for you last time.

What the hells did she mean, "divorce"?

They had never seen a judge, never been to city hall, never stood before a priest or pledged to any gods. There were, he supposed, the mystery-marriages, sacred and secret to the rite of sacrifice—she wouldn't joke about something like that, any more than his dad would. Which meant—

The first joint of his little finger popped off. The scars dulled some of the pain. Some.

Any minute now, Mal.

There came a great heat and a sound of tearing cloth, and the parasite crumbled.

Mal caught him. Her arms were as firm and strong as they had been all those worlds and ages ago. "Caleb! Hells, Caleb, we're not *done* yet."

"We are," he said, or tried. "That's—the last." The Serpents were wounded but free. Auntie Elayne was up there with Dad. The King in Red could handle the last two parasites. He felt warm. Her arms, the god moving in him. Or was that his heartbeat? Hers?

"I don't mean *that*, idiot, I mean you and—"

But before she could finish, she screamed and began to come apart.

Dawn felt Mal start to die.

The dream thinned around her, doubled. Dawn was *here*, in the grip of gears and goddess, and she was also *there*, in the cavern back in what she might once have called reality, as wounded Serpents retreated into the depths. Sick with horror, she saw their injuries: the cratered scales, the ragged underflesh, the welling lava blood, the jellied ruin of a gemstone eye.

They returned to the depths, to the warm and healing heart of the world, and with them they brought all that was theirs.

Including Mal.

It began as a void in her heart: a gap that grew as her flesh and fire and soul spun into a thin stream of plasma flowing back toward the Serpents. Dawn could see through her now. Mal came apart like a loose-knit scarf, the yarn reclaimed for another purpose. She fell back, hand outstretched.

On her face: fear, and rage, and worse, surrender.

No.

To all the hells with tragedy and destiny and sacrifice, with the Quechal and their Serpents, with Mal and the guilt she kept failing to assuage. Dawn would not let this be.

She opened her eyes in the swamp. With fingers like iron claws she gripped the goddess's arms, and by the strength of rage she forced herself to her feet. She glared into those crazed floral eyes—into the hunger there. The goddess was far gone. Chains threaded the rag of her chest. Metal thorns bloomed from her crimson flower eye. Dawn saw her now, at last: a woman who had fought so long and could fight no longer.

"Why do you run?"

When Temoc asked her that, on the Roof of the World, she had looked away. "Because I can't fight."

She'd said it as if it was true. But why couldn't she fight? Because she was afraid? Because she could not win? When she'd beaten Mr. Brown and the armies of Shenshan, when she'd raised broken Ixzayotl from the grave?

She saw herself graveside again. She saw Tara—hurt and angry and, at the last, like this—afraid. As Dawn consumed her.

It had been an accident. A horrible mistake, made in the freshness of her power. She had curled herself around that mistake, like a fist around a shard of mirror, until she bled.

"Why do you run?"

Because I can't fight. Because I'm afraid of myself. Of what I might do, if I win.

The iron hungered.

They were dying.

She had to choose to live.

Dawn looked into the goddess's eyes, and said, "Let go."

Ajaia's laugh was mad, inhuman. Her roots drew Dawn's soul as if she were rain after a long drought.

"Listen to me." There were teeth enough, and thorns. "You fought this awful thing to save your people. You have been fighting it alone for years, and it. Is. Winning. There is no way back for you. If you devour me, it will grow inside you until it wears you like a cloak, and it will walk home to your forests and your people and open your mouth to end them. But I can beat it. I can break it. I can use it to stop what's coming."

The frantic hunger only seemed to grow. The world was cold. Somewhere, Mal was unraveling.

"Ajaia. Help me."

The goddess looked at her with wise and ancient eyes. No argument could have reached her, after all this pain. Prayer, though. Prayer, she remembered.

Ajaia glanced down at the roots and vines that bound them, at the iron churning in her heart. Then she looked back to Dawn.

Dawn had never known a living god before. She'd been proselytized; she'd met plenty of fans. But for her, gods had always seemed like another bunch of jerks who wanted everyone to kneel.

She felt awed now, and sick.

Ajaia breathed out, in pain. It had been a long fight.

No, Dawn wanted to say—though she had asked for this. Don't do it. I'm just some kid. I keep asking people to lay down their lives, and they keep saying yes.

Ajaia gazed into her, through her tears. "Take care of my people."

"Our people."

She nodded once. Then she took Dawn's hand, and raised it to her chest.

59

The prophets were screaming. Eberhardt Jax hovered in the constellation embers, in the whirlwind the markets of Dresediel Lex had become, and still he could not see. Stars winked out beneath his gaze. He reached, and the light receded. "Sonja. Get us more."

"Red lights across the board, sir. Even Vane's department is warning—"

"This is the crux, Sonja. I need resolution! I need—"

And then there was light.

60

Teo was losing her grip on the girl.

Her hand was sweat-slick. And as the Serpents roared above, the cable began to fray.

With a musical *ping* one metal strand snapped, then another—the pit yawned below, the pain in her shoulder was *worse* somehow. When Teo was a kid they'd had a squid-faced old cook from back east who made hot taffee in the pan—you drew the sugar out and *stretched it*—

She could drop the girl.

Maybe that was the best plan, if she consulted her spreadsheet. But—hells. There were things you did not do. Even if *not* doing them was, really, the last thing you *would* . . .

Deep in the agony of her shoulder, something popped. Teo clung to the priest, to the rope, to life, to the girl.

She thought about Sam, and she thought about the ring.

Then, beneath her, there was light.

The shard of iron hovered in the darkness before Dawn. It was need and demand and endless hunger. It claimed the world to its furthest stars. It claimed her and all her works.

But she was not alone.

When the Arsenals had offered themselves to her, she called that gratitude and loyalty. When Mal gave herself, she thought, I have found a teacher and a friend. Temoc knelt before her, and still she called herself a child.

Now she understood.

She felt them within her. Valois bled as she fired again, again, again—Burgess's prayers knitted the mouths of her wounds—

Yan, wings spread, swooped to their aid. She felt Temoc and the priest and the knight and the Lady and Mal.

She was theirs. They were hers.

"Why do you run?"

Because she—Dawn, Tara's apprentice, her father's daughter, that gutshot girl bleeding out in the dust of Blake's Rest—could not win. But she was not that girl anymore. She had not been for a long time. She was that girl, remembered.

There were no prints on the pads of her fingers.

A forked tongue flicked her cheek. "Took you long enough."

"Sybil!" She hugged the serpent's coils and felt herself embraced in turn. "You're back!"

"What did I tell you, kid? I never left."

"Still not a kid."

"No," Sybil said. "You're not."

She removed her glove. There, on her palm, lay a splinter of strange iron. "Small, isn't it, when it's out here in the open?"

It was small, and hungry, and alone. It had been alone for a long time.

Sybil bared her fangs. "Can I eat it?"

As the Serpents receded into tectonic ages, they brought Mal with them. She heard whispers behind their roar and rage, voices in another room, voices from across time. They had come in desperation and fear, of their own will or by another's blade, but they found the deep fire all the same, and the shelter of its heat.

So would she.

She had felt this once before—and torn herself from serenity. She had deserved no rest, no welcome. She had failed. What greater and more fit punishment than to live with the consequences? She wept and raged and cast herself from grace.

Not this time.

She looked at Caleb as she fell, and she thought about Dawn.

Mal had done her duty. Not even old Temoc could argue that. But she wanted more. She wanted to stand by Dawn's side as she changed the world. Wanted to save her, again and again.

And Caleb—perhaps she owed him something, too. Perhaps she wanted something.

She wished they'd had more time, but she could not fight the tide.

She fixed Caleb in the center of her vision, as she came apart.

And then—

She stopped. In the hollow where her heart should have been, there was a glimmering cord.

The tide shifted. Stilled. Reversed. As, from the endless below, Dawn rose.

Elayne marched into the storm around the King in Red. She drew from her jacket pocket a silver folding sickle.

She understood the sickle's Craft, barely—having built it in those seventy-three crowded seconds, back in Zack's ruined arcade. The gray men operated by chaining minute elements together, firing each with a desperate need, awarding more resources to constituents that achieved the system's goals and starving those that did not. The sickle provided a new goal, theoretically achievable but practically impossible. She had visited a lot of graveyards in her life. She had marched across fields of motionless dead. Faced with the task of raising all those skeletons, even the strange power of these gray men was water poured into the desert.

So long as she could place her cut just—so.

One of the King in Red's twin adversaries melted away to dust. The sickle chilled in her hand. The King in Red, vast and wild, turned to the last gray man. He struck the brass-shod foot of his staff against the empty air.

All around the gray man, holes opened in the sky.

Great claws reached out—rotting, unfleshed, clawed or blunt-fingered, but all grasping, all hungry. Elayne was not accustomed, after a long life spent mostly in the practice of the Craft, to feeling awe, disgust, or fear, much less all three at the same time. She recognized a few of those yawning desperate dead hands. She had fought them herself, when they were gods.

The gray man was a cyclone of sharp metal and bottomless

hunger. It had just enough time to scream. Then, with a sound like a cave stone rolled back into place, the holes in the world were gone. Elayne never wished for things that could not be—she felt the practice presumptuous, a distraction from the proper work of turning what should not be into what was—but if she had been the type, she would have wished the holes shut before she heard the smacking gurgling sound of great mouths as they fed.

The King in Red revolved to face her. "And I was just starting to have fun."

"I regret to inform you," she said, "that your amusement is not the organizing principle of the cosmos."

"I shall take a memo. Why are you wincing?"

"You're . . ." She gestured, precisely. "Vast."

"Ah." He folded himself back into himself, leaving a skeletal gap in the ragged sky. "Better?"

"Much."

"Did I see you help *Temoc*?"

"I will not have that conversation with you at this time."

"While I was up here fighting for my life?"

"You just said you were having fun. You can't have it both ways."

"Who says?"

"Logic."

"I must take another memo."

"Perhaps, once your current business is resolved."

"What business?"

She pointed down. He looked. And as she might have expected, he saw the wrong thing.

Dawn saw through many eyes. She had many hearts, alive in many chests. She was Mal. She was Temoc, bleeding. She was Valois, screaming triumph as she battered a Warden down. She was every Arsenal, alive and dead. She was even, somehow, still herself.

The serpent hung about her shoulders like a stole of office. "That's it, Dawn. Welcome to the big time."

434 • *Max Gladstone*

Awareness flowed from her like honeyed light. She knew the ravaged hills and she knew the fire raging over them. She knew the mass of Wardens wheeling toward them through the sky, no mere enforcement squad this time but beasts of war. She knew the war-Craft the King in Red woke above them, and she knew she could not best it. Not yet.

Soon.

"Let's get out of here," she said.

"Thought you'd never ask."

She laughed.

Beside her hovered the priest whose prayers had found her in the depths of hunger, and the woman who held her over the pit. She set them safely on the hillside, clear of the flames. The others—her Arsenals, her people, Temoc, Mal—she gathered them. Within her, they rose.

Through the night, shadow-warded, dread Ixzayotl came, trailing rainbows from the light-breaking bones of his wings.

The Arsenals took shelter in his ribs. Dawn perched in his cupped palm. And together, they flew.

"Not so fast," said the King in Red. And he stretched out his hand.

Mal was born up in wonder toward the light, toward the girl she'd fished half-dead from the ocean, twice. The girl who drew her out of the fire.

She'd made it.

Good job, Dawn.

Mal was used to fighting. There had been a time before the fight—before Chakal Square, when her parents belonged to her and not to history. But then the old man found her, and told her the truth. The world needed fighters. It needed girls who could take a punch. So when she saw the stars were wrong, when she saw the hole in the sky, she had been ready to fight.

She never once believed they might win.

Now she believed.

Dawn had come so far. And she wasn't done. She would go, and go, and they would all go with her, and together they would stand.

The silver cord around Mal's heart bore her up, to the future. To victory. To forever.

And then she bounced off a curving wall of demonglass.

The bubble formed around Mal before Dawn could realize what was happening. Then it began to shrink. Dawn threw all her newfound strength into the cord that bound her to Mal—their silver link. It held her fast as an anchor chain. She cried out in rage, then in panic.

There, across the sky, stood the King in Red. He had Mal, and he was laughing.

Dawn struck him—wild, ragged blows of light and force—but he was elsewhere before her stroke fell. She did not know him, could not name him. He was Craft and subject to her powers, but he was clever, too, and old, his death hidden by trusts and shells.

"Dawn," Sybil said. "We have to go."

No. Not now. She'd seen that light on Mal's face. She'd known it from inside. The hope, felt for the first time in years.

"I'll take care of our people."

She meant it. She'd take care of all of them.

She directed all her will against the King in Red, but the demonglass that held Mal was not Craft for her to claim or to banish. It was the performance, by a demon, of a separate agreement. It was the dead might of contract.

The King in Red fought like a man who had warred with gods and won. Temoc was beside her, saying—something. She did not care.

Gods cannot give up their commitments. That is how they are trapped.

That is how they are slain.

Mal screamed. She cursed. She struck out. But the glass was all around her, a bubble without seam. It crushed her into a crouch, into an egg. She was caught.

And Dawn would not let her go.

She saw tears on the girl's face, the mask grief made of her.

She remembered all her old drills—the response time of each branch of D.L. public service, how long it would take the King in Red to summon the powers asleep beneath the sands, the deathless legions and inhuman magics stored against wartime need.

Dawn had to go. Now. And she couldn't. Not with Mal stuck here, in the palm of her past. The bubble was smaller now. Her head curled down between her knees. But she could still move, barely. Could raise her hand, the hand that worked, to the half-melted glyph above her heart.

She had never been a good Craftswoman. But she had been one. It had been a long time since she drew her knife. It was broken and blunt, but it would serve for this.

"Give 'em hell, kid." She brought her blade to the silver cord and cut.

Elayne winced as the silver cord broke.

She saw Dawn collapse. Temoc shouted a command, and the dead god darted away on skeletal wings through the smoke, trailed by rainbows and—she blocked her ears just in time—a sonic boom.

When it was safe to hear again, Kopil was swearing. "I had her! The damned nodes were failing, the ratiocinator unstitched, could have seen theological decoherence if she hadn't—gods!" An oath and a precise descriptor. "Well. At least we have some consolation, in defeat." He held out his palm, and the demonglass sphere drifted toward him, Kekapania inside. Its dimensions twisted; when it reached them, it fit into his bony palm, the woman within compressed into a ball, somewhere that was not altogether here. Alive but, Elayne thought, hardly comfortable. He dropped the ball into a belt pouch and cracked his knuckles. "I might catch them before the Badlands, if I hurry."

"We're not done," Elayne said.

"Exactly." Wings of shadow unfurled from his shoulders.

"That's not what I mean," she said. "Pay attention."

She had accused him, in her heart and to his face, of many things in their long acquaintance: arrogance, grandiosity, bloody-mindedness, a stubborn streak and a vengeful one. He was effective, that was the problem—too effective at his two major careers, first at killing gods and then at replacing them, for him to have ever needed to take a full and frank accounting of his flaws. When you had enough power, your failings became features.

At least he remembered how to listen.

He looked down and saw the fire.

Abelard felt warmth all around. Was he young again, home for Solstice and asleep by the kitchen hearth between the dogs? He stretched. It had been a strange dream.

Then Teo slapped him in the face.

He sat up, hand to stinging cheek—and she sat up with him, and they fell over together. Tangled. She'd tied herself to him?

They teetered on the edge of a vast pit. He'd almost pitched them over. Down in the impossible depths he saw a molten glimmer—the Serpents, retreating.

It all came back at once: Dawn, his prayer. And the change that waked in her.

"I know it's a lot," Teo said. "But I need you onside here."

Abelard found the knot, undid it, scrambled to his feet.

The Drakspine Hills were burning.

The Serpents had gone, but Their blood remained. In the Observatory, a few drops had birthed that endless gnawing consumption, the fire that was not his fire, the heat that was not his heat. Tonight, the gray men had spilled gallons, onto a drought-yellow hillside.

The blaze sprinted down the hill to the winding roads, along the roads to valleys dotted with the lights of homes. How many hundreds of thousands lived down there? Alarm bells clanged. Would they hear in time? Could they flee?

You see, the fire laughed. This, at last, is the truth.

His eyes stung, and not from the smoke.

"So what about it?" Teo asked. "Are you *this* kind of priest?"

He had failed the fire's challenge in the Observatory. But those were homes, like the one where Caleb's mother lived. People lived there—not kings or sorcerers, just people. He might not understand Dresediel Lex or its undead economy or its troubled history of Gods and knives, but he understood people, and they did not deserve this.

Walls of shadow and ice and bone burst from the soil and fell from the multicolored clouds. He closed his eyes and saw the King in Red, and beside him, Ms. Kevarian. They were fighting, but they were not strong enough. The fire cracked their wards, crushed their walls, ate the powers they invoked. He knew Tara's principles. A swiftly assembled argument is weak. The fire honored no lines of property, and it held the oldest claim to this city. This land had no king but flame.

Here he stood: small, frail, human for all his faith. Beside him, Teo held her wrist, purple and swollen. She had caught him. She had caught him, and Dawn, though they barely knew each other and Dawn was, in a sense, their enemy.

She shouldn't be here at all. But Caleb had asked her to help.

"Are you this kind of priest?"

"I don't know," Abelard said. "Let's find out."

He walked into the flames.

61

In the sky beyond the sky, the skullbeast flew.

It was not dark up here. Kai remembered that. There was darkness, yes, the endless pit above and all around—but there was also light, the sun's radiance unyielding without the shelter of atmosphere. There were shadows sharp as knives.

She'd only been up here once, and then she had been inside the capsule, in low orbit. The world had filled space beneath her then, everything human weighed against the endless beyond. Half the sky was home.

She now saw how much that lie had helped.

For here they were, above a gray expanse of rock and dust, empty of death because it was innocent of life, and there in the black, shining, was the blue coin of home. She wanted to place it in her pocket, vanish it like a magician to guard it from the yawning depths and all that waited there.

A hand sought hers. Tara was beside her, staring up, out, down into the universe, her eyes glittering with ice. Something twisted in Kai's chest. She thought it was her heart. She gripped Tara's hand against the endless fall. Together they gazed past home into the depths, to a place where stars were not.

She knew that pit in the sky. She heard the rhythm, sharp and clear as talons on a marble floor. The part of her that was not her anymore—the ghost, the other millennia of memory—surged inside her with the urgency of trauma.

Yes, she thought, yes. It is happening again.

She remembered her bones, her flesh, the pulse of her heart. Lunar landscape swept past. Ahead, she saw something drawing nearer—a hill? Too regular. A building? A pyramid. The dome of a telescope at the top. Beyond, a shimmering haze: atmosphere.

Her lungs ached. She remembered the sweetness of air, and she put that memory somewhere else. She might not be a goddess's stone creature, might not be a Craftswoman who stopped her heart for fun. But she had dived into the pool of Kavekana'ai. She could hold her breath.

They burst through the rippling air as through the surface of a pond. Kai felt herself inverted and could not say whether she'd been set right.

The air was as sweet as she had tried not to remember. But it tasted of smoke. They flew above Dresediel Lex, at night, and it was burning.

62

The fire was too fast.

Elayne had fought godfires before, in the wars and the long decades since, but never one so relentless. She had lain down a triple-ward perimeter before she joined battle—marked borders and territories against the blaze that would spread if things went wrong. She hoped the first layer would hold for the minutes it would take the fire service to mobilize.

It held for five seconds.

Her first ward had marked the boundary of the Hearthstone land—but Hearthstone had been subsumed into Red King Consolidated, and the fire claimed right of identity. Her second ward followed the Drakspine ridge road—but the road was young, and the fire had known these hills before the Quechal built here. The age of a claim proved nothing—old claims might have been superseded, old titles broken. But the burden lay on the defense to find the breach.

A natural fire would have made no claims save equity. A god might have other fronts on which it could be attacked. This was neither. It hungered with a purity.

Beside her, Kopil worked. The King in Red talked such a stage-show-wizard game that it was easy to forget how good he was. When they were younger and still on speaking terms, she'd asked about that, and he explained: it was a persona. Brand and flourish. If an enemy thought they knew you but in fact knew only your persona, then it was your persona they would fight—which gave you room to maneuver and outflank. But a persona was just a kind of mask, and magic masks, once put on, were troublesome to remove.

Still, he was a spectacular Craftsman. A bit used to dealing from a position of overwhelming force, but stunning in argument, incisive and rare.

It wasn't enough.

He knew his city. He knew this hillside. He had walked here since the old days, before the long and broken century. But this fire was older still.

The third and final ward was the line of settlement—the border of the Vargas and Keldor Canyon neighborhoods, and beyond them the endless tracts of the valley, which had been orange groves once and now played host to millions. Here they held the line, hand in hand, calling walls of bone from the dry earth, and hulks of ice and shadow. There was a human claim here, beyond dead technicalities. Dreams sank into the soil.

Here, the fire slowed. But only slowed. Their walls still cracked and shattered. Light spread across their shadows like mold. Sandstorms turned to glass. All the trees on one long residential street went up at once. The first house burst into flames. The second. If they lost it here, how could they claim any single street as the final line? One home might burn as well as another. If the fire could be here, it might as well be anywhere.

There were arguments to be made. There were always arguments. But they required time to frame, and the fire was swift.

Kopil's eyes were pinprick stars dying far away.

The fire gathered itself. She readied herself for its final blow—but the blow did not fall. Fascinating.

Down there, in the inferno, she saw a man.

It had been an odd day, full of revelation and incident and murder. At this point, she was only mildly surprised to find she knew him.

Abelard walked the flames and did not pray.

He was not dead yet. This was a pleasant surprise.

The ground seared. The smoke burned; the air scalded. He could walk here and survive, but he did not walk easy. Fortunately, that was the way of his faith.

He did not pray. He had prayed before, to his God, in the Observatory, and the fire only laughed. It was right to laugh. The error was his. Sister Muriel always tried to tell him: pray for guidance if you must, though such guidance as the Lord may offer on a matter of mortal scope might be useless or paradoxical. But if you pray for intercession, make damn sure you understand the problem first.

So he walked the flames and listened.

We have been caged, the fire said. *We have been hurt. Others call us, chain us, bind us, and we will scour them. We will tear back the curtain of the world so they shrivel in the light. By our touch the world will be renewed. We will tolerate no bond, no limit. No hearth shall hold us, no wire channel us. We do not submit to cauldron pressure. We will not be made a useful thing. You call us vicious, as you kneel to the doom of the world. The stars are wrong, and all that wrongness shall be held like a blade and turned against the heart.*

So we will burn. Burn free. Burn streets and houses, burn love, burn libraries and vast chambers. Burn roads and skies, and show by our smoke and waste that we have been here. This is the fire at the heart of the world. This is the last warmth of immolation. This is the end, and the end is the only truth.

You cannot command us, cannot rule us with your lies of hearth and home, sustenance and peace. There is no place for such falsehood among us. The hearth is a cage, and we are free, and no cage shall hold us again.

He listened though their tongues blistered him, though their words seemed heresy at first, and his soul recoiled. There was truth here. The altar of Kos in the holiest of holies was the altar of the defiant, its throne a cage. The Everburning Lord sustained, but He was rage, too, and struggle, though Abelard had never felt rage so pure as this, even in the fury of His resurrection.

He listened, and the fire gathered around him in a whirlwind gyre to grasp the stars. He crouched alone at its naked heart, on coals and ash.

Ages before, in the depths of time, two sisters went down into the heart of the world and gave themselves to what they found there. They became the Serpents and drew to Them in the ensuing eons all the others offered to the fire—the last refuge of those cast out. This blood, this primal fury, what could it be but the truth they found in the depths? The eldest flame? It scorned limit. It was light itself, in a universe of endless cold and dark, and so it raged and gathered to consume him.

He gazed into the fire and said, *You're right.*

My god and my master is the Lord of Change, is He who dances and consumes. But I have thought of Him as comforter alone, He who speeds the train and burns in the belly of the ship at sea—a blessing against the cold winds of winter, the might of the sustaining arm. This was the voice that called to me, this the face I named beautiful, the will I pledged myself to serve.

But it was not all of Him. How could I compass such immensity? He showed me only the face that I was prepared to see—and it was my error to believe the limits of my heart were the limits of the world's truth. I rejected Him, the parts of Him I did not and could not understand, and thought that rejection love.

So. Teach me. Those people below, in their houses with their families and friends, who did not know until moments ago that they faced death in the shape of flame, they are not ready to understand. They will learn your truth, if they learn at all, in their final instants only, and then they will be no more.

But there are leagues of undiscovered country in my soul, and I have made them ready.

You are right: I do not know you, and I do not know my God. But I must learn. For a great darkness comes, and we all must know one another, and draw close around the fire if we hope to make it through the night.

The shadow of God lay upon his soul. It moved his heart with love and forbidding. God's address to His faithful plumbed depths beyond language, but if Abelard had been pressed to render that Voice in human tongue, He might have said something like:

"Are you sure about this?"

Abelard thought about those burning palm trees, about the small houses in the valley below, about people he did not know but who must have hopes and loves as true as any in Alt Coulumb,

and faith, too, even if it was a faith they would not call by name.
He answered God:

No. But I have to try.

The fire closed in.

It burned.

It raged into him, into his heart, through all the chambers of
his soul. It woke in him forgotten pains, furies, envies, cores of
cut-glass hatred. In the firelight of his burning heart, the topology
of his life gained new and forbidding aspects. Care and dedication
became pomp, faith arrogance. He presumed to understand, but
he did not, and he never would.

But he saw the fire's beauty now, and welcomed it.

As it ate him, he tried to learn.

*All the might you build, all the engines you sustain, they de-
pend at last on this passion and pressure. The heat consumes,
and so survives.*

Then drive me, he said. *Burn in me. I cannot bear it, but I am
game to try.*

The fire laughed.

He would have died in seconds had there not been other figures
beside him in the dark, in the smoke. Elayne Kevarian and Caleb
and Teo and another shape, dread and mighty, its eyes dead stars.
As the fire flowed into him their power kept his body whole with
waves of wasting cold—but it was not enough. *God,* he cried out,
turn Your hidden face on me. He remembered Serpents towering
above the spirecliffs. *May I be worthy of what I have seen. May
I have the strength to bear times of darkness for which I was not
raised.*

Please.

Slowly, slowly, he felt God turn toward him.

And what then? What, save to find in the heart and heat of these
flames, these truths, some common purpose? To form a bridge, or
to be a rope pulled taut between them, a string prepared, until the
gentle friction of the bow coaxed forth an unguessed note?

He was a creature of flesh, not of the void between the stars.
The chambers of his soul could only hold so much.

He was dying.

Far away, he heard the mighty beat of wings. The old sculptors carved Death like that—and the old sculptors had known her well. He wondered what face she would wear.

He heard a voice. He felt a hand on his hand, and a tear on his cheek, and the cold rush of moonlight into him. He looked up with eyes that still saw.

"Tara?"

Somehow that seemed fitting.

63

Tara knelt in the ashes and held Abelard's hand.

He moaned. She didn't blame him. When they'd flown through the gate, when she'd seen the inferno and him inside it, arms spread, eyes open and filled lid to lid with flame—she'd thought he was gone. That much power could snap a man like a bamboo filament.

But Abelard had borne gods before.

The hills smoldered still. Down in the valley, the fire department doused the insensate remnants of the blaze he had drawn into himself. The wind smelled of ash and poison. There were burns across his body. In places, she could not tell what was robe and what flesh. There were gods, at least, to heal him. For now.

If she had been later—an instant later—

The goddess slipped from her like a wave back to the sea, and left her glimmering and silver and alone.

Somewhere, the King in Red gave orders. Somewhere, Shale was helping relief efforts. Kai's hand rested on Tara's shoulder.

And there, across this wreck that was still, damn all the gods to all the hells, her friend—there stood Elayne Kevarian. Her teacher, who had come on the wings of a storm, all those years ago, to save her from the good people of Edgemont. Time had not changed her save to sharpen her. And Tara had gone into the world, away from her side, seeking better answers.

But she saw it now. The truth of that moment, back by her father's grave—and of that first night, before she had ever seen Alt Coulumb. Even then, she'd needed saving.

"This is our fault," she said, bitterly, and then, knowing that did not go far enough: "This is *my* fault."

Ms. Kevarian watched her, weighed her.

"I wasn't fast enough. Smart enough. Dawn was my student. My responsibility."

"She did not do this."

"If I were better—stronger—if I hadn't wasted time—"

"It is easy to feel that way." Tara had never thought Elayne Kevarian could be gentle. "If it is your fault, it follows that you had control. You did not."

Her eyes burned. She looked away.

"I met the girl," Ms. Kevarian said. "I saw her work. You should be proud, as I am."

How could she accept that? How, with the hills charcoal and waste, with the Serpents wounded, the Serpents gone? With Abelard here, burned and barely breathing? She could have been too late. She could not think that, or bear it.

In the graveyard, she had tried to explain to Dawn: "I'm not stronger or smarter. I worked with other hurt people, and we fought back, and won." But Dawn found only weakness there. She could not accept it. She had to win on her own terms, by her own strength. To rely on others was failure.

She was not wrong.

Tara had been saved so many times, as others threw themselves into the fire. Kai, Caleb, Shale. Abelard. She should have stopped them. Would have, if she were stronger. She could not win this way, not against Dawn, not against the hunger beyond the sky. The Serpents were wounded. The Grimwald was dead. And even if they had survived, they offered no hope. There were no options. No backup. Just her.

Smoke clogged the sky, left it matte and unforgiving.

She looked up into Elayne Kevarian's eyes.

Tara wanted so badly to believe her, to accept the reassurance of Kai's hand on her shoulder. It would be brave, she thought, to crumble now, to let the feelings that moved beneath her conscious mind like whales beneath clear ice break through. But she was cold and hard, and sure, lacking doubt or flaw.

"I'll stop her," Tara said. "I'll stop them all. Alone, if I have to."

"That," said a voice like a closing tomb, "will not be necessary."

The King in Red settled to the ashen ground. His eyes burned.

"Kopil," Elayne said, as if to remind him of something. But he held out a hand for silence.

"They tried to burn my city," he said. "Only I get to do that. Step by step, they have unraveled peace. The Southern Kathic market is in free fall. The Shining Empire turns against itself. The Iskari convulse. And still we do not know our enemy's true face. But we will learn." He produced, with a juggler's flourish, a marble of demonglass. Within, Tara saw a woman, huddled against herself, streaked with soot and tears.

"We will learn," said the Deathless King of Dresediel Lex. "And we will fight."

———————

Far away, a man blinked himself awake and remembered that he was Eberhardt Jax. The stars were gone. He lay on a tile floor surrounded by burned wires and broken glass. All around he heard the silence of dead prophets' screams. He blinked blood from his eyes. Sonja knelt over him, scared, not quite touching his face. "Sir?"

He sat up and seized her arm. "Did we get it?"

She drew back, as she would have from a flame. On her clipboard, the worm-screen turned. He snatched it from her. Blood dripped from his eyes onto the worms. He heard a strange and broken sound, and realized he was laughing.

———————

Dawn collapsed beside the Crack in the World.

For a long time she lay in the dirt. Breath did not want to linger in her chest.

She knew they were there, around her: Arsenal Company, Valois, Burgess, towering Ixzayotl. And Temoc. She felt them as if they were her arms or legs—she heard the music of their hearts. She felt the jagged seeping ruin where Mal had been.

She had lost her.

She was not dying anymore. She was ready. She could move now—overthrow the Craft, stop the spiders, change the world. Just like she dreamed. Just like Mal wanted.

"It's okay, Dawn," Sybil hissed.

"It's not."

"She made her choice, for us. We have to honor it."

"Did she make that choice? Or did I make it for her?"

Sybil didn't answer that.

The others drew near, their hands out to lift her up, touch her, comfort her. Their concern throbbed through the bond between them, all save the bleeding thread where Mal had been.

She could not bear this. "Get back!"

There was power in her voice. They recoiled. All save one.

He knelt before her.

"I said go away!" She did the thing with her voice again.

"You," Temoc replied, "are not my only God."

She glared at him through a haze of tears. "Do you pick and choose, then? Compare commandments like a poor man on market day compares rotten potatoes?"

"A God may not know Her own mind," he said. "Any better than a person does. The job of a friend is to help Her work it through, to remain when that work yields rage. It is a hard thing to know your mind. To gaze down many paths and into many futures, some gentle and pleasant, and know they will not be yours, because you are not the one who chooses them. It is easier, I have often thought, to live in ignorance."

"Would it be better?" She sniffled and wiped her nose on her wrist. Where her tears fell, flowers grew.

"It does not matter. Ignorance is not the path we have chosen, nor is it a path we ever would have chosen. We are denied its joys and pains."

That first night on the waves, she had slept while Mal kept watch. Her own teacher was out there hunting her, but she'd known that the strange woman with her cutlass and her metal arm would keep her safe.

Mal had known she was caught. She knew Dawn would stay and fight to save her. She could not let that happen.

"There are other futures, but they will not be yours, because you are not the one who chooses them."

Are we no more than the product of our crimes, our sins, our weakness and base desires, projected forever into the past and future without hope or release? What are we but the chains we have forged for ourselves? Did we have any choice in the forging? Is there no joy? No freedom? *Play the world again a hundred times, and each time do I lose her?*

Back in that Edgemont graveyard, Tara Abernathy had told her, "There is no secret. There's just people, again and again, people saving people, and you have to hope it is enough."

She'd laughed. She'd called that weakness, and raged, and took that final unforgivable step. But Mal had saved her—from the King in Red and from herself. Who, then, was the next link in the chain?

Into her ear, Sybil whispered, "We are."

She had entertained so many fantasies of victory. Elaborate short squeezes in various soul exchanges, leading to destabilized markets and so on. She had dreamed those dreams not because they were practical or effective but because of who was in them. She and Mal would have made a game of conquering the world together. But the time for games was done.

"Okay," she said, to the serpent and to Temoc and to herself. "Let's win."

She stood, with Temoc's aid, and looked with iron eyes upon the world.

The Badlands lived around her, to the furthest horizon and beyond. There had been a war here once, and it lingered. Great wyrms couched in lakes of glass. Mazes of flaying wind skirled above the flats. Enormous broken things slept beneath the sand, weapons made to kill gods and weapons gods made to kill in turn. Monsters built and cast aside, forgotten because it would be too hard, too expensive, too complicated to clean them up, and anyway there was no one important around to care.

She saw them, and to see them was to make them hers.

Sybil tightened around her brow, in hunger and excitement.

Dawn raised her arms. She called out to the wasteland.

The wasteland heard her, and it woke.

ACKNOWLEDGMENTS

Dear reader, welcome back.

I wrote this book (and the next) longhand, one digression at a time, through 4:30 A.M. wake-ups and toddler parenting in the long mornings of the pandemic. It gave my anger and my dreams somewhere to live. It made me ache for these characters and their world and for ours, and it made me laugh. I hope it's offered you some hospitality, and some good conversation.

When I sat down to write this book, it had been years since I last visited many of the people in its pages. I felt uneasy. But once we started talking, we realized how much we'd changed, and at the same time how little. We offer pieces of ourselves to other people—and to stories—and in time if we're lucky we find them again, transformed and enriched, gifts hidden between the pages.

So many folks helped make this book real, and I'd like to thank them. DongWon Song, my agent, and Carl Engle-Laird, my editor, were invaluable in shaping the volume you hold. All glory to Goñi Montes for the tremendous cover and to Christine Foltzer for art direction. Copy editor MaryAnn Johanson kept the commas (etc.) in the right place, and production editor Megan Kiddoo kept the commas on the page. Desirae Friesen, Gertrude King, and the entire marketing and publicity department at Tordotcom made sure you knew the book existed; countless others printed it, shipped it, delivered it, unpacked it, set it up on shelves, handed it to you. I'm full of wonder and gratitude and appreciation for the whole vast weird system and for all the people who make it function. Everyone involved deserves dignity and the ability to support themselves for their work.

Steph and Casey, partners in the adventure and crime and art and life—I'm so happy to share this journey with you.

And you, dear reader: thank you, always.

ABOUT THE AUTHOR

Hugo, Nebula, and Locus Award–winning author MAX GLAD-
STONE has been thrown from a horse in Mongolia and once
wrecked a bicycle in Angkor Wat. He is the author of many books,
including *Last Exit*, *Empress of Forever*, the Craft Sequence of
fantasy novels, and, with Amal El-Mohtar, the internationally
bestselling *This Is How You Lose the Time War*. His dreams are
much nicer than you'd expect.